"You can't push

Jackson lifted her c
couldn't avoid his ga   were only a
few inches apart.

"What if I am crazy?" Allie's voice broke. "Crazy like a fox?" The first of the fireworks exploded, showering down a glittering red, white and blue light on the meadow below them. The boom echoed in her chest as another exploded to the "oohs" and "ahhs" of the wedding party. She felt scalding tears burn her throat.

Jackson couldn't bear to see Allie like this. He pulled her to him and, dropping his mouth to hers, kissed her. She leaned into him, letting him draw her even closer as the kiss deepened. Fireworks lit the night, booming in a blaze of glittering light before going dark again.

Desire ignited his blood. He wanted Allie like he'd never wanted anyone or anything before.

WEDDING AT
CARDWELL RANCH

BY
B.J. DANIELS

Published in Great Britain 2014
by Mills & Boon, an imprint of Harlequin (UK) Limited,
Eton House, 18-24 Paradise Road, Richmond, Surrey, TW9 1SR

© 2014 Barbara Heinlein

ISBN: 978-0-263-91363-7

46-0714

Harlequin (UK) Limited's policy is to use papers that are natural, renewable and recyclable products and made from wood grown in sustainable forests. The logging and manufacturing processes conform to the legal environmental regulations of the country of origin.

Printed and bound in Spain
by Blackprint CPI, Barcelona

New York Times bestselling author **B.J. Daniels** wrote her first book after a career as an award-winning newspaper journalist and author of thirty-seven published short stories. That first book, *Odd Man Out,* received a four-and-a-half-star review from *RT Book Reviews* and went on to be nominated for Best Intrigue that year. Since then, she has won numerous awards, including a career achievement award for romantic suspense and many nominations and awards for best book.

Daniels lives in Montana with her husband, Parker, and two springer spaniels, Spot and Jem. When she isn't writing, she snowboards, camps, boats and plays tennis. Daniels is a member of Mystery Writers of America, Sisters in Crime, International Thriller Writers, Kiss of Death and Romance Writers of America.

To contact her, write to B.J. Daniels, PO Box 1173, Malta, MT 59538, USA, or e-mail her at bjdaniels@mtintouch. net. Check out her website, www.bjdaniels.com.

This is dedicated to my readers and my Facebook friends who shared their "gaslighting" ideas and proved that they think as creepy me.

If you haven't already, come say hello on my author Facebook page at www.facebook.com/pages/BJ-Daniels/127936587217837.

Thanks for stopping by Cardwell Ranch!

Chapter One

Allison Taylor brushed back a lock of her hair and willed herself not to scream.

"Is something wrong?" her brother-in-law asked from the kitchen doorway, startling her and making her jump.

She dropped the heavy covered pot she'd taken from the pantry a little too hard onto the counter. The lid shifted, but not enough that she could see inside.

"Didn't mean to scare you," Drew Taylor said with a laugh as he lounged against the kitchen door frame. "I was cravin' some of your famous chili, but I think maybe we should go out."

"I just need a minute. If you could see to Natalie…"

"She's still asleep. I just checked." Drew studied her for a long moment. Like his brother, he had russet-brown hair and dark brown eyes and classic good looks. His mother had assured both of her sons that they were wonderful. Fortunately Drew had taken it with a grain of salt—unlike his brother Nick.

"Are you okay, Allie? I've been so worried about you since Nick…"

"I'm fine." She didn't want to talk about her presumed-dead husband. She really just wanted her brother-in-law to go into the other room and leave her alone for a moment.

Drew had been a godsend. She didn't know what she would have done without him, she thought as she pulled a band from her jeans pocket and secured her long, blond hair in a single tail at the back of her head.

When she'd mentioned how nice his brother was to Nick shortly after they married, he'd scoffed.

"Just be glad he likes you. He's about the only one in my family," he had added with a laugh.

"Why don't you let me help you with that," Drew said now as he took a step toward her. He frowned as his gaze went to the pot and the pile of ingredients she'd already stacked up on the counter. The chili pot was the last thing she'd brought into the kitchen from the porch of the small cabin. "You kept the pot?"

So his mother had told him about the incident.

He must think I'm losing my mind just like his mother and sister do.

The worst part was she feared they were right.

Allie looked down at the heavy cast-iron pot with its equally heavy cast-iron lid. Her hand trembled as she reached for the handle. The memory of the last time she'd lifted that lid—and what she'd found inside—sent a shudder through her.

The covered cast-iron casserole pot, enameled white inside and the color of fresh blood on the outside, had been a wedding present from her in-laws.

"She does know how to cook, doesn't she?" her mother-in-law, Mildred, had asked all those years ago as if Allie hadn't been standing there. Mildred was a twig-thin woman who took pride in these things: her petite, slim, fifty-eight-year-old body, her sons and her standing in the community. Her daughter, Sarah, was just the opposite of her mother, overweight and dumpy by comparison. And Mildred was always making that comparison to anyone who would listen, including Sarah.

Mildred was on her fourth husband and lived in one of

the more modest mansions at Big Sky. Of her two sons, Nick had been the baby—and clearly her favorite.

Nick had laughed that day when his mother had asked if his new wife could cook. "She makes pretty good chili, I'll give her that," he told Mildred. "But that's not why I married her." He'd given Allie a side hug, grinning like a fool and making her blush to the roots of her hair.

Nick had liked to say he had the prettiest wife in town. "Just make sure you stay that way," he'd always add. "You start looking like my sister and you can pack your bags."

The red, cast-iron, covered pot she was now reaching for had become her chili pot.

"Allie, I thought you'd thrown that pot away!" Drew reached to stop her, knocking the lid off in the effort. It clattered to the counter.

Allie lunged back, her arm going up protectively to shield her face. But this time the pot was empty. No half-dead squirrel inside it.

"I'm throwing this pot in the trash," Drew announced. "If just the sight of it upsets you—"

"No, your mother will have a fit."

"Let her." He swept pot and lid off the counter and carried it out to the garbage can.

When he came back into the room, he looked at her and shook his head. "Allie, you've got to pull it together. Maybe you should go back to the doctor and see if there is something else he can give you. You're strung like a piano wire."

She shook her head. "I don't need a doctor." She just needed for whatever was happening to her to stop.

His gaze moved past her, his expression going from a concerned frown to a smile. "Hey, girl," he said as his five-year-old niece came into the kitchen. He stepped past Allie to swing Nat into his arms. "I came over to check on the two of you. Mama was going to cook us some dinner but I think we should go out to eat. What do you say?"

Allie started to argue that she couldn't let Drew do any more for them and she sure couldn't afford to go out to eat, but stopped as her daughter said, "Are you sick, Mama?" Her precious daughter looked to her with concern. Allie saw the worry in Nat's angelic face. She'd seen it too much lately. It was bad enough that Natalie had recently lost her father. Now more than ever she needed her mother to be sane.

"I'm fine, sweetie. It's too hot for chili, anyway. So let's go out, why not?" Allie said, relieved and thankful for Drew. Not just for coming by to check on them, but for throwing out the pot. She hadn't because her mother-in-law was upset enough and the Taylors were the only family she had, especially now.

"Just let me freshen up and change," she said as Drew took Nat to look for her shoes.

In the bathroom, Allie locked the door, turned on the shower and stripped off her clothes. She was still sweating from fear, her heart beating hard against her chest.

"You found a what in the chili pot?" her mother-in-law had asked in disbelief when Allie had called her—a huge mistake in retrospect. But at the time, she'd hoped her mother-in-law would understand why she couldn't keep the pot. Why she didn't want it in her house.

"I found a squirrel in that cast-iron pot you gave me. When I picked up the lid—"

"No way would a squirrel get into your cabin, let alone climb under a heavy lid like that. Why would it? You must have imagined it. Are you still on those drugs the doctor gave you after my Nicky died?"

Allie's husband had always been "my Nicky" to his mother while Mildred had insisted Allie call *her* "Mother Taylor."

"No, Mother Taylor, I told you." Allie's own mother had died when she was nineteen. Her father had moved, remarried and started a new family. They'd lost touch. "I quit taking the pills a long time ago."

"I think it's those pills," Mildred had said as if Allie hadn't spoken. "You said they had you seeing things that weren't there."

"The squirrel *was* there. I had to take it out back and—"

"If I were you, I'd talk to your doctor. Why do you need the pills, anyway? It isn't like you're still grieving over my Nicky. Charlotte Reynolds told me she saw you having lunch the other day, you and Natalie, and you were *laughing*."

Allie had closed her eyes, remembering the lunch in question. "I am trying to make things more normal for Nat."

"Well, it looks bad, you having a good time while your poor husband is barely cold in his grave."

She wanted to mention that Nick wasn't in his grave, but knew better than to bring that up. "It's been eight months."

"Like you have to tell me that!" Mildred sniffed and blew her nose. She'd cried constantly over the death of her favorite son and couldn't understand why Allie wasn't still doing the same.

"We all grieve in our own way and I have a young daughter to raise," Allie had said more times than she wanted to recall.

The phone call had ended with Mildred crying and talking about what a wonderful man her Nicky had been. A lie at best. He'd been a lousy husband and an even worse father, but now that he was dead, he would always be the wonderful man Mildred remembered.

After that, she'd learned her lesson. She kept the other crazy things that had been happening to herself. If Mildred knew, she would have her in a straitjacket. And little Nat…? She couldn't bear to think about Mildred having anything to do with raising her daughter.

"So," Drew said as she and Nat sat across from him in a

booth at a local café later that evening. "Did I hear you've gone back to work?"

It was impossible to keep anything a secret in this canyon, Allie thought. She had hoped to keep it from the Taylor family as long as possible.

"Dana Savage called me about doing a Western wedding up at her ranch for her cousin Tag and his soon-to-be wife, Lily." She didn't mention that she'd accepted the job several months ago. Or how badly she needed the money. With the investigation into Nick's presumed death still unresolved, the insurance company was holding off paying her. Not that it would last long if she didn't get back to work.

Her mother-in-law kept mentioning "that big insurance check my Nicky left you," but the insurance money would barely cover a couple years of Natalie's college, if that. And Allie hoped to invest it for that very use.

"I've been doing some work at Cardwell Ranch. Nice people to work for. But are you sure you're up to it?" Drew asked quietly, real concern in his tone. "Mother mentioned that she was worried about you. She said you were still taking the pills and they were making you see things?"

Of course Mildred told Drew and his sister, Sarah, everything. Allie tried not to show her irritation. She had no appetite, but she attempted to eat what she could. She didn't want Drew mentioning to his mother, even accidentally, that she wasn't eating much. Mildred would make it into her not taking care of herself.

"I'm fine. I'm *not* taking the pills. I told your mother—"

He held up his hand. "You don't have to tell me about my mother. She hears only what she wants to hear. I'm on your side. I think going back to work might be the best thing for you. So what do you plan to do with Natalie? I don't have to tell you what Mother is going to say."

"Nat's going with me," Allie said emphatically. "Dana

has children she can play with. As a matter of fact, Dana is going to teach Nat to ride a horse."

Natalie grinned and clapped her small hands excitedly. She was the spitting image of Allie at that age: straight, pale blond hair cut in a bob, green eyes with a pert little nose and deep dimples. Allie got the blond hair from her Scandinavian mother and the green eyes from her Irish father.

There was no sign of the Taylor family in her daughter, something that had caused a lot of speculation from not only Nick, but his mother.

Nat quickly told her uncle that it would be a very gentle horse and Dana's kids Hank and Mary were riding before they were even her age. "The twins are too young to ride yet," she announced.

"Dana wouldn't let Nat do it if she thought it wasn't all right," Allie added.

"I'm sure it will be fine," Drew said, but she could tell that he already knew what her mother-in-law was going to have to say about it. "Cardwell Ranch is where the wedding is going to be, I take it?"

"The wedding will be in a meadow on the ranch with the reception and a lot of other events in the large, old barn."

"You know that we've been invited," Drew said almost in warning.

The canyon was its own little community, with many of the older families—like Dana's—that dated back to the eighteen hundreds before there was even a paved road through it. Mildred Taylor must be delighted to be invited to a wedding of a family that was like old canyon royalty. Mother Taylor might resent the Cardwell clan, say things behind their back, but she would never outright defy them since everyone loved Dana Cardwell Savage and had held great respect for her mother, Mary Justice.

"How are things with you?" Allie asked.

"Everything's fine." He smiled but she'd seen the lines

around his eyes and had heard that his construction company was struggling without Nick.

He'd been so generous with her and Natalie that she feared he was giving away money he didn't have.

She was just thankful when the meal was over and Drew dropped her and Nat off at the small cabin in the Gallatin Canyon where she'd lived with Nick until his disappearance. *The canyon* as it was known, ran from the mouth just south of Gallatin Gateway almost to West Yellowstone, fifty miles of winding road that trailed the river in a deep cut through the mountains.

The drive along the Gallatin River was breathtaking, a winding strip of highway that followed the blue-ribbon trout stream up over the Continental Divide. In the summer as it was now, the Gallatin ran crystal clear over tinted green boulders. Pine trees grew dark and thick along its edge and against the steep mountains. Aspens, their leaves bright green, grew among the pines.

Sheer rock cliffs overlooked the highway and river, with small areas of open land. The canyon had been mostly cattle and dude ranches, a few summer cabins and homes—that was until Big Sky resort and the small town that followed developed at the foot of Lone Mountain.

Luxury houses had sprouted up all around the resort, with Mother Taylor's being one of them. Fortunately, some of the original cabins still remained and the majority of the canyon was National Forest so it would always remain undeveloped.

Allie's was one of the older cabins. Because it was small and not in great shape, Nick had gotten a good deal on it. Being in construction, he'd promised to enlarge it and fix all the things wrong with it. That hadn't happened.

After Drew left, Allie didn't hurry inside the cabin. It was a nice summer night, the stars overhead glittering brightly and a cool breeze coming up from the river.

She had begun to hate the cabin—and her fear of what might be waiting for her inside it. Nick had been such a force of nature to deal with that his presence seemed to have soaked into the walls. Sometimes she swore she could hear his voice. Often she found items of his clothing lying around the house as if he was still there—even though she'd boxed up his things and taken them to the local charity shop months ago.

Just the thought of what might be waiting for her inside the cabin this time made her shudder as she opened the door and stepped in, Nat at her side.

She hadn't heard Nick's voice since she'd quit taking the drugs. Until last night. When she'd come into the living room, half-asleep, she'd found his favorite shirt lying on the floor by the couch. She'd actually thought she smelled his aftershave even though she'd thrown the bottle away.

The cabin looked just as she'd left it. Letting out a sigh of relief, she put Nat to bed and tried to convince herself she hadn't heard Nick's voice last night. Even the shirt that she'd remembered picking up and thinking it felt warm and smelled of Nick before she'd dropped it over the back of the couch was gone this morning, proving the whole incident had been nothing but a bad dream.

"Good night, sweetheart," she said and kissed her daughter's forehead.

"Night," Nat said sleepily and closed her eyes.

Allie felt as if her heart was going to burst when she looked at her precious daughter. She couldn't let Mildred get her hands on Nat. But if the woman thought for a moment that Allie was incapable of raising her daughter...

She quickly turned out the light and tiptoed out of the room. For a moment, she stood in the small living area. Nick's shirt wasn't over the back of the couch so that was a relief.

So many times she had stood here and wished her life

could be different. Nick had been so sweet while they were dating. She'd really thought she'd met her Prince Charming—until after the wedding and she met the real Nick Taylor.

She sighed, remembering her decision soon after the wedding to leave him and have the marriage annulled, but then she'd realized she was pregnant. Had she really been so naive as to think a baby would change Nick into the man she'd thought she'd married?

Shaking her head now, she looked around the cabin, remembering all the ideas she had to fix the place up and make it a home. Nick had hated them all and they had ended up doing nothing to the cabin.

Well, she could do what she wanted now, couldn't she? But she knew, even if she had the money, she didn't have the heart for it. She would never be able to exorcize Nick's ghost from this house. What she really wanted was to sell the cabin and move. She promised herself she would—once everything with Nick's death was settled.

Stepping into her bedroom, she was startled to see a pile of her clothes on her bed. Had she taken them out of the closet earlier when she'd changed to go to dinner? Her heart began to pound. She'd been upset earlier but she wouldn't have just thrown her clothes on the bed like that.

Then how had they gotten there? She'd locked the cabin when she'd left.

Panicked, she raced through the house to see if anything was missing or if any of the doors or windows had been broken into. Everything was just as she'd left it—except for the clothes on her bed.

Reluctantly, she walked back into her bedroom half-afraid the clothes wouldn't still be on the bed. Another hallucination?

The clothes were there. Unfortunately, that didn't come as a complete relief. Tonight at dinner, she'd worn capris, a blouse and sandals since it was June in Montana. Why would she have pulled out what appeared to be almost everything she owned from the closet? No, she realized, not *everything*. These were only the clothes that Nick had bought her.

Tears blurred her eyes as she started to pick up one of the dresses. Like the others, she hated this dress because it reminded her of the times he'd made her wear it and how the night had ended. It was very low cut in the front. She'd felt cheap in it and told him so but he'd only laughed.

"When you've got it, flaunt it," he'd said. "That's what I say."

Why hadn't she gotten rid of these clothes? For the same reason she hadn't thrown out the chili pot after the squirrel incident. She hadn't wanted to upset her mother-in-law. Placating Mother Taylor had begun right after Allie had married her son. It was just so much easier than arguing with the woman.

"Nick said you don't like the dresses he buys you," Mildred had said disapprovingly one day when she'd stopped by the cabin and asked Allie why she wasn't wearing the new dress. "There is nothing wrong with looking nice for your husband."

"The dresses he buys me are just more revealing than I feel comfortable with."

Her mother-in-law had mugged a face. "You'd better loosen up and give my son what he wants or he'll find someone who will."

Now as she reached for the dress on the top of the pile, she told herself she would throw them out, Mother Taylor be damned.

But the moment she touched the dress, she let out a cry of surprise and panic. The fabric had jagged cuts down the front. She stared in horror as she saw other deep, angry-looking slices in the fabric. *Who had done this?*

Her heart in her throat, she picked up another of the dresses Nick had made her wear. Her sewing scissors clattered to the bedroom floor. She stared down at the scissors in horror, then at the pile of destroyed clothing. All of the dresses Nick had bought her had been ruined.

Allie shook her head as she dropped the dress in her hand and took a step back from the bed. Banging into the closed closet doors, she fought to breathe, her heart hammering in her chest. *Who did this?* Who *would* do this? She remembered her brother-in-law calling from out in the hall earlier, asking what was taking her so long before they'd gone to dinner. But that was because she'd taken a shower to get the smell of her own fear off her. It wasn't because she was in here cutting up the clothes her dead husband had made her wear.

Tears welled in her eyes, making the room blur. She shoved that bitter thought away and wiped at her tears. She wouldn't have done this. She *couldn't* have.

Suddenly, she turned and stared at the closed closet door with mounting fear. Slowly, she reached for the knob, her hand trembling. As the closet door came open, she froze. Her eyes widened in new alarm.

A half dozen new outfits hung in the otherwise nearly empty closet, the price tags still on them. As if sleepwalking, Allie reached for one of the tags and stared in shock at the price. Hurriedly, she checked the others. She couldn't afford any of them. So where had they come from?

Not only that, the clothes were what she would call "classic," the type of clothes she'd worn when she'd met Nick. The kind of clothes she'd pleaded with him to let her wear.

"I want other men to look at you and wish they were me," Nick had said, getting angry.

But when she and Nick went out and she wore the clothes and other men did look, Nick had blamed her.

"You must have given him the eye," Nick would say as

they argued on the way home. "Probably flipped your hair like an invitation. Who knows what you do while I'm at work all day."

"I take care of your daughter and your house."

Nick hadn't let her work after they'd gotten married, even though he knew how much she loved her wedding planning business. "Women who work get too uppity. They think they don't need a man. No wife of mine is going to work."

Allie had only the clothes he bought her. She'd purchased little since his death because the money had been so tight. Nick had wanted to know about every cent she'd spent, so she hadn't been able to save any money, either. Nick paid the bills and gave her a grocery allowance. He said he'd buy her whatever she needed.

Now she stared at the beautiful clothes hanging in her closet. Beautiful blouses and tops. Amazing skirts and pants and dresses. Clothes Nick would have taken out in the yard and burned. But Nick was gone.

Or was he? He still hadn't been declared legally dead. That thought scared her more than she wanted to admit. What if he suddenly turned up at her door one night?

Was that what was making her crazy? Maybe she *had* done this. She had yearned for clothing like this and hated the clothes Nick had bought her, so had she subconsciously...

Allie stumbled away from the closet, bumped into the corner of the bed and sat down hard on the floor next to it. Her hand shook as she covered her mouth to keep from screaming. Had she shoplifted these clothes? She couldn't have purchased them. Just as she couldn't have cut up the dresses and not remembered. There had to be another explanation. Someone was playing a horrible trick on her.

But even as she pondered it, more rational thoughts came on its heels. Did she really believe that someone had come into the cabin and done this? Who in their right mind would believe that?

Pushing herself up, she crawled over to where she'd dropped her purse as she tried to remember even the last time she'd written a check. Her checkbook wasn't in her purse. She frowned and realized she must have left it in the desk when she'd paid bills.

Getting up she walked on wobbly legs to the desk in the corner, opened the drawer and took out her checkbook. Her fingers shook with such a tremor that she could barely read what was written in it.

But there it was. A check for more than eight hundred dollars! The handwriting was scrawled, but she knew it had to be hers. She saw the date of the check. *Yesterday?*

She had dropped Nat off for a playdate and then gone into Bozeman… Could she account for the entire afternoon? Her heart pounded as she tried to remember everything she'd done and when she might have bought these clothes. She'd been wandering around in a daze since Nick's death. She couldn't account for every minute of yesterday, but what did that matter? The proof was staring her in the face.

Allie shoved the checkbook into the drawer and tried to pull herself together. She had to think about her daughter.

"You're fine," she whispered to herself. "Once you get back to work…" She couldn't have been more thankful that she had the Cardwell Ranch wedding. More than the money, she needed to do what she loved—planning weddings—and get her mind off everything else.

Once she was out of this house she'd shared with Nick… Yes, then she would be fine. She wouldn't be so…forgetful. What woman wouldn't feel she was losing her mind, considering what she'd been going through?

Chapter Two

"Who's that singing?" five-year-old Ford Cardwell asked as he and his father followed the sound.

Jackson Cardwell had parked the rental SUV down by his cousin Dana's ranch house when they'd arrived, but finding no one at home, they'd headed up the hill toward the barn and the van parked in front of it.

"I have no idea, son," Jackson said, but couldn't help smiling. The voice was young and sweet, the song beautiful. "It sounds like an angel."

"It *is* an angel," Ford cried and pointed past the barn to the corrals.

The girl was about his son's age, but while Ford had taken after the Cardwell side of the family with his dark hair and eyes, this child had pale blond hair and huge green eyes.

When she saw them, she smiled, exposing two deep dimples. Both children were adorable, but this little girl was hands down more angelic-looking and—Jackson would bet—*acting* than Ford.

She wore cowboy boots with a pale green-and-white-polka-dotted, one-piece, short jumpsuit that brought out the emerald-green of her eyes. Jackson saw that the girl was singing to several horses that had come up to the edge of the corral fence.

The girl finished the last of the lyrics before she seemed

to notice them and came running over. "If you're looking for my mother, she's in the barn working."

Next to him, Jackson saw that his son had apparently been struck dumb.

"I'm Nat," the girl announced. "My name is really Natalie, though." She shifted her gaze to the mute Ford. "Everyone calls me Nat, so you can if you want to."

"This is my son, Ford."

Nat eyed Ford for a moment before she stepped forward and took his hand. "Come on, Ford. You'll probably want to see the rest of the animals. There are chickens and rabbits and several mules along with all the horses. Don't worry," she added before Jackson could voice his concern. "We won't get too close. We'll just pet them through the corral fence and feed the horses apples. It's okay. Mrs. Savage showed me how."

"Don't go far," Jackson said as the precocious Nat led his son toward several low-slung buildings. The girl was busy talking as they left. Ford, as far as Jackson could tell, hadn't uttered a word yet.

As he turned back toward the barn, he saw the logo on the side of the van: Weddings by Allie Knight. The logo looked old as did the van.

The girl had said her mother was working in the barn. That must be where the wedding was going to be held. His brother Tag had mentioned something about his wedding to Lily McCabe being very *Western.*

"You mean like Texas meets Montana?" Jackson had joked.

"Something like that. Don't worry. You'll feel right at home."

His brother's wedding wasn't what had him worried. After talking to Tag for a few moments on the phone, he'd known his brother had fallen head over heels for Lily. He was happy for him.

No, what worried Jackson was nailing down the last of the plans before the wedding for the opening of a Texas Boys Barbecue joint in Big Sky, Montana. He had hoped that all of the brothers would be here by now. Laramie and Austin hadn't even flown up to see the space Tag had found, let alone signed off on the deal.

From the time the five brothers had opened their first restaurant in an old house in Houston, they'd sworn they would never venture outside of Texas with their barbecue. Even as their business had grown and they'd opened more restaurants and finally started their own franchise, they had stayed in the state where they'd been raised.

Jackson understood why Tag wanted to open one here. But he feared it had nothing to do with business and everything to do with love and not wanting to leave Montana, where they had all been born.

Before the wedding had seemed the perfect time for all of them to get together and finalize the deal. Hayes had come here last month to see if the restaurant was even feasible. Unfortunately, Hayes had gotten sidetracked, so now it was up to the rest of them to make sure Tag was doing the best thing for the business—and before the wedding, which was only four days away.

He hoped all his brothers arrived soon so they could get this over with. They led such busy lives in Texas that they hardly ever saw each other. Tag had said on the phone he was anxious to show him the building he'd found for the new restaurant. Tag and Hayes had already made arrangements to buy the building without the final okay from the other brothers, something else that made Jackson nervous.

Jackson didn't want this move to cause problems among the five of them. So his mind was miles away as he started to step into the dim darkness inside the barn.

The cool air inside was suddenly filled with a terrified scream. An instant later, a black cat streaked past him and out the barn door.

JACKSON RACED INTO the barn not sure what he was going to find. What he found was a blond-haired woman who shared a striking resemblance to the little girl who'd been singing outside by the corrals.

While Nat had been angelic, this woman was as beautiful as any he'd ever seen. Her long, straight, blond hair was the color of sunshine. It rippled down her slim back. Her eyes, a tantalizing emerald-green, were huge with fear in a face that could stop traffic.

She stood against the barn wall, a box of wedding decorations open at her feet. Her eyes widened in even more alarm when she saw him. She threw a hand over her mouth, cutting off the scream.

"Are you all right?" he asked. She didn't appear to be hurt, just scared. No, not scared, *terrified.* Had she seen a mouse? Or maybe something larger? In Texas it might have been an armadillo. He wasn't sure what kind of critters they had this far north, but something had definitely set her off.

"It was nothing," she said, removing her hand from her mouth. Some of the color slowly returned to her face but he could see that she was still trembling.

"It was *something,*" he assured her.

She shook her head and ventured a look at the large box of decorations at her feet. The lid had been thrown to the side, some of the decorations spilling onto the floor.

He laughed. "Let me guess. That black cat I just saw hightailing it out of here… I'm betting he came out of that box."

Her eyes widened further. *"You saw it?"*

"Raced right past me." He laughed. "You didn't think you imagined it, did you?"

"It happened so fast. I couldn't be sure."

"Must have given you quite a fright."

She let out a nervous laugh and tried to smile, exposing deep dimples. He understood now why his son had gone mute. He felt the same way looking at Natalie's mother. There was an innocence about her, a vulnerability that would make a man feel protective.

Just the thought made him balk. He'd fallen once and wasn't about to get lured into that trap again. Not that there was any chance of that happening. In a few days he would be on a plane back to Texas with his son.

"You know cats," he said, just being polite. "They'll climb into just about anything. They're attracted by pretty things." Just like some cowboys. Not him, though.

"Yes," she said, but didn't sound convinced as she stepped away from the box. She didn't look all that steady on her feet. He started to reach out to her, but stopped himself as she found her footing.

He couldn't help noticing that her eyes were a darker shade of green than her daughter's. "Just a cat. A black one at that," he said, wondering why he felt the need to fill the silence. "You aren't superstitious, are you?"

She shook her head and those emerald eyes brightened. That with the color returning to her cheeks made her even more striking.

This was how he'd fallen for Ford's mother—a pretty face and what had seemed like a sweet disposition in a woman who'd needed him—and look how that had turned out. No, it took more than a pretty face to turn his head after the beating he'd taken from the last one.

"You must be one of Tag's brothers," she said as she wiped her palms on her jeans before extending a hand. Along with jeans, she wore a checked navy shirt, the sleeves rolled up, and cowboy boots. "I'm Allie Taylor, the wedding planner."

Jackson quickly removed his hat, wondering where he'd

left his manners. His mother had raised him better than this. But even as he started to shake her hand, he felt himself hesitate as if he were afraid to touch her.

Ridiculous, he thought as he grasped her small, ice-cold hand in his larger, much warmer one. "Jackson Cardwell. I saw your van outside. But I thought the name on the side—"

"Taylor is my married name." When his gaze went to her empty ring finger, she quickly added, "I'm a widow." She pulled back her hand to rub the spot where her wedding band had resided not that long ago. There was a thin, white line indicating that she hadn't been widowed long. Or she hadn't taken the band off until recently.

"I believe I met your daughter as my son and I were coming in. Natalie?"

"Yes, my baby girl." Her dimpled smile told him everything he needed to know about her relationship with her daughter. He knew that smile and suspected he had one much like it when he talked about Ford.

He felt himself relax a little. There was nothing dangerous about this woman. She was a single parent, just like him. Only she'd lost her husband and he wished he could get rid of his ex indefinitely.

"Your daughter took my son to see the horses. I should probably check on him."

"Don't worry. Nat has a healthy respect for the horses and knows the rules. Also Warren Fitzpatrick, their hired man, is never far away. He's Dana's semi-retired ranch manager. She says he's a fixture around here and loves the kids. That seems to be his job now, to make sure the kids are safe. Not that there aren't others on the ranch watching out for them, as well. Sorry, I talk too much when I'm…nervous." She took a deep breath and let it out slowly. "I want this wedding to be perfect."

He could tell she was still shaken by the black cat episode. "My brother Tag mentioned that Dana and the kids had almost been killed by some crazy woman. It's good she has someone she trusts keeping an eye on the children, even with everyone else on the ranch watching out for them. Don't worry," he said, looking around the barn. "I'm sure the wedding will be perfect."

The barn was huge and yet this felt almost too intimate standing here talking to her. "I was just about to get Ford and go down to the house. Dana told me she was baking a huge batch of chocolate chip cookies and to help ourselves. I believe she said there would also be homemade lemonade when we got here."

Allie smiled and he realized she'd thought it was an invitation. "I really need to get these decorations—"

"Sorry. I'm keeping you from your work." He took a step back. "Those decorations aren't going to put themselves up."

She looked as if she wasn't so sure of that. The cat had definitely put a scare into her, he thought. She didn't seem sure of anything right now. Allie looked again at the box of decorations, no doubt imagining the cat flying out of it at her.

Glancing at her watch, she said, "Oh, I didn't realize it was so late. Nat and I are meeting a friend for lunch. We need to get going."

Jackson was suddenly aware that he'd been holding his hat since shaking Allie's hand. He quickly put it back on as they walked out of the barn door into the bright sunshine. "My son is quite taken with your daughter," he said, again feeling an unusual need to fill the silence.

"How old is he?"

"Ford's five."

"Same age as Nat."

As they emerged into the beautiful late-June day, Jackson saw the two children and waved. As they came running, Nat was chattering away and Ford was hanging on her every word.

"They do seem to have hit it off." Allie sounded surprised and pleased. "Nat's had a hard time lately. I'm glad to see her making a new friend."

Jackson could see that Allie Taylor had been having a hard time, as well. He realized she must have loved her husband very much. He knew he should say something, but for the life of him he couldn't think of what. He couldn't even imagine a happy marriage. As a vehicle came roaring up the road, they both turned, the moment lost.

"Hey, bro," Tanner "Tag" Cardwell called from the rolled down window of his pickup as he swung into the ranch yard. "I see you made it," he said, getting out to come over and shake his brother's hand before he pulled Jackson into a hug. Tag glanced over at Ford and Natalie and added with a laugh, "Like father like son. If there's a pretty female around, you two will find them."

Jackson shook his head. That had been true when he'd met Ford's mother. But since the divorce and the custody battle, he'd been too busy single-handedly raising his son to even think about women. That's why red flags had gone up when he'd met Allie. There was something about her that had pulled at him, something more than her obvious beauty.

"Dana's right behind me with the kids," Tag said. "Why don't I show you and Ford to your cabin, then you can meet everyone." He pointed up in the pines that covered the mountainside. "Let's grab your bags. It's just a short walk."

Jackson turned to say goodbye to Allie, but she and her daughter had already headed for the old van.

"Come on, Nat, we're meeting Belinda for lunch," Allie said as the Cardwell men headed for the cabins on the mountain behind the barn. Working here had been a godsend. Nat was having a wonderful time. She loved Dana's children. Hank was a year older than Nat, with Mary being the same age. Dana's twin boys, Angus and Brick, were just over a year and her sister Stacy's daughter, Ella, was a year and a half. Dana had her hands full but Stacy helped out with the younger ones. All of them loved the animals, especially the horses.

True to her word, Dana had made sure Nat had begun her horseback riding lessons. Nat was a natural, Dana had said, and Allie could see it was true.

Their few days here so far had been perfect.

Until the cat, there hadn't been any other incidents.

Her friend Belinda Andrews was waiting for them at a little Mexican food place near Meadow Village at Big Sky. While other friends had gone by the wayside since she'd married Nick six years ago, Belinda hadn't let Nick run her off. Allie suspected that, like her, she didn't have a lot of friends and Nick, while he'd made it clear he didn't like Belinda, had grudgingly put up with her the times they'd crossed paths.

"I hope we didn't keep you waiting," Allie said as she and Nat met Belinda on the patio. "You didn't have any trouble getting off work for the wedding shoot?" Belinda worked for a local photographer, but freelanced weddings. It was how they'd met back when Allie had her own wedding planning business.

Belinda grinned. "All set for the Tag Cardwell and Lily McCabe wedding. I took Dana up on her offer. I'm moving into one of the guest cabins later today!"

Allie wasn't all that surprised. Dana had offered her a cabin, as well, while she was preparing everything for the wedding. But since she lived just down the highway a few miles, Allie thought it best to remain at home for Nat's sake. Her daughter had had enough changes in her life recently.

"You really are excited about this," Allie said, noticing how nice Belinda looked. Her friend was dressed in a crop top and cut-off jeans, her skin tanned. Her dark hair was piled haphazardly up on her head, silver dangly earrings tinkled from her earlobes and, while she looked makeup free, Allie could tell she wasn't.

Belinda looked enchanting, a trick Allie wished she could pull off, she thought. On the way here, she'd pulled her hair up in a ponytail and even though she'd showered this morning, she'd forgone makeup. Nick was always suspicious when she wore it when he wasn't around so she'd gotten out of the habit.

Inside the café, Nat asked if she could play in the nearby area for kids and Allie said she could as long as she didn't argue about coming back to eat when her meal came.

"You look…pale," Belinda said, studying her after they were seated outside on the patio under an umbrella so they could see Nat. "You haven't had anymore of those…incidents, have you?"

Allie almost laughed at that. "I just need to get more sun," she said and picked up her menu to hide behind.

"I know you too well," Belinda said, dragging down the menu so she could look into her eyes. "What's happened *now?*"

"A black cat jumped out of one of my decoration boxes and scared me just before I came over here. And guess what? Someone else saw it." *So there,* she wanted to say, *I don't need my head examined.*

Belinda nodded, studying her. "A *black* cat?"

"Yes, a *black* cat and I didn't imagine it. One of the Cardwell brothers saw it, as well." She couldn't even voice how much of a relief that had been.

"That's all that's happened?"

"That's it." She had to look down at the menu to pull off the lie and was just glad when Belinda didn't question her further. She hadn't told *anyone* about the shredded dresses from her closet or the new clothes she'd taken back. The sales associate hadn't remembered her, but said the afternoon when the clothing was purchased had been a busy one. None of the other sales associates remembered her, but agreed they'd been too busy to say for sure. She'd ended up keeping two of the outfits to wear while working the rehearsal dinner and the wedding.

"I already moved some of my things into the cabin," Belinda said.

Allie couldn't help being surprised. "Already? Why didn't you stop by the barn and say hello?" Allie had suggested Belinda as the wedding photographer and felt responsible and anxious since this was her first wedding in five years.

"You were busy," her friend said. "We can't keep each other from our jobs, right?"

"Right." She loved that Belinda understood that. In truth, Allie had been hesitant to suggest her friend. She didn't want to have to worry about Belinda, not with everything else that she had going on in her life right now. While her friend was a great photographer, sometimes she got sidetracked if a handsome man was around. But when she'd broached the subject with the bride-to-be, Lily had been delighted that it was one other thing she didn't have to worry about.

Dana had been kind enough to offer Belinda a cabin on the ranch for the five-day affair. "It will make it easier for you to get great shots if you're staying up here and experiencing all the wedding festivities," Dana had said. "And any friend of Allie's is a friend of ours."

She and Belinda had been friends since grade school. Lately they hadn't been as close, probably Allie's fault. Belinda was in between men right now, and much wilder, freer and more outspoken than Allie had ever been. But Belinda didn't have a five-year-old daughter, either.

"You have no idea what this means to me," Belinda said now. "I've been dying to photograph a Western wedding for my portfolio."

"Your portfolio?"

Belinda looked embarrassed as if she'd let the cat out of the bag, so to speak. "I'm thinking about opening my own studio."

"That's great." Allie was happy for her friend, although she'd wondered if Belinda had come into some money because it wouldn't be cheap and as far as she knew Belinda lived from paycheck to paycheck like everyone else she knew.

The waitress came and took their orders. A light breeze stirred the new leaves on the nearby trees. The smell of summer mixed with that of corn tortillas, the most wonderful smell of all, Allie thought. They sipped Mexican Cokes, munched on chips and salsa to the sound of Latin music playing in the background and Allie felt herself begin to relax.

"I wasn't going to bring this up," Belinda said, "but you know that psychic that I've seen off and on?"

Allie fought not to roll her eyes.

"I know you say you don't believe in this stuff, but she said something interesting when I mentioned you."

"You told her about *me?*" Allie hadn't meant for her voice to rise so high. Her daughter looked over. She smiled at Nat and quickly changed her tone. "I really don't want you talking to anyone about me, let alone a…" She tried to come up with a word other than *charlatan*.

Belinda leaned forward, unfazed. "She thinks what's happening to you is because of guilt. Simply put, you feel guilty and it is manifesting itself into these…*incidents.*"

Allie stared at her. Leave it to Belinda to get right to the heart of it.

Her friend lowered her voice as if afraid Nat might be listening. "It makes sense, if you think about it. Nick didn't know you were—" she glanced at Nat "—leaving him and going to file for custody of you-know-who, but *you* did know your plan. Then he goes and gets himself…" She grimaced in place of the word *killed*. "Something like that has to mess with your mind."

"Yes, losing your husband does mess with your mind no matter what kind of marriage you had." Fortunately, the waitress brought their food. Allie called Nat up to the table and, for a few moments, they ate in silence.

"The thing is…" Belinda said between bites.

"Can't we just enjoy our meal?" Allie pleaded.

Her friend waved that suggestion away, but didn't say more until they had finished and Nat had gone back to the play area.

"The psychic thinks there is more to it," Belinda said. "What if Nick *knew* about your…plan?"

"What are you saying?"

"Come on. You've been over Nick for a long time. His death wouldn't make you crazy—"

"I'm not crazy," she protested weakly.

"But what if he *did* know or at least suspected? Come on, Allie. We both know it was so not like Nick to go hunting up into the mountains alone, knowing that the grizzlies were eating everything they could get their paws on before hibernation." She didn't seem to notice Allie wince. "Didn't the ranger say Nick had food in his backpack?"

"He didn't take food to attract a bear, if that's what you're saying. He planned to stay a few days so of course he had food in his backpack."

"I'm not trying to upset you. But if he went up there to end it all, that was his choice. You can't go crazy because you feel guilty."

Her stomach turned at the thought of the backpack she'd been asked to identify. It had been shredded by the grizzly's claws. She'd been horrified to think of what the bear had done to Nick. She would never forget the officer who'd brought her the news.

"From what we've been able to assess at the scene, your husband was attacked by a grizzly and given the tracks and other signs—"

"Signs?"

"Blood, ma'am."

She'd had to sit down. "You're telling me he's...dead?"

"It certainly looks that way," the ranger said. Four days later, the search for Nick Taylor was called off because a winter storm had come in and it was believed that there was little chance he could have survived such an attack without immediate medical attention.

"Nick wouldn't," she managed to say now. In her heart of hearts, the man she knew so well, the man she'd been married to for more than six years, wouldn't purposely go into the woods with a plan to be killed by a grizzly.

But Nick had always been unpredictable. Moody and often depressed, too. The construction business hadn't been doing well even before Nick's death. What would he have done if he'd known she was leaving him and taking his daughter? Hadn't she been suspicious when Nick told her of his plan to go hunting alone? She'd actually thought he might be having an affair and wanted to spend a few days with his mistress. She'd actually hoped that was the case.

"You're going by yourself?" she'd asked. Nick couldn't even watch football by himself.

"I know things haven't been great with us lately," he'd said. That alone had surprised her. She really thought Nick hadn't noticed or cared. "I think a few days apart is just what we both need. I can tell you aren't happy. I promise you there will be changes when I get back and maybe I'll even come home with a nice buck." He'd cupped her face in his hands. "I don't think you know what you mean to me, but I promise to show you when I get back." He'd kissed her then, softly, sweetly, and for a moment, she'd wondered if Nick could change.

"You're wrong about Nick," she said now to Belinda. "If he was going to end it, he would have chosen the least painful way to do it. Not one—" she looked at Nat, who was swinging nearby, humming to herself and seemingly oblivious to their conversation "—that chose him. He had a gun with him he could have used."

"Maybe he didn't get the chance, but you're probably right," Belinda said and grabbed the check. "Let me get this. I didn't mean to upset you. It's just that you need to get a handle on whatever's been going on with you for you-know-who's sake." She cut her eyes to Nat, who headed toward them as they stood to leave.

"You're right about the guilt, though," Allie said, giving her friend that. She'd known as she'd watched Nick leave that day to go up into the mountains that nothing could change him enough to make her stay. She was going to ask him for a divorce when he came back.

Belinda changed the subject. "I saw your brother-in-law, Drew, earlier on the ranch."

Allie nodded. "He mentioned he was working up there. His construction company built the guest cabins."

"I'd forgotten that." Belinda frowned. "I was talking to Lily about photos at the rehearsal dinner. Did you know that Sarah is one of her bridesmaids?"

"My sister-in-law worked with Lily one season at her brother James's Canyon Bar." Allie had the impression that Lily didn't have a lot of female friends. Most of the math professors she knew were male, apparently. "I think James feels sorry for Sarah and you know Lily, she is so sweet."

"I have to hand it to Sarah, putting up with her mother day in and day out," Belinda said.

Allie didn't want to think about it. Along with fewer incidents the past few days, she'd also been blessed with no visits from her mother-in-law and Sarah.

"Sarah's a saint, especially—" Belinda lowered her voice

"—the way Mildred treats her. She is constantly bugging her about her weight and how she is never going to get a husband… It's awful."

Allie agreed.

"I don't understand why she doesn't leave."

"Where would she go and what would she do?" Allie said. "Sarah was in college when Mildred broke her leg. She quit to come home and take care of her mother. Mildred has milked it ever since. It used to annoy Nick, Sarah living in the guesthouse. He thought Sarah was taking advantage of his mother."

"Ha, it's the other way around. Sarah is on twenty-four-hour call. She told me that her mother got her out of bed at 2:00 a.m. one time to heat her some milk because she couldn't sleep. I would have put a pillow over the old nag's face."

Allie laughed and changed the subject. "You look especially nice today," she commented, realizing that her friend had seemed happier lately. It dawned on her why. "There's someone new in your life."

Belinda shrugged. She didn't like to talk about the men she dated because she thought it would jinx things for her. Not talking about them didn't seem to work, either, though. Belinda was so superstitious. Why else would she see a psychic to find out her future?

"This is going to be so much fun, the two of us working together again. Don't worry. I won't get in your way." Belinda took her hand. "I'm sorry I upset you. Sometimes I don't have the brains God gave a rock."

She didn't think that was the way the expression went, but said nothing. Belinda could be so…annoying and yet so sweet. Allie didn't know what she would have done without her the past few years. Belinda had been the only person she would talk freely to about Nick and the trouble between them.

"I'm just worried about you, honey," Belinda said, squeezing her hand. "I really think you should see some-one—"

"I don't need a shrink."

"Not a shrink. Someone more…spiritual who can help you make sense of the things that you say keep happening."

"Things *do* keep happening," she snapped. "I'm not mak-ing them up."

"So talk to this woman," Belinda said just as adamantly. She pressed a business card into Allie's hand.

She glanced at it and groaned. "Your psychic friend?"

"She might be the *only* person who can help you," Be-linda said cryptically. She gripped Allie's hand tighter. "She says she can get you in touch with Nick so you can get past this."

Allie stared at her for a moment before laughing out loud. "You have got to be kidding. What does she use? A Ouija board?"

"Don't laugh. This woman can tell you things that will make the hair on your head stand straight up."

That's all I need, she thought, reminded of Jackson Cardwell asking her if she was superstitious.

"Call her," Belinda said, closing Allie's fingers around the woman's business card. "You need closure, Allie. This woman can give it to you. She's expecting your call."

"I've been expecting your call, as well," said a sharp, older voice.

They both turned to see Mildred and her daughter. From the looks on their faces, they'd been standing there for some time.

Chapter Three

"Want to see the building for Montana's first Texas Boys Barbecue?" Tag asked after they'd dropped Jackson and Ford's luggage off at the small cabin on the side of the mountain and gone down to meet cousin Dana and her brood.

Dana Cardwell Savage was just as Tag had described her. Adorable and sweet and delighted that everyone was coming for the wedding.

"How is your cabin?" she asked after introducing him to her children with husband, Marshal Hud Savage. Hank was the spitting image of his father, Dana said, and six now. Mary was five and looked just like her mom. Then there were the twins, Angus and Brick, just a year and a half old with the same dark hair and eyes as all the Cardwells.

"The cabin is great," Jackson said as Ford instantly bonded with his second cousins. "Thank you so much for letting me stay there."

"Family is why we had them built," Dana said. "My Texas cousins will always have a place to stay when you visit. Or until you find a place to live in Montana when you realize you want to live up here," she added with a wink. "Isn't that right, Tag?"

"I would love to visit, but I'm never leaving Texas," Jackson said.

"Never say never," Tag commented under his breath.

"I was just about to take him down to see the restaurant location."

Ford took off with the other kids into a room full of toys and didn't even look back as his father left. Jackson almost felt as if he were losing his son to Montana and the Cardwell clan.

"Are you sure you don't want to wait until everyone gets here?" he asked as they left.

"Hayes and Laramie are flying in tomorrow. I was hoping you would pick them up at the airport. Austin is apparently on a case tying up some loose ends." He shrugged. Of the five of them, Austin was the loner. He was dedicated to his job and being tied up on a case was nothing new. "Anyway, it's your opinion I want. You're better at this than all three of them put together."

"So you haven't heard from Austin on the deal," Jackson guessed.

Tag shook his head. "You know how he is. He'll go along with whatever everyone else says. Come on," he said with a laugh when Jackson groaned. "I really do want your opinion."

"*Honest* opinion?" Jackson asked.

"Of course."

Jackson glanced around as they drove out of the ranch and down the highway to the turnoff to Big Sky. Being the youngest, he didn't remember anything about Montana. He'd been a baby when his mother had packed up her five sons and taken them to Texas.

Big Sky looked more like a wide spot in the road rather than a town. There were clusters of buildings broken only by sagebrush or golf greens.

"This is the lower Meadow Village," Tag told him. "There is also the Mountain Village higher up the mountain where the ski resort is. You really have to see this place in the winter. It's crazy busy around the holidays. There are a lot of second homes here so the residents fly in and spend a few weeks generally in the summer and the holidays. More and more people, though, are starting to live here year-round. There is opportunity here, Jackson."

Jackson wanted to tell his brother that he didn't need to sell him. He'd go along with whatever the others decided. In fact, he'd already spoken to Hayes about it. Once Hayes got on board, it was clear to Jackson that this was probably a done deal. The holdout, if there was one, would be Austin and only because he wouldn't be available to sign off on the deal. Even Laramie sounded as if he thought the restaurant was a good idea.

"Where does Harlan live?" Jackson asked as they drove past mansions, condos and some tiny old cabins that must have been there before anyone even dreamed of a Big Sky. He had only a vague recollection of his father from those few times Harlan had visited Texas when he was growing up.

"He lives in one of those cabins back there, the older ones. We can stop by his place if you like. More than likely he and Uncle Angus are down at the Corral Bar. It's their favorite watering hole. Maybe we could have a beer with them later."

"I'm sure I'll see him soon enough." Harlan was a stranger who hadn't even made Jackson's wedding, not that the marriage had lasted long, anyway. But he felt no tie to the man who'd fathered him and doubted he ever would. It was only when he thought about Ford that he had regrets. It would have been nice for Ford to have a grandfather. His ex-wife's family had no interest in Ford. So the only family his son had in Texas was Jackson's mother, Rosalee Cardwell and his brother Laramie. Tag had already moved to Montana and Hayes would be moving here soon.

"I'm getting to know Dad," Tag said. "He's pretty remarkable."

"Tell me about your wedding planner," Jackson said,

changing the subject then regretting the topic he'd picked when his brother grinned over at him. "I'm just curious about her." He hadn't told anyone about the cat or the terrified woman he'd found in the barn earlier. Her reaction seemed over the top given it had only been a cat. Though it *had* been a black one. Maybe she *was* superstitious.

"Allie's great. Dana suggested her. That's our Dana, always trying to help those in need. Allie lost her husband eight months ago. Terrible thing. He was hunting in the mountains and apparently killed by a grizzly bear."

"Apparently?"

"They never found his body. They think the bear dragged the body off somewhere. Won't be the first time remains have turned up years later in the mountains—if they turn up at all. They found his backpack and enough blood that he can be declared legally dead but I guess the insurance company has been dragging its feet."

Jackson thought of Allie and her little girl, Nat. "How horrible for them."

"Yeah, she's been having a hard time both emotionally and financially according to Dana, who suggested her for our wedding planner because of it. But Lily loves Allie and, of course, Natalie. That little girl is so darned bright."

"Yeah, Ford is definitely taken with her." But his thoughts were on Allie and her reaction to the cat flying out of that box of wedding decorations. It must have scared her half out of her wits in the emotional state she was in. "That was nice of Dana to hire her."

"Allie worked as a wedding planner before she married Nick Taylor. Dana offered Allie and Nat one of the new guest ranch cabins where we're staying. But I guess she thinks it would be better for Natalie to stay in their own home."

"Where do Allie and her daughter live now?"

"An old cabin down by the river. I'll show you on the

way back." Tag swung into a small complex and turned off the engine. "Welcome to the site of the next Texas Boys Barbecue joint."

"I THOUGHT YOU had a job," Mildred said to Allie over the sound of brass horns playing cantina music at the Mexican café.

"They allow lunch breaks," she said. "But I really need to get back." She excused herself to go to the ladies' room.

Mildred turned to Natalie, leaned down and pinched her cheek. "How is my sweetie today? Grandma misses you. When are you coming to my house?"

In the restroom, Allie splashed cold water on her face and tried to calm down. How much had they heard?

Enough that they had been looking at her strangely. Or was that all in her mind, as well? But if they heard Belinda trying to get her to see a psychic so she could reach Nick on the other side… Allie could well imagine what they would think.

She hurried, not wanting to leave Natalie with her grandmother for long. She hated it, but Mildred seemed to nag the child all the time about not spending enough time with her.

Leaving the restroom, she saw that Sarah and her mother hadn't taken a seat. Instead, they were standing at the take-out counter. There was no avoiding talking to them again.

"I couldn't help but overhear your…friend suggesting you see a…psychic?" Mother Taylor said, leaving no doubt that they had been listening. "Surely she meant a psychiatrist, which indicates that you are still having those hallucinations." She quirked an eyebrow, waiting for an answer.

"Belinda was only joking. I'm feeling much better, thank you."

Mildred's expression said she wasn't buying a minute of it. "Sarah, I left my sweater in the car."

"I'll get it, Mother." Sarah turned and headed for their vehicle parked out front.

"How is this…job of yours going?" Mildred asked. "I've never understood what wedding planners do."

Allie had actually told her once, listing about fifty things she did but Mildred clearly hadn't been listening.

"I'll have to tell you sometime," she said now. "But I need to get back to it. Come on, Natalie."

"You should let me have her for the rest of the day," Mildred said. "In fact, she can spend the night at my house."

"I'm sorry, but Natalie is getting horseback riding lessons this afternoon," Allie lied. "She's having a wonderful time with Dana's children."

"Well, she can still—"

"Not only that, I also prefer to have Nat with me right now. It's hard enough without Nick." Another lie followed by the biggest truth of all, "I need my daughter right now."

Mildred looked surprised. "That's the first time I've heard you mention my Nicky in months." She seemed about to cry. Sarah returned with her sweater, slipping it around her shoulders without even a thank-you from Mildred.

Nearby, Belinda was finishing up their bill.

"I really should get back to work." Allie tried to step past her mother-in-law, but the older woman grabbed her arm. "I worry that you are ill-equipped to take care of yourself, let alone a child. I need Natalie more than you do. I—"

Allie jerked her arm free. "Natalie would be heartbroken if she was late to her horseback riding lesson." She hurried to her daughter, picked up her purse off the table and, taking Nat's hand, left the restaurant, trying hard not to run.

She told herself to calm down. Any sign of her being upset and her in-laws would view it as her being unable to take care of Nat. But all she wanted was to get away and as quickly as possible.

But as she and Nat reached her van and she dug in her

purse for her keys, she realized they weren't there. Her heart began to pound. Since Nick's death, she was constantly losing her keys, her purse, her sunglasses…her mind.

"Forgetfulness is very common after a traumatic event," the doctor had told her when she'd gotten an appointment at her in-laws' insistence.

"It scares me. I try to remind myself where I put things so this doesn't happen, but when I go back to get whatever it was…I'm always so positive that's where I left it. Instead, I find it in some…strange place I could never imagine."

The doctor had chuckled and pulled out his prescription pad. "How are you sleeping?" He didn't even wait for her to answer. "I think once you start sleeping through the night, you're going to find that these instances of forgetfulness will go away."

The pills had only made it worse, though, she thought now as she frantically searched for her van keys. She could feel Nat watching her, looking worried. Sometimes it felt as if her five-year-old was taking care of her instead of the other way around.

"It's okay, sweetheart. Mama just misplaced her keys. I'm sure they're in here…."

"Looking for these?" The young waitress from the café came out the door, holding up her keys.

"Where did you find them?" Allie asked, thinking they must have fallen out of her purse at the table and ended up on the floor. That could happen to anyone.

"In the bathroom sink."

Allie stared at her.

"You must have dropped them while you were washing your hands," the young woman said with a shrug as she handed them over.

As if that was likely. She hadn't even taken her purse to

the restroom, had she? But she had it now and she couldn't remember. She'd been so upset to see Sarah and Mildred.

"Nat, what was Grandmother saying to you in the restaurant?"

"She wanted me to go to her house but I told her I couldn't. I'm going horseback riding when we get to the ranch," Nat announced. "Dana is taking me and the other kids." Her lower lip came out for a moment. "Grandma said she was really sad I wasn't going with her."

"Yes," Allie said as, with trembling fingers, she opened the van door. Tears stung her eyes. "But today is a happy day so *we* aren't going to be sad, right? There are lots of other days that you can spend with your grandmother." Nat brightened as she strapped her into her seat.

Just a few more minutes and she and Nat would be out of here. But as she started the van, she looked up to find Mother Taylor watching her from beside Sarah's pearl-white SUV. It was clear from her expression that she'd witnessed the lost-key episode.

From the front steps of the restaurant, Belinda waved then made the universal sign to telephone.

Allie knew Belinda didn't mean call her. Reaching in her pocket, she half expected the psychic's business card to be missing. But it was still there, she realized with sagging relief. As crazy as the idea of reaching Nick beyond the grave was, she'd do *anything* to make this stop.

WHEN ALLIE AND her daughter returned, Jackson was watching her from inside his cousin's two-story ranch house.

"She lost her husband some months back," Dana said, joining him at the window.

"I wasn't—"

"He went up into the mountains during hunting season," she continued, ignoring his attempt to deny he'd been wondering about Allie. "They found his backpack and his rifle and grizzly tracks."

"Tag mentioned it." Tag had pointed out Allie's small, old cabin by the river on their way back to the ranch. It looked as if it needed work. Hadn't Tag mentioned that her husband was in construction? "Tag said they never found her husband's body."

Dana shook her head. "But Nick's backpack was shredded and his rifle was half-buried in the dirt with grizzly tracks all around it. When he didn't show up after a few days and they had no luck finding him..."

"His remains will probably turn up someday," Hud said as he came in from the kitchen. Dana's husband, Hud, was the marshal in the canyon—just as his father had been before him. "About thirty years ago now, a hiker found a human skeleton of a man. He still hasn't been identified so who knows how long he'd been out there in the mountains."

"That must make it even harder for her," Jackson said.

"It was one reason I was so glad when she decided to take the job as wedding planner."

He watched Allie reappear to get a box out of the van. She seemed nervous, even upset. He wondered if something had happened at lunch. Now at least he understood why she had overreacted with the black cat.

Hud kissed his wife, saying he had to get back to work, leaving Dana and Jackson alone.

"Our fathers are setting up their equipment on the bandstand in the barn," Dana said. "Have you seen Harlan yet?"

"No," Jackson admitted. "Guess there is no time like the present, huh?"

Jackson hadn't seen his father in several years, and even then Harlan hadn't seemed to know how to act around him—or his other sons, for that matter. As they entered the barn, Tag joining them, he saw his father and uncle standing on the makeshift stage, guitars in their hands, and was surprised when he remembered a song his father had once sung to him.

He didn't know how old he'd been at the time, but he recalled Harlan coming into his bedroom one night in Texas and playing a song on his guitar for him. He remembered being touched by the music and his father's voice.

On stage, the two brothers began playing their guitars in earnest. His father began singing. It was the voice Jackson remembered and it was like being transported back to his childhood. It rattled him more than he wanted to admit. He'd thought he and his father had no connection. But just hearing Harlan sing made him realize that he'd been lying to himself about not only the lack of connection, but also his need for it.

Harlan suddenly broke off at the sight of his sons. He stared through the dim barn for a moment, then put down his guitar to bound off the stage and come toward Jackson. He seemed young and very handsome, belying his age, Jackson thought. A man in his prime.

"Jackson," he said, holding out his hand. His father's hand was large and strong, the skin dry, callused and warm. "Glad you made it. So where are the rest of your brothers?"

"They're supposed to fly in tomorrow. At least Laramie and Hayes are," Tag said. "Austin... Well, he said he would do his best to make it. He's tied up on a case, but I'm sure you know how that goes." At Christmas, Tag had found out what their father did besides drink beer and play guitar—and shared that amazing news with them. Both Harlan and his brother Angus had worked undercover as government agents and still might, even though they were reportedly retired.

"Duty calls sometimes," Harlan agreed. "I'm glad I'm retired."

"Until the next time someone gets into trouble and needs help," Tag said.

Harlan merely smiled in answer.

Jackson was glad to see that his brother and their father could joke. Tag, being the oldest, remembered the years living in Montana and their father more than his brothers.

"The old man isn't so bad," Tag had told them after his visit at Christmas. "He's starting to grow on me."

Jackson had laughed, but he'd been a little jealous. He would love for his son to have a grandfather. He couldn't imagine, though, how Harlan could be a part of his only grandson's life, even if he wanted to. Texas and Montana were just too far apart. And Harlan probably had no interest, anyway.

"Where's that bride-to-be?" Uncle Angus asked Tag as he hopped off the stage and came toward them.

"Last minute preparations for the wedding," Tag said. "You can't believe the lists she's made. It's the mathematician in her. She's so much more organized than I am. Which reminds me, Jackson and I have to drive down to Bozeman to pick up the rings."

"It took a wedding to get you Cardwell boys to Montana, I see." Uncle Angus threw an arm around Jackson. "So how are you liking it up here? I saw that boy of yours. Dana's got him riding horses already. You're going to have one devil of a time getting him to go back to Texas after this."

Didn't Jackson know it. He'd hardly seen his son all day. Even now Ford had been too busy to give Jackson more than a quick wave from the corral where he'd been with the kids and the hired man, Walker.

"Ford is going to sleep like a baby tonight after all this fresh air, sunshine and high altitude," Jackson said. "He's not the only one," he added with a laugh.

"It's good for him," Harlan said. "I was talking to him earlier. He's taken with that little girl."

"Like father like son," Tag said under his breath as Allie came in from the back of the barn.

Jackson saw her expression. "I think I'd better go check on my son," he said as he walked toward Allie. He didn't have time to think about what he was about to do. He moved to her, taking her arm and leading her back out of the barn. "What's wrong?"

For a moment she looked as if she were going to deny anything was. But then tears filled her eyes. He walked her around the far side of the barn. He could hear Dana out by the corral instructing the kids in horseback riding lessons. Inside the barn, his father and uncle struck up another tune.

"It's nothing, really," she said and brushed at her tears. "I've been so forgetful lately. I didn't remember that the band would be setting up this afternoon."

He saw that she held a date book in her trembling hand.

"It wasn't written down in your date book?"

She glanced at her book. "It was but for some reason I marked it out."

"No big deal, right?"

"It's just that I don't remember doing it."

He could see that she was still upset and wondered if there wasn't something more going on. He reminded himself that Allie had lost her husband only months ago. Who knew what kind of emotional roller coaster that had left her on.

"You need to cut yourself more slack," he said. "We all forget things."

She nodded, but he could see she was still worried. No, not worried, scared. He thought of the black cat and had a feeling it hadn't been her first scare like that.

"I feel like such a fool," she said.

Instinctively, he put his arm around her. "Give yourself time. It's going to be all right."

She looked so forlorn that taking her in his arms seemed not only the natural thing to do at that moment, but the only thing to do under the circumstances. At first she felt board-stiff in his arms, then after a moment she seemed to melt into him. She buried her face into his chest as if he were an anchor in a fierce storm.

Suddenly, she broke the embrace and stepped back. He followed her gaze to one of the cabins on the mountainside behind him and the man standing there.

"Who is that?" he asked, instantly put off by the scowling man.

"My brother-in-law, Drew. He's doing some repairs on the ranch. He and Nick owned a construction company together. They built the guest cabins."

The man's scowl had turned into a cold stare. Jackson saw Allie's reaction. "We weren't doing anything wrong."

She shook her head as the man headed down the mountainside to his pickup parked in the pines. "He's just very protective." Allie looked as if she had the weight of the world on her shoulders again.

Jackson watched her brother-in-law slowly drive out of the ranch. Allie wasn't the only one the man was glaring at.

"I need to get back inside," she said and turned away.

He wanted to go after her. He also wanted to put his fist into her brother-in-law's face. Protective my butt, he thought. He wanted to tell Allie to ignore all of it. Wanted... Hell, that was just it. He didn't know what he wanted at the moment. Even if he did, he couldn't have it. He warned himself to stay away from Allie Taylor. Far away. He was only here for the wedding. While he felt for the woman, he couldn't help her.

"There you are," Tag said as he came up behind them. "Ready to go with me to Bozeman to get the rings?"

Jackson glanced toward the barn door Allie was stepping through. "Ready."

Chapter Four

As Jackson started to leave with his brother, he turned to look back at the barn. Just inside the door he saw Allie. All his survival instincts told him to keep going, but his mother had raised a Texas cowboy with a code of honor. Or at least she'd tried. Something was wrong and he couldn't walk away.

"Give me just a minute," he said and ran back. As he entered the barn, he saw Allie frantically searching for something in the corner of the barn. His father and brother were still playing at the far end, completely unaware of them.

"What are you looking for?"

She seemed embarrassed that he'd caught her. He noticed that she'd gone pale and looked upset. "I know I put my purse right there with my keys in it."

He glanced at the empty table. "Maybe it fell under it." He bent down to look under the red-and-white-checked tablecloth. "The barn is looking great, by the way. You've done a beautiful job."

She didn't seem to hear him. She was moving from table to table, searching for her purse. He could see that she was getting more anxious by the moment. "I know I put it right there so I wouldn't forget it when I left."

"Here it is," Jackson said as he spied what he assumed had to be her purse not on a table, but in one of the empty boxes that had held the decorations.

She rushed to him and took the purse and hurriedly looked inside, pulling out her keys with obvious relief.

"You would have found it the moment you started loading the boxes into your van," he said, seeing that she was still shaken.

She nodded. "Thank you. I'm not usually like this."

"No need to apologize. I hate losing things. It drives me crazy."

She let out a humorless laugh. "Crazy, yes." She took a deep breath and let it out slowly. Tears welled in her eyes.

"Hey, it's okay."

He wanted to comfort her, but kept his distance after what had happened earlier. "It really is okay."

She shook her head as the music stopped and quickly wiped her eyes, apologizing again. She looked embarrassed and he wished there was something he could say to put her at ease.

"Earlier, I was just trying to comfort you. It was just a hug," he said.

She met his gaze. "One I definitely needed. You have been so kind…."

"I'm not kind."

She laughed and shook her head. "Are you always so self-deprecating?"

"No, just truthful."

"Well, thank you." She clutched the keys in her hand as if afraid she would lose them if she let them out of her sight.

At the sound of people approaching, she stepped away from him.

"Let me load those boxes in your van. I insist," he said before she could protest.

As Dana, Lily and the kids came through the barn door they stopped to admire what Allie had accomplished. There were lots of oohs and ahhs. But it was Lily whose face lit up as she took in the way the barn was being transformed.

Jackson shifted his gaze to Allie's face as she humbly accepted their praise. Dana introduced Jackson to Lily. He could see right away why his brother had fallen for the woman.

"Please come stay at one of the guest cabins for the rest of the wedding festivities," Dana was saying to Allie.

"It is so generous of you to offer the cabin," Allie said, looking shocked at the offer.

"Not at all. It will make it easier for you so you don't have to drive back and forth. Also I'm being selfish. The kids adore Natalie. It will make the wedding a lot more fun for them."

Allie, clearly fighting tears of gratitude, said she would think about it. Jackson felt his heartstrings pulled just watching. "I'll work hard to make this wedding as perfect as it can be. I won't let you down."

Lily gave her a hug. "Allie, it's already perfect!"

Jackson was surprised that Lily McCabe had agreed to a Western wedding. According to the lowdown he'd heard, Lily taught mathematics at Montana State University. She'd spent her younger years at expensive boarding schools after having been born into money.

Jackson wondered if the woman had ever even been on a horse—before she met the Cardwells. Apparently, Allie was worried that a Western wedding was the last thing a woman like Lily McCabe would want.

"Are you sure this is what *you* want?" Allie asked Lily. "After all, it is *your* wedding."

Lily laughed. "Just to see the look on my parents' faces will make it all worthwhile." At Allie's horrified look, she quickly added, "I'm kidding. Though that is part of it. But when you marry into the Cardwell family, you marry into ranching and all that it comes with. I want this wedding to be a celebration of that.

"This is going to be the best wedding ever," Lily said as

she looked around the barn. "Look at me," she said, holding out her hands. "I'm actually shaking I'm so excited." She stepped to Allie and gave her another hug. "Thank you so much."

Allie appeared taken aback for a moment by Lily's sudden show of affection. The woman really was becoming more like the Cardwells every day. Or at least Dana Cardwell. That wasn't a bad thing, he thought.

"We should probably talk about the other arrangements. When is your final dress fitting?"

"Tomorrow. The dress is absolutely perfect, and the boots!" Lily laughed. "I'm so glad Dana suggested red boots. I love them!"

This was going to be like no wedding Allie had ever planned, Jackson thought. The Cardwells went all out, that was for sure.

He looked around the barn, seeing through the eyes of the guests who would be arriving for the wedding. Allie had found a wonderful wedding cake topper of a cowboy and his bride dancing that was engraved with the words: *For the rest of my life.* Tag had said that Lily had cried when she'd seen it.

The cake was a little harder to nail, according to Tag. Jackson mentally shook his head at even the memory of his brother discussing wedding cakes with him. Apparently, there were cake designs resembling hats and boots, covered wagons and cowhide, lassoes and lariats, spurs and belt buckles and horses and saddles. Some cakes had a version of all of them, which he could just imagine would have thrown his brother for a loop, he thought now, grinning to himself.

"I like simple better," Lily had said when faced with all the options. "It's the mathematician in me."

Allie had apparently kept looking until she found what she thought might be the perfect one. It was an elegant white, frosted, tiered cake with white roses and ribbons in a similar design as Lily's Western wedding dress.

"I love it," Lily had gushed. "It's perfect."

They decided on white roses and daisies for her bouquet. Bouquets of daisies would be on each of the tables, the vases old boots, with the tables covered with red-checked cloths and matching napkins.

Jackson's gaze returned to Allie. She seemed to glow under the compliments, giving him a glimpse of the self-assured woman he suspected she'd been before the tragedy.

"Jackson?"

He turned to find Tag standing next to him, grinning.

"I guess you didn't hear me. Must have had your mind somewhere else." Tag glanced in Allie's direction and then wisely jumped back as Jackson took a playful swing at him as they left the barn.

"You sure waited until the last minute," Jackson said to his brother as they headed for Tag's vehicle. "Putting off the rings…" He shook his head. "You sure you want to go through with this?"

His brother laughed. "More sure than I have been about anything in my life. Come on, let's go."

"I'll see if Ford wants to come along," Jackson said. "I think that's enough cowboying for one day."

But when he reached the corral, he found his son wearing a straw Western hat and atop a huge horse. Jackson felt his pulse jump at the sight and his first instinct was to insist Ford get down from there right away.

But when he got a good look at his son's face, his words died on a breath. He'd never seen Ford this happy. His cheeks were flushed, his eyes bright. He looked…proud.

"Look at me," he called to his father.

All Jackson could do was nod as his son rode past him. He was incapable of words at that moment.

"Don't worry about your son," his father said as he joined him at the corral fence. "I'll look after him until you get back."

ALLIE LISTENED TO Jackson and Tag joking with each other as they left the barn. Jackson Cardwell must think her the most foolish woman ever, screaming over nothing more than a cat, messing up her date book and panicking because she'd misplaced her purse.

But what had her still upset was the hug. It had felt so good to be in Jackson's arms. It had been so long since anyone had held her like that. She'd felt such an overwhelming need…

And then Drew had seen them. She'd been surprised by the look on his face. He'd seemed…angry and upset as if she was cheating on Nick. Once this investigation was over, maybe they could all put Nick to rest. In the meantime, she just hoped Drew didn't go to his mother with this.

Instinctively, she knew that Jackson wouldn't say anything. Not about her incidents or about the hug.

Dana announced she was taking the kids down to the house for naptime. Allie could tell that Nat had wanted to go down to the house—but for lemonade and cookies. Nat probably needed a nap, as well, but Allie couldn't take her up to the cabin right now. She had work to do if she hoped to have the barn ready for the rehearsal dinner tomorrow night.

"I really need your help," she told her daughter. Nat was always ready to give a helping hand. Well, she was before the Cardwell Ranch and all the animals, not to mention other kids to play with.

"Okay, Mama." She glanced back at the barn door wistfully, though. Nat had always wanted brothers and sisters, but they hadn't been in Allie's plans. She knew she could take care of one child without any help from Nick. He'd wanted a boy and insisted they try for another child soon after Nat was born.

Allie almost laughed. Guilt? She had so much of it where Nick and his family were concerned. She had wanted to enjoy her baby girl so she'd gone on the pill behind Nick's back. It had been more than dishonest. He would have killed her if he had found out. The more time that went by, the less she wanted another child with her husband so she'd stayed on the pill. Even Nick's tantrums about her not getting pregnant were easier to take than having another child with him.

She hadn't even told Belinda, which was good since her friend was shocked when she told her she was leaving Nick and moving far away.

"Divorcing him is one thing," Belinda had said. "But I don't see how you can keep his kid from him or keep Nat from his family."

"Nick wanted a son. He barely takes notice of Nat. The only time he notices her is when other people are around and then he plays too rough with her. When she cries, he tells her to toughen up."

"So you're going to ask for sole custody? Isn't Nick going to fight you?"

Allie knew it would be just like Nick to fight for Nat out of meanness and his family would back him up. "I'm going to move to Florida. I've already lined up a couple of jobs down there. They pay a lot more than here. I really doubt Nick will bother flying that far to see Nat—at least more than a few times."

"You really are going to leave him," Belinda had said. "When?"

"Soon." That had been late summer. She'd desperately wanted a new start. Nick would be occupied with hunting season in the fall so maybe he wouldn't put up much of a fight.

Had Belinda said something to Nick? Or had he just seen something in Allie that told him he had lost her?

"How can I help you, Mama?" Nat asked, dragging her from her thoughts.

Allie handed her daughter one end of a rope garland adorned with tiny lights in the shape of boots. "Let's string this up," she suggested. "And see how pretty it looks along the wall."

Nat's eyes lit up. "It's going to be beautiful," she said. *Beautiful* was her latest favorite word. To her, most everything was beautiful.

Allie yearned for that kind of innocence again—if she'd ever had it. But maybe she could find it for her daughter. She had options. She could find work anywhere as a wedding planner, but did she want to uproot her daughter from what little family she had? Nat loved her Uncle Drew and Sarah could be very sweet. Mildred, even as ungrandmotherly as she was, was Nat's only grandmother.

Allie tried to concentrate on her work. The barn was taking shape. She'd found tiny cowboy boot lights to put over the bar area. Saddles on milk cans had been pulled up to the bar for extra seating.

Beverages would be chilling in a metal trough filled with ice. Drinks would be served in Mason jars and lanterns would hang from the rafters for light. A few bales of hay would be brought in around the bandstand.

When they'd finished, Allie plugged in the last of the lights and Nat squealed with delight.

She checked her watch. "Come on," she told her daughter. "We've done enough today. We need to go into town for a few things. Tomorrow your aunt Megan will be coming to help." Nat clapped in response. She loved her auntie Megan, Allie's half sister.

After Allie's mother died, her father had moved away, remarried and had other children. Allie had lost touch with her father, as well as his new family. But about a year ago, her stepsister Megan had found her. Ten years younger, Megan was now twenty-three and a recent graduate in design. When she'd shown an interest in working on the Cardwell Ranch wedding, Allie had jumped at it.

"I really could use the help, but when can you come down?" Megan lived in Missoula and had just given her two weeks' notice at her job.

"Go ahead and start without me. I'll be there within a few days of the wedding. That should be enough time, shouldn't it?"

"Perfect," Allie had told her. "Natalie and I will start. I'll save the fun stuff for you." Natalie loved Megan, who was cute and young and always up for doing something fun with her niece.

The thought of Megan's arrival tomorrow had brightened Natalie for a moment, but Allie now saw her looking longingly at the Savage house.

"How about we have something to eat while we're in Bozeman?" Allie suggested.

Nat's eyes widened with new interest as she asked if they could go to her favorite fast-food burger place. The Taylors had introduced her daughter to fast food, something Allie had tried to keep at a minimum.

But this evening, she decided to make an exception. She loved seeing how happy her daughter was. Nat's cheeks were pink from the fresh air and sunshine.

All the way into town, she talked excitedly about the horses and the other kids. This wedding planner job at Cardwell Ranch was turning out to be a good thing for both of them, Allie thought as they drove home.

By the time they reached the cabin Nat had fallen asleep in her car seat and didn't even wake up when Allie parked out front. Deciding to take in the items she'd purchased first, then bring in her daughter, Allie stepped into the cabin and stopped dead.

At the end of the hall, light flickered. A candle. She hadn't lit a candle. Not since Nick. He liked her in candlelight. The smell of the candle and the light reminded her of the last time they'd had sex. Not made love. They hadn't made love since before Natalie was born.

As she started down the hallway, she told herself that she'd thrown all the candles away. Even if she'd missed one, she wouldn't have left a candle burning.

She stopped in the bedroom doorway. Nick's shirt was back, spread on the bed as if he were in it, lying there waiting for her. The smell of the sweet-scented candle made her nauseous. She fought the panicked need to run.

"Mama?" Nat's sleepy voice wavered with concern. "Did Daddy come back?" Not just concern. Anxiety. Nick scared her with his moodiness and surly behavior. Nat was smart. She had picked up on the tension between her parents.

Allie turned to wrap her arms around her daughter. The warmth of her five-year-old, Nat's breath on her neck, the solid feel of the ground under her feet, those were the things she concentrated on as she carried Natalie down the hallway to her room.

Her daughter's room had always been her haven. It was the only room in the house that Nick hadn't cared what she did with. So she'd painted it sky-blue, adding white floating clouds, then trees and finally a river as green and sunlit as the one out Nat's window.

Nick had stuck his head in the door while she was painting it. She'd seen his expression. He'd been impressed—and he hadn't wanted to be—before he snapped, "You going to cook dinner or what?" He seemed to avoid the room after that, which was fine with her.

Now, she lay down on the bed with Nat. It had been her

daughter's idea to put stars on the ceiling, the kind that shone only at night with the lights out.

"I like horses," Nat said with a sigh. "Ms. Savage says a horse can tell your mood and that if you aren't in a good one, you'll get bucked off." She looked at her mother. "Do you think that's true?"

"I think if Ms. Savage says it is, then it is."

Nat smiled as if she liked the answer.

Allie could tell she was dog-tired, but fighting sleep.

"I'm going to ride Rocket tomorrow," Natalie said.

"Rocket? That sounds like an awfully fast horse." She saw that Nat's eyelids had closed. She watched her daughter sleep for a few moments, then eased out of bed.

After covering her, she opened the window a few inches to let the cool summer night air into the stuffy room. Spending time with her daughter made her feel better, but also reminded her how important it was that she not let anyone know about the things that had been happening to her.

She thought of Jackson Cardwell and the black cat that had somehow gotten into her box of decorations. She hadn't imagined that. She smiled to herself. Such a small thing and yet…

This time, she went straight to her bedroom, snuffed out the candle and opened the window, thankful for the breeze that quickly replaced the sweet, cloying scent with the fresh night air.

On the way out of the room, she grabbed Nick's shirt and took both the shirt and the candle to the trash, but changed her mind. Dropping only the candle in the trash, she took the shirt over to the fireplace. Would burning Nick's favorite shirt mean she was crazy?

Too bad, she thought as she dropped the shirt on the grate and added several pieces of kindling and some newspaper. Allie hesitated for only a moment before lighting the paper with a match. It caught fire, crackling to life and forcing her to step back. She watched the blaze destroy the shirt and reached for the poker, determined that not a scrap of it would be left.

She had to get control of her life. She thought of Jackson Cardwell and his kindness. He had no idea how much it meant to her.

As she watched the flames take the last of Nick's shirt, she told herself at least this would be the last she'd see of that blamed shirt.

Chapter Five

Jackson met Hayes and Laramie at the airport, but while it was good to see them, he was distracted.

They talked about the barbecue restaurant and Harlan and the wedding before McKenzie showed up while they were waiting for their luggage to pick up Hayes. Hayes had been in Texas tying up things with the sale of his business.

Jackson had heard their relationship was serious, but seeing McKenzie and Hayes together, he saw just how serious. Another brother falling in love in Montana, he thought with a shake of his head. Hayes and McKenzie would be joining them later tonight at the ranch for dinner.

He and Laramie ended up making the drive to Cardwell Ranch alone. Laramie talked about the financial benefits of the new barbecue restaurant and Jackson tuned him out. He couldn't get his mind off Allie Taylor.

Maybe it was because he'd been through so much with his ex, but he felt like a kindred spirit. The woman was going through her own private hell. He wished there was something he could do.

"Are you listening?" Laramie asked.

"Sure."

"I forget how little interest my brothers have in the actual running of this corporation."

"Don't let it hurt your feelings. I just have something else on my mind."

"A woman."

"Why would you say that, knowing me?"

Laramie looked over at him. "I was joking. You swore off women after Juliet, right? At least that's what you... Wait a minute, has something changed?"

"Nothing." He said it too sharply, making his brother's eyebrow shoot up.

Laramie fell silent for a moment, but Jackson could feel him watching him out of the corner of his eye.

"Is this your first wedding since...you and Juliet split?" Laramie asked carefully.

Jackson shook his head at his brother's attempt at diplomacy. "It's not the wedding. There's this...person I met who I'm worried about."

"Ah. Is this person—"

"It's a woman, all right? But it isn't like that."

"Hey," Laramie said, holding up his hands. "I just walked in. If you don't want to tell me—"

"She lost her husband some months ago and she has a little girl the same age as Ford and she's struggling."

Laramie nodded. "Okay."

"She's the wedding planner."

His brother's eyebrow shot up again.

"I'll just be glad when this wedding is over," Jackson said and thought he meant it. "By the way, when is Mom flying in?" At his brother's hesitation, he demanded, "What's going on with Mom?"

ALLIE HAD UNPACKED more boxes of decorations by the time she heard a vehicle pull up the next morning. Natalie, who had been coloring quietly while her mother worked, went running when she spotted her aunt Megan. Allie smiled as Megan picked Nat up and swung her around, both of them laughing. It was a wonderful sound. Megan had a way with Natalie. Clearly, she loved kids.

"Sorry I'm so late, but I'm here and ready to go to work." Megan was dressed in a T-shirt, jeans and athletic shoes. She had taken after their father and had the Irish green eyes with the dark hair and complexion. She was nothing short of adorable, sweet and cute. "Wow, the barn is already looking great," she exclaimed as she walked around, Natalie holding her hand and beaming up at her.

"I helped Mama with the lights," Nat said.

"I knew it," Megan said. "I can see your handiwork." She grinned down at her niece. "Did I hear you can now ride a horse?"

Natalie quickly told her all about the horses, naming each as she explained how to ride a horse. "You have to hang on to the reins."

"I would imagine you do," Megan agreed.

"Maybe you can ride with us," Nat suggested.

"Maybe I can. But right now I need to help your mom."

Just then Dana stuck her head in the barn doorway and called to Natalie. Allie introduced Dana to her stepsister, then watched as her daughter scurried off for an afternoon ride with her friends. She gave a thankful smile to Dana as they left.

"Just tell me what to do," Megan said and Allie did, even more thankful for the help. They went to work on the small details Allie knew Megan would enjoy.

Belinda stopped by to say hello to Megan and give Allie an update on the photos. She'd met with Lily that morning, had made out a list of photo ideas and sounded excited.

Allie was surprised when she overheard Belinda and Megan discussing a recent lunch. While the three of them had spent some time together since Megan had come back into Allie's life, she hadn't known that Belinda and Megan had become friends.

She felt jealous. She knew it was silly. They were both

single and probably had more in common than with Allie, who felt as if she'd been married forever.

"How are you doing?" Megan asked after Belinda left.

"Fine."

"No, really."

Allie studied her stepsister for a moment. They'd become close, but she hadn't wanted to share what was going on. It was embarrassing and the fewer people who knew she was losing her mind the better, right?

"It's been rough." Megan didn't know that she had been planning to leave Nick. As far as her sister had known, Allie had been happily married. Now Allie regretted that she hadn't been more honest with Megan.

"But I'm doing okay now," she said as she handed Megan another gift bag to fill. "It's good to be working again. I love doing this." She glanced around the barn feeling a sense of satisfaction.

"Well, I'm glad I'm here now," Megan said. "This is good for Natalie, too."

Good for all of us, Allie thought.

JACKSON LOOKED AT his brother aghast. "Mom's dating?" He should have known that if their mom confided in anyone it would be Laramie. The sensible one, was what she called him, and swore that out of all her sons, Laramie was the only one who she could depend on to be honest with her.

Laramie cleared his throat. "It's a little more than dating. She's on her honeymoon."

"Her *what?*"

"She wanted it to be a surprise."

"Well, it sure as hell is that. Who did she marry?"

"His name is Franklin Wellington the Fourth. He's wealthy, handsome, very nice guy, actually."

"*You've* met him?"

"He and Mom are flying in just before the wedding on his private jet. It's bigger than ours."

"Laramie, I can't believe you would keep this from the rest of us, let alone that Mom would."

"She didn't want to take away from Tag's wedding but they had already scheduled theirs before Tag announced his." Laramie shrugged. "Hey, she's deliriously happy and hoping we will all be happy for her."

Jackson couldn't believe this. Rosalee Cardwell hadn't just started dating after all these years, she'd gotten married?

"I wonder how Dad will take it?" Laramie said. "We all thought Mom had been pining away for him all these years...."

"Maybe she was."

"Well, not anymore."

"BUT YOU *HAVE* to go on the horseback ride," Natalie cried.

As he stepped into the cool shade, Jackson saw Allie look around the barn for help, finding none. Hayes was off somewhere with his girlfriend, McKenzie, Tag was down by the river writing his vows, Lily was picking her parents up at the airport, Laramie had restaurant business and Hud was at the marshal's office, working. There had still been no word from Austin. Or their mother.

Wanting to spend some time with his son, Jackson had agreed to go on the short horseback ride with Dana and the kids that would include lunch on the mountain.

"Dana promised she would find you a very gentle horse, in other words, a really *old* one," Megan joked.

Natalie was doing her "please-Mama-please" face.

"Even my dad is going to ride," Ford said, making everyone laugh.

Allie looked at the boy. "Your dad is a cowboy."

Ford shook his head. "He can't even rope a cow. He tried

once at our neighbor's place and he was really bad at it. So it's okay if you're really bad at riding a horse."

Jackson smiled and ruffled his son's hair. "You really should come along, Allie."

"I have too much work to—"

"I will stay here and get things organized for tomorrow," Megan said. "No more arguments. Go on the ride with your daughter. Go." She shooed her toward the barn door.

"I guess I'm going on the horseback ride," Allie said. The kids cheered. She met Jackson's gaze as they walked toward the corral where Dana and her ranch hand, Walker, were saddling horses. "I've never been on a horse," she whispered confidentially to Jackson.

"Neither had your daughter and look at her now," he said as he watched Ford and Natalie saddle up. They both had to climb up the fence to get on their horses, but they now sat eagerly waiting in their saddles.

"I'll help you," Jackson said as he took Allie's horse's reins from Dana. He demonstrated how to get into the saddle then gave her a boost.

"It's so high up here," she said as she put her boot toes into the stirrups.

"Enjoy the view," Jackson said and swung up onto his horse.

They rode up the mountain, the kids chattering away, Dana giving instructions to them as they went.

After a short while, Jackson noticed that Allie seemed to have relaxed a little. She was looking around as if enjoying the ride and when they stopped in a wide meadow, he saw her patting her horse's neck and talking softly to it.

"I'm afraid to ask what you just said to your horse," he joked as he moved closer. Her horse had wandered over to some tall grass away from the others.

"Just thanking him for not bucking me off," she admitted shyly.

"Probably a good idea, but your horse is a she. A mare."

"Oh, hopefully, she wasn't insulted." Allie actually smiled. The afternoon sun lit her face along with the smile.

He felt his heart do a loop-de-loop. He tried to rein it back in as he looked into her eyes. That tantalizing green was deep and dark, inviting, and yet he knew a man could drown in those eyes.

Suddenly, Allie's horse shied. In the next second it took off as if it had been shot from a cannon. To her credit, she hadn't let go of her reins, but she grabbed the saddlehorn and let out a cry as the mare raced out of the meadow headed for the road.

Jackson spurred his horse and raced after her. He could hear the startled cries of the others behind him. He'd been riding since he was a boy, so he knew how to handle his horse. But Allie, he could see, was having trouble staying in the saddle with her horse at a full gallop.

He pushed his harder and managed to catch her, riding alongside until he could reach over and grab her reins. The horses lunged along for a moment. Next to him Allie started to fall. He grabbed for her, pulling her from her saddle and into his arms as he released her reins and brought his own horse up short.

Allie slid down his horse to the ground. He dismounted and dropped beside her. "Are you all right?"

"I think so. What happened?"

He didn't know. One minute her horse was munching on grass, the next it had taken off like a shot.

Jackson could see that she was shaken. She sat down on the ground as if her legs would no longer hold her. He could hear the others riding toward them. When Allie heard her daughter calling to her, she hurriedly got to her feet, clearly wanting to reassure Natalie.

"Wow, that was some ride," Allie said as her daughter came up.

"Are you all right?" Dana asked, dismounting and joining her.

"I'm fine, really," she assured her and moved to her daughter, still in the saddle, to smile up at her.

"What happened?" Dana asked Jackson.

"I don't know."

"This is a good spot to have lunch," Dana announced more cheerfully than Jackson knew she felt.

"I'll go catch the horse." He swung back up into the saddle and took off after the mare. "I'll be right back for lunch. Don't let Ford eat all the sandwiches."

ALLIE HAD NO idea why the horse had reacted like that. She hated that she was the one who'd upset everyone.

"Are you sure you didn't spur your horse?" Natalie asked, still upset.

"She isn't wearing spurs," Ford pointed out.

"Maybe a bee stung your horse," Natalie suggested.

Dana felt bad. "I wanted your first horseback riding experience to be a pleasant one," she lamented.

"It was. It is," Allie reassured her although in truth, she wasn't looking forward to getting back on the horse. But she knew she had to for Natalie's sake. The kids had been scared enough as it was.

Dana had spread out the lunch on a large blanket with the kids all helping when Jackson rode up, trailing her horse. The mare looked calm now, but Allie wasn't sure she would ever trust it again.

Jackson met her gaze as he dismounted. Dana was already on her feet, heading for him. Allie left the kids to join them.

"What is it?" Dana asked, keeping her voice down.

Jackson looked to Allie as if he didn't want to say in front of her.

"Did I do something to the horse to make her do that?" she asked, fearing that she had.

His expression softened as he shook his head. "You didn't do *anything.*" He looked at Dana. "Someone shot the mare." He moved so Dana could see the bloody spot on the horse. "Looks like a small caliber. Probably a .22. Fortunately, the shooter must have been some distance away or it could have been worse. The bullet barely broke the horse's hide. Just enough to spook the mare."

"We've had teenagers on four-wheelers using the old logging roads on the ranch," Dana said. "I heard shots a few days ago." Suddenly, all the color drained from Dana's face. "Allie could have been killed," she whispered. "Or one of the kids. When we get back, I'll call Hud."

JACKSON INSISTED ON riding right beside Allie on the way back down the mountain. He could tell that Allie had been happy to get off the horse once they reached the corral.

"Thank you for saving me," she said. "It seems like you keep doing that, doesn't it?" He must have looked panicked by the thought because she quickly added, "I'm fine now. I will try not to need saving again." She flashed him a smile and disappeared into the barn.

"Ready?" Tag said soon after Jackson had finished helping unsaddle the horses and put the tack away.

Dana had taken the kids down to the house to play, saying they all needed some downtime. He could tell that she was still upset and anxious to call Hud. "Don't forget the barbecue and dance tonight," she reminded him. "Then tomorrow is the bachelor party, right?"

Jackson groaned. He'd forgotten that Tag had been waiting for them all to arrive so they could have the party. The last thing he needed was a party. Allie's horse taking off like that... It had left him shaken, as well. Dana was convinced it had been teenagers who'd shot the horse. He hoped that was all it had been.

"Glad you're back," Tag said. "We're all going down to the Corral for a beer. Come on. At least four of us are here. We'll be back in time for dinner."

Ford was busy with the kids and Dana. "Are you sure he isn't too much?" Jackson asked his cousin. "I feel like I've been dumping him on you since we got here."

She laughed. "Are you kidding? My children adore having their cousin around. They've actually all been getting along better than usual. Go have a drink with your brothers. Enjoy yourself, Jackson. I suspect you get little time without Ford."

It was true. And yet he missed his son. He told himself again that he would be glad when they got back to Texas. But seeing how much fun Ford was having on the ranch, he doubted his son would feel the same.

ALLIE STARED AT her date book, heart racing. She'd been feeling off balance since her near-death experience on the horse. When she'd told Megan and Belinda about it on her return to the barn, they'd been aghast.

She'd recounted her tale right up to where Jackson had returned with the mare and the news that it had been shot.

"That's horrible," Megan said. "I'm so glad you didn't get bucked off. Was the mare all right?"

Belinda's response was, "So Jackson saved you? Wow, how romantic is that?"

Needing to work, Allie had shooed Belinda out of the barn and she and Megan had worked quietly for several hours before she'd glanced at her watch and realized something was wrong.

"The caterer," Allie said. "Did she happen to call?"

Megan shook her head. "No, why?"

"Her crew should have been here by now. I had no idea

it was so late." Allie could feel the panic growing. "And when I checked my date book…"

"What?" Megan asked.

"I wouldn't have canceled." But even as she was saying it, she was dialing the caterer's number.

A woman answered and Allie quickly asked about the dinner that was to be served at Cardwell Ranch tonight.

"We have you down for the reception in a few days, but… Wait a minute. It looks as if you did book it."

Allie felt relief wash through her, though it did nothing to relieve the panic. She had a ranch full of people to be fed and no caterer for the barbecue.

"I'm sorry. It says here that you called to cancel it yesterday."

"That's not possible. It couldn't have been me."

"Is your name Allie Taylor?"

She felt her heart drop. "Yes."

"It says here that you personally called."

Allie dropped into one of the chairs. She wanted to argue with the woman, but what good would it do? The damage was done. And anyway, she couldn't be sure she hadn't called. She couldn't be sure of anything.

"Just make sure that the caterers will be here on the Fourth of July for the wedding reception and that no one, and I mean not even me, can cancel it. Can you do that for me?" Her voice broke and she saw Megan looking at her with concern.

As she disconnected, she fought tears. "What am I going to do?"

"What's wrong?"

Her head snapped up at the sound of Jackson's voice. "I thought you were having beers with your brothers?"

"A couple beers is all I can handle. So come on, what's going on?"

She wiped at her eyes, standing to turn her back to him until she could gain control. What the man must think of her.

"The caterer accidentally got canceled. Looks like we might have to try to find a restaurant tonight," Megan said, reaching for her phone.

"Don't be ridiculous," Jackson said, turning Allie to look at him. "You have some of the best barbecue experts in the country right here on the ranch. I'll run down to the market and get some ribs while my brothers get the fire going. It's going to be fine."

This last statement Allie could tell was directed at her. She met his gaze, all her gratitude in that one look.

Jackson tipped his hat and gave her a smile. "It's going to be better than fine. You'll see."

"I HOPE YOU don't mind," Allie heard Jackson tell Dana and Lily. "I changed Allie's plans. I thought it would be fun if the Cardwell boys barbecued."

Dana was delighted and so was Lily. They insisted she, Natalie, Megan and Belinda stay and Allie soon found herself getting caught up in the revelry.

The Texas Boys Barbecue brothers went to work making dinner. Allie felt awful that they had to cook, but soon saw how much fun they were having.

They joked and played around while their father and Dana's provided the music. All the ranch hands and neighbors ended up being invited and pretty soon it had turned into a party. She noticed that even Drew, who'd been working at one of the cabins, had been invited to join them.

The barbecue was amazing and a lot more fun than the one Allie had originally planned. Everyone complimented the food and the new restaurant was toasted as a welcome addition to Big Sky.

Allie did her best to stay in the background. The day had left her feeling beaten up from her wild horseback ride to the foul-up with the caterer, along with her other misadventures. She was just happy to sit on the sidelines. Megan and Belinda were having a ball dancing with some of the ranch hands. All the kids were dancing, as well. At one point, she saw Jackson showing Ford how to do the swing with Natalie.

Someone stepped in front of her, blocking her view of the dance floor. She looked up to see Drew.

"I don't believe you've danced all night," he said.

"I'm really not—"

"What? You won't dance with your own brother-in-law? I guess you don't need me anymore now that you have the Cardwells. Or is it just one Cardwell?"

She realized he'd had too much to drink. "Drew, that isn't—"

"Excuse me," Jackson said, suddenly appearing beside her. "I believe this dance is mine." He reached for Allie's hand.

Drew started to argue, but Jackson didn't give him a chance before he pulled Allie out onto the dance floor. The song was a slow one. He took her in his arms and pulled her close.

"You really have to quit saving me," she said only half joking.

"Sorry, but I could see you needed help," Jackson said. "Your brother-in-law is more than a little protective, Allie."

She didn't want to talk about Drew. She closed her eyes for a moment. It felt good in the cowboy's arms. She couldn't remember the last time she'd danced, but that felt good, too, moving to the slow country song. "You saved my life earlier and then saved my bacon tonight. Natalie thinks you're a cowboy superhero. I'm beginning to wonder myself."

He gave her a grin and a shrug. "It weren't nothin', ma'am," he said, heavy on the Texas drawl. "Actually, I don't know why my brothers and I hadn't thought of it before. You did me a favor. I'd missed cooking with them. It was fun."

"Did I hear there is a bachelor party tomorrow night?"

Jackson groaned. "Hayes is in charge. I hate to think." He laughed softly. "Then the rehearsal and dinner the next night and finally the wedding." He shook his head as if he couldn't wait for it to be over.

Allie had felt the same way—before she'd met Jackson Cardwell.

Drew appeared just then. "Cuttin' in," he said, slurring his words as he pried himself between the two of them.

Jackson seemed to hesitate, but Allie didn't want trouble. She stepped into Drew's arms and let him dance her away from the Texas cowboy.

"What the hell do you think you're doing?" Drew demanded as he pulled her closer. "My brother is barely cold in his grave and here you are actin' like—"

"The wedding planner?" She broke away from him as the song ended. "Sorry, but I'm calling it a night. I have a lot of work to do tomorrow." With that she went to get Natalie. It was time to go home.

Chapter Six

Allie was getting ready to go to the ranch the next morning when she heard a vehicle pull up. She glanced out groaning when she saw it was Drew. Even more disturbing, he had his mother with him. As she watched them climb out, she braced herself for the worst. Drew had been acting strangely since he'd seen her with Jackson that first time.

"Hi," she said opening the door before either of them could knock. "You just caught me heading out."

"We *hoped* to catch you," Mildred said. "We're taking Natalie for the day so you can get some work done."

Not may we, but *we're taking*. "I'm sorry but Natalie already has plans."

Mildred's eyebrow shot up. "Natalie is five. Her plans can change."

"Natalie is going with the Cardwells—"

"The Cardwells aren't family," Mildred spat.

No, Allie thought, *but I wish they were.* "If you had just called—"

"I'm sure Nat would rather spend the day with her grandmother than whatever you have planned for—" Mildred broke off at the sound of a vehicle coming up the road toward them.

Who now? Allie wondered, fearing she was about to lose this battle with her in-laws—and break her daughter's heart. Her pulse did a little leap as she recognized the SUV as the one Jackson Cardwell had been driving yesterday. But what was he doing here? Allie had said she would bring Nat to the ranch.

Jackson parked and got out, Ford right behind him. He seemed to take in the scene before he asked, "Is there a problem?"

"Nothing to do with you," Drew said.

"Jackson Cardwell," he said and held out his hand. "I don't believe we've been formally introduced."

Drew was slow to take it. "Drew Taylor." Allie could see her brother-in-law sizing up Jackson. While they were both a few inches over six feet and both strong-looking, Jackson had the broader shoulders and looked as if he could take Drew in a fair fight.

Mildred crossed her arms over her chest and said, "We're here to pick up my granddaughter."

"That's why *I'm* here," Jackson said. Just then Natalie came to the door. She was dressed for the rodeo in her Western shirt, jeans and new red cowboy boots. Allie had braided her hair into two plaits that trailed down her back. A straw cowboy hat was perched on her head, her smile huge.

"I'm going to the rodeo with Ford and Hank and Mary," Nat announced excitedly. Oblivious to what was going on, she added, "I've never been to a rodeo before."

"Hop into the rig with Ford. I borrowed a carseat from Dana," Jackson said before either Drew or Mildred could argue otherwise.

With a wave, Nat hurried past her grandmother and uncle and taking Ford's hand, the two ran toward the SUV.

Allie held her breath as she saw Drew ball his hands into fists. She'd never seen him like this and realized Jackson was right. This was more than him being protective.

Jackson looked as if he expected Drew to take a swing—and was almost daring him to. The tension between the two men was thick as fresh-churned butter. Surely it wouldn't come to blows.

"Are you ready?" Jackson said to her, making her blink in surprise. "Dana gave me your ticket for the rodeo."

He *knew* she wasn't planning to go. This wedding had to be perfect and let's face it, she hadn't been herself for some time now.

"Going to a rodeo is part of this so-called wedding planning?" Mildred demanded. She lifted a brow. "I heard it also entails dancing with the guests."

"All in a day's work," Jackson said and met Allie's gaze. "We should get going. Don't want to be late." He looked to Drew. "Nice to meet you." Then turned to Mildred. "You must be Allie's mother-in-law."

"Mildred." Her lips were pursed so tightly that the word barely came out.

"I just need to grab my purse," Allie said, taking advantage of Jackson's rescue, even though she knew it would cost her.

When she came back out, Jackson was waiting for her. He tipped his hat to Drew and Mildred as Allie locked the cabin door behind her. She noticed that Mother Taylor and Drew were still standing where she'd left them, both looking infuriated.

She hated antagonizing them for fear what could happen if they ever decided to try to take Natalive from her. If they knew about just a few of the so-called incidents...

Like Nat, Allie slipped past them out to the SUV and didn't let out the breath she'd been holding until she was seated in the passenger seat.

"That looked like an ambush back there," Jackson said as they drove away.

She glanced back knowing she might have escaped this time, but there would be retribution. "They mean well."

JACKSON GLANCED OVER at her. "Do they?"

She looked away. "With Nick gone... Well, we're all adjusting to it. I'm sure they feel all they have left of him is Nat. They just want to see more of her."

He could see that she felt guilty. His ex and her family had used guilt on him like a club. He remembered that beat-up, rotten feeling and hated to see her going through it.

In the backseat, Natalie was telling Ford about something her horse had done yesterday during her ride. They both started laughing the way only kids can do. He loved the sound.

"Thank you for the rescue, but I really can't go to the rodeo. You can drop me at the ranch," Allie said, clearly nervous. "I need to check on things."

"You've done a great job. A few hours away at the rodeo is your reward. Dana's orders. She's the one who sent me to get you, knowing you wouldn't come unless I did."

"I really should be working."

"When was the last time you were at a rodeo?" he asked.

She chewed at her lower lip for a moment. "I think I went with some friends when I was in the fifth grade."

He smiled over at her. "Well, then it is high time you went again."

"I want an elephant ear!" Ford cried from the backseat.

"An elephant ear?" Nat repeated and began to giggle.

"So Nat's never been to a rodeo, either?" Jackson asked.

"No, I guess she hasn't."

"Well, she is going today and she and her mother are going to have elephant ears!" he announced. The kids laughed happily. He was glad to hear Ford explaining that an elephant ear really was just fried bread with sugar and cinnamon on it, but that it was really good.

Allie seemed to relax, but he saw her checking her side mirror. Did she think her in-laws would chase her down? He wouldn't have been surprised. They'd been more than overbearing. He had seen how they dominated Allie. It made him wonder what her husband had been like.

When they reached the rodeo grounds, Dana and Hud were waiting along with the kids and Tag and Lily and Hayes and McKenzie and Laramie.

"Oh, I'm so glad you decided to come along," Dana said when she saw Allie. "Jackson said he wasn't sure he could convince you, but he was darned sure going to try." She glanced at her cousin. "He must be pretty persuasive."

"Yes, he is," Allie said and smiled.

Jackson felt a little piece of his heart float up at that smile.

Easy, Texas cowboy, he warned himself.

But even as he thought it, he had to admit that he was getting into the habit of rescuing this woman—and enjoying it. Allie needed protecting. How badly she needed it, he didn't yet know.

It was the least he could do—until the wedding. And then he and Ford were headed back to Texas. Allie Taylor would be on her own.

Just the thought made him scared for her.

ALLIE COULDN'T REMEMBER the last time she'd had so much fun. The rodeo was thrilling, the elephant ear delicious and the Cardwells a very fun family. She'd ended up sitting next to Jackson, their children in front of them.

"I want to be a barrel racer," Natalie announced.

"We'll have to set up some barrels at the ranch," Dana said. "Natalie's a natural in the saddle. She'd make a great barrel racer."

"Well, I'm not riding the bulls," Ford said and everyone laughed.

"Glad you came along?" Jackson asked Allie as he offered some of his popcorn.

She'd already eaten a huge elephant ear and loved every

bite, but she still took a handful of popcorn and smiled. "I am. This is fun."

"You deserve some fun."

Allie wasn't so sure about that. She wasn't sure what she deserved, wasn't that the problem? She leaned back against the bleachers, breathing in the summer day and wishing this would never end.

But it did end and the crowd began to make their way to the parking lot in a swell of people. That's when she saw him.

Nick. He was moving through the crowd. She'd seen him because he was going in the wrong direction—in their direction. He wore a dark-colored baseball cap, his features lost in the shadow of the cap's bill. She got only a glimpse—Suddenly, he turned as if headed for the parking lot, as well. She sat up, telling herself her eyes were deceiving her. Nick was dead and yet—

"Allie, what it is?" Jackson asked.

In the past when she'd caught glimpses of him, she'd frozen, too shocked to move. She sprang to her feet and pushed her way down the grandstand steps until she reached the ground. Forcing her way through the crowd, she kept Nick in sight ahead of her. He was moving fast as if he wanted to get away.

Not this time, she thought, as she felt herself gaining on him. She could see the back of his head. He was wearing his MSU Bobcat navy ball cap, just like the one he'd been wearing the day he left to go up into the mountains—and his favorite shirt, the one she'd burned.

Her heart pounded harder against her ribs. She told herself she wasn't losing her mind. She couldn't explain any of this, but she knew what she was seeing. Nick. She was within yards of him, only a few people between them. She could almost reach out and grab his sleeve—

Suddenly, someone grabbed her arm, spinning her

around. She stumbled over backward, falling against the person in front of her, tripping on her own feet before hitting the ground. The fall knocked the air from her lungs and skinned her elbow, worse, her pride. The crowd opened a little around her as several people stopped to see if she was all right.

But it was Jackson who rushed to help her up. "Allie, are you all right?"

All she could do was shake her head as the man she thought was Nick disappeared into the crowd.

"WHAT'S GOING ON?" Jackson asked, seeing how upset she was. Had he said or done something that would make her take off like that?

She shook her head again as if unable to speak. He could tell *something* had happened. Drawing her aside, he asked her again. The kids had gone on ahead with Dana and her children.

"Allie, talk to me."

She looked up at him, those green eyes filling with tears. "I saw my husband, Nick. At least I think I saw him." She looked shocked as she darted a glance at the crowd, clearly expecting to see her dead husband again.

"You must think I'm crazy. *I* think I'm crazy. But I saw Nick. I know it couldn't be him, but it looked so much like him…." She shivered, even though the July day was hot. "He was wearing his new ball cap and his favorite shirt, the one I burned…" She began to cry.

"Hey," he said, taking her shoulders in his hands to turn her toward him. "I don't think you're crazy. I think you've had a horrible loss that—"

"I didn't *love* him. I was *leaving* him." The words tumbled out in a rush. "I…I…*hated* him. I *wanted* him gone, not dead!"

Jackson started to pull her into his arms, but she bolted

and was quickly swept up in the exiting crowd. He stood for a moment, letting her words sink in. Now, more than ever, he thought he understood why she was letting little things upset her. Guilt was a powerful thing. It explained a lot, especially with her relationship with her in-laws that he'd glimpsed that morning. How long had they been browbeating her? he wondered. Maybe her whole marriage.

He found himself more curious about her husband, Nick Taylor. And even more about Allie. Common sense told him to keep his distance. The wedding was only days away, then he and Ford would be flying back to Houston.

Maybe it was because he'd gone through a bad marriage, but he felt for her even more now. Like her, he was raising his child alone. Like her, he was disillusioned and he'd certainly gone through a time with his ex when he thought he was losing his mind. He'd also wished his ex dead more than once.

ALLIE CAUGHT UP to Dana as she was loading all the kids into her Suburban. Hud had brought his own rig since he had to stop by the marshal's office.

"Mind if I catch a ride with you?" Allie asked. "Jackson had some errands to run in town." The truth was that after her outburst, she was embarrassed and knew Dana had room for her and Nat in the Suburban.

"Of course not."

Allie had stopped long enough to go into the ladies' room and wash her face and calm down. She knew everyone had seen her take off like a crazy woman. She felt embarrassed and sick at heart, but mostly she was bone-deep scared.

When she'd seen Jackson heading for the parking lot, she'd motioned that she and Nat were going with Dana. He'd merely nodded, probably glad.

Dana didn't comment on Allie's red eyes or her impromptu exit earlier, though as she joined them at the Suburban. Instead, Dana made small talk about the rodeo, the weather, the upcoming wedding.

They were almost back to the ranch before Dana asked, "How are things going?" over the chatter of the kids in the back of the SUV.

Allie could tell that she wasn't just making conversation anymore. She really wanted to know. "It's been hard. I guess it's no secret that I've been struggling."

Dana reached over and squeezed her hand. "I know. I feel so bad about yesterday. I'm just so glad you weren't hurt." She smiled. "You did a great job of staying on that horse, though. I told Natalie how proud I was of you."

Allie thought of Jackson. He'd saved her life yesterday. She remembered the feel of his arms as he'd pulled her from the horse—and again on the dance floor last night. Shoving away the memory, she reminded herself that once the wedding was over, he and Ford would be leaving. She was going to have to start saving herself.

"Did Hud find out anything about who might have shot the horse?" she asked, remembering Hud talking to the vet when he'd stopped by to make sure the mare was all right.

"Nothing yet, but he is going to start gating the roads on the ranch. We can't keep people from the forest service property that borders the ranch, but we can keep them at a distance by closing off the ranch property. In the meantime, if there is anything I can do to help you…"

"Dana, you've already done so much. Letting Natalie come to the ranch and teaching her to ride…" Allie felt overwhelmed at Dana's generosity.

"Let's see if you thank me when she's constantly bugging you about buying her a horse," Dana joked. "Seriously, she can always come up to the ranch and ride. And if someday you do want a horse for her…"

"Thank you. For everything."

"I love what you've done to the barn," Dana said, changing the subject. "It is beyond my expectations and Lily can't say enough about it. I'm getting so excited, but then I'm a sucker for weddings."

"Me, too," Allie admitted. "They are so beautiful. There is so much hope and love in the air. It's all like a wonderful dream."

"Or fantasy," Dana joked. "Nothing about the wedding day is like marriage, especially four children later."

No, Allie thought, but then she'd had a small wedding in Mother Taylor's backyard. She should have known then how the marriage was going to go.

"Have you given any more thought to moving up to a guest cabin?" Dana asked.

"I have. Like I said, I'm touched by the offer. But Natalie has been through so many changes with Nick's death, I think staying at the cabin in her own bed might be best. We'll see, though. She is having such a great time at the ranch and as the wedding gets closer…"

"Just know that I saved a cabin for you and Natalie," Dana said. "And don't worry about your daughter. We have already adopted her into the family. The kids love her and Ford…." She laughed and lowered her voice, even though the kids weren't paying any attention behind them. "Have you noticed how tongue-tied he gets around her?"

They both laughed, Allie feeling blessed because she felt as if she, too, had been adopted into the family. The Cardwells were so different from the Taylors. She pushed that thought away. Just as she did the memory of that instant when she would have sworn she saw Nick at the rodeo.

Every time she thought she was getting better, stronger, something would happen to make her afraid she really was losing her mind.

"HEY," BELINDA SAID, seeming surprised when Allie and Nat walked into the barn that afternoon. "Where have you been? I thought you'd be here working."

"We went to the rodeo!" Natalie said. "And now I'm

going to go ride a horse!" With that she ran out of the barn to join the other kids and Dana.

"You went to the rodeo?"

"You sound like my in-laws," Allie said. "Yes, I was invited, I went and now I will do the last-minute arrangements for the rehearsal dinner tomorrow and it will all be fine."

Belinda lifted a brow. "Wow, what a change from the woman who was panicking because she couldn't find her keys the other day. Have you been drinking?"

"I'm taking my life back." She told her friend about the candle, Nick's shirt and what she did with it. Also about chasing the man she thought was Nick at the rodeo. "I almost caught him. If someone hadn't grabbed my arm…"

Belinda's eyes widened in alarm. "Sorry, but doesn't that sound a little…"

"Crazy? Believe me, I know. But I was sick of just taking it and doing nothing."

"I can see you thinking you saw someone who looked like Nick at the rodeo…."

"He was wearing his favorite shirt and his new ball cap."

Belinda stared at her. "The shirt you'd burned a few nights ago, right?"

Allie regretted telling her friend. "I know it doesn't make any sense. But all these things that have been happening? I'm not imagining them." From her friend's expression, she was glad she hadn't told her about the dresses or the new clothes she'd found in her closet.

"Sweetie," Belinda asked tentatively. "Did you give any more thought to making that call I suggested?"

"No and right now I have work to do."

"Don't we all. Some of us didn't spend the day at the rodeo."

Her friend actually sounded jealous. Allie put it out of her mind. She had to concentrate on the wedding. The barn looked beautiful. After the rehearsal dinner tomorrow night, she would get ready for the wedding. All she had to do was hold it together until then.

Megan came in with her list of last-minute things that needed to be tended to before the wedding rehearsal.

"I'll meet you down in the meadow in a few minutes." Left alone, Allie looked around the barn. She was a little sad it would be over. Jackson and Ford would be returning to Texas. Nat was really going to miss them.

And so are you.

ALLIE WASN'T SURE what awakened her. Dana had insisted she take the rest of the day off and spend it with Natalie.

"You have accomplished so much," Dana had argued. "Tomorrow is another day. The men are all going with Tag for his bachelor party tonight. I plan to turn in early with the kids. Trust me. We all need some downtime before the wedding."

Emotionally exhausted, Allie had agreed. She and Nat had come back to the cabin and gone down to the river until dinner. Nat loved building rock dams and playing in the water.

After dinner even Natalie was exhausted from the full day. After Allie had put her down to sleep, she'd turned in herself with a book. But only a few pages in, she had turned out the light and gone to sleep.

Now, startled awake, she lay listening to the wind that had come up during the night. It was groaning in the boughs of the pine trees next to the cabin. Through the window, she could see the pines swaying and smell the nearby river. She caught only glimpses of the moon in a sky filled with stars as she lay listening.

Since Nick's death she didn't sleep well. The cabin often woke her with its creaks and groans. Sometimes she would hear a thump as if something had fallen and yet when she'd gone to investigate, she would find nothing.

One time, she'd found the front door standing open. She had stared at it in shock, chilled by the cold air rushing in—and the knowledge that she distinctly remembered locking it before going to bed. Only a crazy woman would leave the front door wide open.

Now, though, all she heard was the wind in the pines, a pleasant sound, a safe sound. She tried to reassure herself that everything was fine. She thought of her day with the Cardwell family and remembered how Jackson had saved her by having the Cardwell brothers make their famous Texas barbecue for supper. She smiled at the memory of the brothers in their Texas Boys Barbecue aprons joking around as they cooked.

She'd overheard one of the brothers say he was glad to see Jackson loosening up a little. Allie found herself watching him earlier at the rodeo, wondering how he was doing as a single father. She didn't feel as if she'd done very well so far as a single mother.

Ford was having a sleepover at the main house at the ranch again tonight. Allie knew if Nat had known about it, she would have wanted to stay, as well. But she suspected that Dana had realized that she needed her daughter with her tonight. What a day! First a run-in earlier with Mildred and Drew... Allie felt a chill at the memory. They had both been so furious and no doubt hurt, as well. Then thinking she saw Nick. She shook her head and, closing her eyes, tried to will herself to go back to sleep. If she got to thinking about any of that—

A small thump made her freeze. She heard it again and quickly swung her legs over the side of the bed. The sound had come from down the hall toward the bedroom where Natalie was sleeping.

Allie didn't bother with her slippers or her robe; she was too anxious as she heard another thump. She snapped on the hall light as she rushed down the short, narrow hallway to her daughter's room. The door she'd left open was now closed. She stopped in front of it, her heart pounding. The wind. It must have blown it shut. But surely she hadn't left Nat's window open that much.

She grabbed the knob and turned, shoving the door open with a force that sent her stumbling into the small room. The moon and starlight poured in through the gaping open window to paint the bedroom in silver as the wind slammed a loose shutter against the side of the cabin with a thump.

Allie felt her eyes widen as a scream climbed her throat. Nat's bed was empty.

Chapter Seven

Jackson felt at loose ends after the bachelor party. Part of the reason, he told himself, was because he'd spent so little time with his son. Back in Texas on their small ranch, he and Ford were inseparable. It was good to see his son having so much fun with other children, but he missed him.

Tonight Ford was having a sleepover at the main house with Dana's brood. He'd wanted to say no when Dana had asked, but he had seen that Ford had his heart set and Jackson had no choice but to attend Tag's bachelor party.

Fortunately, it had been a mild one, bar-hopping from the Corral to Lily's brother's bar at Big Sky, The Canyon Bar. They'd laughed and joked about their childhoods growing up in Texas and talked about Tag's upcoming wedding and bugged Hayes about his plans with McKenzie. Hayes only grinned in answer.

Hud, as designated driver, got them all home just after midnight, where they parted company and headed to their respective cabins. That was hours ago. Jackson had slept for a while before the wind had awakened him.

Now, alone with only his thoughts, he kept circling back to Allie. She'd had fun at the rodeo—until she'd thought she'd seen her dead husband. He blamed her in-laws. He figured they'd been laying a guilt trip on her ever since Nick Taylor had been presumed dead. Her run-in with them that morning must have made her think she saw Nick. He wanted to throttle them for the way they treated Allie and shuddered at the thought of them having anything to do with raising Natalie.

Allie was too nice. Did she really believe they meant well? Like hell, he thought now. They'd been in the wrong and yet they'd made her feel badly. It reminded him too much of the way his ex had done him.

It had been fun cooking with his brothers again—just as they had when they'd started their first barbecue restaurant. Allie'd had fun at the barbecue, too. He'd seen her laughing and smiling with the family. He'd enjoyed himself, as well. Of course Austin still hadn't arrived. But it was nice being with the others.

As much as he'd enjoyed the day, he felt too antsy to sleep and admitted it wasn't just Ford who was the problem. He tried to go back to sleep, but knew it was impossible. He had too much on his mind. Except for the wind in the pines, the ranch was quiet as he decided to go for a walk.

Overhead the Montana sky was a dazzling glitter of starlight with the moon peeking in and out of the clouds. The mountains rose on each side of the canyon, blacker than midnight. A breeze stirred the dark pines, sending a whisper through the night.

As he neared his rental SUV, he decided to go for a ride. He hadn't had that much to drink earlier and, after sleeping for a few hours, felt fine to drive.

But not far down the road, he found himself slowing as he neared Allie's cabin. The cabin was small and sat back from the highway on the river.

He would have driven on past, if a light hadn't come on inside the cabin.

Something about that light coming on in the wee hours of the morning sent a shiver through him. He would have said he had a premonition, if he believed in them. Instead, he didn't question what made him turn down her road.

Just as he pulled up to the cabin, Allie came running out.

At first he thought she'd seen him turn into her yard and that was why she'd come running out with a flashlight. But one look at her wild expression, her bare feet and her clothed in nothing but her nightgown, and he knew why he'd turned into her cabin.

"Allie?" he called to her as he jumped out. "Allie, what's wrong?"

She didn't seem to hear him. She ran toward the side of the cabin as if searching furiously as her flashlight beam darted into the darkness. He had to run after her as she headed around the back of the cabin. He grabbed her arm, thinking she might be having a nightmare and was walking in her sleep.

"Allie, what's wrong?"

"Nat! She's gone!"

He instantly thought of the fast-moving river not many yards out the back door. His gaze went to Allie's feet. "Get some shoes on. I'll check behind the house."

Taking her flashlight, he pushed her toward the front door before running around to the back of the cabin. He could hear and smell the river on the other side of a stand of pines. The July night was cool, almost cold this close to the river. Through the dark boughs, he caught glimpses of the Gallatin River. It shone in the moon and starlight, a ribbon of silver that had spent eons carving its way through the granite canyon walls.

As he reached the dense pines, his mind was racing. Had Natalie gotten up in the night and come outside? Maybe half-asleep, would she head for the river?

"Natalie!" he called. The only answer was the rush of the river and moan of the wind in the pine boughs overhead.

At the edge of the river, he shone the flashlight beam along the edge of the bank. No tracks in the soft earth. He flicked the light up and down the area between the pines, then out over the water. Exposed boulders shone in the light as the fast water rushed over and around them.

If Natalie had come down here and gone into the swift current...

At the sound of a vehicle engine starting up, he swung his flashlight beam in time to see a dark-colored pickup take off out of the pines. Had someone kidnapped Natalie? His first thought was the Taylors.

As he ran back toward the cabin, he tried to tell himself it had probably been teenagers parked down by the river making out. Once inside, he found Allie. She'd pulled on sandals and a robe and had just been heading out again. She looked panicked, her cheeks wet with tears.

"You're sure she isn't somewhere in the house," he said, thinking about a time that he'd fallen asleep under his bed while his mother had turned the house upside down looking for him.

The cabin was small. It took only a moment to search everywhere except Nat's room. As he neared the door to the child's bedroom, he felt the cool air and knew before he pushed open the door that her window was wide open, the wind billowing the curtains.

He could see the river and pines through the open window next to the bed. No screen. What looked like fresh soil and several dried pine needles were on the floor next to the bed. As he started to step into the room, a sound came from under the covers on the bed.

Jackson was at the bed in two long strides, pulling back the covers to find a sleeping Natalie Taylor curled there.

Had she been there the whole time and Allie had somehow missed her?

Allie stumbled into the room and fell to her knees next to her daughter's bed. She pulled Nat to her, snuggling her face into the sleeping child.

Jackson stepped out of the room to leave them alone for

a moment. His heart was still racing, his fear now for Allie rather than Nat.

A few minutes later, Allie came out of her daughter's room. He could see that she'd been crying again.

"She's such a sound sleeper. I called for her. I swear she wasn't in her bed."

"I believe you."

"I checked her room. I looked under her bed...." The tears began to fall again. "I looked in her closet. I called her name. *She wasn't there.* She wasn't anywhere in the cabin."

"It's all right," Jackson said as he stepped to her and put his arms around her.

Her voice broke as she tried to speak again. "What if she was there the whole time?" she whispered against his chest. He could feel her trembling and crying with both relief and this new fear. "She can sleep through anything. Maybe—"

"Did you leave the window open?"

"I cracked it just a little so she could get fresh air...."

"Natalie isn't strong enough to open that old window all the way like that."

Allie pulled back to look up at him, tears welling in her green eyes. "I *must* have opened it. I *must* have—"

He thought of the pickup he'd seen leaving. "There's something I need to check," he said, picking up the flashlight from where he'd laid it down just moments before. "Stay here with Natalie."

Outside he moved along the side of the house to the back, shining the flashlight ahead of him. He suspected what he would find so he wasn't all that surprised to discover the boot prints in the soft dirt outside Nat's window.

Jackson knelt down next to the prints. A man-size boot. He shone the light a few feet away. The tracks had come up to the window, the print a partial as if the man had sneaked up on the toes of his boots. But when the prints retreated from the child's window, the prints were full boot tracks, deep in the dirt as if he'd been carrying something. The tracks disappeared into the dried needles of the pines, then reappeared, this time headed back to the house. When the man had returned Natalie to her bed—and left dried pine needles and dirt on the bedroom floor.

ALLIE SAT ON the edge of her daughter's bed. She'd always loved watching Natalie sleep. There was something so incredibly sweet about her that was heightened when she slept. The sleep of angels, she thought as she watched the rise and fall of her daughter's chest.

Outside the now closed window, Jackson's shadow appeared and disappeared. A few minutes later, she heard him come back into the cabin. He came directly down the hall, stopping in Nat's bedroom doorway as if he knew she would be sitting on the side of the bed, watching her daughter sleep. That was where he would have been if it had been his son who'd gone missing, he thought.

She was still so shaken and scared. Not for Natalie, who was safe in her bed, but for herself. How could she have thought her daughter was missing? She really was losing her mind. Tucking Nat in, she checked to make sure the window was locked and left the room, propping the door open.

Jackson followed her into the small living room. She held her breath as she met his gaze. He was the one person who had made her feel as if she was going to be all right. He'd seen the black cat. He'd sympathized with her when she'd told him about misplacing her car keys and messing up her date book.

But earlier he'd looked at her as if she were a hysterical woman half out of her mind. She *had* been. Maybe she *was* unstable. When she'd found Nat's bed empty— Just the thought made her blood run cold again.

"I swear to you she wasn't in her bed." She could hear how close she was to breaking down again.

He must have, too, because he reached over and gripped her arm. "You didn't imagine it any more than you did the black cat."

She stared at him. "How can you say that?"

"Someone was outside Natalie's window tonight. There were fresh tracks where he'd stood. He took Natalie."

Her heart began to thunder in her ears. "Someone tried to…" She couldn't bring herself to say the words as she imagined a shadowed man taking her baby girl out through the window. "But why…?"

"He must have heard me coming and changed his mind," Jackson said.

"Changed his mind?" This all felt too surreal. First Nick's death then all the insane incidents, now someone had tried to take her child?

"Why don't you sit down," Jackson suggested.

She nodded and sank into the closest chair. He took one and pulled it next to hers.

"Is there someone who would want to take your daughter?" he asked.

Again she stared at him, unable to speak for a moment. "Why would anyone want to kidnap Natalie? I don't have any money."

He seemed to hesitate. "What about your husband's family?"

JACKSON SAW THAT he'd voiced her fear. He'd seen the way her in-laws had been just that morning. It wasn't much of a stretch that they would try to take Natalie. But through an open window in the middle of the night?

"They've made no secret that they want to see her more, but to steal her from her bed and scare me like this?"

Scare her. He saw her eyes widen in alarm and he took a guess. "There have been other instances when something happened that scared you?"

Her wide, green eyes filled with tears. "It was nothing. Probably just my imagination. I haven't been myself since…"

"Tell me about the incidents."

She swallowed and seemed to brace herself. "I found a squirrel in my cast-iron pot that has a lid."

"A live squirrel?"

"Half dead. I know it sounds crazy. How could a squirrel get under a heavy lid like that?"

"It couldn't. What else?"

She blinked as if stunned that he believed her, but it seemed to free her voice. "My husband used to buy me clothes I didn't like. I found them all cut up but I don't remember doing it. My brother-in-law took Nat and me out for dinner and when I got back they were lying on the bed and there were new clothes in the closet, eight hundred dollars' worth, like I would have bought if…"

"If you had bought them. Did you?"

She hesitated. "I don't think so but there was a check missing from my checkbook and when I took them back to the store, the clerks didn't remember who'd purchased them."

"No one was ever around when any of these things happened?"

She shook her head. "When I told my mother-in-law about the squirrel in the pot…she thought I was still taking the drugs the doctor gave me right after Nick's death. The drugs did make me see things that weren't there…." Her words fell away as if she'd just then realized something. "Unless the things *had* been there."

Allie looked up at him, tears shimmering in her eyes. "Like the black cat…. I wasn't sure I'd even seen it until you…"

It broke his heart. For months after her husband's death, she'd been going through this with no one who believed her.

"I don't think you imagined any of these things that have been happening to you," he said, reaching for her hand. "I think someone wants you to *believe* you are losing your mind. What would happen if you were?"

She didn't hesitate an instant. "I would lose Natalie."

As RELIEVED AS she was, Allie had trouble believing what he was saying. She got up and started to make a fire.

"Let me do that," Jackson said, taking a handful of kindling from her.

Allie moved restlessly around the room as he got the blaze going. "You think it's someone in Nick's family?"

"That would be my guess. It's clear they want Natalie, especially your mother-in-law. Would her son, Drew, help her?"

She shook her head. "Nick would do whatever his mother wanted. But Drew…" She didn't want to believe it, but he seemed to have turned against her lately. She felt sick at the thought that she might have been wrong about him all this time.

"You must think I'm such a fool."

"My mother said be careful what family you're marrying into. I didn't listen. I didn't even *know* the woman I was really marrying. But then she hid it well—until we were married."

"I know exactly what you're saying."

His chuckle held no humor. "I learned the hard way."

"So did I. I would have left Nick, if he hadn't disappeared…. I suppose you heard that he went hiking up in the mountains late last fall and was believed killed by a grizzly."

He nodded. "I'm sorry. You must have all kinds of conflicting emotions under the circumstances."

Allie let out a sigh. "You have no idea. Or maybe you do. My friend Belinda says my so-called incidents are brought on by my guilt. She's even suggested that I see a psychic to try to contact Nick on the other side to make the guilt go away."

He shook his head. "I think there is a very sane explanation that has nothing to do with guilt, and the last thing you need is some charlatan who'll only take your money."

She laughed. "That was exactly what I thought." She couldn't believe how much better she felt. She hadn't felt strong for so long. Fear had weakened her, but Jackson's words brought out some of the old Allie, that strong young woman who'd foolishly married Nick Taylor.

He hadn't broken her at first. It had taken a few years before she'd realized what he'd done to her. She no longer had her own ideas—if they didn't agree with his. He dressed her, told her what friends he liked and which ones he didn't.

He'd basically taken over her life, but always making it seem as if he were doing her a favor since he knew best. And she had loved him. At least at first so she'd gone along because she hadn't wanted to upset him. Nick could be scary when he was mad. She'd learned not to set him off.

When Nick had been nice, he'd been so sweet that she had been lulled into thinking that if she was just a little more accommodating he would be sweet all the time.

"Belinda thinks Nick knew that I was leaving him and went up in the mountains to…"

"Kill himself? What do you think?" Jackson asked.

"Nick did say he wanted to change and that he was sorry about the way he'd acted, but…"

"You didn't believe it?"

She shook her head. "The Nick I knew couldn't change even if he'd wanted to."

So why had Nick Taylor gone up into the mountains last fall and never come back? Jackson wondered.

The fact that his body hadn't been found made Jackson more than a little suspicious. If the man had purposely gone to the mountains intending to die and leave his wife and child alone, then he was a coward. If he set the whole thing up and was now trying to have his wife committed…

The timing bothered him. His stomach roiled with anger at the thought. "Is there any chance he knew of your plans?"

"I didn't think so. For months I'd been picking up any change he left lying around. I also had been skimping on groceries so I could save a little. He might have noticed." She looked away guiltily. "I also took money out of his wallet if he'd been drinking. I figured he wouldn't know how much he spent. He never said anything."

Jackson hoped this bastard was alive because he planned to punch him before the man went to prison for what he was doing to this woman. Not letting her have her own money was a sin in any marriage, no matter what some head-of-the household types said.

"I hate to even ask this, but is there any chance—"

"Nick is still alive?" She stood and paced around the room. "That would explain it, wouldn't it? Why I think I see him or why I smell his aftershave in the house, even though I threw out the bottle months ago. Why when I start feeling better, he shows up."

"Like at the rodeo?" Jackson asked, feeling his skin crawl at the thought of the bastard. "This only happens when there is no one else around who sees him, right?"

She nodded. "It all happens in a split second so I can't be sure. At the rodeo, though, I almost caught him. Just a few more yards…" Allie's eyes suddenly widened. "I remember now. Someone grabbed my arm and spun me around. That's why I fell."

"You think it was someone who didn't want you to catch him."

"Did you see anyone you recognized in the crowd before you found me?"

He thought for a moment. "I wasn't looking for anyone

but you, I'm sorry. Allie, all of this is classic gaslighting. Someone wants to unnerve you, to make you think you're imagining things, to make you doubt your own reality and ultimately make you doubt your own sanity."

She met his gaze. Her eyes filled with tears. "You think it's Nick?"

"I think it's a possibility. If he suspected you were going to leave him and take Natalie…he might have staged his death. He had the most to lose if you left him and with his body never being found…"

NICK ALIVE? ALLIE felt a chill move through her. Her husband had been a ghost, haunting her from his mountain grave for months. Now he had taken on an even more malevolent spirit.

She got up and threw another log on the fire. But not even the hot flames could chase away the icy cold that had filled her at the thought of Nick still alive. Not just alive but stalking her, trying to make her think she was crazy. Still, why—

"You think he's after Natalie," she said and frowned. "He's never cared that much about her. He wanted a son and when he didn't get one…"

"Believe me. I know what it's like to have a vindictive spouse who would do anything to hurt me—including taking a child she didn't really want."

"Oh, Jackson, I'm so sorry."

"If your husband is alive, you can bet he is behind all of this."

If Nick really was alive, then Drew would know. It would also explain why Drew was being so protective and acting jealous over Jackson.

Jackson stepped to her. "There is one thing you can count on. It's going to get worse. Nick will have to escalate his plan. He probably has a story already planned for when he comes stumbling out of the mountains after being attacked and having no memory for months. But that story won't hold up if it goes on much longer. I don't want to scare you, but if whoever is behind this can't drive you crazy, they might get desperate and decide the best way to get Natalie is to get rid of her mother for good."

She shuddered.

"Sorry," he said. "I know it seems like a leap…"

Jackson looked to the dark window before returning his gaze to her. "But if your husband is alive, then you have to assume he is watching your every move."

If Nick wasn't, then Drew was doing it for him, she realized. "You really think it's possible?" she asked in a whisper as if not only was he watching but he was listening, as well.

"Given what has been happening to you and the fact that his body was never found?" Jackson nodded. "But if he is alive, we can't let him know that we're on to him."

We. That had such a wonderful sound. She had felt so alone in all this. Suddenly, she wasn't. Jackson believed her. He didn't think she was crazy. Far from it. He thought all of this was happening because someone wanted her to *believe* she was crazy. Maybe not just *someone,* but the man she'd married.

She swallowed back the bile that rose in her throat at the thought of how far her husband had gone and to what end? "He must have known I was leaving him and taking Natalie."

"That would be my guess. With you in the nuthouse, he could reappear and take your daughter."

The thought of Natalie with a man who would do something like that turned her blood to ice.

"But if he is alive, then—" Jackson seemed to hesitate "—then I really can't see how he could have pulled this off without help."

Allie knew what he was saying. Not just Drew but Mildred and Sarah might be in on this. "His brother, Drew, has been around a lot since Nick...disappeared and has helped out financially until the investigation is over. His mother's never liked me and didn't believe me when I've told her about only some of the things that have been happening. Or at least she pretended not to."

Jackson nodded. "What about Drew's sister, Sarah?"

"She's afraid of Mother Taylor, not that I can blame her."

He looked away for a moment. "What about the two women working with you on the wedding?"

"*Belinda and Megan?* Belinda's the only friend who stuck with me after I married Nick. He tried to run her off but she wasn't having any of it." Allie didn't want to believe it. Refused to. She shook her head. "She's been on my side against them. And Megan? She's my *stepsister* I never knew until..."

"Until?" he prompted.

"I guess it was right before Nick died. Megan contacted me. She was just finishing up her college degree at the University of Montana in Missoula. After my mother died, my father remarried several times and had more children. He moved away and I lost track of him and my step-siblings. Megan was like a gift coming into our lives when she did. Nat adores her. I adore her. You can't think she is somehow involved in any of this."

Jackson didn't say anything. He didn't have to. His skepticism was written all over his face. "It's the timing that bothers me."

She nodded. He thought she was naive. She'd always been too trusting. Isn't that what Nick had told her time and time again?

Allie quickly turned away as she felt hot tears scald her eyes. All of this was just too much. She thought of her daughter and hurriedly wiped at her tears. Straightening her back, she felt a surge of anger and turned back to face Jackson.

"Whoever is doing this, they aren't going to win. What do we do?" she asked.

"We catch them. Do you have a photograph of Nick?"

As she left the room, she noticed that the sun had come up. She came back with a snapshot. "This is the only one I could find. It's one of Nick and his brother, Drew. Nick is the one on the right."

Jackson looked down at the photo. "They look alike."

"Do they?" she said, looking at the snapshot he was holding. "I guess they do a little," she said, surprised that she hadn't noticed it because their personalities were so different. "Drew was always the quiet one. Nick was his mother's favorite. I'm sure that had something to do with why he was so cocky and smart-mouthed. Drew was the one always standing back watching."

"Did Drew resent that?" Jackson asked.

Allie frowned. "I don't know. He didn't seem to. Just the other day he was telling me how hard it was to keep the business going without Nick."

Jackson turned thoughtful for a moment. "You mentioned something about Belinda wanting you to see some psychic so you could reach Nick on the other side? I think you should do it."

Allie blinked in surprise. "Seriously? You don't think I'm messed up enough?"

"It's Belinda's idea, right? If she is involved, then this séance with the psychic is a trap. But since we are on to them now, it would help to know what they have planned for you. I suspect it won't be pleasant, though. I'm sure it is supposed to push you over the edge, if you aren't already dangling there. Do you think you can handle it?"

She raised her chin, her eyes dry, resolve burning in her like a blazing fire. She thought of the people who had been tricking her for months. Anger boiled up inside her along with a steely determination. She hadn't felt this strong in years. "I can handle it."

Jackson smiled at her. "Good." He checked his watch. "Give the psychic a call. Calling this early she will think you are desperate to see her, exactly what we want her to think."

Allie dug the card out, glad now that she'd saved it. She took a breath, let it out and dialed the number. Jackson stepped closer so he could hear.

She was surprised when a young-sounding woman answered after three rings.

"I'm sorry to call so early but I need your help. My friend Belinda suggested I call you." Jackson gave her a thumbs-up.

"You must be Allie. I was hoping you'd call. You're in danger—and so is your daughter. I need to see you as soon as possible."

"Is today too soon, then?" Allie asked.

"Why don't you come this evening, say about eight? Will that work for you?"

Allie met Jackson's gaze. He nodded. "That would be fine. I hope you can help me."

"I will do my best but ultimately it will be up to the spirits."

Jackson swore softly as Allie disconnected. "Spirits my ass. Between now and then, I will try to find out everything I can about the people with access to you." He reached over and took her hand. "Don't worry. We're going to catch these bastards."

Chapter Eight

When Jackson returned to the ranch, he found his brothers, told them what he thought was going on and asked for their help. He no longer kidded himself that he wasn't involved.

"I can talk to the cops about what they found in the mountains," Hayes said. "You say Nick Taylor's body still hasn't been found? Isn't that odd? He died late last fall and even with hikers in the area, no remains have turned up?"

"No, that's what makes me suspicious," Jackson said. "His claw-shredded backpack and rifle were discovered at the scene with grizzly prints in the dirt and enough blood to make them believe he was killed there. But still no remains of any kind."

Hayes nodded. "I'll get right on it."

"What can I do?" Laramie asked.

"Financials on everyone involved including Allie's friend Belinda Andrews and her stepsister, Megan Knight, as well as all of the Taylor family. Nick and his brother, Drew, were partners in a construction company called Gallatin Canyon Specialty Construction."

"You got it," Laramie said. "What about Allie herself?"

"Sure, and Nick, just in case he had something going on that she didn't know about," Jackson said.

"Wait a minute," Tag said. "What about me?"

"You, brother dear, are getting married. You just concentrate on your lovely bride-to-be," Jackson told him. Tag started to object. "If you're going to be hanging around the ranch here, then do me a favor. Keep an eye on Drew Taylor. He's apparently doing some repairs here."

Jackson stopped by the barn to find Allie and Megan hard at work putting together centerpieces for the tables. Allie pretended she needed something from her van and got up to go outside with him.

"No more trouble last night?" he asked, seeing worry in her gaze.

"None. I'm just having a hard time believing any of that happened last night." She glanced around as if she expected Nick to materialize before her gaze came back to him. Or maybe she was worried about her brother-in-law, Drew, seeing them together again. "I can't believe Belinda or Megan—"

"Have you seen Belinda?"

"She had to go into Bozeman. She left about twenty minutes ago, why?"

He shook his head. "You better get back inside. Try not to let on that you're suspicious."

She sighed. "You don't know how hard that is."

"I can imagine." He gave her an encouraging smile. "Just be your usual sweet self." He loved it when she returned his smile and those gorgeous dimples of hers showed.

As she went back into the barn and rejoined Megan, he headed up the hillside. Belinda was staying in the last guest-house to the east. Each cabin was set away from the others in the dense pines for the most privacy.

A cool pine-scented breeze restlessly moved the boughs over his head as he walked on the bed of dried needles toward Belinda's cabin. He could hear the roar of the river and occasionally the sound of a semi shifting down on the highway far below. A squirrel chattered at him as he passed, breaking the tranquility.

He was almost to her cabin when he heard the crack of a twig behind him and spun around in surprise.

His brother Hayes grinned. "I would imagine the cabin will be locked," he said as he stepped on past to climb the steps to the small porch and try the door. "Yep, I know your lock-picking skills are rusty at best." He pulled out his tool set.

Jackson climbed the steps and elbowed his brother out of the way. "I told Dana I was locked out. She gave me the master key." He laughed and opened the door.

"You know I do this for a living, right?" his brother asked.

"I'd heard that. But are you any good?"

Hayes shot him a grin and headed for the log dresser in the room with the unmade bed.

Jackson glanced around the main room of the cabin and spotted Belinda's camera bag. He could hear his brother searching the bedroom as he carefully unzipped the bag. There were the usual items found in a professional photographer's large bag. He carefully took out the camera, lens and plastic filter containers and was about to put everything back, thinking there was nothing to find when he saw the corner of a photo protruding from one of the lower pockets.

"What did you find?" Hayes asked as he returned after searching both bedrooms.

Jackson drew out the photos and thumbed through them. They were shots taken with apparent friends. Each photo had Belinda smiling at the camera with her arm around different friends, all women. He was thinking how there wasn't one of her and Allie, when he came to the last photo and caught his breath.

"Who is that?" Hayes asked.

"Allie's husband, Nick, and her best friend Belinda Andrews. Allie said that Nick never liked Belinda." The snapshot had been taken in the woods along a trail. There was a sign in the distance that said Grouse Creek Trail. Nick had his arm possessively around Belinda. Both were smiling at each other rather than the camera the way lovers do.

"Apparently, they liked each other a lot more than Allie knew," Hayes said. "But you know what is really interesting about that photo? That trailhead sign behind them."

"Let me guess. Up that trail is where Nick Taylor was believed to have been killed."

WHEN THEY'D FINISHED the centerpieces, Allie sent Megan into Bozeman for an order of wedding items that had been delayed. It had been difficult working with her and suspecting her of horrible things. Allie was relieved when she was finally alone in the barn.

Everything was coming along on schedule. It had been Dana's idea to start days early. "I don't want you to feel any pressure and if you need extra help, you just let me know," Dana had said.

"No, I'm sure that will be fine."

"I want you to have some free time to go for a horseback ride or just spend it on the ranch with your daughter."

"You are so thoughtful," Allie had said.

"Not at all. I just know what it's like with a little one, even though Natalie isn't so little anymore," she said with a laugh. "I promise I will keep your daughter busy so you can work and not have to worry about her having a good time."

Dana had been good to her word. Allie stepped outside the barn now to check on Natalie only to find her on the back of a horse about to take a short ride up the road for another picnic with Dana and the other children.

"Come along," Dana encouraged. "Warren would be happy to saddle you a horse. You know what they say about almost falling off a horse, don't you?" she asked with a smile. "You have to get back on."

Allie laughed, thinking that was exactly what she was

doing with her life, thanks to Jackson. She was tempted to go on the ride until she saw him headed her way. "Next time."

"We're going to hold you to it," Dana said. "In fact, we're all going on a ride tomorrow before the rehearsal dinner. Plan on coming along." With that they rode off, the kids waving and cheering as they disappeared into the pines.

Jackson waved to his son, making the same promise before he continued on down the mountainside toward her.

When she saw his expression, her heart fell. He'd discovered something and whatever it was, it wasn't good.

"Let's go up to my cabin," Jackson said as he glanced around. "We can talk there."

They made the short hike up the mountainside. His cabin faced the river, sheltered in the pines and was several dozen yards from the closest cabin where his brothers were staying together.

"What is it?" Allie asked the moment they were inside.

Jackson handed her a snapshot in answer.

She looked down at her smiling husband and her best friend. There was no doubt what she was looking at but still she was shocked and found it hard to believe. For more than six years Belinda and Nick had acted as if they couldn't stand each other. Had it been a lie the entire time?

"When was this taken?" she asked.

Jackson shook his head. "There isn't a date. I found it in her camera bag with a lot of other photos of her with friends."

Allie raised an eyebrow. "You aren't going to try to convince me that they are just friends."

He shook his head. "You weren't at all suspicious?"

She laughed as she made her way to the couch and sat down. The ground under her feet no longer felt stable. "Nick always said I was too trusting. Belinda was the only friend who could put up with Nick. So I guess a part of me suspected that Nick liked her more than he let on."

"I'm sorry."

"Don't be. I stopped loving Nick Taylor the year we got married. If I hadn't gotten pregnant with Nat…" She tossed the photo on the coffee table in front of her.

"She was the only one you told about your plans to leave Nick?" he asked as he took a seat across from her.

Allie let out a laugh. "So of course she told him."

"More than likely," he agreed. "There's more." He took a breath and let it out as he studied her. "You sure you want to hear all of this?"

She sat up straighter. "Let me have it."

"I got my brothers to help me. They have the expertise in their chosen fields that we needed. Hayes talked to the cops who had a copy of Nick's file with reports from the hiker who found the backpack and rifle to the warden who investigated the initial scene. He reported that there was sufficient evidence to assume that Nick was dead based on the shredded backpack and the amount of blood soaked into the pine needles."

"So…he's dead?"

"Or he made it look that way," Jackson said. "No DNA was tested at the scene because there didn't appear to be a need to do so. But there are still a lot of questions. No shots were fired from the rifle, leading the investigators to believe he didn't have time to get off a shot before he was attacked by the bear. Or he could have staged the whole thing. But the incidents you've been having with things disappearing and reappearing, those can't be Nick. If he's alive, he has to keep his head down."

"So we're back to my in-laws and Belinda and Megan."

"I'm afraid so. Belinda, if involved with Nick, would be the obvious one. Was she around before any of the incidents happened?"

Allie thought back to when her keys had ended up in the bathroom sink at the Mexican restaurant. She'd left her purse at the table, but then Sarah and her mother had been there, too. She sighed, still refusing to believe it, even after seeing the photo. "Yes, but Belinda wouldn't—"

"Wouldn't have an affair with your husband behind your back?"

"She's been so *worried* about me."

Jackson raised a brow.

Allie hugged herself against the thought of what he was saying. Belinda *had* apparently betrayed her with Nick. Maybe Jackson was right. Then she remembered something. "Belinda has a new man in her life. I know the signs. She starts dressing up and, I don't know, acting different. The man can't be Nick. That photo doesn't look recent of her and Nick. Why would she be acting as if there was someone new if it was Nick all these months?"

"Maybe he's been hiding out and has only now returned to the canyon."

That thought turned her stomach. "If he's come back…"

"Then whoever has been gaslighting you must be planning on stepping up their plan," Jackson said.

She turned to look at him as a shiver raced through her. "The psychic. Maybe this is their grand finale, so to speak, and they have something big planned tonight to finally send me to the loony bin."

"Maybe you shouldn't go—"

"No. Whatever they have planned, it won't work. They've done their best to drive me crazy. I know now what they're up to. I'll be fine."

"I sure hope so," Jackson said.

"WHAT IS THE lowdown on the Taylor family?" Jackson asked Hud after dinner that evening at the ranch. They'd had beef steaks cooked on a pitchfork in the fire and eaten on the wide porch at the front of the house. The night had been beautiful, but Jackson was too antsy to appreciate it. He was worried about Allie.

She'd dropped Natalie by before she and Belinda had left. He hadn't had a chance to speak with her without raising suspicion. All he could do was try his best to find out who was behind the things that had been happening to her.

"Old canyon family," Hud said. "Questionable how they made their money. It was rumored that the patriarch killed someone and stole his gold." Hud shrugged. "Mildred? She married into it just months before Bud Taylor died in a car accident. She's kept the name even though she's been through several more husbands. I believe she is on number four now. Didn't take his name, though. He's fifteen, twenty years older and spends most of his time with his grown children back in Chicago."

"And the daughter?"

"Sarah?" Hud frowned. "Never been married that I know of. Lives in the guesthouse behind her mother's. No visible means of support."

"The brothers had a construction company together?"

"They did. Nick was the driving force. With him gone, I don't think Drew is working all that much."

"Just between you and me, Allie was planning to leave Nick Taylor before he went up in the mountain and disappeared," Jackson said, taking the marshal into his confidence.

Hud looked over at him. "What are you getting at?"

"Is there any chance Nick Taylor is alive?"

Hud frowned. "You must have some reason to believe he is."

"Someone has been gaslighting Allie."

"For what purpose?"

"I think someone, probably in the Taylor family, wants to take Natalie away from her."

"YOU SEEM BETTER," Belinda noted on the drive out of the canyon. She'd insisted on driving Allie to the psychic's house, saying she didn't trust Allie to drive herself if the psychic said anything that upset her.

Allie had been quiet most of the drive. "*Do* I seem better?" Did her friend seem disappointed in that?

"Maybe this isn't necessary."

That surprised her. "I thought you were the one who said I had to talk to this psychic?"

"I thought it would help."

"And now?" Allie asked.

"I don't want her to upset you when you seem to be doing so well."

"That's sweet, but I'm committed…so to speak."

Belinda nodded and kept driving. "Seriously, you seem so different and the only thing that has changed that I can tell is Jackson Cardwell showing up."

Allie laughed. "Just like you to think it has to be a man. Maybe I'm just getting control of my life."

Her friend looked skeptical. "Only a few days ago you were burning Nick's favorite shirt so it didn't turn up again."

"Didn't I tell you? The shirt *did* turn up again. I found it hanging in the shower this morning. Now I ask you, how is that possible?"

"You're sure you burned it? Maybe you just—"

"Dreamed it?" Allie smiled. That was what they wanted her to think. She looked over at Belinda, worried her old friend was up to her neck in this, whatever it was.

Allie fought the urge to confront her and demand to know who else was behind it. But Belinda turned down a narrow road, slowing to a stop in front of a small house with a faint porch light on.

Showtime, Allie thought as she tried to swallow the lump in her throat.

Chapter Nine

Belinda's apartment house was an old, five-story brick one a few blocks off Main Street in Bozeman.

Laramie waited in the car as lookout while Jackson and Hayes went inside. There was no password entry required. They simply walked in through the front door and took the elevator up to the third floor to room 3B. It was just as Allie had described it, an apartment at the back, the door recessed so even if someone had been home on the floor of four apartments, they wouldn't have seen Hayes pick the lock.

"You're fast," Jackson said, impressed.

Hayes merely smiled and handed him a pair of latex gloves. "I'm also smart. If you're right and Nick Taylor is alive and this becomes a criminal case… You get the idea. It was different up on the ranch. This, my brother, is breaking and entering."

Jackson pulled on the gloves and opened the door. As he started to draw his flashlight out of his pocket, Hayes snapped on an overhead light.

"What the—"

"Jackson," his brother said and motioned toward the window. The curtains were open, the apartment looking out onto another apartment building. While most of the curtains were drawn in those facing this way, several were open.

Hayes stepped to the window and closed the curtains.

"Nothing more suspicious than two dudes sneaking around in a woman's apartment with flashlights."

He had a point. "Let's make this quick."

"I'm with you," Hayes said and suggested the best place to start.

"If I didn't know better, I'd think you'd done this before," Jackson joked.

Hayes didn't answer.

In the bedroom in the bottom drawer of the bureau under a bunch of sweaters, Jackson found more photos of Belinda and Nick, but left them where he'd found them.

"So you think I'm right and Nick is alive," Jackson said.

Hayes shrugged.

Jackson finished the search of the bedroom, following his brother's instructions to try to leave everything as he had found it.

"Find anything?" he asked Hayes when he'd finished.

"She recently came into thirty-eight thousand dollars," Hayes said, thumbing through a stack of bank statements he'd taken from a drawer.

"Maybe it's a trust fund or an inheritance."

"Maybe. Or blackmail money or money Nick had hidden from Allie," Hayes said as he put everything back. "Laramie would probably be able to find out what it was if we had more time. Did you put the photos back?"

"All except one. I want to show it to Allie. It looks more recent to me."

Hayes looked as if he thought that was a bad idea. "You're messing with evidence," he reminded him.

"I'll take that chance," Jackson said.

His brother shook his head as he turned out the light and moved to the window to open the curtains like he'd found them.

"Does anyone else know how involved you are with the wedding planner?" Silence. "I didn't think so. Better not let cousin Dana find out or there will be hell to pay. She is very protective of people she cares about. She cares about that woman and her child. If you—"

"I'm not going to hurt her." He couldn't see his brother's expression in the dark. He didn't have to.

ALLIE BRACED HERSELF. She hadn't shared her fears about the visit with the psychic with Jackson before she'd left. She hadn't had to. She'd seen the expression on his face as he watched her leave. He was terrified for her.

For months someone had been trying to push her over the edge of sanity. She had a bad feeling that the psychic was part of the master plan, a shocker that was aimed at driving her insane. By now, they probably thought she was hanging on by a thread. While she was stronger, thanks to Jackson and his determination that she was perfectly sane and those around her were the problem, there was a part of her that wasn't so sure about that.

Just this morning, she'd stepped into the bathroom, opened the shower curtain and let out a cry of shock and disbelief. Nick's favorite shirt was hanging there, the same shirt she'd burned in the fireplace a few nights ago. Or at least one exactly like it. Worse, she smelled his aftershave and when she opened the medicine cabinet, there it was in the spot where he always kept it—right next to his razor, both of which she had thrown out months ago.

Had he hoped she would cut her wrists? Because it had crossed her mind. If it hadn't been for Natalie…and now Jackson…

"Remember, you're that strong woman you were before you met Nick Taylor," Jackson had said earlier.

She'd smiled because she could only vaguely remember that woman. But she wanted desperately to reacquaint herself with her. Now all she could do was be strong for her daughter. She couldn't let these people get their hands on Natalie.

Belinda parked in front of a small house and looked over at her. "Ready?"

Allie could hear reluctance in her friend's voice. If Jackson was right and Nick was behind this, then Allie suspected he was forcing Belinda to go through with the plan no matter what.

But that's what she had to find out. If Nick was alive. She opened her car door and climbed out. The night air was cool and scented with fresh-cut hay from a nearby field. It struck her how remote this house was. The closest other residence had been up the road a good half mile.

If a person was to scream, no one would hear, Allie thought, then warned herself not to bother screaming. Belinda and the psychic were probably hoping for just such a reaction.

"I was surprised when you agreed to do this," Belinda said now, studying her as she joined Allie on the path to the house.

"I told you. I would do anything to make whatever is happening to me stop." Allie took a deep breath and let it out. "Let's get this over with."

They walked up the short sidewalk and Belinda knocked. Allie noticed that there weren't any other vehicles around except for an old station wagon parked in the open, equally old garage. If Nick was here he'd either been dropped off or he'd parked in the trees at the back of the property.

The door was opened by a small, unintimidating woman wearing a tie-dyed T-shirt and worn jeans. Her feet were bare. Allie had been expecting a woman in a bright caftan wearing some sort of headdress. She was a little disappointed.

"Please come in," the woman said in what sounded like a European accent. "I am Katrina," she said with a slight nod. "It is so nice to meet you, Allie. Please follow me. Your friend can stay here."

Belinda moved to a couch in what Allie assumed was the sparsely furnished living area.

Allie followed the woman down a dim hallway and through a door into a small room dominated by a table and two chairs. The table was bare.

Katrina closed the door, making the room feel even smaller. She took a seat behind the desk and motioned Allie into the chair on the opposite side.

This felt silly and it was all Allie could do not to laugh. She and a friend in the fifth grade had stopped at the fortune teller's booth at the fair one time—her friend Willow's idea, not hers.

"I want to know if I am going to marry Curt," her friend had said.

Allie could have told her that there was a good chance she wasn't going to marry some boy in her fifth grade class.

The fortune teller had told them they would have long, happy lives and marry their true loves. Five dollars each later they were standing outside the woman's booth. Willow had been so excited, believing what the fortune teller had said was that she would marry Curt. She'd clearly read what she wanted into the woman's words.

Willow didn't marry Curt but maybe she had found her true love since she'd moved away in sixth grade when her father was transferred. Allie hadn't had a happy life nor had she apparently married her true love and now here she was again sitting across from some woman who she feared really might know her future because she was about to control it.

"I understand you want me to try to reach your husband who has passed over," Katrina said. "I have to warn you that I am not always able to reach the other side, but I will try since your friend seems to think if I can reach…"

"Nick," Allie supplied.

"Yes, that it will give you some peace." The woman hesitated. "I hope that will be the case. It isn't always, I must warn you. Do you want to continue?"

Allie swallowed and nodded.

"Give me your hands. I need you to think of your husband." Katrina dimmed the lights and reached across the table to take Allie's hands in hers. "It helps if you will close your eyes and try to envision your husband."

That was about the last thing Allie wanted to do, but as Katrina closed hers, Allie did the same. She couldn't help but think of Nick and wonder if he was watching her at this very moment.

"WHILE WE'RE BREAKING the law, there is one other place I'd like to have a look before we head back," Jackson said to his brothers.

Hayes looked disapproving. "What part of breaking and entering don't you understand?"

"You can wait in the car."

Gallatin Canyon Specialty Construction was located on the outskirts of town next to a gravel pit. The industrial area was dark this time of the night as Jackson pulled in with his lights out and parked.

"Allie said the company hasn't been doing very well without Nick and wasn't doing that well even before Nick allegedly died," Jackson said. "I just want to take a look at the books."

"Good thing you brought me along," Laramie said. "You did mean, you want me to take a look, right?"

Jackson laughed. "Yeah, if you don't mind."

Hayes sighed and they all got out and walked toward the trailer that served as the office. Hayes unlocked the door then said, "I'll stand guard. Make it quick," before disappearing into the darkness.

"You do realize you might be jeopardizing everything by doing this," Laramie said. "Is this woman worth it?"

Jackson didn't answer as he pulled on the latex gloves Hayes had shoved at him in the car and handed his brother a pair before turning on a light and pointing at the file cabinets.

It wasn't until they were all three back in the car and headed south toward Cardwell Ranch that Jackson asked his brother what he'd found, if anything.

After Laramie tried to explain it in fiduciary terms, Hayes snapped, "The bottom line, please."

Laramie sighed. "It is clear why you all leave the business part of Texas Boys Barbecue up to me. All right, here it is. Drew Taylor is broke and has been siphoning off the money from the business before the sale."

"Sale?" Jackson said.

"While not of general knowledge, Drew has been trying to sell the business through a company in other states."

"That's suspicious," Hayes said.

"Is his mother involved in the construction business?" Jackson asked.

Laramie chuckled. "Excellent question. I believe she might have been a silent partner, which I take to mean she provided some of the money. Until recently, Drew was writing her a check each month."

"Think she knows what her son is up to?" Hayes asked.

"Doubtful. According to Allie, Mother Taylor rules the roost. Everyone is afraid of her."

"Sounds like our boy Drew is planning to escape in the dark of night," Hayes commented and Jackson agreed.

"As for the rest of the people you asked me to look at the finances of, Mildred Taylor is fine as long as her old, absentee husband sends her a check each month. She and her daughter live off the old man. Nick wasn't much of a breadwinner. Montana winters slow down construction, apparently. But he did okay. After his death, there wasn't much in his personal account."

"So the thirty-eight thousand Belinda just received wasn't from Nick, then," Hayes said.

Laramie continued, "Nick did, however, leave a hundred-thousand-dollar insurance policy, which is supposed to pay out any day once Nick has finally been ruled legally deceased."

"A hundred thousand?" Jackson exclaimed. "That doesn't seem like enough money to put Allie into the nuthouse for."

Laramie and Hayes agreed. "There could be other insurance policies I'm not aware of."

"What about Megan Knight?" Jackson asked.

"Just finished college, has thousands of dollars in student loans," Laramie said. "Majored in psychology so unless she goes to grad school…"

"What do you all make of this?" Jackson asked.

"Well," his brother Laramie said. "I've always said follow the money. That will usually take you to the source of the problem."

"SO WE HAVE Drew siphoning money from the business and Belinda coming into some money and Megan needing money to pay off her student loans," Jackson said. "So which of them has motive to want Allie in the nuthouse?"

"Your guess is as good as mine," Hayes said. "That photo you took from Belinda's apartment of her and Nick? The lovebirds didn't look like they were getting along."

"Wait a minute," Laramie said from the backseat. "Are you thinking with Nick gone, Drew and Belinda hooked up?"

"Good question," Jackson said.

"I've heard of stranger things happening," Hayes said.

"Or maybe it's blackmail money," Jackson said. "Maybe

Belinda has something on Drew and he's the source of the thirty-eight thousand."

"Or Drew is simply taking money from the business and giving it to Belinda to give to Nick," Hayes threw in.

"Which would mean that Drew knows Nick is alive," Jackson said.

"Or at least he has been led to believe his brother is alive according to Belinda," Hayes said.

"You two are making my head spin," Laramie cried and both brothers laughed. "No wonder I prefer facts and figures. They are so much less confusing."

"He's right," Hayes said. "It could be simple. Nick's dead, Belinda got her money from another source entirely and Drew is blowing his on beer."

As they reached Cardwell Ranch, Jackson glanced at the time. "Let's hope Allie gets some answers tonight," he said, unable to keep the worry out of his voice. "Who knows what horrors they have planned for her."

"ALLIE."

Nick's voice made Allie jump, but Katrina held tight to her hands. Goose bumps skittered over her skin as Nick spoke again.

"Allie?" His voice seemed to be coming from far away.

"We're here, Nick," Katrina said after she'd spent a good five minutes with her eyes closed, calling up Nick's spirit. "Is there something you want to say to Allie?"

She heard him groan. The sound sent her heart pounding even harder. Somehow it was more chilling than his saying her name.

"Please, Nick, do you have a message for Allie?"

Another groan, this one sounding farther away. Katrina seemed anxious as if she feared she was going to lose Nick before he said whatever it was he wanted to say.

Allie doubted that was going to happen, but maybe the

woman would try to drag this out, get more money from her by making her come back again.

She tried to pull away, but Katrina tightened her hold, pulling her forward so her elbows rested on the table.

"Nick, please, give your wife the peace she desperately needs."

Another groan. "Allie, *why?*" The last word was so ghostly that Allie felt her skin crawl. At that moment, she believed it was Nick calling to her from the grave.

"What are you asking?" Katrina called out to him.

Silence. It was so heavy that it pressed against Allie's chest until she thought she couldn't breathe.

Then a groan as forlorn as any she'd ever heard filled the small room. She shivered. "Allie," Nick said in a voice that broke. "Why did you kill me?"

Chapter Ten

Allie jerked her hands free and stumbled to her feet. She didn't realize she'd made a sound until she realized she was whimpering.

As the lights came up, she saw that Katrina was staring at her in shock as if whoever was behind this hadn't taken her into their confidence. Either that, or she was a good actress.

Allie rushed out of the room and down the hallway. Belinda wasn't in the living room where she'd been told to wait. Opening the door, Allie ran outside, stopping only when she reached Belinda's car.

None of that was real. But it had been Nick's voice; there was no doubt about that. He was either alive…or they'd somehow gotten a recording of Nick's voice. *That wasn't Nick speaking from his grave.* Intellectually, she knew that. But just hearing Nick's voice and those horrible groans…

Belinda came bursting out of the house. Allie turned to see Katrina standing at the doorway looking stunned. Or was that, too, an act?

"Allie?" Belinda ran to her looking scared. "What happened in there?"

She ignored the question. "Where were you?"

Belinda seemed taken aback by her tone, if not her question. "I had to go to the bathroom. I was just down the hall. Are you all right?"

"I want to go." Katrina was still standing in the doorway.

Allie reached for the door handle but the car was locked. "Belinda, I want to *go*."

"Okay, just a sec." She groped in her purse for her keys.

"Can't find them?" Allie taunted with a sneer. "Maybe you left them in the bathroom sink."

Belinda glanced up in surprise, frowning as if confused. "No, I have them. Honey, are you sure you're all right?"

Allie laughed. "How can you seriously ask that?"

Belinda stared at her for a moment before she opened the car doors and went around and slid behind the wheel.

They rode in silence for a few minutes before Belinda said, "I'm sorry. Clearly, you're upset. I thought—"

"What did you think?" Allie demanded.

Belinda shot her a glance before returning to her driving. "I seriously thought this might help."

"Really? Was it your idea or Nick's?"

"Nick's?" She shot her another quick look.

"I *know,* Belinda." Silence. "I know about you and Nick." Belinda started to deny it, but Allie cut her off. "You two had me going for a while, I'll give you that. I really did think I was losing my mind. But not anymore. How long have you and Nick been having an affair?"

"Allie—"

"I don't have to ask whose plan this was. It has Nick written all over it."

"Honey, I honestly don't know what you're talking about."

"No?" Allie reached into her pocket and pulled out the photo of Belinda and Nick standing next to the trailhead sign at Grouse Creek. "As you've often said, a picture is worth a thousand words."

Belinda groaned, not unlike Nick had back at the alleged psychic's. "It isn't what you think."

Allie laughed again as she put the photo back in her pocket. "It never is."

"I'm sorry." She sounded as if she were crying, but Allie could feel no compassion for her.

"What was the point of all that back there?" Allie demanded as they left the Gallatin Valley behind and entered the dark, narrow canyon.

"I swear I don't know what you're talking about. What happened in there that has you so angry and upset?"

"Don't play dumb, Belinda. It doesn't become you. But tell me, what's next?" Allie demanded. "You failed to make me crazy enough that you could take Natalie. Is it the insurance money? Is that what you're planning to use to open your own studio? But in order to get it, you're going to have to kill me. Is that the next part of your plot, Belinda?"

The woman gasped and shot her a wide-eyed look. "You sure you aren't crazy, because you are certainly talking that way. That photo of me and Nick? That was before he met and married you. I broke up with him. Why do you think he didn't like me? Why do you think he put up with me? Because I threatened to tell you about the two of us." She took a breath and let it out. "As for me trying to make you think you were crazy…" Belinda waved a hand through the air. "That's ridiculous. I'm the one who has been trying to help you. I should have told you about me and Nick, but it was water under the bridge. And Nick's insurance money? I don't need it. Remember I told you about my eccentric aunt Ethel? Well, it seems she'd been socking money away in her underwear drawer for years. Thirty-eight thousand of it was left to me, tax free. That's what I plan to use to start my own photo studio. Allie, no matter what you think, I'm your *friend*."

She had thought so, but now she didn't know what to believe. "How did you come up with the idea of me going to see Katrina?" she challenged.

Belinda drove in silence, the canyon highway a dark ribbon along the edge of the river. "I told you. I'd seen

Katrina a few times. But the idea for you to go see her so you could try to reach Nick and get closure? That was your sister *Megan*'s idea."

JACKSON FOUND HIMSELF walking the floor of his cabin until he couldn't take it anymore. Finally, he heard the sound of a vehicle, saw the headlights coming up the road and hurried down to the barn where Allie had left her van.

He waited in the shadows as both women got out of Belinda's car, neither speaking as they parted ways.

"Are you all right?" Jackson asked Allie as he stepped from the shadows. She jumped, surprised, and he mentally kicked himself for scaring her. "I'm sorry. I've been pacing the floor. I was so worried about you."

Her features softened. "I'm okay." She looked drained.

"If you don't want to talk about it tonight…"

Allie gave him a wane smile. "Natalie is staying with your family and I'm not going to be able to sleep, anyway."

"Do you mind coming up to my cabin?"

She shook her head and let him lead her up the mountainside through the pines. It was only a little after ten, but most everyone had turned in for the night so there was little light or sound on the ranch. Under the thick pine boughs, it was cool and dark and smelled of summer.

Jackson realized he was going to miss that smell when he returned to Texas. He didn't want to think about what else he might miss.

Once inside the cabin, they took a seat on the couch, turning to face each other. It was warm in the cabin away from the chill of the Montana summer night. Without prompting, Allie began to relate what had happened slowly as if she was exhausted. He didn't doubt she was.

He hated putting her through this. She told him about the ride to the psychic's and Belinda's apparent hesitancy to let her go through with it. Then she told him about Katrina and the small remote house.

"It all felt silly and like a waste of time, until I heard Nick's voice."

He looked at her and felt his heart drop. Hearing her husband's voice had clearly upset her. It surprised him that whoever was behind this had gone that far.

"You're sure it was Nick's voice."

She nodded. "It sounded as if it was far away and yet close."

"Could it have been a recording?"

"Possibly. His words were halting as if hard for him to speak and he...groaned." She shuddered. "It was an awful sound, unearthly."

"I'm so sorry. After you left, I regretted telling you to go." He sighed. "I was afraid it would just upset you and accomplish nothing."

"It gets worse. Nick...accused me of...killing him."

"*What?* That's ridiculous. I thought a grizzly killed him."

She shrugged. "The psychic believed it. You should have seen her face."

"Allie, the woman was in on it. This was just another ploy. You knew that going in."

"But I didn't know I would hear his voice. I didn't know he would ask me why I'd killed him. I didn't..." The tears came in a rush, dissolving the rest of whatever she was going to say.

Jackson pulled her to him. She buried her face into his chest. "None of this is real, Allie. Are you listening to me? None of it. They just want you to believe it is."

After a few moments, the sobs stopped. He handed her a tissue from the box by the couch and she got up and moved to the window. His cabin view was the rock cliff across the valley and a ribbon of Gallatin River below it.

As he got up, he moved to stand behind her. He could see starlight on that stretch of visible river. It shone like silver.

"If Nick is alive and I believe he is, then he has tried to do everything he can to make you think you're losing your mind. It hasn't worked. This isn't going to work, either. You're stronger than that."

"Am I?" she asked with a laugh. "I am when I'm with you, but..."

He turned her to face him. "You just needed someone to believe in you. I believe in you, Allie."

She looked up at him, her green eyes full of hope and trust and—

His gaze went to her mouth. Lowering his head, he kissed her.

A LOW MOAN escaped her lips. As he drew her closer, Allie closed her eyes, relishing in the feel of her body against his. It had been so long since a man had kissed her let alone held her. She couldn't remember the last time she'd made love. Nick had seemed to lose interest in her toward the end, which had been more than fine with her.

She banished all thoughts of Nick as she lost herself in Jackson's kiss. Her arms looped around his neck. She could feel her heart pounding next to his. Her breasts felt heavy, her nipples hard and aching as he deepened the kiss. A bolt of desire like none she'd ever known shot through her veins as he broke off the kiss to plant a trail of kisses down the column of her neck to the top of her breasts.

At her cry of arousal, Jackson pulled back to look into her eyes. "I've told myself all the reasons we shouldn't do this, but I want to make love to you."

"Yes," she said breathlessly, throwing caution to the wind. She wanted him, wanted to feel his bare skin against her own, to taste his mouth on hers again, to look up at him as he lowered himself onto her. She ached for his gentle touch, needed desperately to know the tenderness of love-making she'd never experienced with Nick but sensed in Jackson.

He swept her up in his arms and carried her to the bedroom, kicking the door closed before he carefully lowered her to the bed. She looked into his dark eyes as he lay down next to her. He touched her face with his fingertips, then slipped his hand around to the nape of her neck and drew her to him.

His kiss was slow and sensual. She could feel him fighting his own need as if determined to take it slow as he undid one button of her blouse, then another. She wanted to scream, unable to stand the barrier of their clothing between them. Grabbing his shirt, she pulled each side apart. The snaps sung as the Western shirt fell open exposing his tanned skin and the hard muscles under it.

She pressed her hands to his warm flesh as he undid the last button on her blouse. She heard his intake of breath an instant before she felt his fingertips skim across the tops of her breasts. Pushing her onto her back, he dropped his mouth to the hard points of her nipples, sucking gently through the thin, sheer fabric of her bra.

She arched against his mouth, felt him suck harder as his hand moved to the buttons of her jeans. With agonizing deliberate movements, he slowly undid the buttons of her jeans and slipped his hand beneath her panties. She cried out and fumbled at the zipper of his jeans.

"Please," she begged. "I need you."

"Not yet." His voice broke with the sound of his own need. "Not yet."

His hand dipped deeper into her panties. She arched against it, feeling the wet slickness of his fingers. He'd barely touched her when she felt the release.

"Oh, Allie," he said as if he, too, hadn't made love for a very long time. He shifted to the side to pull off her jeans and panties. She heard him shed the rest of his own clothing and then he was back, his body melding with hers in a rhythm as old as life itself.

THEY MADE LOVE twice more before the dawn. Jackson dozed off at some point, but woke to find Allie sleeping in his arms.

She looked more peaceful than she had since he'd met her. Like him, he suspected she hadn't made love with anyone for a very long time—much longer than her husband had allegedly been dead.

He cursed Nick Taylor. How could the fool not want this woman? How could the man mistreat someone so wonderful, not to mention ignore a child like Natalie? When he found the bastard…

When is it that you plan to find him?

The thought stopped him cold. There were only two more days until the wedding. He and Ford had tickets to fly out the following day.

He couldn't leave Allie now when she needed him the most. But how could he stay? He had Ford to think about. His son would be starting kindergarten next month. Jackson wasn't ready. He'd received a list from the school of the supplies his son would need, but he hadn't seen any reason to get them yet, thinking there was plenty of time. Same with the boy's new clothes.

He thought of his small ranch in Texas. Most of the land was leased, but he still had a house down there in the summer heat. He couldn't stay away indefinitely. What if he couldn't find Nick Taylor before Ford's school started?

His thoughts whirling, he looked down at Allie curled up next him and felt a pull so strong that it made him ache. What was he going to do?

Whatever it was, he couldn't think straight lying next to

this beautiful, naked woman. As he tried to pull free, she rolled away some, but didn't wake.

Slipping out of bed, he quickly dressed and stepped outside. The fresh Montana morning air helped a little. Earlier he'd heard voices down by the main house. He hoped to catch his brothers as he headed down the mountain. He needed desperately to talk to one of them, even though he had had a bad feeling what they were going to say to him. He'd been saying the same thing to himself since waking up next to Allie this morning.

ALLIE WOKE TO an empty bed. For a moment, she didn't know where she was. As last night came back to her with Jackson, she hugged herself. The lovemaking had been… amazing. This was what she'd been missing out on with Nick. Jackson had been so tender and yet so…passionate.

She lay back listening, thinking he must be in the bathroom or maybe the small kitchen. After a few minutes, she sat up. The cabin was too quiet. Surely Jackson hadn't left.

Slipping her feet over the side of the bed, she tiptoed out of the bedroom. The bathroom was empty. So was the living room and kitchen. Moving to the front window, she glanced out on the porch. No Jackson.

For a moment, she stood staring out at the view, trying to understand what this meant. Had he finally come to his senses? That was definitely one explanation.

Had he realized they had no future? That was another.

Hurrying into the bathroom, she showered, and, forced to put on the clothes she'd worn the night before, dressed. Fortunately, she'd been wearing jeans, a tank top and a blouse. She tucked the blouse into her large shoulder bag, pulled her wet hair up into a ponytail and looked at herself in the mirror.

Her cheeks were flushed from the lovemaking and the hot shower. Her skin still tingled at even the thought of

Jackson's touch. She swallowed. Hadn't she warned herself last night of all the reasons they shouldn't make love?

At a knock on the cabin door, she jumped. Her heart leaped to her throat as she saw a dark, large shadow move on the porch beyond the curtains. Jackson wouldn't knock. Maybe it was one of his brothers.

She held her breath, hoping he would go away. She didn't want to be caught here, even though she knew his brothers wouldn't tell anyone.

Another knock.

"Jackson?" Drew Taylor's voice made her cringe. She put her hand over her mouth to keep from crying out in surprise. "I need to check something in your cabin." She heard him try the door and felt her heart drop. What if Jackson had left the door open?

She was already backing up, frantically trying to decide where she could hide, when she heard Drew try the knob. Locked.

He swore, thumped around on the porch for a moment then retreated down the steps.

Allie finally had to let out the breath she'd been holding. If Drew had caught her here... What would he have done? Tell Nick. But what would a man who had faked his death do to stop his plan from working? She thought of Jackson and felt her heart drop. She'd put Jackson's life in danger, as well.

She waited until she was sure Drew had gone before she cautiously moved to the door, opened it and peered out. She could see nothing but pines as she slipped out and hurried across the mountainside, planning to slip into the barn as if she'd come to work early.

With luck, no one would be the wiser.

Allie didn't see Drew. But he saw her.

Chapter Eleven

Dana was sitting on the porch as Jackson approached the house. She motioned for him to join her.

"Where is everyone?" he asked, taking the rocker next to her.

"Early morning ride. Hud took everyone including the kids. Quiet, isn't it?" She glanced over at him. "How are you this morning?"

"Fine." He would have said great, but he had a bad feeling where Dana was headed with the conversation.

"I'm worried about Allie," she said, looking past him to the mountainside.

He glanced back toward the cabins in time to see Allie hurrying toward the barn from the direction of his cabin.

"Is she all right?"

In truth, he didn't know how she was. He regretted leaving before she'd awakened, but he'd needed to get out of there. "I—"

"She's been through so much. I would hate to see her get hurt. Wouldn't you?"

He felt as if she'd slapped him. He closed his eyes for a moment before he turned to look at her. "I told myself not to get involved, but…"

"So now you are involved?" Dana frowned. "She's in trouble, isn't she?"

Jackson nodded. "I have to help her." Even if it meant

staying in Montana longer, he couldn't abandon her. Isn't that what had scared the hell out of him when he'd awakened this morning? He was in deep, how deep, he didn't want to admit. "She's going through some things right now but she's working so hard on the wedding, it will be fine."

Dana studied him openly. "You care about her."

"I'm not going to hurt her."

"I hope not." She gave him a pat on the shoulder as she rose and went inside the house.

Jackson sat looking after his cousin, mentally kicking himself. *"What the hell are you doing?"*

"I was going to ask you the same thing." Laramie came walking up.

As he climbed the porch, Jackson said, "I thought you went riding with the others."

"I've been working," his brother said as he took a seat next to him. He shook his head. "I hope you know what you're doing, Jackson." He sighed and pulled out a sheet of paper. "Allie's mother spent the last seven years of her life in a mental institution. Paranoid schizophrenia."

As ALLIE SLIPPED into the barn, she was surprised to see Belinda setting up her gear for a shoot. She'd half expected Belinda to be gone after their argument last night. In fact, Allie had almost called several photographers she knew to see if they could possibly fill in at the last minute.

"So you're still here," she said as she approached Belinda.

"Where did you think I would be?"

"I wasn't sure. I thought you might have quit."

Belinda shook her head. "You really do have so little faith in me. I'm amazed. I'm the one who has stuck by you all these years. I'm sorry about…everything. But I'm here to do a job I love. Surely you understand that."

Allie did and said as much. "If I've underestimated you—"

Her friend laughed. "Or overestimated me given that you

think I'm capable of some diabolical plot to destroy you. And what? Steal your cabin on the river? Steal Nick's insurance money?" Her eyes widened. "Or was it steal Natalie?" Belinda looked aghast. "Oh, Allie, no wonder you're so upset. I get it now."

She felt tears rush her eyes as Belinda pulled her into a stiff, awkward hug.

"No matter what you believe, I'm still your friend," Belinda said as she broke the embrace and left the barn, passing Megan who looked bewildered as she came in.

Allie waited until she and Megan were alone before she spoke to her stepsister about what Belinda had told her. She didn't want to believe Megan had anything to do with the psychic or what had happened last night. Either Belinda was lying or there had to be another explanation.

"I need to ask you something."

"You sound so serious," Megan said. "What is it?"

"Was it your idea for me to see the psychic?"

Megan frowned. "I guess I was the one who suggested it. When Belinda told me about some of the things you'd been going through, I thought— Allie, why are you so upset?"

Allie had turned away, unable to look at her sister. Now she turned back, just as unable to hide her disappointment. "Why would you do that?"

"I just told you. I thought it would help."

"Trying to reach Nick on…the other side?" she demanded. "You can't be serious."

"A girl I knew at college lost her mother before the two of them could work some things out. She went to a psychic and was able to put some of the issues to rest. I thought…" Her gaze locked with her sister's. "I wanted to help you. I couldn't bear the things Belinda was telling me. It sounded as if you'd been going through hell. If I was wrong, I'm sorry."

Allie studied her for a moment. "You would never betray me, would you, Megan?"

"What a strange question to ask me."

"This past year since you came into my life and Natalie's… It's meant so much to both of us. Tell me you wouldn't betray that trust."

Megan frowned. "Does this have something to do with Jackson Cardwell? Is he the one putting these ideas in your head?"

"He has a theory about the so-called incidents I've been having," Allie confided. "He thinks someone is trying to make me think I'm crazy in order to take Natalie from me."

"That sounds…crazy in itself. Allie, I hate to say this, but you are starting to sound like your—"

"Don't say it," Allie cried. Wasn't that her real underlying fear, the one that had haunted her her whole life? That she was becoming sick like her mother? She rubbed a hand over the back of her neck. What was she sure of right now? She'd thought Jackson, but after this morning… "I know it sounds crazy, but if it's true, I have to find out who is behind it."

"And Jackson is *helping* you?" Megan said and frowned. "Or is he complicating things even more? You aren't…falling for him, are you?"

JACKSON WASN'T SURE what he was going to say to Allie. He felt like a heel for leaving her alone this morning. She must be furious with him. No, he thought, not Allie. She would be hurt, and that made him feel worse than if she was angry.

He headed for the barn to apologize to her. Once inside, though, he didn't see Allie.

"She said she had to run an errand," Megan told him with a shrug.

Glancing outside, he saw her van still parked where it had been last night. "Did she go on foot?"

"Her brother-in-law offered her a ride."

"Drew?" Jackson felt his heart race at the thought of Allie alone with that man. "Do you know where they went?"

Megan shook her head and kept working.

"You don't like me," he said, stepping farther into the barn. "Why is that?"

"I don't think you're good for my sister."

"Based on what?" he had to ask. "We have barely met."

"She told me about this crazy idea you have that someone is causing these incidents she's been having."

"You disagree?"

Megan gave him an impatient look. "I know the Taylors. The last thing they want is a five-year-old to raise."

"So you think what's been happening to Allie is all in her head?"

She put down what she'd been working on and gave him her full attention for the first time. "You just met her. You don't know anything about her. I love my stepsister, but I don't think she has been completely honest with you. Did you know that her mother spent her last years in a mental hospital? Or that she killed herself?"

"You aren't trying to tell me it runs in the family."

Megan raised a brow. "Allie's been through a lot. She has some issues she hasn't gotten past, including the fact that she wanted her husband gone. So she already told you about that, huh?" He nodded. "Did she also tell you that she bought a gun just before Nick went up into the mountains? That's right. I wonder what happened to it." She shrugged. "Like I said, I love Allie and Nat, but I also know that Allie hated her husband and would have done anything to escape him."

ALLIE HAD BEEN on her way to her van when Drew had suddenly appeared next to her.

"Where you off to?" he'd asked.

"I just have to pick up some ribbon at the store," she'd said, trying to act normal. What a joke. She hadn't felt *normal* in so long, she'd forgotten what it felt like. Worse, she feared that Drew would find out about last night. The Taylors wouldn't hesitate to use it against her, claiming it proved what a terrible mother she was.

Allie felt guilty enough. Her husband had been dead only months and here she was making love with another man. Did it matter that she hadn't loved Nick for years? She had a child to think about and Jackson Cardwell would be leaving in two days' time. Then what?

It would be just her and Nat and the Taylors.

"I'll give you a ride," Drew said. She started to argue but he stopped her. "It would be stupid to take your van when I'm going that way, anyway. You pick up your ribbon. I'll pick up the chalk I need next door at the hardware store. We'll be back here before you know it."

All her instincts warned her not to get into the pickup with him, but she couldn't think of a reason not to accept the ride without acting paranoid. Did she really think he would take her somewhere other than the store and what? Attack her?

She climbed into the passenger side of the pickup and remembered something Nick had said not long before he'd left to go hunting that day.

"You're so damned trusting, Allie. I worry about you. Don't you get tired of being so nice?" He'd laughed and pretended he was joking as he pulled her close and kissed the top of her head. "Don't change. It's refreshing."

It also had made it easier for him to control her.

"You want to know something crazy?" Drew said as he started the engine and drove down the road toward Big Sky. "When I got here this morning, your van was where you'd left it last night. There was dew on the window. I checked the motor. It hadn't been moved and even more interesting, you were nowhere to be found."

She didn't look at him as he roared down the road. Ahead

she could see the bridge that spanned the Gallatin River. Why hadn't she listened to her instincts and not gotten into the vehicle with Drew?

"It was like a mystery. I love mysteries. Did I ever tell you that?"

A recent rainstorm had washed out some of the road just before the bridge, leaving deep ruts that were to be filled this afternoon. Couldn't have the wedding guests being jarred by the ruts.

"I saw you come out of Jackson Cardwell's cabin this morning." Drew swore as he braked for the ruts. "You slut." He started to backhand her, but had to brake harder as he hit the first rut so his hand went back to the wheel before it reached its mark. "How could you screw—"

Allie unsnapped her seat belt and grabbed the door handle.

As the door swung open, Drew hit the brakes even harder, slamming her into the door as she jumped. She hit the soft earth at the side of the road, lost her footing and fell into the ditch.

Drew stopped the truck. She heard his door open and the shocks groan as he climbed out. By then she was on her feet and headed into the pines next to the road, running, even though her right ankle ached.

"Allie!" Drew yelled from the roadbed. "You could have killed yourself. You're crazy, you know that?"

She kept running through the pines. Her brother-in-law was right. She had been stupid. Stupid to get into the truck with him when all her instincts had been telling her not to, and crazy to jump out.

Behind her, she heard the truck engine rev, then the pickup rumble over the bridge. She slowed to catch her breath then limped the rest of the way back to the barn, telling herself she was through being naive and trusting.

JACKSON DIDN'T SEE Allie until that evening at the wedding rehearsal so he had no chance to get her alone. "We need to talk," he whispered in those few seconds he managed to get her somewhat alone.

She met his gaze. "Look, I think I already know what you're going to say."

"I doubt that." She wore a multicolored skirt and top that accentuated her lush body. "You look beautiful. That top brings out the green in your eyes."

"Thank you." Something glinted in those eyes for a moment. "Jackson—"

"I know. This isn't the place. But can we please talk later? It's important."

She nodded, though reluctantly.

He mentally kicked himself for running out on her this morning as he stood there, wanting to say more, but not able to find the right words.

Allie excused herself. He watched her head for the preacher as the rehearsal was about to begin. Was she limping?

All day he'd stewed over what Megan had told him. She was wrong about Allie, but he could understand why she felt the way she did. Maybe she really did love her sister. Or maybe not.

Belinda was busy behind her camera, shooting as they all went to their places. As one of the best men, Jackson was in a position to watch the others. He hadn't seen much of Sarah Taylor. But Sarah, her mother and brother would be at the rehearsal dinner tonight. He watched Sarah enter the barn and start up the aisle toward the steps to where the preacher was standing along with the best men and the groom.

An overweight woman with dull, brown hair pulled severely back from her face, Sarah seemed somewhere else, oblivious to what was happening. Either that or bored. Four more bridesmaids entered and took their places.

Harlan and Angus broke into "Here Comes the Bride" on their guitars and Lily came out of a small-framed building next to the meadow with her father and mother. Jackson hadn't met either of them yet but he wanted to laugh when he saw them looking as if in horror. Lily was smiling from ear to ear. So was her brother Ace from the sidelines. But clearly her parents hadn't expected this kind of wedding for their only daughter.

Jackson looked over at Allie. She really was beautiful. She glanced to the parking lot and quickly looked away as if she'd seen something that frightened her.

He followed her gaze. Drew Taylor stood lounging against his pickup, a malicious smirk on his face as if he was up to something.

THE REHEARSAL WENT off without a hitch. Allie tried to breathe a sigh of relief. Dana had booked an Italian restaurant in Bozeman for the night of the rehearsal dinner. "I know it's not the way things are normally done," she'd said with a laugh. But Lily and I discussed it."

Dana had insisted anyone involved in the wedding had to be there so that meant Allie and Natalie as well as Megan and Belinda.

They'd just gotten to the restaurant when Allie heard a strident voice behind her say, "There you are."

She bristled but didn't turn, putting off facing her mother-in-law as long as possible.

"Sarah thinks you're avoiding us," Mildred said. "But why would you do that?"

Allie turned, planting a smile on her face. "I wouldn't."

"Hmmm," her mother-in-law said. She gave Allie the once-over. "You look different."

Allie remembered that she was wearing one of two

outfits that she hadn't taken back to the store. This one was a multicolored top and skirt that Jackson had said brought out the green in her eyes. She loved it and while it was more expensive than she could really afford, she'd needed something to wear tonight.

"Where did you get that outfit?" Mildred asked, eyeing her with suspicion.

"I found it in my closet," Allie said honestly.

"Really?"

Allie felt a hand take hers and looked up to see Jackson.

"I saved you a spot down here," he said and led her to the other end of the table, away from the Taylors.

Dana had insisted that there be no prearranged seating. "Let everyone sit where they want. I like people to be comfortable." Lily had seemed relieved that she could sit by Tag, away from her parents.

Allie was grateful to Jackson for saving her. Dinner was served and the conversation around the table was light with lots of laughter and joking. She was glad Jackson didn't try to talk to her about last night.

It had been a mistake in so many ways. But tomorrow after the wedding, they would say goodbye and he and Ford would fly out the next day. She told herself that once the wedding was over, everything would be all right.

A part of her knew she was only kidding herself. There hadn't been any more incidents, no misplaced keys, no Nick sightings, no "black cat" scares and that almost worried her. What had changed? Or was Nick and whomever he had helping him just waiting to ambush her?

She had a feeling that the séance with the psychic hadn't produced the results they'd wanted. Now she, too, was waiting. Waiting for the other shoe to drop.

Just let it drop after the wedding, she prayed. Jackson and Ford would be back in Texas. Whatever was planned for her, she felt she could handle it once this job was over.

The one thing Jackson had done was made her feel stronger, more sure of herself. He'd also reminded her that she was a woman with needs that had long gone unmet until last night.

"Stop telling stories on me," Tag pleaded at the dinner table across from her. "Lily is going to change her mind about marrying me."

"Not a chance, cowboy," Lily said next to him before she'd kissed him to hoots and hollers.

Even Sarah seemed to be enjoying herself with the other bridesmaids since they had all worked together at Lily's brother's bar.

Allie avoided looking down the table to see how the Taylors were doing. She was so thankful to be sitting as far away from them as possible, especially Drew. To think that she'd trusted him and thought he'd really had her and Nat's best interest at heart. She'd felt his eyes on her all night. The few times she'd met his gaze, he'd scowled at her.

She glanced over at the children's table to see her daughter also enjoying herself. Dana's sister Stacy had the children at a separate table. Allie saw that her daughter was being on her best behavior. So ladylike, she was even using the manners Allie had taught her. She felt a swell of pride and told herself that she and Natalie were going to be all right no matter what happened after the wedding.

To her surprise, her eyes welled with tears and she quickly excused herself to go to the ladies' room. The bathroom was past an empty section of the restaurant, then down a long hallway. She was glad that no one had followed her. She needed a few minutes alone.

Inside the bathroom, she pulled herself together. Last night with Jackson had meant more to her than she'd admitted. It had hurt this morning when he hadn't been there, but she could understand why he'd panicked. Neither of them took that kind of intimacy lightly.

Feeling better, she left the bathroom. As she reached the

empty section of the restaurant, Drew stepped in front of her, startling her. She could smell the alcohol on him. The way he was standing... She recognized that stance after five years of being married to his brother.

Drew was looking for a fight. How had she thought the brothers were different? Because she hadn't seen this side of Drew. Until now.

"You *jumped* out of my truck. What the hell was that? Do I scare you, Allie?" he asked, slurring his words and blocking her way.

"Please, Drew, don't make a scene."

He laughed. "Oh, you don't want Dana to know that you slept with her cousin?"

"Drew—"

"Don't bother to lie to me," he said as he stepped toward her, shoving her back. "I *saw* you." His voice broke. "How can you do this to my brother?"

"Nick's...gone."

"And forgotten. Is that it?" He forced her back against the wall, caging her with one hand on each side of her.

"Please, Drew—"

"If Nick really was out of the picture..." He belched. "You have to know I've always wanted you," he said drunkenly. Before she could stop him, he bent down and tried to kiss her.

She turned her head to the side. He kissed her hair, then angrily grabbed her jaw in one hand. His fingers squeezed painfully as he turned her to face him.

"What? Am I not good enough for you?"

"Drew—"

Suddenly he was jerked away. Allie blinked as Jackson hauled back and swung. His fist connected with Drew's jaw and he went down hard, crashing into a table.

"Are you all right?" Jackson asked, stepping to her.

She nodded and glanced at her brother-in-law. He was

trying to get up, but he seemed to take one look at Jackson and decided to stay down.

"You'll pay for that!" he threatened as she and Jackson headed back toward their table. Allie knew he wasn't talking to Jackson. She would pay.

"If he bothers you again—" Jackson said as if reading her mind.

"Don't worry about me."

"How can I not?" he demanded. "That was about me, wasn't it?"

"Drew was just looking for a reason."

"And I provided it."

"He saw me leaving your cabin this morning," she said. "I don't think he's told anyone, but he will. I just wanted to warn you. I'm afraid what Nick might do to you."

"Allie, I don't give a damn about any of that. What I'm sorry about was leaving you this morning," he said, bringing her up short as he stopped and turned her to face him. "There is so much I want to say to you—"

"Oh, there you are," Mildred Taylor said as she approached. "I was just looking for Drew. I thought you might have seen him. Allie, you look terrible. I knew this job was going to be too much for you."

Natalie and Ford came running toward them. Mildred began to say something about giving Allie and Nat a ride home, but then Drew appeared, rubbing his jaw.

"Drew, whatever happened to you?" Mildred cried.

"I still need to talk to you," Jackson whispered to Allie, who was bending down to catch her daughter up into her arms.

"After the wedding," she said as she lifted Natalie, hugging her tightly. "Tonight I just need to take my daughter home."

Jackson wanted to stop her. But she was right. The wedding was the important thing right now. After that...

Chapter Twelve

Wedding Day. Allie woke at the crack of dawn. She couldn't help being nervous and excited. The wedding was to be held in a beautiful meadow near the house. Those attending had been told to wear Western attire as the seating at the wedding would be hay bales.

Drew had constructed an arch for the bride and groom to stand under with the preacher. Allie had walked through everything with the bride and groom, the caterer and the musicians. The barn was ready for the reception that would follow. But she still wanted to get to the ranch early to make sure she hadn't forgotten anything.

The last few days had felt like a roller-coaster ride. Today, she needed calm. Jackson hadn't tried to contact her after she and Natalie left the restaurant with Dana and family last night and she was glad. She needed time with her daughter.

Natalie hadn't slept in her own bed for several nights now. Allie made sure her daughter's window was locked as she put her to bed. She checked the other windows and the door. Then, realizing that any of the Taylors could have a key to her cabin, she pushed a straight-back chair under the doorknob.

She and Natalie hadn't been disturbed all night. At least not by intruders. In bed last night, Allie couldn't help but think about Jackson. And Nick.

"Please, just let me get through this wedding," she'd prayed and had finally fallen asleep.

Now as she drove into the ranch, she saw that Dana and the kids were waiting for Natalie.

"We have a fun morning planned," Dana said with a wink. "You don't have to worry about anything today."

Allie wished that was true. She looked down at the meadow to see that Megan was up early. She was sitting on a hay bale looking as if she were staring at the arch. Imagining her own wedding? Allie wondered as she approached.

"Good morning," she said and joined her sister on the bale.

"It's perfect. Drew really did do a good job," Megan said.

The arch had been made out of natural wood that blended in beautifully with its surroundings. Allie had asked Lily if she wanted it decorated with flowers.

"There will be enough wildflowers in the meadow and I will be carrying a bouquet. I think that is more than enough."

She had agreed and was happy that Lily preferred the more minimalist look.

"Have you been up to the barn?" Allie asked.

"Not yet." Megan finally looked over at her. "How are you?"

"Fine."

Her sister eyed her. "You can lean on me. I'm here for you and Natalie."

Allie hugged her, closing her eyes and praying it was true. She couldn't bear the thought of Megan betraying not only her but Natalie, as well.

Together they walked up to the barn. Allie turned on the lights and gasped.

JACKSON HAD TOSSED and turned all night—after he'd finally dropped off to sleep. He felt as if he'd let Allie down. Or maybe worse, gotten involved with her in the first place, knowing he would be leaving soon.

She wasn't out of the woods yet. She had to know that whoever was messing with her mind wasn't through. He still believed it had to be Nick. He had the most to gain. It scared Jackson to think that whoever was behind this might try to use Tag's wedding to put the last nail in Allie's coffin, so to speak.

His fear, since realizing what was going on, was that if they couldn't drive her crazy, they might actually try to kill her.

He was just getting dressed when he heard the knock at his cabin door. His mood instantly lifted as he thought it might be Allie. She'd said she would talk to him *after* the wedding. Maybe she had changed her mind. He sure hoped so.

Jackson couldn't hide his disappointment when he opened the door and saw his brothers standing there.

"I found something that I think might interest you," Laramie said and he stepped back to let them enter.

"Shouldn't you be getting ready for your wedding?" he asked Tag, who laughed and said, "I have been getting ready for months now. I just want this damned wedding over."

They took a seat while he remained standing. From the expressions on their faces, they hadn't brought good news.

"Nick and his brother, Drew, took out life insurance policies on each other through their construction business," Laramie said.

"That isn't unusual, right?" he asked.

"They purchased million-dollar policies and made each other the beneficiary, but Nick purchased another half million and made Allie the beneficiary."

Jackson let out a low whistle. "All Allie knew about was the hundred-thousand-dollar policy." He saw Hayes lift a brow. "She didn't kill her husband."

"Whether she knew or not about the policies, I believe it supports your theory that Nick is alive and trying to get that money," Laramie said.

"It hasn't paid out yet, right?"

"She should be getting the checks next week."

Jackson raked a hand through his hair. Allie was bound to have been notified. Maybe it had slipped her mind. "You're sure she is the beneficiary?"

Laramie nodded.

"Who gets the money if Allie is declared incompetent?"

"Her daughter, Natalie."

Jackson groaned. "Then this is why Nick is trying to have Allie committed. He, and whoever he is working with, would get the money and Natalie."

"Only if Nick is alive and *stays* dead," Hayes pointed out.

"If Nick stays dead the money would be used at the discretion of Natalie's *guardian*."

Jackson looked at his brother, an ache starting at heart level. "Who is her guardian?"

"Megan Knight. The policy was changed eight months ago—just before Nick Taylor went up into the mountains hunting and a guardian was added."

ALLIE COULDN'T EVEN scream. Her voice had caught in her throat at the sight in the barn. Last night when she'd left, the barn had been ready for the reception except for putting out the fresh vases of flowers at each setting. The tables had been covered with the checked tablecloths and all the overhead lanterns had been in place along with the decorations on the walls and in the rafters.

"Oh, my word," Megan said next to her.

Allie still couldn't speak. Someone had ripped the tablecloths from the tables and piled them in the middle of the dance floor. The old boots that served as centerpieces that would hold the fresh flowers were arranged on the floor in a circle as if the invisible people in them were dancing.

Megan was the first one to move. She rushed to the table-cloths and, bending down, picked up the top one. "They've all been shredded." She turned to look at Allie, concern in her gaze.

"You can't think I did this."

Her sister looked at the tablecloth in her hand before returning her gaze to Allie. "This looks like a cry for help."

Allie shook her head. "It's someone who hates me."

"Hates you? Oh, Allie."

"What's happened?"

She swung around to see Jackson standing in the doorway. Tears filled her eyes. She wanted to run out the barn door and keep running, but he stepped to her and took one of her hands.

"I was afraid they weren't done with you," he said. "How bad is it?" he asked Megan.

"The tablecloths are ruined. Fortunately, whoever did this didn't do anything to the lanterns or the other decorations in the rafters. Probably couldn't reach them since the ladders have all been packed away." This last was directed at Allie, her meaning clear.

"Tag already ordered tablecloths for the restaurant," Jackson said, pulling out his cell phone. "I'll see if they've come in. We can have this fixed quickly if they have." He spoke into the phone for a moment. When he disconnected, he smiled at Allie and said, "Tag will bring up the red-checked cloths right away. With their help, we'll have it fixed before anyone else hears about it."

Allie went weak with relief as he quickly got rid of the ruined tablecloths and Tag showed up with new ones from the restaurant. With the Cardwell brothers' help, the problem was solved within minutes.

"I want at least two people here watching this barn until the wedding is over," Jackson said.

"I'll talk to Dana and see if there are a couple of ranch hands who can help," Laramie said.

"That really isn't necessary," Megan said. "I will stay here to make sure nothing else happens."

Jackson shook his head. "I'm not taking any chances. I'll feel better if you aren't left alone here. Whoever is doing this… Well, I think it might get dangerous before it's over."

"Why don't you just admit that you think I'm involved in this," Megan said and looked sadly at her sister. "Apparently, you aren't the only one who's paranoid." She sighed. "Whatever you need me to do. I don't want anything to spoil this wedding."

JACKSON HAD PLANNED to talk to Allie about the insurance policies, but he realized it could wait until after the wedding. Allie's spirit seemed buoyed once the barn was ready again and a ranch hand stayed behind with Megan to make sure nothing else went wrong.

He was having a hard time making sense of the insurance policy news. Why would Nick Taylor change the guardian from his brother to Allie's stepsister, Megan? The obvious answer would be if the two were in cahoots.

That would break Allie's heart, but a part of her had to know that her sister thought all of this was in her head. Megan had given him the impression that she was ready to step in as more than Natalie's guardian.

Jackson reminded himself that it was his brother's wedding day. As much as he didn't like weddings and hadn't attended one since his marriage had ended, he tried to concentrate on being there for Tag. He couldn't help being in awe as Allie went into wedding-planner mode. He admired the way she handled herself, even with all the stress she was under in her personal life. The day took on a feeling of celebration; after all it was the Fourth of July.

At the house, Allie made sure they were all ready, the men dressed in Western attire and boots, before she went to help the bride. Jackson had seen his father and uncle with their guitars heading for the meadow. They would be playing the "Wedding March" as well as accompanying several singers who would be performing. He just hoped everything went smoothly for Tag and Lily's sake, as well as Allie's.

"Look who's here," Laramie said, sounding too cheerful.

Jackson turned to see his mother on the arm of a nice-looking gray-haired Texas oilman. Franklin Wellington IV had oil written all over him. Jackson tried not to hold it against the man as he and his brothers took turns hugging their mother and wishing her well before shaking hands with Franklin.

His mother *did* look deliriously happy, Jackson had to admit, and Franklin was downright friendly and nice.

"Time to go," Allie said, sticking her head into the room where he and his brothers had been waiting.

Jackson introduced her to his mother and Franklin. He saw his mother lift a brow in the direction of Laramie and groaned inwardly. She would trust Laramie to tell her why she was being introduced to the wedding planner.

Allie didn't notice the interplay as she smiled at Tag. "Your bride looks absolutely beautiful and you don't look so bad yourself."

She was quite pretty, as well, in her navy dress with the white piping. She'd pulled her hair up. Silver earrings dangled at her lobes. She looked professional and yet as sexy as any woman he'd ever known. He felt a sense of pride in her, admiring her strength as well as her beauty. She'd been through so much.

Hell, he thought as he took his place, I *am* falling for her. That realization shook him to the soles of his boots.

In the meadow, his father and uncle began to play the "Wedding March" at Allie's nod. Compared to most, the wedding was small since Tag and Lily knew few people in Big Sky. But old canyon friends had come who had known the Cardwells, Savages and Justices for years.

As Lily appeared, Jackson agreed with Allie. She looked beautiful. He heard his brother's intake of breath and felt his heart soar at the look on Tag's face when he saw his bride-to-be. For a man who had sworn off weddings, Jackson had to admit, he was touched by this one.

The ceremony was wonderfully short, the music perfect and when Tag kissed the bride, Jackson felt his gaze searching for Allie. She was standing by a tree at the edge of the meadow. She was smiling, her expression one of happy contentment. She'd gotten them married.

Now if they could just get through the reception without any more trouble, he thought.

AT THE RECEPTION, Jackson watched the Taylor family sitting at a table away from the others. Mildred had a smile plastered on her face, but behind it he could see that she was sizing up everyone in the room. Her insecurities were showing as she leaned over and said something to her daughter.

Whatever her mother said to her, Sarah merely nodded. She didn't seem to have any interest in the guests, unlike her mother. Instead, she was watching Allie. What was it that Jackson caught in her gaze? Jealousy? Everyone at the wedding had been complimenting Allie on the job she'd done. Sarah couldn't have missed that.

Nor, according to Hud, had Sarah ever been married. She had to be in her late thirties. Was she thinking that it might never happen for her? Or was she content with living next to her mother and basically becoming her mother's caregiver?

Sarah reached for one of the boot-shaped cookies with Tag and Lily's wedding date on them. Her mother slapped her hand, making Sarah scowl at her before she took two cookies.

He wondered what grudges bubbled just below the surface in any family situation, let alone a wedding. Weddings, he thought, probably brought out the best and worst of people, depending how happy or unhappy you were in your own life.

As happy as he was for Tag, it still reminded him of his own sorry marriage. What did this wedding do to the Taylor clan? he wondered as he studied them. It certainly didn't seem to be bringing out any joy, that was for sure.

But his side of the family were having a wonderful time. He watched his brother Tag dancing with his bride. Their mother was dancing with her new husband, both women looking radiant. It really was a joyous day. Dana and Hud had all the kids out on the floor dancing.

Jackson thought the only thing that could make this day better would be if he could get the wedding planner to dance with him.

ALLIE TRIED TO breathe a little easier. The wedding had gone off without a hitch. Lily had been exquisite and Tag as handsome as any Cardwell, which was saying a lot. Allie had teared up like a lot of the guests when the two had exchanged their vows. She'd always loved weddings. This one would remain her favorite for years to come.

When the bride and groom kissed, she'd seen Jackson looking for her. Their eyes had locked for a long moment. She'd pulled away first, a lump in her throat, an ache in her heart. The wedding was over. There was nothing keeping Jackson and Ford in Montana.

Whoever had been trying to gaslight her, as Jackson had called it, hadn't succeeded. Maybe now they would give up trying. She certainly hoped so. If Nick was alive, then she should find out soon. The insurance check for the hundred thousand would be deposited into her account next week.

She'd already made plans for most of it to go into an inter-est-bearing account for Natalie's college.

Allie wondered what would happen then. If Nick was alive, would he just show up at her door? Or would the media be involved with reporters and photographers snapping photos of him outside the cabin as he returned from his ordeal?

All she knew was that the only way Nick could get his hands on the insurance money would be if he killed her. That thought unnerved her as she surveyed the reception. Belinda was busy shooting each event along with some can-did shots of guests. Allie had to hand it to her, she appeared to be doing a great job.

Everything looked beautiful. Megan had taken care of the flowers in the boot vases, put the attendees' gifts on the tables and made sure the bar was open and serving. Appe-tizers were out. Allie checked to make sure the caterer was ready then looked around for her daughter. Nat was with the other kids and Dana. Allie had bought her a special dress for the wedding. Natalie looked beautiful and she knew it because she seemed to glow.

Her tomboy daughter loved getting dressed up. She smiled at the thought. She was thinking that they should dress up more when Mildred Taylor let out a scream at a table near the dance floor and stumbled to her feet.

Allie saw that she was clutching her cell phone, her other hand over her mouth.

"What is it?" Dana demanded, moving quickly to the Taylors' table.

"It's *my Nicky*," Mildred cried, her gaze going to Allie, who froze thinking it was already happening. She was so sure she knew what her mother-in-law was about to say, that she thought she'd misunderstood.

"His body has been found," Mildred managed to say be-tween sobs. She cried harder. "They say he was *murdered*."

Chapter Thirteen

Pandemonium broke out with Mildred Taylor shrieking uncontrollably and everyone trying to calm her down.

Jackson looked over at Allie. All the color had bled from her face. He moved quickly to her. "Let's get you out of here," he said, taking her hand. "You look like you could use some fresh air."

"I'll see to Natalie," Dana said nearby as she motioned for Jackson and Allie to go.

Allie looked as if she were in shock. "It just won't end," she said in a breathless rush as he ushered her outside. "It just won't end."

"I'm so sorry," Jackson said, his mind reeling, as well.

"I was so sure he was *alive.*" She met his gaze. "I thought…"

"We both thought he was alive. I'm as floored as you are." He realized that wasn't possible. Nick Taylor had been her husband, even if he had been a bad one, she would still be shocked and upset by this news. He was the father of her child.

"Nick was *murdered?* How is that possible? They found his backpack and his gun and the grizzly tracks."

"We need to wait until we have all the details," he said as his brothers Hayes and Laramie joined them.

"We're headed down to the police station now," Hayes said. "I'll let you know as soon as I have any information."

"Thank you." Jackson swallowed the lump in his throat. His brothers had been so great through his divorce and custody battle, and now this. He couldn't have been more grateful for them.

"The police will be looking for me," Allie said, her eyes widening.

He saw the fear in her eyes and at first had misunderstood it then he remembered what had happened at the psychic's. "No one believes you killed your husband."

"*Someone* already does."

"That's crazy. How could whoever was behind the séance know that Nick was even murdered unless they did the killing?"

She shook her head. "Mildred has blamed me for his death all along. Belinda thought I drove him to kill himself. Don't you see? They didn't have to know it was true. They just wanted me to feel responsible. Now that it *is* true... Even dead, he's going to ruin my life."

The last of the sun's rays slipped behind the mountains to the west, pitching the canyon in cool twilight. Inside the barn, the reception was continuing thanks to Megan and Dana, who had taken over.

"I need to go back in."

"No." Jackson stopped her with a hand on her arm. "You did a great job. No one expects you to do any more. You don't have to worry about any of that."

She met his gaze. "I don't understand what's going on."

"My brothers will find out. Allie, I'm sorry I left you the other morning. I...panicked. But I'm not leaving you now."

Allie shook her head and took a step back from him. "This isn't your problem. You should never have gotten involved because it's only going to get worse."

He remembered what Laramie had told him about the insurance policy and realized she was right. The money would definitely interest the police. He looked toward the barn. Some guests had come out into the evening air to admire the sunset.

"Please, come up to my cabin with me so we have some privacy. There's something important I need to tell you." He saw her expression and realized that she'd misunderstood.

She looked toward the barn, then up the mountain in the direction of his cabin.

"I just need to talk to you," he assured her.

"That wasn't what I…" She met his gaze. "Jackson, I've caused you enough grief as it is. If the Taylors come looking for me—"

"Let me worry about your in-laws. As for Drew, he won't be bothering you as long as I'm around."

She smiled at that. They both knew that once he left she would again be at the mercy of not just Drew but also the rest of the Taylor family.

He wanted to tell her he wouldn't leave her. But he couldn't make that promise, could he?

She was on her own and she knew it.

"Come on," he said and reached for her hand.

DARKNESS CAME ON quickly in the narrow canyon because of the steep mountains on each side. Allie could hear the fireworks vendors getting ready for the wedding grand finale and glanced at her watch. They were right on time. Maybe she wasn't as necessary as she'd thought since everything seemed to be going on schedule without her.

Overhead the pines swayed in the summer night's breeze. Jackson was so close she could smell his woodsy aftershave and remember his mouth on hers. The perfect summer night. Wasn't that what she'd been thinking earlier before her mother-in-law had started screaming?

Nick was dead. Murdered.

For days now she'd believed he was alive and behind all

the weird things that had been happening to her. Now how did she explain it?

Jackson stopped on the porch. "We can talk privately here, if you would be more comfortable not going inside." He must have seen the answer in her expression because he let go of her hand and moved to the edge of the porch.

Inside the cabin she would remember the two of them making love in his big, log-framed bed. Her skin ached at the memory of his touch.

"Allie, I hate to bring this up now, but the police will ask you…" He leaned against the porch railing, Allie just feet away. "Were you aware that your husband and brother-in-law took out life insurance policies on each other when they started their construction business?"

"No, but what does that have to do with me?"

"They purchased million-dollar policies and made the other brother the beneficiary, but Nick purchased another half million and made you beneficiary. He never mentioned it to you?"

She shook her head, shocked by the news and even more shocked by how it would look. "You think a million and a half dollars in insurance money gives me a motive for killing him."

"I don't, but I think the police might, given that just before your husband went up into the mountains on his hunting trip, he changed the beneficiary of his million-dollar insurance policy from Drew to you."

Allie didn't think anything else could surprise her. "Why would he do that?" Her eyes filled with tears as a reason came to her. She moved to the opposite railing and looked out across the darkening canyon. "Maybe he did go up there to kill himself," she said, her back to Jackson.

"Hayes will find out why they think he was murdered. In the meantime—"

All the ramifications of this news hit her like a battering ram. "What happens if I'm dead?" She had been looking out into the darkness, but now swung her gaze on him. "Who inherits the money?"

"Natalie. The money would be used for her care until she was twenty-one, at which time her guardian—"

"Her *guardian?*"

"Nick named a guardian in case of your...death or incarceration."

Allie's voice broke. *"Who?"*

"Originally Drew was listed as guardian on the policies, but Nick changed that, too, right before he headed for the mountains." He met her gaze. "Megan, as your next closest kin, even though she isn't a blood relative."

She staggered under the weight of it. She couldn't deal with this now. She had the wedding. "The fireworks show is about to start," she said. "I have to finish—"

"I'm sure Dana will see that the rest of the wedding goes off like it is supposed to," Jackson said, blocking her escape. "No one expects you to continue, given what's happened."

"I took the job. I want to finish it," Allie said, hugging herself against the evening chill. "I thought you would understand that."

"I do. But—" His cell phone rang. "It's Hayes." He took the call.

She had no choice but to wait. She had to know what he'd found out at the police station. As she waited, she watched the lights of Big Sky glitter in the growing darkness that fell over the canyon. A breeze seemed to grow in the shadowed pines. The boughs began to move as if with the music still playing down in the barn.

After a moment, Jackson thanked his brother and disconnected. She remained looking off into the distance, her back to him, as he said, "Nick Taylor's remains were found in a shallow grave. There was a .45 bullet lodged in his skull. The trajectory of the bullet based on where it entered and exited, along with the fact that it appears someone tried to hide the body... It's being investigated as a homicide."

She felt a jolt when he mentioned that the bullet was a .45 caliber and knew Jackson would have seen it. Still, she didn't turn.

"Megan told me you bought a gun and that it disappeared from the cabin," he said. She could feel his gaze on her, burning into her back. He thought he knew her. She could imagine what was going through his mind. He would desperately want to believe she had nothing to do with her husband's murder. "Was the gun you purchased a—"

"Forty-five?" She nodded as she turned to look at him. "Everyone will believe I killed him. You're not even sure anymore, are you?"

"Allie—" He took a step toward her, but she held up her hand to ward him off. It had grown dark enough that she couldn't make out his expression unless he came closer, which was a godsend. She couldn't bear to see the disappointment in his face.

Below them on the mountain everyone was coming out of the barn to gather in the meadow for the fireworks. She suddenly ached to see her daughter. Natalie had been all that had kept her sane for so long. Right now, she desperately needed to hold her.

What would happen to Natalie now? She was trembling with fear at the thought that came to her and would no doubt have already come to the police—and eventually Jackson. She didn't want to be around when that happened.

"With my husband dead, that is three insurance policies for more than a million and a half," she said. "Mother Taylor is convinced I've made up all the stories about someone gaslighting me, as you call it. She thinks I have some plot to make myself rich at her poor Nicky's expense. I'm sure she's shared all of that with the police by now. Maybe I did it."

He stepped to her and took her shoulders in his hands.

"Don't. You didn't kill your husband and you *know* damned well that I believe you."

"Your ex-wife, she was a liar and con woman, right? Isn't that why you were so afraid to get involved with me? What makes you so sure I'm not just like her?"

"You can't push me away." He lifted her chin with his fingers so she couldn't avoid his gaze. Their faces were only a few inches apart. "You aren't like her."

"What if I'm crazy?" Her voice broke. "Crazy like a fox?" The first of the fireworks exploded, showering down a glittering red, white and blue light on the meadow below them. The boom echoed in her chest as another exploded to the oos and ahs of the wedding party. She felt scalding tears burn her throat. "What if Mother Taylor is right and all of this is some subconscious plot I have to not only free myself of Nick, but walk away with a million and a half dollars, as well?"

JACKSON COULDN'T BEAR to see Allie like this. He pulled her to him and, dropping his mouth to hers, kissed her. She leaned into him, letting him draw her even closer as the kiss deepened. Fireworks lit the night, booming in a blaze of glittering light before going dark again.

Desire ignited his blood. He wanted Allie like he'd never wanted anyone or anything before. She melted into him, warm and lush in his arms, a moan escaping her lips.

Then suddenly he felt her stiffen. She broke away. "I can't keep doing this," she cried and, tearing herself from his arms, took off down the steps and through the trees toward the barn.

He started after her, but a voice from the darkness stopped him.

"Let her go."

He turned to find his brother Laramie standing in the

nearby trees. More fireworks exploded below them. "What are you doing, little brother?"

"I'm in love with her." The words were out, more honest than he'd been with even himself—let alone Allie.

"Is that right?" Laramie moved to him in a burst of booming light from the meadow below. "So what are you going to do about it?"

Jackson shook his head. "I…I haven't gotten that far yet."

"Oh, I think you've gotten quite far already." Laramie sighed. "I don't want to see you jump into anything. Not again."

"She is nothing like Juliet."

His brother raised a brow. "I knew one day you would fall in love again. It was bound to happen, but Jackson, this is too fast. This woman has too many problems. Hayes and I just came from the police station. They are going to be questioning her about her husband's murder. It doesn't look good."

"She had nothing to do with his death."

"She owns a .45 pistol, the one they suspect is the murder weapon."

Jackson sighed and looked toward the meadow below. It was cast in darkness. Had the fireworks show already ended? "She did but whoever is trying to have her committed, took it to set her up. You know as well as I do that someone has been gaslighting her."

Laramie shook his head. "We only know what Allie has been telling you."

His first instinct was to get angry with his brother, but he understood what Laramie was saying. There was no proof. Instead, the evidence against her was stacking up.

"I believe her and I'm going to help her," he said as he stepped past his brother.

"I just hope you aren't making a mistake," Laramie said behind him as Jackson started down the mountainside.

He'd only taken a few steps when he saw people running all over and heard Allie screaming Natalie's name. He took off running toward her.

"What's wrong?" he demanded when he reached her.

"Nat's gone!" Allie cried.

Chapter Fourteen

"She *can't* be gone," Jackson said. "She was with Dana, right?"

"Dana said the kids were all together, but after one of the fireworks went off, she looked over and Nat wasn't with them. She asked Hank and he said she spilled her lemonade on her dress and went to the bathroom to try to wash it off. Dana ran up to the house and the barn, but she wasn't there." Allie began to cry. "She found this, though." She held up the tie that had been on Nat's dress. "Natalie might have gone looking for me. Or someone took her—"

"Allie," he said, taking her shoulders in his hands. "Even if she left the meadow to go to the house, she couldn't have gotten far. We'll find her."

The search of the ranch area began quickly with everyone from the wedding party out looking for the child.

"I turned my back for just a moment," Dana said, sounding as distraught as Allie when Jackson caught up with her.

"It's not your fault. If anyone is to blame, it's me. I've been trying to help Allie and have only made things worse. I need to know something," he said as he watched the searchers coming off the mountain from the cabins. No Natalie. "Did you see anyone go toward the house about the time you realized she was gone?"

She shook her head. "You mean Drew or his mother? They both left earlier to go talk to the police."

"What about his sister, Sarah? Have you seen her?"

Dana frowned. "She didn't leave with them, now that I think about it, and I haven't seen her since Nat went missing."

Jackson spotted Belinda trying to comfort Allie down by the main house. "How about Megan?"

She shook her head. "I haven't seen either of them." Dana looked worried. "You don't think—"

He did think. He ran down the slope toward the house and Allie. "Did either of you see Sarah or Megan?"

They looked at him in surprise.

"They left together not long after the fireworks started," Belinda said. "Sarah said she had a headache and asked Megan to give her a ride."

Jackson looked at Allie. "You know where Sarah lives, right?"

"You think they took Nat?" Allie looked even more frightened.

"Belinda, stay here and keep us informed if the searchers find Nat. Come on. Let's see if they have Natalie or might have seen her since they left about the time she went missing."

EACH BREATH WAS a labor as Allie stared out the windshield into the darkness ahead. She fought not to break down but it took all of her strength. She'd never been so frightened or felt so helpless. All she could do was pray that Natalie was safe.

"If they took her, then I'm sure they wouldn't hurt her," she said, needing desperately to believe that. "Sarah might have thought it was getting too late for Natalie to be out. Or maybe Nat's dress was so wet—"

"We're going to find her." Jackson sounded convinced of that.

She glanced over at him. His strong hands gripped the

wheel as he drove too fast. He was as scared as she was, she realized. Like her, he must be blaming himself. If the two of them hadn't left the wedding…

"Tell me where to turn. I don't know where they live."

"Take a left at the Big Sky resort turnoff. Mother Taylor… Mildred lives up the mountain."

"They don't have that much of a head start," he said, sounding as if he was trying to reassure himself as much as her.

"This is all my fault." She didn't realize she'd said the words aloud until he spoke.

"No, if anyone is to blame it's me," he said as he reached over and squeezed her hand. "You have been going through so much and all I did was complicate things for you."

She let out a nervous laugh. "Are you kidding? I would have been in a straitjacket by now if it wasn't for you. I still might end up there, but at least I had this time when there was someone who believed me."

"I *still* believe you. You're not crazy. Nor did you have anything to do with your husband's death. You're being set up and, if it is the last thing I do, I'm going to prove it."

Allie couldn't help but smile over at him. "Thank you but I can't ask you to keep—"

"You're not asking. There's something else I need to say." He glanced over at her before making the turn at Big Sky then turned back to his driving. "I hadn't been with another woman since my ex. I didn't *want* anyone. The mere thought of getting involved again… Then I met you," he said shooting her a quick look as they raced up the mountain toward Big Sky Resort.

"Turn at the next left when we reach the top of the mountain," she said, not sure she wanted to hear what he had to say.

"I hadn't felt anything like that in so long and then we made love and…"

She really didn't need him to let her down easy. Not right now. All she wanted to think about was Natalie. If he was just doing this to keep her from worrying... "You don't have to explain."

"I do. I panicked because making love with you was so amazing and meant so much and..." He shook his head. "I...I just needed time to digest it all. And, truthfully, I was scared. Ford's mom did a number on me. Admittedly, we were both young, too young to get married, let alone have a child together. I had this crazy idea that we wanted the same things. Turned out she wanted money, a big house, a good time. When she got pregnant with Ford..." He slowed to make the turn.

"It's up this road about a mile. Turn left when you see the sign for Elk Ridge."

He nodded. "Juliet didn't want the baby. I talked her into having Ford. She hated me for it, said it was going to ruin her figure." He shook his head at the memory. "I thought that after he was born, her mothering instincts would kick in. My mistake. She resented him even more than she did me. She basically handed him to me and went out with her friends."

"I can't imagine."

He glanced over at her. "No, *you* can't." He sighed. "After that, she started staying out all night, wouldn't come home for days. Fortunately, the barbecue businesses took off like crazy so I could stay home with Ford. I asked for a divorce only to find out that my wife liked being a Cardwell and didn't want to give up what she had, which was basically no responsibilities, but lots of money and freedom to do whatever she wanted."

"Keep going up this road," she told him. Then after a moment, said, "She didn't want a divorce."

"No. She said that if I pushed it, she would take Ford."

"How horrible," Allie cried. Hadn't that been her fear

with Nick? Hadn't she worried that he would be a bastard and try to hurt them both when she told him she was leaving him?

"After the battle I fought to keep my son, I was...broken."

"I understand. The last thing you wanted was to get involved with a woman who only reminded you of what you'd been through."

He glanced over at her. "That was part of it." He didn't say more as he reached the turnoff for Mildred Taylor's house and the guesthouse where her daughter, Sarah, lived. He turned down it and Mildred's house came into view.

JACKSON HAD ALMOST told Allie how he felt about her. That he loved her. But as he'd turned and seen Mildred Taylor's big house, he'd realized the timing was all wrong. First they had to find Natalie.

He prayed she would be here, safe. But if so, did the Taylors seriously think they could get away with this? Had they told someone they were taking Natalie and the person just forgot or couldn't find Allie and left? Was there a logical explanation for this?

He hoped it was just a misunderstanding. But in his heart, he didn't believe for a minute that Allie had imagined the things that had been happening to her. Someone was behind this and they weren't finished with Allie yet. What scared him was that one of them could have murdered Nick.

His heart began to pound harder as he pulled in front of the large stone-and-log house set back against the mountainside. There were two vehicles parked in front and the lights were on inside the massive house. He parked and opened his door, anxious to put Nat in her mother's arms. Allie was out her door the moment he stopped.

"Who all lives here?" Jackson asked as he caught up to her.

"Just Mildred in the main house. Sarah stays in the guesthouse behind it. Drew lives down in Gateway but he stays with his mother a lot up here. That's his pickup parked next to Mildred's SUV so he must be here."

As Jackson passed Mildred's SUV, he touched the hood. Still warm. They at least hadn't been here long.

"What does Sarah drive?" he asked, glancing toward the dark guesthouse.

"A pearl-white SUV. I don't see it."

At Allie's knock, he heard movement inside the house. If they were trying to hide Natalie, it wouldn't do them any good. He looked back down the mountainside telling himself that if Natalie was in this house, he'd find her.

Drew opened the door and looked surprised to see them standing there.

"Where is Natalie?" Allie cried as she pushed past him.

"Natalie?" Drew barely got the word out before Jackson pushed past him, as well. The two of them stormed into the main part of the house.

Mildred was seated on one of the large leather couches facing the window in the living room, a glass of wine in her hand. She looked up in surprise.

"Where is she?" Allie demanded. "I know you have my daughter."

"Natalie?" Mildred asked, frowning. "You can't *find* her?"

"They seem to think we have her," Drew said, closing the front door and joining them. "We've been at the police station. Why would you think we had Natalie?"

"Allie, stay here. I'll search the house," Jackson said.

"You most certainly will not," Mildred cried. "I'll call the cops."

"Call the cops, but I suspect the marshal is already on his way here," he told her and wasn't surprised when Drew stepped in front of him as if to block his way.

"You really want to do this now? Your niece is missing.

If you don't have her, then we need to be out looking for her, not seeing who is tougher between you and me."

"We don't have her," Drew said, "and you're not—"

Jackson hit him and didn't wait around to see if he got up.

He stormed through the house, calling Nat's name. There were a lot of rooms, a lot of closets, a lot of places to look. But it didn't take him long to realize she wasn't here. Whatever they might have done with her, she wasn't in this house.

"I'm going to have you arrested for trespassing and barging into our house and attacking my son," Mildred threatened but hadn't made the call when he returned. Drew had a package of frozen peas he was holding to his eye as he came out of the kitchen.

"Mildred swears she hasn't seen Sarah," Allie told him.

"Well, Natalie isn't here. I think we should still check the guesthouse."

"You planning to break in?" Drew asked. "Or would you like me to get the key?"

Mildred pushed to her feet. "Drew, you are most certainly not going to—"

"Shut up, Mother," he snapped. "Aren't you listening? Natalie is missing. If I can help find her, I will. What I'd like to know is why you aren't upset about it. If you know where Nat is, Mother, you'd better tell me right now."

Jackson felt his cell phone vibrate, checked it and said, "I just got a text that the marshal is on his way. Mrs. Taylor, you could be looking at felony kidnapping," he warned.

ALLIE STARED AT HER mother-in-law, seeing a pathetic, lonely woman who now looked trapped.

"She's not in the guesthouse," Mildred said. "She's *fine*. She's with Sarah and Megan."

"Where?" Allie demanded, her heart breaking at the

thought of Megan being involved in this. "Why would they take her?"

Mildred met her gaze. "Because you're an unfit mother. Megan told me all about your mother and her family. Crazy, all of them. And you? You see things and do things that prove you can't raise my Nicky's baby girl. She needs *family*. Natalie needs her *grandmother*," she said before bursting into tears.

"Call them and tell them to bring Natalie back," Jackson ordered.

"He's right, Mother. Natalie belongs with her mother."

"How can you say that?" Mildred cried, turning on her son. "I told you about all the crazy things she's been doing. Did you know she cut up all those lovely dresses my Nicky had bought her? She never liked them and with him gone—" Mildred stopped as if she felt Allie staring at her in shock. "She's *crazy*. Just look at her!"

"The dresses. I never told anyone other than Jackson about finding them cut up on my bed," Allie said, surprised by how normal her voice sounded. Even more surprised by the relief she felt. "It was the night Drew took Natalie and me to dinner. *You?* You bought the clothes in the closet that I found. No wonder you asked me about what I was wearing at the rehearsal dinner. You knew where I kept my checkbook in the desk drawer. Nick would have told you about the kind of clothes I liked. Forging my signature on a check wouldn't have been hard, not for a woman who has been forging her husband's signature on checks for years."

Mildred gasped. "Where would you get an idea like that?"

"*Your Nicky* told me. You've been stealing from the elderly man you married to keep up the lifestyle you believe you deserve. But you don't deserve my daughter."

"Is that true, Mother?" Drew asked with a groan.

"Never mind that cheap bastard. Men never stay so yes, I took advantage while it lasted and now he's divorcing me. Happy?" Mildred thrust her finger at Allie. "But you, you killed my Nicky!"

"How can you say that?" Allie demanded. "You can't really believe I followed him up into the mountains."

"You *paid* someone to kill him. I know you did," the older woman argued. "When I came over that weekend, you were packing up some of Nicky's belongings. You knew he was dead before we even heard."

"That was just some things he left out before he went hunting."

"She's lying," Mildred cried as she looked from Jackson to Drew. "She knew Nicky wasn't coming back. She was packing. I saw that she'd cleaned out the closet before she closed the bedroom door."

"I was packing my own things and Natalie's," Allie said. "I was planning to leave Nick. Ask Belinda. She'll tell you. I wanted a divorce."

Mildred looked shocked. "Why would you want to leave my Nicky? You must have found another man."

"No," Allie said, shaking her head. "I know how much you loved him but I didn't see the same man you did. Nick wasn't any happier than I was in the marriage."

"Oh, I have to sit down," Mildred cried. "Can't you see? She had every reason to want Nicky dead. She's admitted it."

"Make the call to your daughter, Mrs. Taylor," Jackson said, handing her his phone.

At the sound of a siren headed toward the house, Mildred took his phone.

"You'll get your daughter back, but only temporarily," her mother-in-law spat after making the call. "Once you go to prison for my Nicky's murder, you will get what you deserve and I will get my Nicky's baby."

"And all Nick's insurance money," Jackson said. "Isn't that what this is really about?"

Mildred didn't answer as Marshal Hud Savage pulled up out front.

Chapter Fifteen

Emotionally exhausted, all Allie could think about was holding her daughter. They'd all waited, the marshal included, until Megan and Sarah brought Natalie to the Taylor house.

Allie swept her daughter up into her arms, hugging her so tightly that Natalie cried, "Mama, you're squishing me!"

Hud took Mildred, Drew, Megan and Sarah down to the marshal's office to question them.

"Why don't you come stay at the ranch," Jackson suggested, but all Allie wanted to do was take her daughter home. "Okay, I'll drop you off there. I can give you a ride to the ranch in the morning to pick up your van."

She looked into his dark eyes and touched his arm. "Thank you."

They didn't talk on the drive to her cabin. Natalie fell asleep after complaining that she'd missed most of the fireworks. Apparently, Sarah and Megan had told her they were taking her to see her mama and that it was important.

As they drove, pockets of fireworks were going off around them. Allie had forgotten it was the Fourth of July. Even the wedding seemed like it had been a long time ago.

"If you need anything…" Jackson said after he'd insisted on carrying Natalie into her bed. He moved to the cabin door. "I'm here for you, Allie."

She could only nod, her emotions long spent.

"I'll see you tomorrow."

Allie doubted that. Jackson and Ford would be flying out. She told herself that she and Natalie were safe as she locked the front door, leaned against it and listened to Jackson drive away.

But in her heart she knew they wouldn't be safe until Nick's killer was caught.

"I RUINED TAG and Lily's wedding," Jackson said with a groan the next morning at breakfast.

"You did not," Dana said, patting his hand as she finished serving a huge ranch breakfast of elk steaks, biscuits and gravy, fried potatoes and eggs. She had invited them all down, saying that she knew it had been a rough night. Hud had left for his office first thing this morning.

The wedding couple had stayed at Big Sky Resort last night and flown out this morning to an undisclosed location for their two-week-long honeymoon.

"They loved everything about the wedding," Dana said. "They were just worried about Allie after Mildred's announcement and then concerned for Natalie. I'm just so thankful that she was found and is fine. I can't imagine what Sarah and Megan were thinking."

Jackson had filled everyone in on what had happened at the Taylors' and how apparently Mildred, Sarah and Megan had been gaslighting Allie.

"Oh, Allie must be heartbroken to find out her stepsister was in on it," Dana said.

"I'm sure Hud will sort it out," Jackson said as he watched his son eating breakfast with the Savage clan at the kid table. Ford, he noticed, had come out of his shell. Jackson couldn't believe the change in the boy from when they had arrived at the ranch. Montana had been good for his son.

"Natalie is safe and so is Allie, at least for the moment," he said. "The problem is Nick's murder," he said, dropping his voice, even though he doubted the kids could hear, given the amount of noise they were making at their table.

"They still don't know who killed him?" Dana asked.

Jackson shook his head. "Mildred is convinced Allie paid someone to do it. The police want to talk to her."

"You sound worried," Dana noted. "And your brothers haven't said a word," she said, looking from Hayes to Laramie and finally Jackson. "Why is that?"

"They've been helping me do some investigating," he admitted.

Dana rolled her eyes. "I should have known that was what was going on." She glanced at Hayes and Laramie. "You found something that makes her look guilty?"

"Someone is setting her up," Jackson said.

"The same people who tried to drive her crazy?" she asked.

"Maybe not. There could be more going on here than even we know." Jackson couldn't help sounding worried as he got to his feet. "Hayes and I are going to take her van to her. She called this morning. A homicide detective from Bozeman wants to see her."

ALLIE HAD AWAKENED in Natalie's bed to the sound of the phone. She'd expected it to be Jackson. That sent her heart lifting like helium. But as she reminded herself he was leaving today, her moment of euphoria evaporated.

Reaching for the receiver, she had a bad feeling it wasn't going to be good news. "We would like to ask you a few questions," the homicide detective told her. "When would be a good time?"

After she'd hung up, she'd called Jackson and told him the news.

"You knew this was coming. It's nothing to worry about," he'd told her, but she'd heard concern in his voice. "Do you want me to go with you?"

"No. This is something I have to do alone. Anyway, aren't you flying out today?"

Silence, then, "I canceled our flight."

"You shouldn't have done that," she said after a moment.

"Allie, I can't leave yet. I saw that the key is in the van. Hayes and I will bring it over."

"There is no hurry. I don't see the homicide detective until later."

Their conversation had felt awkward and ended just as badly. Allie told herself she couldn't keep leaning on Jackson. She knew now what Mildred and her daughter and Megan had done to her. She could understand Sarah going along with whatever her mother said, but Megan?

She'd felt like family. But then so had Drew.

Allie made Natalie her favorite pancakes when she woke up, then they went for a walk down by the river. Nat did love to throw rocks into the water. Allie watched the ripples they made, thinking about Jackson and the ripples he'd made in her life.

After a while, they walked back to the cabin. Dana had called saying she would love to take Natalie while Allie went to talk to the detective.

"If you trust me with her. I wouldn't blame you if you didn't. Just let me know."

Allie called Dana right back. "I would always trust you with Natalie and she would love to see the kids, not to mention Sugar, the horse."

Dana laughed and Allie could hear tears in her voice. "I was afraid you would never forgive me."

"There is nothing to forgive. Megan and Sarah took advantage of the fireworks show and the wedding."

"What were they thinking? Did they really believe they could get away with keeping her?"

"I suppose they thought I would come unglued, which

I did, proving that I was unbalanced. If it hadn't been for Jackson…" She really hadn't meant to go there.

"Is Natalie all right?"

"She didn't even realize anything was amiss. Apparently, they told her they were taking her to me, but when they reached Megan's motel room, they told her I was going to meet them there. Nat ended up falling asleep. So she had no idea what was going on."

"Thank goodness."

"I'll drop Nat off on my way, if that's okay."

"That's wonderful. We can't wait to see her. Tell her to wear her boots. We'll go for a ride."

"YOU NEED TO take the hint," Hayes said as he and Jackson drove away from Allie's cabin. They'd dropped off the van, Allie had thanked them and that was that, so Jackson knew what his brother was getting at. "Allie is handling all of this fine. I'm not sure there is anything you can do from here on out."

"You think she had him killed?" Jackson demanded.

Hayes shrugged. "I don't know her as well as you think you do. I don't think she paid anyone to do it. But if she gave Drew any kind of opening with her, I think he would have killed his brother for her—and the insurance money."

"She wasn't in cahoots with Drew. And stop doing that," he snapped as his brother shrugged again. "Do you realize how cynical you've become? Worse, does McKenzie?"

Hayes smiled. "Speaking of McKenzie… I'm opening a private investigator business here."

"You think that's a newsflash?" Jackson laughed. "We've all seen that coming for a mile. So when is the wedding?"

"I'm thinking we might elope. I'm not sure the family can live through another Cardwell Ranch wedding."

"Which reminds me, still no word from Austin?"

"You know our brother when he's on a case. But I am a little worried about him. I really thought he'd make Tag's wedding."

"Yeah, me too. Maybe I'll give a call down there. Knowing him, he probably didn't list any of us as emergency contacts."

ALLIE TRIED TO get comfortable in the chair the homicide detectives offered her. The room was like any office, no bare lightbulb shining into her eyes, no cops threatening her. But she still shifted in her chair.

On the drive here, she'd tried to concentrate on who might have killed Nick. Belinda had been up that trail with Nick when the two of them had been dating. Drew usually went hunting with his brother. Had Drew gone this time, as well, gotten in an argument with Nick and killed him?

She shuddered at the path her thoughts had taken. Did she really think someone in Nick's own family had killed him?

Better that than to think that her stepsister, Megan, had. Allie felt sick at the thought. Her sister had called this morning but Allie hadn't picked up.

"I need to explain," Megan had said on voice mail. "I did what I did for Natalie's sake. I love you and my niece. I really believed I was protecting you both. I had no idea Mildred and Sarah were doing those things to you, making you behave the way they told me you were. Please call me so we can talk about this."

The larger of the two homicide detectives cleared his voice. His name tag read Benson. "We need to know where you were the weekend your husband went up into the mountains."

"I was home that whole weekend."

"Did you talk to anyone? Anyone stop by?"

Allie tried to remember. Her mind was spinning. They

thought she'd had something to do with Nick's death? Of course they did, given the insurance policies and her mother-in-law's rantings and ravings.

Just yesterday, she'd been sure that Nick was alive. Jackson had been convinced, as well. She'd been even more convinced when she'd heard his voice at the séance. Nick's voice accusing her of killing him. She shivered at the memory.

"Mrs. Taylor?" the smaller of the two, whose name tag read Evans, asked.

She blinked. No one called her Mrs. Taylor. Mrs. Taylor was Nick's mother. "Please, call me Allie. I just need a moment to think." Had anyone stopped by that weekend?

Fighting all her conflicting thoughts, she tried to remember. Nick had left early, having packed the night before. He'd seemed excited about the prospect of going alone on this hunt. Why hadn't she noticed that something was wrong right there? It was the first red flag.

Had anyone stopped by? No. She frowned. She'd tried to call Belinda but hadn't been able to reach her, she recalled now. She'd wanted to tell her what Nick had said about making some changes when he returned from his hunting trip. She'd had misgivings about the trip even then and she'd needed to talk to someone. Had she worried that he might be thinking of killing himself?

"I don't remember anyone stopping by," she said, trying to keep her thoughts on the question. She ticked off everyone on her fingers. "I couldn't reach my friend Belinda." Had she tried Megan? "Or my stepsister, Megan. And my in-laws. I think that was the weekend that Mildred and Sarah went on a shopping trip to Billings. Drew... I don't know where he was. I didn't talk to him."

She looked up to see that both detectives were studying her. They were making her even more nervous.

"I was alone with my daughter that whole weekend." She

had no alibi. But they didn't really think she'd followed Nick up in the mountains and killed him, did they?

"Was it unusual for your husband to go hunting alone?"

"Very. I didn't think he had. I thought he was having an affair. I was surprised when I learned that he really had gone into the mountains."

The detectives shared a look before the lead one asked, "Did you have any reason to believe your husband was having an affair?"

"No. I guess it was wishful thinking. It would have made it easier for me."

The two shared another look. "Easier?"

She met the smaller detective's gaze. "I was going to leave Nick." Why not admit it? They probably already knew this after talking to her in-laws and Belinda and Megan. "But I didn't want him dead. You asked what I was doing that weekend? I didn't leave the house. I had my five-year-old daughter to take care of that weekend and I was busy packing."

"When were you planning to tell him?" Benson asked.

"As soon as he returned."

Evans picked up a sheet of paper from the desk. "Mrs. Tay— Excuse me, Allie, you own a .45 pistol?"

Chapter Sixteen

The gun. What had she been thinking when she'd bought it? Had she really thought that pulling it on Nick would be a good idea? She'd wanted something to protect herself for when she told him she was leaving.

Now she saw how ridiculous that was. Nick would have taken it away from her, knowing she couldn't shoot him and then he would have been so furious....

"Yes, I bought the gun for protection."

Benson raised a brow. "Protection? Against whom?"

"I was planning to leave my husband. My daughter and I would be alone—"

"But you hadn't left him yet," Evans pointed out. "So why buy a .45 pistol only days before your husband was to go on his hunting trip?"

"I...I...was afraid of how Nick was going to take it when he returned and I told him I was leaving him. Sometimes he scares me."

The two detectives exchanged another look.

"But it was impulsive and silly because Nick would have known I couldn't use it on him. He would have taken it away from me and..." She swallowed.

"You were afraid of your husband," Benson said.

"Sometimes."

"Where is the gun now?" Evans asked.

"I don't know. When I heard that Nick had been killed

with a .45, I looked for it, but it was gone." Allie could see the disbelief written all over their faces. Hadn't she known when she looked that it would be gone?

"I think someone is trying to set me up for his murder," she blurted out and instantly regretted it when she saw their expressions. Apparently, they'd heard this type of defense before.

"You're saying someone took the gun to frame you?" Benson asked. "Who knew you'd bought it?"

Allie met his gaze. "I didn't tell anyone, if that is what you're asking."

"Who had access to your house?" Evans asked.

"It's an old cabin. I don't know how many people might have a key. Nick was always going to change the locks…"

"Your in-laws? Did they have keys?" Benson asked.

"Yes."

"Friends?"

"Belinda and my stepsister, Megan, know where there's a key to get in."

"Where did you keep the gun that someone could have found it? You have a five-year-old. I assume you didn't just leave the gun lying around," Benson asked.

"Of course not. I put it on the top shelf of the closet. It wasn't loaded."

"But there were cartridges for it with the gun?"

She nodded.

"When was the last time you saw it?" Evans asked.

"The day I bought it. I put it on the shelf behind some shoe boxes… I'd forgotten all about it with Nick's…death… and all."

"So you were just going to leave him," Evans said. "This man who you said scared you sometimes, you were going to allow him to have joint custody of your child?"

"It hadn't gotten that far. I guess it would have been up to the court—"

"Oh, so you'd already seen a lawyer about a divorce?" Benson asked.

"Not yet. I couldn't afford to see one until I got a job and Nick wouldn't allow me to work."

The detectives exchanged looks.

"Was your husband abusive?" Benson asked not unkindly.

Allie hesitated. "He was…controlling."

"And he scared you," Evans said.

"Yes, sometimes. What is it you want me to say? He wasn't a good husband or father to our daughter. And yes, sometimes he scared me."

"Mrs. Taylor, did you kill your husband?" Evans asked.

"No. I told you. I could never—"

"Did you get your brother-in-law, Drew, or someone else close to you to do the killing for you?" Benson asked.

"*No!* I didn't want to be married to Nick anymore but I didn't want him dead."

Evans leaned forward. "But look how it turned out. Nick is no longer around to scare you, even sometimes. Your daughter is safe from him. And you are a wealthy woman thanks to his insurance money. Better than a divorce and a lengthy battle over your daughter, wouldn't you say?"

Allie felt as if the detectives had beaten her as she stumbled out of the police station. For a moment she forgot where she'd parked the van. Panic sent her blood pressure soaring before she spotted it. There it was, right where she'd left it. And there was…

"Jackson?"

He pushed off the van and moved quickly to her. "I had to see you before I left."

She frowned, still feeling off balance. "I thought you weren't flying out yet?"

"It's my brother Austin. He's a sheriff's deputy in Texas. He's been shot. He's critical. I have to fly out now. Franklin and Mom already left. Hayes, Laramie and I are taking the corporate jet as soon as I get to the airport."

"I'm so sorry, Jackson. Does Tag know?"

"We weren't able to reach him. He and Lily wanted their honeymoon to be a secret… Ford is staying with Dana until I get back. But I couldn't leave without seeing you. Are you all right?"

She started to say she was fine, but she couldn't get the lie past her lips. Her eyes filled with tears. "They think I killed Nick. Everyone does."

"Not me," he said and pulled her into his arms. "When I get back, we'll sort this out. I'm sorry I have to go."

She pulled back, brushed at her tears. "I'll say a prayer for your brother." As he ran to his rented SUV, she turned in time to see Detective Evans watching her from the front of the building. He looked like a man who'd just received a gift he hadn't expected. Jackson Cardwell. Another motive as to why she'd want her husband gone for good.

THE JET OWNED by the corporation was waiting on the tarmac when Jackson arrived at the airport. He ran to climb aboard and Laramie alerted the captain that they were ready.

"Have you heard any more from Mom or the hospital?" Jackson asked as he buckled up.

"I just got off the phone with Mom," Hayes said. "Austin's still in surgery." His tone was sufficient for Jackson to know it didn't look good.

"Do we know what happened?" he asked as the plane began to taxi out to the runway.

"You know how hard it is to get anything out of the sheriff's department down there," Hayes said. "But I got the impression he was on one of the dangerous cases he seems to like so well." He raked a hand through his hair. "There was a woman involved. He'd apparently gone into a drug cartel to get her out."

"That sounds just like Austin," Jackson said with a sigh as the jet engine roared and the plane began to race down the runway. "Did he get her out?"

"Don't know. Doubtful, though, since some illegal immigrants found him after he'd been shot and got him to a gas station near the border."

Hayes shook his head. "Some of the same illegal immigrants his department is trying to catch and send back over the border. What a mess down there. I'm glad I'm done with it."

His brothers looked at him in surprise as the plane lifted off the ground.

"McKenzie and I signed the papers on a ranch in the canyon not far from Cardwell Ranch. When I get back, we're eloping. She's already looking for some office space for me at Big Sky to open a private investigation office up here."

"Congratulations," Laramie said.

"Have you told Mom?" Jackson asked. "I'm wondering how she is going to feel losing another son to Montana?" The plane fell silent as he realized she might be losing another son at this very moment, one that not even Montana got a chance to claim.

Speaking of Montana, he thought as he looked out the window at the mountains below them. He'd hated leaving Allie, especially as upset as she'd been. He promised himself he would return to the canyon just as soon as he knew his brother was going to be all right.

He said a prayer for Austin and one for Allie, as well.

DANA HAD CALLED to say she was taking the kids on a horseback ride and that Allie could pick Natalie up later, if that was all right. Ford apparently was very upset and worried about his uncle Austin, so Dana was trying to take their minds off everything for a while.

Not wanting to go back to an empty cabin, Allie had

busied herself with errands she'd put off since the wedding preparation. It was late afternoon by the time she got home. She'd called the ranch only to find out that Dana and the kids had gone to get ice cream and would be back soon.

Allie was carrying in groceries and her other purchases when she heard the vehicle pull up. She'd hoped to get everything put away before she went to pick up Natalie. She carried the bags into the cabin, dumping them on the kitchen counter, before she glanced out the window to see her mother-and sister-in-law pull up. She groaned as the two got out and came to the door.

For just an instant, she thought about not answering their knock, but they must have seen her carrying in her groceries. Mildred wasn't one to take the hint and go away.

"I just got back from the police station," she said as she opened the door. "I'm really not in the mood for visitors." She couldn't believe either of them would have the gall to show their faces around here after what they'd done. Well, they weren't coming in. Whatever they had to say, they could say it on the front step.

Allie had already talked to Hud this morning. He'd questioned all of them last night, but had had to let them all go. Maybe they had come by to apologize, but Allie doubted it.

"I just got a call from the police," Mildred said indignantly. "Why would you tell them that Sarah and I went to Billings the weekend my Nicky was killed?"

"I thought you had." She knew she shouldn't have been surprised. No apology for what they had tried to do to her.

"We'd planned to go, but Sarah was sick that whole weekend." She sniffed. "I was alone when I got the call about my Nicky." She glared at her daughter for a moment. "Sarah had taken my car down to the drugstore to get more medicine since her car was in the shop. I couldn't even leave the house to go to Drew." Mildred sighed.

"I'm sorry you were alone, Mother. I came right back. I

couldn't have been gone more than five minutes after you got the call," Sarah said.

"That was the longest five minutes of my life," Mildred said with another sniff.

"I guess I had forgotten the two of you hadn't gone to Billings, but I'm sure you straightened it out with the police," Allie said. "And Sarah couldn't have known that would be the time you would get the call about Nick," Allie pointed out.

Sarah gave her a grateful smile, then added, "I hate to ask, but do you happen to have a cola in your fridge?"

"Oh, for crying out loud, Sarah, how many times have I told you that stuff is horrible for you?" her mother demanded.

"Help yourself," Allie said, moving to the side of the doorway to let her pass. She saw that the sun had disappeared behind Lone Mountain, casting the canyon in a cool darkness. Where had this day gone? "I hate to run you off, but I have to go pick up Natalie."

"Once this foolishness is over, I hope you'll forgive me and let me spend some time with my granddaughter," Mildred said.

As Sarah came out with a can of cola, Allie moved aside again to let her pass, hoping they would now leave.

Mildred looked in the yard at Nick's pickup, where it had been parked since someone from the forest service had found it at the trailhead and had it dropped off. "Why are you driving that awful van of yours? You should either drive Nicky's pickup or sell it. Terrible waste to just let it sit."

Allie planned to sell the pickup but she'd been waiting, hoping in time Mildred wouldn't get so upset about it.

"I'd like to buy it," Sarah said, making them both turn to look at her in surprise.

"What in the world do you need with Nicky's pickup?"

Mildred demanded. "I'm not giving you the money for it and I couldn't bear looking at it every day."

"It was just a thought," Sarah said as she started toward her SUV. The young woman took so much grief from her mother.

Her gaze went to Nick's pickup. The keys were probably still in it, she realized. As Sarah climbed behind the wheel and waited for her mother to get into the passenger side of the SUV, Allie walked out to the pickup, opened the door and reached inside to pull the keys.

The pickup smelled like Nick's aftershave and made her a little sick to her stomach. She pocketed the keys as she hurriedly closed the door. The truck was Nick's baby. He loved it more than he did either her or Natalie. That's why she was surprised as she started to step away to see that the right rear panel near the back was dented. She moved to the dent and ran her fingers over it. That would have to be fixed before she could sell it since the rest of the truck was in mint condition.

Just something else to take care of, she thought as she dusted what looked like chalky white flakes off her fingers. She looked up and saw that her in-laws hadn't left. Mildred was going on about something. Sarah was bent toward the passenger seat apparently helping her mother buckle up. Mildred was probably giving her hell, Allie thought.

When Sarah straightened, she looked up from behind the wheel and seemed surprised to see Allie standing by Nick's truck. Her surprise gave way to sadness as she looked past Allie to her brother's pickup.

Was it possible Sarah really did want Nick's pickup for sentimental reasons? Maybe she should have it. Allie had never thought Sarah and her brother were that close. Well, at least Nick hadn't been that crazy about his sister. He'd been even more disparaging than his mother toward Sarah.

Allie met her sister-in-law's dark gaze for a moment,

feeling again sorry for her. Maybe she would just give her the pickup. She waved as Sarah began to pull away, relieved they were finally leaving.

Her cell phone rang. She hoped it was Jackson with news of his brother. She said a silent prayer for Austin before she saw that it was Dana.

"Is everything all right?" Allie asked, instantly afraid.

"Ford is still upset about his uncle. Natalie told him that you were picking her up soon…"

Allie knew what was coming. She couldn't bear the thought. She wanted Natalie home with her. The way things were going, she feared she might soon be under arrest for Nick's murder. She didn't know how much time she and Nat had together.

"Natalie wishes to speak with you," Dana said before Allie could say no.

"Mama?" Just the sound of her daughter's voice made her smile. "Please say I can stay. Ford is very sad about his uncle. Please let me stay."

"Maybe Ford could come stay with you—"

"We're all going to sleep in the living room in front of the fire. Mrs. Savage said we could. She is going to make popcorn. It is Mary and Hank's favorite."

Allie closed her eyes, picturing how perfect it would be in front of Dana's fireplace in that big living room with the smell of popcorn and the sound of children's laughter. She wanted to sleep right in the middle of all of them.

"Of course you need to stay for your new friend," she heard herself say as tears burned her eyes. "Tell Mrs. Savage that I will pick you up first thing in the morning. I love you."

"I love you, too, Mama." And Natalie was gone, the phone passed to Dana who said, "I'm sorry. This was the kids' idea."

"It's fine."

"What about you? How did it go with the police?"

"As expected. They think I killed Nick. Or at least got someone to do it for me."

"That's ridiculous. Allie, listen, you shouldn't be alone. Why don't you come stay here tonight? I think you need your daughter. Do you like butter on your popcorn? Come whenever you want. Or take a little time for yourself. If you're like me, when was the last time you got a nice leisurely bath without being interrupted? Whatever you need, but bring your pjs. We're having a pajama party. Right now the kids all want to go help feed the animals. See you later."

As THE JET touched down just outside of Houston, Hayes got the call from their mother. Jackson watched his expression, waiting for the news. Relief flooded his brother's face. He gave thumbs up and disconnected.

"Mom says Austin is out of surgery. The doctor says he should make it."

Jackson let out the breath he'd been holding. As the plane taxied toward the private plan terminal, he put in a call to Allie. It went straight to voice mail.

He left a message, telling her the good news, then asking her to call when she got the message. "I'm worried about you." As he disconnected, he realized he'd been worried the entire flight about both his brother and Allie.

"I can't reach Allie."

His brothers looked at him in concern as the plane neared the small brightly lit terminal. It was already dark here, but it would still be light in Montana.

"Call Dana," Hayes said. "She's probably over there."

He called. "No answer."

"They probably went for a horseback ride," Laramie said. "Wasn't that what Ford told you they were going to do the last time you talked to him?"

Jackson nodded, telling himself his brother was probably

right. He glanced at Hayes. He understood what Laramie couldn't really grasp. Laramie was a businessman. Hayes was a former sheriff's deputy, a private investigation. He understood Jackson's concern. There was a killer still loose in Montana.

The plane came to a stop. Jackson tried Allie again. The call again went straight to voice mail. He got Mildred Taylor's number and called her.

"Have you seen Allie?" he asked. He couldn't explain his fear, just a feeling in the pit of his stomach that was growing with each passing minute.

"Earlier. She wouldn't even let me in her house." She sniffed. "She was on her way to Cardwell Ranch to pick up Natalie the last I saw of her. Driving that old van. Why she doesn't drive Nickie's pickup I will never—"

He disconnected and tried Dana. Still no answer. He tried Allie again. Then he called the marshal's office in Big Sky.

"Marshal Savage is unavailable," the dispatcher told him.

"Is there anyone there who can do a welfare check?"

"Not at the moment. Do you want me to have the marshal call you when he comes in?"

Jackson started to give the dispatcher his number but Hayes stopped him.

"Take the plane," Hayes said. "Mother said it would be hours before we could even see Austin. I'll keep you informed of his progress."

"Are you kidding?" Laramie demanded. "What is it with you and this woman? Have you forgotten that she's the number one suspect in her husband's murder?"

"She didn't kill him," Jackson and Hayes said in unison.

"Let us know as soon as you hear something," Hayes said.

Jackson hugged his brother, relieved that he understood. He moved to cockpit and asked the pilot how long before they could get the plane back in the air. As Hayes and Laramie disembarked, he sat down again and buckled his seatbelt, trying to remain calm.

He had no reason to believe anything had happened. And yet…that bad feeling he'd gotten when her phone had gone to voice mail had only increased with each passing second. His every instinct told him that Allie was in real trouble.

Chapter Seventeen

Allie had taken a hot bath, but had kept it short. She was
too anxious to see her daughter. She changed her clothes,
relieved she was going to Dana's. She really didn't want to
be alone tonight. She'd heard Natalie's happy chatter in the
background and couldn't wait to reach the ranch.

In fact, she had started out the door when she realized
she didn't have her purse or her van keys. Leaving the door
open, she turned back remembering that she'd left them on
the small table between the living room and kitchen when
she brought in her groceries earlier.

She was sure she'd left her purse on the table, but it
wasn't there. As she started to search for it, she began to
have that awful feeling again. Her mind reeled. Mildred
wasn't still fooling with her, was she? No Mildred hadn't
come into the cabin. But Sarah had. Why would Sarah hide
her purse? It made no sense.

Racking her brain, she moved through the small cabin.
The purse wasn't anywhere. On her way back through, she
realized she must have left it in the van. She was so used
to leaving her purse on that small table, she'd thought she
remembered doing it again.

She started toward the open door when a dark figure suddenly filled the doorway. The scream that rose in her throat
came out a sharp cry before she could stop it.

"Drew, you scared me. I didn't hear you drive up."

"My truck's down the river a ways. I was fishing...."

The lie was so obvious that he didn't bother finishing it. He wasn't dressed for fishing nor was he carrying a rod.

"The truth is, I wanted to talk to you and after everything that's happened, I thought you'd chase me off before I could have my say."

"Drew, this isn't a good time. I was just leaving."

He laughed. "That's exactly why I didn't drive up in your yard. I figured you'd say something just like that."

"Well, in this case, it's true. Natalie is waiting for me. I'm staying at Cardwell Ranch tonight. Dana is going to be wondering where I am if I don't—"

"This won't take long." He took a breath. "I'm so sorry for everything."

Allie felt her blood heat to boiling. No one in this family ever listened to her. How dare he insist she hear him out when she just told him she was leaving? "You and your mother tried to drive me insane."

"I didn't know anything about that, I swear," Drew cried. "Mother told me that you had already forgotten about Nick. It was breaking her heart. She said you needed to be reminded and if you saw someone who looked like Nick..."

"You expect me to believe that?"

He shrugged. "It's true. I did it just to shut her up. You know how Mother is."

She did. She also knew arguing about this now was a waste of time and breath. She glanced at the clock on the mantel. "I really need to go."

"Just give me another minute, please. Also I wanted to apologize for the other night. I had too much to drink." He shook his head. "I don't know what I was thinking. But you have to know, I've always liked you." He looked at her shyly. "I would have done anything for you and now the cops think I killed Nick for you."

Her pulse jumped, her heart a thunder in her chest. "That's ridiculous."

"That's what I told them. I could never hurt my brother. I loved Nick. But I have to tell you, I was jealous of him when he married you."

"Drew, I really don't have time to get into this right—"

"Don't get me wrong," he said as if she hadn't spoken. "If I thought there was chance with you…"

A ripple of panic ran up her spine. "There isn't, Drew."

"Right. Jackson Cardwell."

"That isn't the reason."

"Right," he said sarcastically. His jaw tightened, his expression going dark. She'd been married to his brother long enough to know the signs. Nick could go from charming to furious and frightening in seconds. Apparently so could his brother.

"Drew—"

"What if I did kill him for you, Allie?" He stepped toward her. "What if I knew where he would be up that trail? What if I wanted to save you from him? You think I don't know how he was with you?" He let out a laugh. "Jackson Cardwell isn't the only knight in shining armor who wants to come to your rescue."

She didn't want to hear his confession and feared that was exactly what she was hearing. "Drew, I would never want you to hurt your brother for any reason, especially for me."

"Oh yea? But what if I did, Allie? Wouldn't you owe me something?"

He took another a step toward her.

She tried to hold her ground but Drew was much stronger, much larger, much scarier. With Nick, she'd learned that standing up to him only made things worse. But she was determined that this man wasn't going to touch her. She'd backed down too many times with Nick.

"This isn't happening, Drew." She stepped to the side

and picked up the poker from the fireplace. "It's time for you to go."

She could almost read his mind. He was pretty sure he could get the poker away from her before she did much bodily harm to him. She lifted it, ready to swing, when she heard a vehicle come into the yard.

Drew heard it to. "Jackson Cardwell to the rescue again?"

But it couldn't be Jackson. He was in Texas by now.

Allie was relieved to see his sister Sarah stick her head in the door. "I hope I'm not interrupting anything," she said into the tense silence.

"Not at all," Allie assured her sister-in-law. Her voice sounded more normal than she'd thought it would. Had Drew just confessed to killing Nick? "Drew was just leaving."

"We're not through talking about this," he said as he started for the door.

"Oh, I think we already covered the subject. Goodbye Drew."

"Is everything all right?" Sarah asked as Allie returned the poker to its spot next to the fireplace. She stepped in and closed the door behind her.

"Fine. You didn't happen to see my purse when you were here earlier, did you? Dana is expecting me and I can't seem to find it."

"No. You still haven't picked up Natalie?"

"No, Dana invited me for a sleepover with the kids. I was just heading there when Drew arrived."

"I didn't see his truck," Sarah said glancing toward the window.

"He said he parked it down river where he was fishing." She glanced around the living room one more time. "I need to find my purse and get going."

"Your purse? Oh, that explains why you didn't answer

your cell phone. I tried to call you," Sarah said. "Do you want me to help you look?"

"No, maybe I'll just take Nick's truck." The idea repulsed her, but she was anxious to get to the ranch. "I'm sure my purse will turn up. Oh, that's right, I was going out to check the van and see if I left it there when Drew showed up."

"So you're off to a kids sleepover?"

Allie knew she should be more upset with Sarah for taking Natalie last night, but Sarah had always done her mother's bidding. Allie couldn't help but feel sorry for the woman.

"Nat wanted to spend the night over there for Ford. He's upset about his uncle Austin who was shot down in Texas. His brothers should be at the hospital by now. No wonder I haven't heard anything with my cell phone missing."

"Natalie and Ford sure hit it off, didn't they? It's too bad Nat doesn't have a sibling. I always thought you and Nick would have another child."

Allie found Nick's truck keys in her jacket pocket and held them up. "If you still want Nick's truck, you can have it. I was planning to sell it. But the back side panel is dented." She frowned. "It's odd that Nick didn't mention it. You know how he was about truck…"

Her thoughts tumbled over each other in a matter of an instant as her gaze went to her fingers and she remembered the white flakes she'd brushed off the dent. It hadn't registered at the time. The dent. The white paint from the vehicle that had hit it. Pearl white on Nick's black pickup.

Nick would have been out of his mind if someone had hit his pickup. So it couldn't have happened before his hunting trip, which meant it happened where? At the trailhead?

ANOTHER VEHICLE MUST have hit the pickup. Allie's thoughts fell into a straight, heart-stopping line. A pearl-white vehi-

cle like the one Sarah was having repaired the day the call
came about Nick's death.

Allie felt the hair rise on the back of her neck as she
looked up and saw Sarah's expression.

"I knew you would figure it out the minute I saw you
standing next to the dent in Nick's pickup. Nick was so particular about his truck. One little scratch and he would have
been losing his mind. Isn't that what you were realizing?"

"Oh Sarah," she said, her heart breaking.

"That's all you have to say to the woman who killed
your husband?" she asked as she pulled Allie's .45 out of
her pocket and pointed the barrel at Allie's heart.

JACKSON HAD LEFT his rental car at the Bozeman airport. The
moment the jet landed he ran to it and headed up the canyon. He tried Allie again. Still no answer. He left a message
just in case there was a good reason she wasn't taking calls.

The only reason he could come up with was that she was
at Dana's with the kids and didn't want to be disturbed. But
she would have taken his calls. She would have wanted to
know how Austin was doing.

He tried Dana and was relieved when at least she answered. "I'm looking for Allie. Have you seen her?"

"Not yet. I talked to her earlier. I told her to take a nice
hot, long bath and relax, then come over for a sleepover."
He could hear Dana let out a surprised sound. "I didn't realize it was so late. She should have been here by now."

"Her calls are going straight to voice mail."

"I'm sure she's just running late…" Dana sounded worried. "How is Austin?"

"He's out of surgery. The doctor said he should make it.
I left Hayes and Laramie in Houston."

"Where are you now?"

"On my way to Allie's cabin. If you hear from her, will
you please call me?"

He disconnected and drove as fast as he could through the winding narrow canyon. Something was wrong. Dana felt it, too. He prayed that Allie was all right. But feared she wasn't.

Realizing his greatest fear, he called Drew's number. When he'd heard the part Allie's brother-in-law had played in gaslighting her, he'd wanted to punch Drew again. He didn't trust the man, sensed he was a lot like Nick had been; another reason to hate the bastard.

But Jackson also worried that Drew might have killed Nick. The problem was motive. He wouldn't benefit from his brother's death since Nick had changed his beneficiaries on his insurance policy. Or was there something else Drew wanted more than money?

It came to him in a flash. Allie. If he had her, he would also have Nick's money and Nick's life.

Drew answered on the third ring. "What?" He sounded drunk.

Jackson's pulse jumped. "Have you seen Allie?"

"Who the hell is this?"

"Jackson Cardwell." He heard Drew's sneer even on the phone.

"What do *you* want? Just call to rub it in? Well, you haven't got Allie yet so I wouldn't go counting your chickens—"

His heart was pounding like a war drum. "Is she with you?"

Drew laughed. "She's having a sleepover but not with me. Not yet."

"She isn't at the sleepover. When did you see her?"

Finally picking up on Jackson's concern, he said, "She was with my sister at the cabin."

Jackson frowned. "Your sister?"

"They both think I killed Nick. But Sarah had more of a motive than I do. She hated Nick, especially since he'd been trying to get Mother to kick her out. Sarah might look sweet, but I have a scar from when we were kids. She hit me with a tire iron. A tire iron! Can you believe that?"

Jackson saw the turnoff ahead. As he took it, his headlights flashed on the cabin down the road. There were three vehicles parked out front. Nick's black pickup. Allie's van. Sarah's pearl-white SUV.

Chapter Eighteen

"I don't understand," Allie said. "Why would you kill your brother?"

Sarah smiled. "Sweet, lovable *Nickie?* You of all people know what he was like. You had to know the way he talked about me."

Allie couldn't deny it. "He was cruel and insensitive, but—"

"He was trying to get Mother to kick me out without a cent!" Her face reddened with anger. "I gave up my life to take care of her and Nickie is in her ear telling her I am nothing but a parasite and that if she ever wants to see me get married, she has to kick me out and force me to make it on my own. Can you believe that?"

She could. Nick was often worried about any money that would be coming to him via his mother. He was afraid Sarah would get the lion's share because his mother felt sorry for her.

"He was jealous," Allie said. "He was afraid you were becoming her favorite just because she depends on you so much."

Sarah laughed. "Her *favorite?* She can't stand the sight of me. She'd marry me off in a heartbeat if she could find someone to take me off her hands."

"That isn't true. You know she would be lost without you." With a start, Allie realized that Mildred was going to get a chance to see what life was like without Sarah once Sarah went to prison. That is, unless she got away with murdering Nick. With Allie out of the way, Sarah just might.

"I still can't believe you killed him," Allie said as she searched her mind for anything within reach of where she was standing that she could use to defend herself. Something dawned on her. "How did you get my gun?"

"Mother had sent me to your cabin to see if you still had that pink sweater she gave you for Christmas. You never wore it and it was driving her crazy. I told her pink didn't look good on you, but she got it on sale... You know how she is."

Oh yes, she knew. That ugly pink sweater. Allie had put the gun under it behind the shoe boxes.

"When I found the gun, I took it. I was thinking I would try to scare Nick. After all, we have the same genes. He should have known I could be as heartless as him. But Nick had always underestimated me. I tried to talk to him, but he went off on women, you in particular."

Allie blinked in surprise. *"Me?"*

"He said some women needed to be kept in their place and that you thought you were going to leave him and take his child. He had news for you. He laughed, saying how you'd been stealing small amounts of his money thinking he wouldn't notice but he was on to you. He'd given you a few days to think about what you were doing, but when he came back there were going to be big changes. He was going to take you in hand. He said, 'I'll kill her before I'll let her leave me.' Then he told me to get out of his way and took off up the trail."

So Nick hadn't been promising to change, she thought. He was going to change her when he got back. Allie felt sick to her stomach, imagining what Nick would have been like if he had ever returned home to find her packing to leave him.

"His parting shot was to yell back at me. 'You big fat ugly pig. Go home to your mommy because when I get back your butt is out of that guesthouse.' Then he laughed and disappeared into the trees."

"Oh, Sarah, I'm so sorry. Nick was horrible. If you tell the police all of this—and I will back you up—I'm sure they will—"

"Will what? Let me go? You can't be that naive. I'll go to prison."

Allie had a crazy thought that prison would be preferable to living with Mildred Taylor.

"No, Allie, there is another way. You are the only one who knows what I did."

"If you kill me, they'll eventually catch you and since this will be cold-blooded murder, you will never get out of prison. Don't throw your life away because of Nick."

"I'm going to make you a deal," Sarah said. "I will spare your daughter if you do what I say."

"What? You would hurt Natalie?" Allie's terror ramped up as she realized this was a woman who felt no remorse for killing her own brother. Nor would she feel any for killing her sister-in-law now. That she could even think of hurting Natalie…

"Do you know why I look like I do?" Sarah asked. "I made myself fat after my mother's first divorce when I was just a little older than Natalie." She stepped closer, making Allie take a step back. "My stepfather thought I was adorable and couldn't keep his hands off me. My other stepfathers were just as bad until I gained enough weight that, like my mother, they only had contempt for me."

Allie couldn't hold back the tears. "I'm so sorry. I had no idea."

"No one did. My mother knew, though." Her eyebrow

shot up. "That surprises you?" She laughed. "You really have no idea what *Mother Taylor* is capable of doing or why she dotes on her granddaughter. This latest husband is divorcing her, but there will be another husband, one who will think your little Natalie is adorable. Think about that. You do what I say and I will make sure what happened to me doesn't happen to Nat."

Allie was too stunned almost to breathe. What was Sarah saying?

"That's right, Mother Taylor *needs* Natalie," her sister-in-law said. "Now you can either take this gun and shoot yourself or I will shoot you. But if I have to do it, I will probably get caught as you say and go to prison. Imagine what will happen to Natalie without me here to protect her. Oh, and don't even think about turning the gun on me because trust me I will take you with me and Natalie will have a new grandpa, one who will adore her."

Allie couldn't bear the choice Sarah was demanding she make. "Natalie needs me," she pleaded as she looked at the .45 her sister-in-law held out to her.

"She needs me more. Just imagine the danger Natalie would have been in if I hadn't warned you."

"Don't you think I suspected something was wrong at that house? I didn't like Natalie going there. I didn't trust your family."

"With good reason as it turns out. You have good mothering instincts. I wonder what my life would have been like if I'd had a good mother?"

Allie's heart went out to her even though the woman was determined she would die tonight. "I'm so sorry. Sarah, but we don't have to do this. I won't tell the police about the dent in the pickup."

"You're too honest. Every time you saw me, we would both know." She shook her head. "One day you would have to clear your conscience. You know what would happen to me if I went to prison. No, this is the best way. Think of your daughter."

How could she think of anything else? That's when she heard the vehicle approaching.

Sarah got a strange look on her face as she cocked her head at the sound of the motor roaring up into the yard. "This has to end now," she said.

Allie couldn't imagine who had just driven up. Dana and the kids? She couldn't take the chance that someone else would walk into this.

She grabbed for the gun.

JACKSON HIT THE door running. He told himself he was going to look like a damned fool barging in like this. But all his instincts told him something was very wrong.

As he burst through the door, he saw Allie and Sarah. Then he saw the gun they were struggling over.

The sound of the report in the tiny cabin was deafening. Jackson jumped between them going for the gun that Sarah still gripped in her hands. The silence after the gunshot was shattered as Allie began to scream.

Jackson fought to get the gun out of Sarah's hands. She was stronger than she looked. Her eyes were wide. She smiled at him as she managed to pull the trigger a second time.

The second silence after the gunshot was much louder.

"Allie, are you hit?" Jackson cried as he wrenched the gun from Sarah's hand.

She looked at him, tears in her eyes, and shook her head.

For a moment all three of them stood there, then Sarah fell to her knees, Allie dropping to the floor with her, to take the woman in her arms.

"She killed herself," Allie said to Jackson. "She could have killed me, but she turned the gun on herself." Still holding Sarah, Allie began to cry.

   Jackson pulled out the phone, tapped in 911 and asked
for an ambulance and the marshal, but one look at Sarah
and he also asked for the coroner.

Epilogue

Be careful who you marry—including the family you marry into. That had been Jackson's mother's advice when he'd married Juliet. He hadn't listened. But Allie's in-laws made Juliet's look like a dream family.

"If you want to file charges," Marshal Hud Savage was saying. "You can get your mother-in-law for trespassing, vandalism, criminal mischief…but as far as the gaslighting…"

"I don't want to file charges," Allie said. "The real harm she's done… Well, there isn't a law against it, at least not for Mildred. And like you said, no way to prove it. How is Mildred?"

After what Allie had told him, Jackson hoped the woman was going through her own private hell. She deserved much worse.

"She's shocked, devastated, but knowing Mildred, she'll bounce back," Hud said. "How are you doing?"

"I'm okay. I'm just glad it's over."

Jackson could see the weight of all this on her. He wanted to scoop her and Natalie up and take them far away from this mess. But he knew the timing was all wrong. Allie had to deal with this before she would be free of Nick and his family.

"I did talk to the psychic Belinda took you to," Hud said. "She claims she didn't know what was planned. Mildred had given her a recording of Nick's voice that had been digitally altered with Drew helping with any extra words that were needed. She alleges she was as shocked as anyone when Nick said what he did."

"I believe her," Allie said.

"As for who shot your horse up in the mountains..." Hud rubbed a hand over his face. "I've arrested Drew for that. I can't hold him for long without evidence, but he does own a .22 caliber rifle and he did have access to the ranch."

"So that whole family gets off scot-free?" Jackson demanded.

Hud raised a brow. "I wouldn't say scot-free. I'd love to throw the book at Mildred and Drew, believe me. But neither will see jail time I'm afraid. Their justice will have to come when they meet their maker." Hud shook his head and turned to Jackson. "I heard Austin is recovering fine."

"It was touch and go for a while, but he's tough. The doctor said he will be released from the hospital in a week or so, but he is looking at weeks if not months before he can go back to work. He might actually get up to Montana to see the Texas Boys Barbecue joint before the grand opening."

"I suppose you're headed back to Texas then?" Hud asked. "Dana said Ford will be starting kindergarten this year?"

Jackson nodded. "I suppose I need to get a few things sorted out fairly soon."

ALLIE COULDN'T FACE the cabin. She had nothing but bad memories there. So she'd been so relieved when Dana had insisted she and Natalie stay in one of the cabins. All but one of them was now free since Laramie had gone back to Texas, and Hayes and McKenzie had bought a ranch down the highway with a large house that they were remodeling. Only Jackson and Ford were still in their cabin, not that

Ford spent much time there since he was having so much fun with his cousins.

The same with Natalie. Allie hardly saw her over the next few days. She'd gotten through the funerals of Sarah and a second one for Nick. Mildred had tried to make her feel guilty about Sarah's death. But when Mildred started insisting that Natalie come stay with her, Allie had finally had to explain to her mother-in-law that she wouldn't be seeing Nat and why.

Of course Mildred denied everything, insisting Sarah had been a liar and blamed everything on her poor mother.

"We're done," Allie said. "No matter what I decide to do in the future, you're not going to be a part of my life or Natalie's."

"I'll take you to court, I'll…" Mildred had burst into tears. "How can you be so cruel to me? It's because you have all my Nickie's money now. I can't hold my head up in this canyon anymore, my husband is divorcing me, Drew is selling out and leaving… Where am I supposed to go?"

"I don't care as long as I never have to see you." Allie had walked away from her and hadn't looked back.

"I don't want Nick's insurance money," she'd told Dana the day she and Natalie had moved into one of the ranch cabins.

"Use just what you need and put the rest away for Natalie. Who knows what a good education will cost by the time Nat goes to college? Then put that family behind you."

But it was her own family that Allie was struggling to put behind her, she thought as she saw Megan drive up in the ranch yard. Megan had been calling her almost every day. She hadn't wanted to talk to her. She didn't want to now, but she knew she had to deal with it, no matter how painful it was.

Stepping out on the porch, she watched her half sister get out of the car. Natalie, who'd been playing with the kids, saw her aunt and ran to her. Allie watched Megan hug Natalie to her and felt a lump form in her throat.

"We can talk out here," she told Megan as Natalie went to join her friends.

Allie took a seat on the porch swing. Megan remained standing. Allie saw that she'd been crying.

"I used to ask about you when I was little," Megan said. "I'd seen photographs of you and you were so pretty." She let out a chuckle. "I was so jealous of your green eyes and your dimples. I remember asking Dad why I got brown eyes and no holes in my cheeks."

Allie said nothing, just letting her talk, but her heart ached as she listened.

"I always wanted to be you," Megan said. "Dad wouldn't talk about your mother, so that made me all the more curious about what had happened to her. When I found out... I was half afraid when I met you, but then you were so sweet. And Natalie—" she waved a hand through the air, her face splitting into a huge smile "—I fell in love with her the moment I saw her. But I guess I was looking for cracks in your sanity even before Nick was killed and Mildred began telling me things. I'm sorry. Can you ever forgive me?"

Allie had thought that what she couldn't do was ever trust Megan again, especially with Natalie. But as she looked at her stepsister, she knew she had to for Natalie's sake. She rose from the chair and stepped to her sister to pull her into her arms.

They both began to cry, hugging each other tightly. There was something to this family thing, Allie thought. They might not be related by blood, but Allie couldn't cut Megan out of their lives, no matter where the future led them.

ALLIE WATCHED HER sister with Natalie and the kids. Megan, at twenty-three, was still a kid herself, she thought as she watched her playing tag with them. She knew she'd made the right decision and felt good about it.

She felt freer than she had in years. She'd also made up with Belinda. They would never be as close, not after her friend had kept her relationship with Nick from her. But they would remain friends and Allie was glad of it.

Belinda said she wanted her to meet the man in her life. Maybe Allie would, since it seemed that this time the relationship was serious.

Drew had tried to talk to her at the funeral, but she'd told him what she'd told his mother. She never wanted to see either of them again and with both of them leaving the canyon, she probably never would.

Beyond that, she didn't know. She would sell the cabin, Nick's pickup, everything she owned and start over. She just didn't know where yet, she thought as she saw Jackson coming up the mountainside.

He took off his Stetson as he approached the steps to her cabin and looked up at her. "Allie," he said. "I was hoping we could talk."

She motioned him up onto the porch. He looked so bashful. She smiled at the sight of his handsome face. The cowboy had saved her more times than she could count. He'd coming riding in on his white horse like something out of a fairytale and stolen her heart like an old-time outlaw.

"What did you want to talk about?" she asked. He seemed as tongue tied as Ford had been when he'd met Natalie.

"I…I…" He swallowed. "I love you."

Her eyes filled with tears. Those were the three little words she had ached to hear. Her heart pounded as she stepped to him. "I love you, Jackson."

He let out a whoop and picking her up, spun her around. As he set her down, he was still laughing. "Run away with me?"

"Anywhere."

"Texas?"

"If that's where you want to go."

"Well, here is the problem. You know my father, Harlan? I think he might just make a better grandfather than he ever did a father. I want Ford to have that."

She smiled. "Montana?"

"This is where I was born. I guess it is calling back my whole family. Did I tell you that my mother's new husband, Franklin, owns some land in the state? They're going to be spending half the year here. Hayes and McKenzie bought a place up the road and Tag and Lily will be living close by, as well. Dana said we can stay on the ranch until we find a place. The only thing we have to do is make sure our kids are in school next month."

"Montana it is then."

"Wait a minute." He looked shy again as he dropped to one knee. She noticed he had on new jeans and a nice Western dress shirt. Reaching into his pocket, he pulled out a ring box. "You're going to think I'm nuts. I bought this the day Tag and I went to pick up his rings for the wedding. I saw it and I thought, 'It's the same color as Allie's eyes.' Damned if I knew what I was going to do with it. Until now." He took a breath and let it out. "Would you marry me, Allie?"

She stared down at the beautiful emerald-green engagement ring set between two sparkling diamonds and felt her eyes widen. "It's the most beautiful thing I have ever seen."

He laughed. "No, honey, that would be you," he said as he put the ring on her finger, then drew her close and kissed her. "I can't wait to tell the kids. I have a feeling Ford and Natalie are going to like living in Montana on their very own ranch, with their very own horses and lots of family around them."

Allie felt like pinching herself. She'd been through so much, but in the end she'd gotten something she'd never dreamed of, a loving man she could depend on and love with all her heart. For so long, she'd been afraid to hope that dreams could come true.

She smiled as Jackson took her hand and they went to tell the kids the news.

* * * * *

"Alex, I have something to tell you," she said.

"Your tone of voice worries me."

"It's nothing bad. It's about that 'virus' I was fighting in February." She took another deep breath. "Do you remember that big fight we had in January?"

"Yeah," he said, "I do. I can't remember what it was about, though."

"It doesn't matter now," she said. "What's important is how we made up the next day," she added.

She could feel him staring at her. Was he remembering that night? They'd made love with a vengeance, downstairs in front of a blazing fire, and had slept there all night. "I've been trying to tell you this since you got home," she added. "I was wrong about the cause of my nausea. Brace yourself. I'm about four months pregnant."

She could see the whites of his eyes widen. "Say that again," he whispered.

"We're going to have a baby."

STRANDED

BY
ALICE SHARPE

Published in Great Britain 2014
by Mills & Boon, an imprint of Harlequin (UK) Limited,
Eton House, 18-24 Paradise Road, Richmond, Surrey, TW9 1SR

© 2014 Alice Sharpe

ISBN: 978-0-263-91363-7

46-0714

Harlequin (UK) Limited's policy is to use papers that are natural, renewable and recyclable products and made from wood grown in sustainable forests. The logging and manufacturing processes conform to the legal environmental regulations of the country of origin.

Printed and bound in Spain
by Blackprint CPI, Barcelona

Alice Sharpe met her husband-to-be on a cold, foggy beach in Northern California. One year later they were married. Their union has survived the rearing of two children, a handful of earthquakes registering over 6.5, numerous cats and a few special dogs, the latest of which is a yellow Lab named Annie Rose. Alice and her husband now live in a small rural town in Oregon, where she devotes the majority of her time to pursuing her second love, writing.

This book is dedicated to sweet Ruby Rose.
Welcome, baby.

Prologue

February

To Alex Foster, the flight between Blunt Falls, Montana, and Shatterhorn, Nevada, felt ill-fated from the get-go. The unexpected deteriorating weather was just the latest obstacle, but at least it was one that could be managed by some decent flying skills and a deviation from his flight plan.

He yawned and rubbed his eyes, fighting a growing fatigue he couldn't afford. Unscrewing the cap on a new bottle of the vitamin-enhanced water he carried when he piloted his plane, he took a long swallow. The numbers on the charts swam before his eyes and he blinked, performed a few fuzzy calculations and changed radio frequencies to the Bozeman, Montana beacon. He banked the plane toward the east, hoping to avoid the worst of the system and arrive just a little late.

No big deal. Nate would explain the facts of life when it came to flying to their friend Mike. And Mike's issues would be there in two hours or two days—they weren't going away anytime soon. The poor guy had been devastated by the incident all three men shared last Labor Day when a lone teenage gunman had shot and killed four kids in a random attack at a Nevada shopping mall.

Since then, Mike had been gathering data he believed hinted at a conspiracy. This meeting would let them review what Mike had learned and maybe, hopefully, help him get past some of his wild ideas.

A glimpse out the Cessna window revealed nothing but icy-white sky that seemed to swirl in his head. He climbed higher, hoping to find less turbulent air. He was kind of glad Jessica hadn't come along. She'd claimed she was fighting a virus and he'd accused her of making it up so she wouldn't have to be with him. Maybe some time apart would help, he didn't know. However, now, with his vision blurring and his stomach turning, he considered he might owe her an apology.

He yawned again and took another swallow of the drink as he tried to quench his thirst.

After thirty more minutes, the break in the weather he'd anticipated still hadn't materialized. His eyes drifted shut and he opened them quickly, making himself sit up straighter. As he did periodically, he glanced at the control panel. It took him a second to actually register what he saw.

The oil-pressure indicator showed a rapid decline toward the red zone. He stared at the gauge with disbelief, then tapped the glass. At that moment he became aware of a burning odor and peered out the window where he found oil flying over the coaming. Liquid drops hit the windshield and crawled away, leaving portentous snail-like tracks on the glass.

A quick check of the gauge showed pressure still falling. He flipped the radio frequencies again, but the unit was now silent. He tore off the headphones as flames flared from the engine compartment. Almost simultaneously, he pulled the handle to turn off the fuel tanks and yanked on the fire extinguisher lever. Smoke billowed from under the cowling, but dissipated at once.

And then the engine seized.

The fire was out but the plane was dead.

Disaster was imminent. He was off his flight plan, somewhere over the Bitterroot Mountains in the middle of the Rockies. He had an EPIRB aboard and knew the emergency beacon would signal once activated by a crash, but unlike the newer models that communicated with satellites, his older unit required a search plane to fly directly overhead. Would anyone look for him this far afield from his expected route?

The plane began losing altitude. He spiraled down through the clouds, into the storm. Visibility cleared for a few seconds and he saw a large snow-covered meadow to the north. He quickly corrected his course to aim for that, going into a glide, pushing the yoke ahead to avoid a stall.

Seconds seemed to drag and then everything sped up as the ground once again appeared closer than ever. The plane skimmed over the snowy treetops ringing the meadow and shuddered as it made its first bounce. That was immediately followed by the scream of twisted metal as the landing-gear struts tore from their housings. The wounded plane skimmed along the snow on its belly, racing into the middle of the meadow, snow flying at the windshield.

At last the Cessna came to an abrupt and sudden stop. Alex flew forward into the instrument panel. His chest impacted with the yoke, his left leg caught and twisted in the mangled metal below. The outside of the cabin was covered with snow. He wiped something from his eyes— blood—then immediately struggled with the door, pushing against the buildup, knowing he had to get it open before it froze shut. He almost choked on relief as weak daylight flooded the cabin.

A strange cracking noise drove ice picks through his nervous system. The noise came again and he recognized it for what it was. With horror, he looked down to find water rising over his shoes. As quick as he'd ever done anything in his life, he grabbed his backpack and the medical kit and threw both through the open door. He undid his seat belt, took a steadying breath and screamed with pain as he ruthlessly extricated his leg. There was blood everywhere but he'd have lots of time to worry about that later. If there was a later...

Clenching his teeth, he used his upper-body strength to pull himself through the open door.

This was no meadow; this was a lake covered with ice and the plane, heavy with unspent fuel, had broken through. He scrambled out the door and landed on his gear. The fall sent a stab of unbearable agony racing from his heel to his groin, and he had to struggle to keep from passing out. Priority one: keep himself and his gear from going into the water. Get away, get away, as fast as possible, beat the cracks spreading out around him. His hands were clumsy as he tied things together and then he dragged himself away from the wreck, using his elbows for traction, trailing his gear from his belt, the fissures continuing to open up all around him.

Chapter One

Three Months Later

Jessica's cell phone rang as she sat at her desk grading a math quiz. She jumped in her seat and swallowed a lump of panic as she dug the device from the jacket hanging over the back of her chair. You'd think after all this time a ringing phone wouldn't cause this fearful knee-jerk reaction, but it did and it probably always would. Until they found his body, anyway. Or until she knew the truth.

She clicked it on and said, "Yes?" in a breathless voice because she didn't recognize the number on the screen and that was always nerve-racking. How many times had she imagined learning news of Alex's fate from a stranger? Almost as many times as she'd imagined him calling her himself from some secret spot in Middle America where he'd gone to start a life without her. That was the trouble when a husband simply vanished. You never knew if he was dead or alive; you lived in limbo. Any closure would be better than none.

The caller was a salesman wanting to know if she needed new drainpipes and she got rid of him right away. The truth was, her house was in limbo, too. If it wasn't for Billy Summers and his sweet-natured persistence in helping her with chores, she imagined she would just let the place crumble around her.

And that had to end. She had to get a grip. Maybe it was time to think about selling the house, getting something smaller. Could she do that? Not yet. But the question nagged her: What would she do if Alex walked through the door?

The sun beating through the high windows made the room too warm. She folded her arms on her desk and rested her forehead against her hands, closing her eyes. Restless nights usually caught up with her in the late afternoon, and apparently today was no exception. The school was mostly empty now, but occasional footsteps moving in the halls gave her a reassuring feeling of not being alone as did the faint whirring and beeping of distant machines set to automatic timers.

Thank goodness the school term was almost finished and she'd been allowed to back out of teaching summer school this year. She loved the kids in her remedial classes at Blunt Falls High, but she needed time away from them and everyone else. Who would have guessed constant pity could be so exhausting? She closed her eyes and let her mind drift for a while.

A nearby noise jerked her out of her stupor and she looked up to find a stranger standing in her open doorway. As the school was very strict about allowing unauthorized people on the campus, this man had to be someone's father, but he didn't look like any other parent she'd met at this school. He was tall and dark, thin, with uncut hair and a full beard. Dark glasses covered his eyes. His jeans and corduroy shirt appeared too big for his frame, while his face and hands were weathered looking. There was a healed abrasion across one cheekbone and another slashing across what she could see of his forehead. As he moved into the class, she detected a definite hitch in his left leg.

She found herself on her feet without consciously deciding to rise. "May I help you?"

He took off the dark glasses, folding them away as he continued moving between the desks. The look in his hazel eyes pinned her to the floor and she all but stopped breathing as her throat closed.

And then he was right beside her, taking her hands, looking at her as though he'd never seen her before. He brought her right hand up to his face and laid her palm against his hairy cheek. His eyes sparkled with tears.

"Alex?" she murmured, searching his face with a disbelieving intensity. "Oh, my God. Alex?"

His nod was almost imperceptible. His tears moistened her fingertips. "Are you real or am I dreaming?" she mumbled.

"If you're dreaming, then so am I," he said, his voice choked with emotion.

She forgot to wonder how she would feel or react and just flung herself against him. Tears of relief filled her eyes as he held her. She finally pushed herself away. "How is this possible?" she asked. "Where have you been?"

He pulled her back against him, burying his face against her neck, holding her tight as if he'd never let her go. "I crashed in the Bitterroots," he said. "I've just been trying to stay alive until the snow melted so I could get back."

"I thought you were dead," she said. "Or maybe even worse, that you…"

She stopped short.

"I can't believe I'm holding you," he whispered.

She leaned back to gaze up at him, smoothing his hair

away from his brow with trembling fingers, trying to find the man she married under the scars and hair. "Are you all right? You're limping. And your poor face." She searched his eyes for answers.

Instead of providing them, he tugged her back to his chest, and this time his lips landed on hers. Even when times were tough between them, the physical connection had been quicksilver and so it still was, all the sweeter for the fact that until a few minutes before, she'd thought she'd never see him again.

A woman's voice cut in from the open doorway and they both turned to find the school's principal, Silvia Greenspan. "I'm sorry to interrupt you guys," she said. It appeared she knew Alex was at the school, had probably spoken to him when he came onto the campus. She smiled at them both fondly as she added, "There are tons of reporters outside. Alex, I think someone in the office got excited and alerted the local television channel that you'd reappeared here at the school. I don't know how long we can hold them back." She turned and left, her footsteps clicking in retreat as she hurried back down the hall.

"How did you get to Blunt Falls?" Jessica asked.

"Doris and Duke Booker brought me. They're the people who more or less rescued me."

"Rescued you! Alex, what happened?"

"Later, okay?" He looked at her longingly. "There's so much I need to tell you."

"I know," she said, her mind still grappling with his offhand comment about being rescued. "Me, too."

"I'm sorry about the fight we had before I left. It was my fault."

"Not now," she said, straightening his collar. "You have to go talk to the press."

He shook his head. "No."

"What do you mean, no? Everyone is going to be so relieved to hear you're home safe and sound."

"They can wait," he said. He gestured at her cluttered desk. "Anything here need to go home with you?"

"These tests," she said, picking up the math papers she'd been grading. He retrieved her briefcase from the closet and held it open for her as she deposited the papers. "Why are we running away?"

"Because," he said, sounding like one of her students. "There's a back way out of here through the gym, isn't there?"

"Yes, but—"

"But nothing," he interrupted as he took her jacket from her chair and draped it over her shoulders. "Where's your purse?"

"I'll get it," she said as she unlocked the desk drawer where she kept it during classes. "Why don't you want to talk to the newspeople? What's wrong?"

"Nothing is wrong, not like that. I just think we have the right to reconnect before the blitz. Don't you?"

"Yes," she said, nodding, suddenly realizing he was right. There were so many things she had to tell him about the past three months, things he needed to understand, things that would redefine what he thought he knew about the world, things she didn't want him hearing from someone holding a camera on his face. And, she realized with a jolt of panic, there were things she needed to take care of, too. Things she didn't want him to see.

She followed him toward the door, his limp a visual reminder of the struggle he must have endured. "Hurry," she added as they raced down the hall and out the back of the gym toward the baseball field, which they could circle to access the parking lot.

It was a tremendous relief to slide behind the wheel of

her car. "Duck your head," she muttered, driving out of
the lot. Their path led them past two or three television
vans with satellite dishes on their roofs and a growing
crowd of people milling about. Alex didn't sit up again
until they were half a mile away and she gave him the
all clear. Their gazes met and he smiled but she knew
it wouldn't be long before reporters figured out they'd
slipped away.

And it wasn't as though they'd be hard to find.

"NOTHING MUCH HAS CHANGED," Alex said in wonder as he
followed Jessica into the house and closed the front door
behind them. It seemed surreal that for the past one hundred and three days he'd been living in the most primi-
tive of conditions while his wife, his house, his job—his
world—existed right here as it always had. At the time,
emerged as he was in basic survival, all this had seemed
like a distant fantasy he'd never live to revisit, but here it
had been all along, chugging away without him, apparently none the worse for his absence.

The same thing had happened when he'd been de-
ployed in the army, only then he'd been shot at, as well.
On the other hand, he hadn't been alone and there was a
lot to be said for companionship.

The house was a newer one, built in a cluster of similar
houses located in a small wooded area a few miles outside of Blunt Falls. They'd bought it with plans to fill the
rooms upstairs with their children and had pictured them
running through the trees and splashing in the shallow
stream at the bottom of the gulch with the neighborhood
kids as playmates. But that had never happened. Oh, the
neighbors' families grew all right, but theirs didn't and
now, in some ways, the houses all around them, strewn
with tricycles and sandboxes, formed a painful reminder

that things didn't always work out the way you thought they would.

Now the house welcomed him back with years of memories, and he stood by the big rock fireplace just trying to center himself. Meanwhile, Jessica closed the drapes and turned to face him. She'd deposited her purse and briefcase on the chair nearest the door, much as she always had and now stood looking up the stairs as though she wanted to dash up to their room.

He reached for her hand. "We won't have long before they track us down," he said.

She looked at him and nodded. "Good point."

"I'm a little beat," he said with a smile. "Let's go sit at the table like we used to. Let's talk."

"Yes," she said, nodding. "Okay."

He claimed the chair facing the living-room door and patted the one beside it. She entered the dining room behind him, her brown eyes velvety, enhanced by the oversize cream tunic she wore over slim black jeans.

She looked good, her auburn hair longer than it had been in a while, combed straight back from her oval-shaped face which was devoid of makeup as it almost always was. He'd been afraid he'd find her worn-out and grief stricken, but instead she seemed almost luminescent. His disappearance didn't seem to have hurt her.

Well, why should it have? They'd been whisper close to a separation for most of the past year, so caught up in their different lives that they'd become like that old saying, "Ships passing in the night." In fact, for the past three months his greatest fear had been that she would be relieved he'd vanished. No more fights, no more disappointments, no stress. Just over. And who was to say that that isn't what happened? Maybe she'd moved on, maybe she'd even found someone else.

Maybe he should stop borrowing trouble....

"Are you hungry?" she asked, standing behind the chair he'd patted. It provided a good view of the garden and he'd already noticed the plethora of bushes and flowers that bloomed with an intensity he didn't remember ever seeing before. Some plants were absolutely covered with buds, promising radiant blossoms in the weeks to come. She must have spent hours out there tending that garden, loving it.

"The Bookers stuffed me," he said, a bit distracted by the beauty sweeping across the yard toward the doors. He pulled his attention back to her. "They grow or hunt just about everything they eat. My poor digestive tract is probably struggling to cope after existing on three-plus months of pretty much nothing but fish."

She slid a basket of clothes across the table and started folding them. He got the distinct impression she was keeping her hands busy. Either that, or she was creating a barrier by positioning the basket between them. "Where did you meet these people?" she asked.

"I literally stumbled into their garden and collapsed in their asparagus patch."

She stopped folding a lacy bra and stared at him. He tore his gaze away from the undergarment and all the memories it provoked as she said, "You're not making any sense. Where have you been for three months? What exactly happened to you?"

He told her about the storm and the dead engine, ending with the crash far off his reported route and the immediate sinking of the plane. He touched on his nightmare crawl across the lake to the relative safety of the shore and how he'd managed to live through the first night by digging out a trench around the base of a tree and covering it over with evergreen boughs.

"I can't believe you survived," she said when he paused. "Did you ever see a search plane?"

"Once," he said, all but wincing at the memory. "I woke up to the sound of an engine and scrambled out of my hole like a crippled badger."

"When was this?"

"Two days after the crash. I had to grab the makeshift crutches to get out into the clear where they could see me. The emergency beacon I carried went down with the Cessna."

She almost rolled her eyes and he smiled. "I know, I know. You asked me to update my equipment a hundred times."

"Two hundred," she said.

"Well, you were obviously right. Anyway, by the time I got out from under the trees, they were gone and they didn't come back."

"That must have been horrible," she said, visibly shuddering. "How is your leg now?"

"Pretty good. I'll probably limp for the rest of my life, but considering everything, that's not so bad."

She nodded. "Okay, now tell me how you ended up in an asparagus patch."

He shrugged as though it was all no big deal. The actuality of it was a whole different matter. "I waited until the snow started to melt, smoked a bunch of fish, broke camp and stared downhill, following a stream that fed from the lake. After a few days, I ran into tended land, though I didn't see a house. There was this big, tall fence surrounding some seedlings so I went through the gate to see if anything was mature enough to eat yet. I found a few strawberries, gobbled them up and must have passed out or fallen asleep because the next thing I knew, an older woman was shaking me awake. She told me her name was Doris and that she and her husband, Duke, had built themselves a place just over the rise. They nursed me for a day or so and then they insisted on driving me home and that took another two days."

"Thank heavens she found you," Jessica said. "You should see a doctor about your leg."

"I will. Right now, it's enough just to be sitting here." He ran a hand across his hairy chin and added, "I need a shave and my own clothes. Duke lent me these."

"They sound like incredibly kind people. But, Alex, why didn't you phone me?"

"They don't have a phone," he said. "No television, no internet, no electricity. They're the back-to-nature type. I did call my parents on the way, though."

"But not me."

Did that bother her? Was she thinking that in the months before he disappeared he'd often not reported in as often as he should because it always seemed to come with an argument or apathy, either one of them hard to take? "I didn't want you to find out about me over a phone," he said gently. "I wanted to see you. I wanted to look in your eyes, to know if it mattered to you that I was alive."

"Of course it matters to me," she said, brow furling. "What a terrible thing to say."

"You know what I mean, Jess."

She nodded as she bit her lip and took a deep breath.

"Still," he continued, gesturing at the wall phone. "I'm kind of surprised that thing isn't ringing off the hook. Mom has had time to tell all the relatives by now."

"I have it switched to message only," she said. "I had to. It felt like every call was a possible ambush. I had to be able to deal with people on my own terms, at least once I was inside this house." She met his gaze and smoothed back her hair. "I'm sorry, Alex, that must sound selfish to you."

"No," he said gently, patting the chair again as she finished folding the laundry. "No, it sounds like survival, that's all."

She sat down next to him, their knees all but touching. He ached to fold her in his arms. He wanted to tell her that he'd been thinking of little else but her for weeks and weeks and that he wanted them to be together, to make things work. But she was distant and jittery and he wasn't brave enough to admit his feelings and have them dashed in his face.

For that matter, dare he trust his feelings? The past several days had been a roller coaster of a ride, exhausting on all levels. Being back was strange and wonderful and truth be known, scary as hell.

He caught her studying his face and wished he'd taken Duke Booker up on his offer for a shave and a haircut so he'd look a little more like he had before.

"There are things you need to know," she said.

He braced himself. Here it came. She'd moved on.

She shook her head as she added, "Maybe you should call Nate and get him to tell you."

"Nate?" What did his best friend have to do with her?

"He's been so concerned about you," she said.

"I can imagine," Alex murmured, trying to imagine what it must have been like for Nate to keep waiting for a plane that never arrived. They'd met in the army, had both ended up with careers in law enforcement, Nate as a deputy in Arizona and Alex a police detective in Blunt Falls. Now they were fishing buddies when the opportunity allowed.

"What does Nate need to tell me that you can't?" he asked.

She shook her head. "Okay, I'll try to explain. Before people start asking you questions, you've got to know a few things. There are a lot of people, Nate included, who don't think your plane crash was an accident."

He frowned. "What?"

"Right around the time your plane disappeared, Nate was almost killed. That's why he couldn't join the search to try to find you. Worse than all that, though, is that Mike Donovan was murdered."

"Mike is dead?"

"Yes. I'm sorry."

Mike wasn't a close pal, like Nate, but Alex had cared for him all the same. Head spinning, he murmured, "Nate thinks all three of us were targeted by the same person?"

"Yes, a man in Shatterhorn who sang your accolades after the mall incident. Everyone refers to him simply as The Shatterhorn Killer and not by name, a tribute to those he killed or caused to die. Anyway, he's dead now, thanks to an unidentified driver Nate saw purposefully run him down with a car. This same man was also behind the shooting at the Shatterhorn mall and apparently, him and others like him have been responsible for all sorts of mayhem occurring on national holidays around the country. Remember that incident in Hawaii last Pearl Harbor Day where some angry kid shot and killed those off-duty soldiers on the beach? Things like that. Everyday events shattered by violence. And everyone is certain something is going to happen this Memorial Day, too."

Alex stared at her a moment, trying to make sense of all this. "But you said the guy was run over."

"There are apparently others. Even if this man wasn't in Blunt Falls when your plane was sabotaged, he could have hired someone to help him do it."

Alex simply couldn't wrap his head around any of it.

The lonely austerity of the mountains suddenly seemed like the epicenter of civilization and this place a jungle. "Why would anyone do this?" he asked.

"Oh, it's complicated, Alex. Something about creating terror for people engaged in normal, ordinary situations so they won't support any kind of weapon control. It's domestic terrorism but with a spin. They call themselves patriots and they recruit malcontent kids to do the dirty work. It's been in the news lately, but I've been a little distracted.... Nate can tell you more and I know the FBI and FAA are going to want to talk to you, too."

Welcome home, he thought. Here all this time he'd assumed he'd been in an everyday kind of plane crash, no intrigue, no drama, just rotten luck and maybe a bad gasket or something. And now he was hearing someone may have tried to murder him.

The fact was the day of the crash was something of a blur. He hadn't felt very good; he'd thought he was getting Jessica's flu. He'd been tired and thirsty and out of it, and then the plunging oil pressure, so sudden and dramatic and final.

Could that have been caused by someone tampering with his plane? But he'd had the required maintenance performed on the plane—in fact, he was a stickler for that. He'd also conducted a preflight check. He could vaguely remember doing it although like everything else about that day, the recollection was hazy.

"We don't know for sure that your crash was premeditated, but it's awfully coincidental," Jessica said, and he wasn't positive but it sounded to him as though she was trying to ease some of his shock.

"Yeah," he said. He took a deep breath before trying to shy away from all of this for a moment. "How about you?" he asked. "How have you been? Did anyone try to harm you?"

"No, I've been fine," she said, and then shook her head. "That's not true. I've been a wreck."

"In some odd way, I'm glad to hear it," he admitted. He took a deep breath. "I've had all sorts of time to regret what I said that last morning. I shouldn't have even suggested you were lying to me about having the flu."

"I wasn't making it up, you know. I really did feel sick."

"I know. I think I had a touch of it, too. It's just that we'd been going our own ways so often that it was beginning to feel like we'd never hook back up."

"I know," she said.

"You began to say something earlier," he added. "Something like, there being something worse than me being dead. You stopped yourself. What were you going to say? What would have been worse than me being dead?"

She blinked a few times and he could almost see the wheels turning in her head. "I don't remember where I was going with that," she said at last.

Their gazes met and she looked away. She may not have been lying about having a virus but she was lying now, he was sure of it. He wanted to demand she explain, but he couldn't bring himself to further distance her. The warmth they'd shared in her classroom had evaporated as soon as they hit the house. How ironic would it be to survive what he'd survived just to lose everything that really mattered?

But had he really thought he could waltz back in here and erase the past year or two of tension between them with a few kisses and an apology?

"We can try again," he said very softly, searching her face.

"Try again? What do you mean?" she asked.

"Having a baby. I know you said before that you were finished hoping but I've been thinking about that, too. The doctor might have been wrong. We could consult another specialist."

"Please, Alex," she said, staring into his eyes. "This is all too much. An hour ago I thought I'd never see you again. There are things we need to discuss." She smiled and added, "That's a real understatement."

There was a sudden knock on the front door and they both turned their heads and stared into the living room as though expecting an invasion.

"I think our time before the blitz is about up," he said as the doorbell chimed. He could hear voices coming from outside and more knocks seemed to rattle the windows. "Continue with what you were saying," he urged.

"Not now, not like this," she said with a shake of her head. She pushed a few strands of hair away from her face and smiled. "Later, okay? I'll go stick these clothes in the bedroom. Will you answer the door?"

"Might as well get it over with," he said as he got to his feet. But for a second he stood there watching Jessica hurry into the kitchen with the basket on her hip. He knew she would take the back stairs up to their bedroom.

What he didn't know was what she was trying to tell him.

Chapter Two

Jessica's laptop sat on her desk. With barely a pause, she set the laundry basket aside and opened the computer. Within a few seconds, she was at her Facebook page where she spent several minutes deleting a post she'd made almost two months earlier and which she hoped and prayed Alex would never know existed.

What she'd written had seemed reasonable at the time, like turning over every rock, but now in light of what she knew, it seemed the very essence of double-crossing on her part.

She deleted all pertinent comments from friends and family and closed the laptop, able to really take a breath for the first time in an hour. Then she moved to the window and pulled aside the drape. From this vantage point, she could see all the media trucks parked outside. Several neighbors had wandered over, apparently curious about what was going on. Alex, a lone, weathered-looking figure, stood on the front lawn facing the crowd, his back to Jessica. After months of solitude, what must this day be like for him?

She hurried down the stairs, pausing to take a deep breath before going outside. They'd been a team once upon a time, like right after their marriage when no life-altering disappointments had pushed them apart. Could they be a team again?

Well, one thing was for sure. There was far too much at stake not to at least try. It was time to join Alex.

She stood to the side as he skirted questions, explaining how he'd survived and how he'd finally been able to get home. But reporters asking him about his plane and what went wrong got vague answers and he flatly refused to comment on the possibility of sabotage. He said it was too soon to talk like that, he needed more information.

Jessica was proud of the way he handled himself but not surprised. He could be a very articulate and commanding man when he wanted to be. Those qualities had drawn her to him in the first place and as she listened to him now, she once again wondered how they had grown so far apart.

When he saw her standing near, he extended his arm to welcome her to stand beside him and she did. Flashbulbs popped at the reunited, happy couple and she smiled as best she could.

Much later that night, she woke up in the middle of a dream whose details vanished upon opening her eyes. She reached across the sheets as she had done so many times before, knowing this time, finally, she would find Alex. When her fingers met nothing but rumpled sheets and blanket, she sat up and switched on the light.

For one blinding moment, she thought she'd dreamed Alex coming home. No, there on the chair was the corduroy shirt he'd borrowed from Duke Booker.

She got out of bed and shrugged on her robe, then went looking for him. The house was dark and silent and though she switched on enough lights to see where she was going, she couldn't find him anywhere. The garage still held his truck, which had been sitting in the same spot since she'd reclaimed it from the airport parking lot a few days after he vanished. That left only one place she could think of.

She didn't turn on the outside light. Closing the glass patio door behind her, she called his name into the dark and he responded at once. "Over here," he said, his voice coming from way back in the yard where it was deeply shadowed despite the moon overhead. However, she'd spent the past several restless weeks wandering around the garden at all times of the day and night and had no trouble finding her way.

Moonlight shone off the white roses that had just started to bloom. Some of the lilacs were still in flower, as well, and they added a deep, rich perfume to the night air.

Even though it was late May, temperatures dropped at night in Blunt Falls, and Jessica shivered in her thin robe. She used his voice as a guide until her vision adjusted to the dark, and then she could see him sitting on the rock wall that surrounded the pond where every spring, mallards raised their families.

"What are you doing out here at 3:00 a.m.?" she asked, but she knew. All evening she'd watched him pace the living room, turning away from his image on the television news, perusing the bookcase without touching a book, staring out the windows like a trapped animal. He'd taken a long walk after a supper he barely touched and, though he hadn't asked her not to come, she could tell he wanted to be alone. She'd determined to come clean with him right after the news conference, but his remote demeanor had kept her lips sealed.

She knew all the revelations she'd had to tell him in such a hurry weighed heavily on his mind, especially when he hadn't been able to reach Nate. But what else could she do? He had to know what had happened in his absence and it wasn't as if the rest of the world would give him a chance to recover from his ordeal before telling him all the gory details. After switching the phone back on, their evening had consisted of one call after the other until they finally turned it off again.

She'd gone to bed before him, worn-out from the day and exhausted trying to figure out where they went from here. He'd changed so much over the years and the horrible thing was that she wasn't sure exactly when it had happened. It was easy to blame their problems on not being able to have a child, but plenty of marriages thrived through much worse.

She knew things had gone downhill after the mall shooting in Shatterhorn where he and Nate had been involved in trying to stop a teenage gunman. He'd come home shaken to the core but he wouldn't talk to her about it. She'd seen the pictures in the newspaper, though—the broken glass, the blood spatters, the candlelight vigils.... No one came away from something like that without scars. But it had hurt her that he couldn't trust her with his feelings. Impatient with him, she'd allowed him to retreat even further into his work and his world.

But maybe it was even before that, even before the fertility doctors had told them to set their sights on something besides a big family unless they were open to adoption. Alex had refused to even entertain the thought of adoption and that had cut her as deep as her body's inability to conceive a child.

With nothing to say to one another and with each nursing their own disappointments, it had been easier to let go than hold on. There had been times while he was missing that she felt almost at peace with things and that now shamed her down to her toes.

"I couldn't sleep," he said softly.

She sat down on the rocks beside him, brushing aside the tulips and the forsythia. "It's hard being back, isn't it?"

He laughed under his breath. "It's all I wanted for months, to escape the snow and the outdoors and quiet—things I now miss in some ways." He put his hand over hers. "But don't think I'd rather be there than here. You know that, right?"

"Right," she said softly.

"We'll work things out," he said as if he'd been thinking about the same things she'd been thinking about.

"I hope we can," she said.

There was a moment of silence as they both folded their hands in their own laps and stared into the night. "You've really kept the yard up nice," he finally said.

"You can see it in the dark?" she teased.

"Almost. It seems to glow. But really, I noticed it earlier today. I've never seen anything like it. How did you manage it all by yourself?

"I didn't," she admitted. "Do you remember Billy Summers?"

"The kid who does odd jobs at the airfield? What about him?"

"After you...didn't come home...he showed up on the doorstep. I hadn't seen him since he graduated from high school and that has to be at least three years ago now. He'd heard about your plane disappearing and he wanted to know if he could help me. I refused at first, but he kept coming back and offering. I started giving him odd jobs. He proved to be very reliable, especially when it came to the yard."

"I would never have guessed that of Billy Summers."

"I know. He was a surprise. I told him about how I

always bought flowers for the veterans' graves on Memorial Day and he offered to plant some if I would tell him how. He brought me some little index cards and I wrote the directions down for him in simple words. I saw him checking the instructions all the time, but I don't really think they were necessary. He seems to have a way with plants. Anyway, we owe the flowers to Billy."

"And we'll be able to skip the last-minute dash to the big-box store to order flowers for Memorial Day," Alex said.

She nodded and bit her lip. She'd been about to tell Alex that all last week she'd planned to honor his memory and years of service, as well. He didn't need to hear that. "Alex, I have something to tell you," she said.

"Your tone of voice worries me."

"It's nothing bad. It's about that 'virus' I was fighting in February." She took another deep breath. "Do you remember that big fight we had in January?"

"Yeah," he said, "I do. I can't remember what it was about, though."

"It doesn't matter now," she said, but she could have enlightened him. He'd been working extra shifts, coming home late and grumpy. Talk about water under the bridge. "What's important is how we made up the next day," she added.

She could feel him staring at her. Was he remembering that night? They'd made love with a vengeance, downstairs in front of a blazing fire and slept there all night. "I've been trying to tell you this since you got home," she said. "I was wrong about the cause of my nausea. Brace yourself. I'm about four months pregnant."

She could see the whites of his eyes widen. "Say that again," he whispered.

"We're going to have a baby," she said, wishing she

had waited until morning to tell him so she could see the expression on his face.

"I can't believe this," he said, springing to his feet. "Four months? Are you okay, shouldn't you be lying down or something?"

"No. The doctor said if it's going to stick, it's going to stick."

"You shouldn't be working every day, should you?" he asked, and she could hear the panic in his voice. She understood how he felt, how amazing this must seem to him. It was the same to her, the difference being that she'd had months to get used to the idea, she'd spoken to the doctor, she knew what was going on.

"Summer vacation is coming and then the baby is due in October and with you home, I won't go back to work right away. Really, Alex, everything is fine. What I wanted to explain is that I found out about it a week or two after you disappeared. And that's why I got on Facebook. See—"

He interrupted her by pulling her to her feet and crushing her in his arms. "This is absolutely wonderful! I can hardly believe it. I promise you I'll do everything I can to make you happy. I love you."

She closed her eyes and held on to him. In a way, it was like he'd finally come home.

AFTER LAYING AWAKE for what seemed like hours, Alex got up quietly the next morning. He'd been rising with the sun and it felt unnatural to lie there when he could see daylight filtering through the curtains.

Besides, there was a lot on his mind.

Mentally he made a list. Call Nate. Make sure he still had a job on the Blunt Falls police force. Get checked out by the doctor.

He looked down at Jessica's slumbering face and added the most important thing of all: win back his wife before his baby was born.

She was so beautiful with her hair spilling over her pillow like a billowing russet-colored cloud, her lashes sweeping her cheeks, her peachy lips soft and yielding. No wonder she glowed. She was having a baby, his baby, after eight years of trying. He knew what it meant to her, he knew what it meant to him. And the urge to protect her at all costs surged through his body.

He had to pull himself together. Just as he'd planned for and worked toward walking out of the mountains every single day of his exile, he now had to put that behind him and work at moving forward in his marriage, in his job, in his life. What's done was done. He couldn't erase the past, but he could learn from it.

His reflection in the mirror wasn't particularly inspiring. The healed gashes across his cheek and forehead caused by the Cessna's broken windshield hadn't healed perfectly. But inside he knew he was stronger and more focused than he'd ever been and it was time to put all that energy to work.

The first thing he did was call Nate in Arizona. Again. The phone switched immediately to message and he wasn't sure if there was any point in leaving one. Nate had a habit of disappearing into the wild with his horse and a dog or two for days on end, fishing and camping, no phone, no interruptions.

On the other hand, Alex knew his best friend would appreciate knowing he was back from the dead, so he left a message. Then he went downstairs to start a pot of coffee for Jessica, something he'd dreamed about doing over and over again, only this time it was for real. He found the bag of coffee beans where they'd always been, but they were labeled as decaf, he supposed in deference to her pregnancy. Still, the freshly ground beans smelled like heaven on earth and even the familiar perking sounds were like music. He didn't like to drink the stuff, but he used to make her a cup and carry it upstairs to her bed every morning when they were first married. He wasn't sure when that had stopped.

For himself, he dared hope he might find one of his favorite drinks in the back of the fridge where he left it months ago. Unless Jessica had thrown it out, of course. He opened the refrigerator quickly, wondering how long it would be before things like electricity would stop amazing him, dug behind a giant jar of pickles and came up with an icy bottle of Vita-Drink.

Happy days. It tasted great.

A light rapping on the glass kitchen door finally got through to him. Only friends and family came around the back like this and he braced himself for another homecoming as he went to see who it was.

He opened the door when he saw his partner on the police force, Detective Dylan Hobart. At the sight of Alex, Dylan's rugged face split into a giant grin. He wasn't wearing his usual jeans and T-shirt covered with an old military-looking vest adorned with patches and badges he'd earned as a former marine. Instead he wore a tight T-shirt and a leather jacket that fit him like a glove. He might be approaching forty-five, but he wasn't going without a struggle.

"If you aren't a sight for sore eyes," Dylan cried as he wrapped Alex in a one-armed bear hug. Then he pushed him away and stared at his face. "Holy cow, what happened to you? Damn, man, you've lost weight!"

Alex laughed. "You try eating nothing but fish for three months straight and see if you maintain all that mass." Dylan lived and breathed to lift weights and work out and he had the physique to prove it.

Dylan now produced the morning newspaper from where he'd apparently folded it into his rear pocket. "You're all over the place, man," he said, tapping the newsprint where Alex glimpsed a picture of himself and Jessica standing on the front lawn. He'd still had the beard when the picture was taken though he'd shaved it off later last night. He touched his smooth jaw and felt a little naked.

"I tried calling," Dylan said, "and then I thought, what the hell, I'm going over there and see that loser with my own eyes. I can't believe you walked out of those mountains. Are you really okay?"

Alex assured him he was fine. But Dylan's next question was more difficult to answer.

"What happened? I mean, I imagine you are sick to death of being asked this question, but did you drive your plane into a mountain or something? The article didn't really say."

"I made some coffee for Jess," Alex said, pouring his partner a mug. "Warning—it's decaf." They sat opposite each other at the counter. Alex drank the last of his water, and sighed. "I'm not sure what happened," he said.

"What do you mean?"

"A lot went down all at once. The oil leaked out of the engine somehow and then the engine froze and I'd been flying all over hell and breakfast trying to skirt a weather front. I landed on a lake and the plane sank. I was hurt, and so that confused the issue, too. Pretty much end of story."

"Pretty much beginning of story you mean," Dylan said with a knowing look in his light blue eyes.

"Whatever, the point is I survived."

"Have you spoken with the FAA about it? Given what happened to your buddies in Shatterhorn, we had our share of speculation around here after you went missing. There were some who thought your plane was rigged to crash. It seems kind of far-fetched to me, though."

"I just don't know," Alex said. "I made a few calls last night. Someone named Struthers from the FBI is coming today. I'll listen to what he has to say."

"Well," Dylan added, "I guess the important thing is you're home."

"No kidding," Alex said with feeling. "Especially now. I found out last night that Jess is going to have a baby."

Dylan's lips curled into a smile. "That's great news. Are you and she...well, I know things were rocky—"

"We're going to work things out," Alex said with no equivocation in his voice. He would do what he had to do. He would figure out how to show Jessica she was the center of his universe.

"That's great. You're going to be a daddy! That must be why she posted that comment on Facebook. I wondered. Wow, man, she must be so excited."

"We both are," Alex said, then asked, "What comment?" Hadn't she mentioned something about Facebook the night before?

"She didn't tell you?" He took out his phone and spent a minute getting to the site he wanted. "This is her page, but the comment is gone."

"What did it say?" Alex asked.

"No big deal. Just asked you to contact her if you could."

"What?"

"It just said that if you were reading what she'd written, would you contact her because there was something important you needed to know. It must have been the baby, don't you think?"

Alex nodded as he adjusted his expression to hide how shocked he was by this revelation. Was that what she'd meant when she told him that she'd thought he was something worse than dead? That he was what—hiding? Did she really think he would run out on her like a coward?

"They didn't replace you at work," Dylan said as though unaware of the bomb he'd just detonated in Alex's gut. "It's been slow, so it's been fine, but lately things are picking up a little. You know, the weather warms up and all the crazies come out. There was talk they were going to promote Kit Anderson but they haven't done it yet. Chief Quill quit right after you disappeared when he was caught taking bribes. The mayor appointed Frank Smyth to fill the position until he makes a permanent decision. As far as I know, they've got you on the books as being on some kind of emergency leave."

Alex made himself concentrate on the conversation. "I'm surprised the mayor chose Frank instead of you to act as chief."

"Yeah, I was, too. But Frank likes the business end of things and getting his picture in the paper, you know what he's like. He probably sweet-talked the mayor and that's nothing I would do unless he was twenty, gorgeous and a she."

Alex nodded. He didn't know Frank all that well even though they'd worked side by side on occasion. Frankly, the new chief was something of an enigma to Alex. Touchy on one hand, egotistical on the other, never shy about tooting his own horn. It was hard to imagine him as the chief. On the other hand, Alex was grateful the guy had held open his job.

"You're probably going to break Kit's heart but he'll

live through it," Dylan said. "I don't care how many classes he's been taking, I don't think he could pass the detective test, anyway."

They both turned as Jessica entered the kitchen. She'd wrapped a kimono around herself and Alex's gaze immediately dropped to her midsection where he tried to discern a bulge. She smiled at him and his gaze flew to her face. "It doesn't show too much yet," she said.

He tried out a smile and wished they were alone so he could ask her about the Facebook thing.

"Morning, Dylan," she said as she poured herself a cup of coffee. "It's good to see you."

"Sorry to barge in so early. I just had to look at this guy with my own eyes," he said. "I swear, I hate to say it, but I never thought I'd see him again."

"It's hard to believe he's home," she said.

Dylan turned back to Alex. "It says in the newspaper that you hurt your leg."

"No big deal," Alex said. "Besides, Jess has already heard all the gory details. Let's not bore her with more."

"Come off it," she protested. "You've barely told me anything."

"And that's because you have more important things to think about," he said as he got up from his stool and offered it to her. He suddenly realized he hadn't delivered her coffee because he let himself get sidetracked by Dylan. Oh, well, there was always tomorrow.

"More important than your survival? I don't think so," she said.

"The fact is I did survive. Hey, here's some good news. Dylan says my job is still open."

She shook her head as she glanced at Dylan. "He's in protective mode," she said. "I may not survive it."

"I'm not worried," Dylan said. "We spend a lot of

time driving around together. I'll get sick of his stories by the end."

"That's true, you will," Alex said. The phone rang and he added, "I have a feeling that's Nate calling me back. I need to talk to him and it might take a while. Later, okay?"

"Sure," Dylan said as Alex sprinted off to grab the phone before the answering machine came on.

"I'D BETTER BE on my way," Dylan said. But he paused with his hand on the knob and looked back at Jessica. "I'm so glad things are finally working out for you two."

Dylan was such a strong, physically honed individual that there were times Jessica found being in the same room with him a little overwhelming. She knew he was divorced, liked fast cars and dated a lot of younger women but never the same one for very long. It always seemed his romances started out hot and heavy and then tapered off.

"I know you've had a rough time the last year or so," he added.

She really did not want to talk about her relationship with her husband, at least not with Dylan, so she smiled brightly. "That's all behind us now," she said.

He cocked his eyebrows as though he thought she was being very naive. Exactly what had Alex told him? Whatever it was, she didn't want to know, but she could imagine. Hadn't she discussed her struggling marriage with her girlfriends? There was no reason Alex shouldn't have done the same. "Do you work tonight?" she asked.

"Not unless something terrible happens," he said. "Knock on wood."

"Then why don't you come back around six o'clock.

Bring along anyone from the office who's free. We'll have a little surprise party for Alex."

"Do you think he'll like that?" Dylan said.

"I think it might be easier for him to see people in an informal situation. He can bring everyone up to speed at the same time and not have to keep going over things."

"That sounds reasonable," Dylan said. "Why don't you make it potluck. I'll bring one of those veggie trays."

"Okay. Tell everyone to park around the block and come in the back way through the garden."

"You got it."

After he left, she went in search of Alex. She found he'd closed himself in the den and what she could hear of his voice sounded low and guarded.

A few minutes later, he emerged from the den and seemed surprised to find her standing there.

"I take it that was Nate?" she said.

"Yeah."

"I bet he's relieved to hear you're okay."

He put his arm around her and kissed the top of her head. "Yeah, of course."

"Did he explain things better than I did?" she asked as they started back toward the kitchen.

"He just gave me a few more facts. He talked about the B-Strong organization which was used as a front, stuff like that. And he says the authorities can't place the guy who killed Mike as being in Blunt Falls last February."

"Which means he must have had an accomplice here," she said.

"Exactly. Nate says the FBI hasn't found anyone, though. Oh, you'll be relieved to hear the concern about a Memorial Day attack seems to be centered on Seattle, Washington, not here."

"I'm not relieved about anything," she said stubbornly.

He stared into her eyes. "Nate has had a hard time. That shooting at the mall really gutted him. He thought he should be able to save those kids…and then he was injured and in the hospital. The authorities are going to be hell-bent on finding out if my plane was sabotaged but even if it was, it doesn't seem to me that it has a whole lot of bearing on the here and now."

"But we don't know that," she said. She bit her lip and added, "I get the feeling you're giving me the kid-glove treatment," she said. "I can be pregnant and concerned about other things at the same time, you know. I'm pretty good at multitasking."

"I don't want to argue with you," he said. "Just let me take care of this and you take care of our baby."

"Listen carefully," she said, her voice soft. "We drifted apart before, partly because our dreams of having children weren't coming true. Now they are, but you're using him or her as an excuse to push me away again. I don't want to live like that, Alex. You have to let me share your life."

"I know," he said. "That goes two ways."

"What does that mean?"

"It means you have to let me share yours, too."

"I'm not the one refusing to talk about things," she said defiantly.

He stared into her eyes and she had the feeling there was something he wanted to say. But he shook his head. He didn't say it but it was as clear as day. He didn't want to fight, he didn't want to risk alienating her, but that's exactly what he was doing.

She needed to think. "Are you hungry?" she asked him. "Would you like an omelet?"

"Sure. And maybe I could take you to dinner tonight so you don't have to cook."

"Let's just stay in," she said.

"Just the two of us," he said. "Sounds cozy."

Chapter Three

An hour later Alex came into the kitchen from the backyard where he'd been fixing a broken screen. As he paused to grab another Vita-Drink, he heard voices coming from the living room. A second after that, Jessica called his name.

A tall man with light brown skin and close-cut black hair stood in the living room beside her. He wore a very tailored dark suit accented with an equally sober steel-gray tie. His hand clutched the handle of a briefcase and to Alex's eyes, he had Federal Agent written all over him.

"Alex, this is Agent Struthers," Jessica said.

Alex offered his hand. They adjourned to the den where Alex once again told his story about the crash and walking out of the mountains. And once again, he had to face the fact that his memory of the minutes preceding the actual impact were hazy.

"I don't know if the plane was sabotaged," he finished. "I don't see how it could have been. I plan on visiting the mechanic out at the field to ask him if he has any ideas."

The agent, who had seated himself across the desk, thumbed through his notes. "You're talking about Anthony Machi of High Mountain Aviation and Maintenance?"

"Yes."

"The FAA, Homeland Security, the Transportation Department as well the FBI also spoke with Mr. Machi. Without any details of what actually occurred, he was unable to do more than speculate, of course. Now about the plane. It's totally submerged?"

"Yes. Nate Matthews is a deputy in Arizona and a friend of mine. He suggests we fly back to the lake and dive on the wreck. We're both certified and Nate's Arizona fishing buddy is a diver with the FAA."

"The FAA will raise the plane. You should get in touch with them before you do anything yourself," the agent said. "You'll need to pinpoint the exact location on one of their aerial maps."

"I already called them this morning. I'll go by later today," Alex said as he slid a look over at Jessica. She was doing exactly what he knew she'd be doing: glowering. "I was going to tell you all this," he said to her.

She looked away from him.

"There's one more thing we need to discuss," the agent said as he opened a different folder and perused the information inside. "First of all, you know about Mike Donovan's notebook, right? The one your friend Nate Matthews found?"

"Yes," Alex said. "Nate told me Mike kept the notebook to catalog his investigation into who was really behind the mall shooting. That's why we were getting together that weekend. Mike thought he was on the trail of a conspiracy."

"Yes," Struthers agreed. "And as it turns out, he was absolutely right. Mr. Donovan had written 'Seattle' on one of the pages along with the name of the man who appeared to head the B-Strong group that supposedly ran programs for strengthening young men's characters. There was also a date that happens to correspond to this coming Memorial Day. The current thinking is that something the Shatterhorn Killer set in motion is going to occur in Seattle in a few short days."

"But the Shatterhorn Killer is dead," Alex said.

Struthers nodded. "Which brings me to a recent development. As part of our investigation, we're running a wiretap on a suspect phone in Seattle. I was contacted because this person received a call from a former employee of the Shatterhorn Killer. There was mention of a contact in Blunt Falls which is why it was called to my attention. Since you're thought to have been a target of these people and the timing suggests your reappearance may have triggered the call, you need to be on the alert."

"Someone who worked for the killer in Nevada?"

"As his secretary, yes. He disappeared right after the parade on President's Day after destroying evidence. We looked for him, of course. There's some speculation he was the driver of the car who struck and killed his supposed employer." Struthers looked through his papers again and showed Alex a photograph of a bald sixty-something-year-old man with a haughty look in his slate eyes. "While he was in Shatterhorn, he used the name William Tucker but we now know that was a stolen identity. We're also pretty sure he shaved his head and isn't really bald. We're not sure what his part was or if it was pivotal. The fact he's been in contact with a man assumed to be involved in a similar militia group in the northwest is what's troubling."

This time when Jessica looked at Alex it was with horror in her eyes instead of impatience. "How do you guys know it was the same man?" she asked.

"He referred to himself as 'aka William Tucker.'"

"And in this conversation, they mentioned a nameless third person, someone here in Blunt Falls?" Alex asked.

"Yes."

Jessica hugged herself. "Is this about money or something? What does someone here have to gain?"

"It's not about money," Struthers said. "These people work for ideals, not cash. And it seems to be bipartisan, as well. This is across-the-board terrorism."

"We have an alarm system in the house and we'll be sure to use it," Alex said.

"Just be cautious. Our experience with this strain of domestic militia is that they use any means to make their point, no matter who they kill or maim."

"And what about the threat of a Memorial Day massacre of sorts? Is that still on people's minds?"

"Of course. This is the first national holiday since the killer's botched attempt to gun down people at an Idaho parade on President's Day. Now with this latest news of a contact here in Blunt Falls, everyone is gearing up to safeguard any festivities."

"Blunt Falls always has a parade on Memorial Day," Jessica commented.

He checked his papers again. "I see we've discussed this with the mayor and the chief of police, a Mr. Frank Smyth. Measures are being taken both here and in Seattle. Frankly, police all over the country are gearing up with extra precautions." Struthers shook his head. "The truth is no one is safe anywhere until this current crop of lunatics is put out of business."

"And are you any closer to accomplishing that goal?" Jessica asked.

"We look into every allegation and possibility. It's like any war on terror—many of the victories go unheralded, but that doesn't mean they aren't significant. But malls and parades and both foot and auto races—

anything where people gather in large numbers—are being watched."

Alex nodded as he attempted to return the photo, but Struthers shook his head. "You keep it. If you see this guy, call us."

"Do you want us to show it around?"

"Couldn't hurt," the agent said. "But tell people not to approach him, just to get in contact with the FBI. We don't know yet if this man is dangerous or a loose cannon or what exactly he is."

Alex put the photo in his desk, then walked to Jessica's side and laid a hand on her shoulder as he stared into her eyes. It suddenly seemed totally irrelevant that she had somehow doubted his plane crash, that she'd written that damn comment on Facebook for the world to see. He couldn't bear to see pain or fear on her face and he sure as hell wasn't going to go out of his way to create more of it. "I would never let anyone hurt you or our baby," he said softly.

She looked up at him. "Oh, Alex, it's not me or the baby I'm worried about. It's you."

AFTER THE AGENT LEFT, Jessica insisted she needed to work on the test papers she'd brought home from school and promised to lock all the doors and turn on the alarm system. On a whim, he called his doctor who was also a friend. "I've been reading about your triumphant return," Josh Woodward said. "Sounds as if I should check you out."

"That's why I'm calling," Alex said. "I want to go back to work as soon as possible and that means I need a once-over from you. I know it's Saturday, but is there any chance we could do it today?"

"Well, the clinic is open for free vaccinations this

afternoon which means there will be a limited staff present. Sure, I'll meet you down there in an hour. You'll have to come back in the next week or so for blood work and any tests I might want to run."

"That's fine, Josh. I'll see you in an hour."

The afternoon was filled with steps toward reaching his goal of getting back to work. After meeting with the doctor, Alex braved the mall to replace the cell phone he'd lost during his months in the mountains, and to get a haircut. Then he took the doctor's clearance to the precinct where he found the place running on a skeleton crew. Maybe crime was lurking on the threshold of Blunt Falls like the FBI warned, or maybe it wasn't. The sparsely occupied office certainly seemed to suggest the latter.

He left his medical clearance on Chief Smyth's desk, before calling Jessica to tell her he was on his way home. He was not going to fall into the old pattern of coming and going as he pleased, leaving her to guess when he'd show up. She asked him to stop by the store and that's how he found himself peering into the freezer case of their local megamart. He needed something called Moonie Mocha Fudge Ripple. He was determined to find the exact ice cream Jessica had asked for as it was his first experience with the cravings of pregnancy and he didn't want to blow it.

Of course it was chocolate, what else would it be? He finally found the right one and bought two. Then he added a couple of jars of pickles and some anchovies to the order, hoping she'd find that funny, hoping it would ease some of the tension between them.

He paused before going inside the house, determined that tonight he would be honest and clear with her. She deserved no less and, face it, unless he learned how to trust her, sooner or later she was going to walk away and not look back, and that thought was so terrible it made him ache.

He suspected anyone who had lived through years of trying to have a baby didn't take a moment of pregnancy for granted, never assumed everything would turn out right. The worry was always there. He could see it in Jessica's eyes and he could feel it in his own heart.

A minute later, he unlocked his front door and stopped short. A crowd had gathered in the room and they were all staring at him, all grinning. He was so flabbergasted to find his living room full of people that he couldn't make sense of it. And then they yelled "Surprise!" at the same moment and the faces took identities—neighbors, fellow officers and friends from years before. Jessica approached and he handed her the grocery bag as the room instantly filled with music and noise.

"You didn't really need this stuff, did you?" he asked.

"Not really. People were still arriving when you called so I gave you an errand. Are you surprised?"

"I'm stunned," he said truthfully.

"I hope it's okay," she added, her brow furrowed a little. "Your family wanted to come but it was too far away for such short notice. They wanted me to tell you they're coming to Blunt Falls right after Memorial Day."

"I know. My mother called me twice."

"You can't blame her for being relieved you're alive and well."

"I realize that. And everything here is perfect," he assured her, anxious to chase away her worry. So what if he would have preferred a quiet evening alone with her? He leaned down and kissed her soft cheek and people applauded, of all things.

"I like your haircut," she added, then kissed his cheek and went to put away the ice cream.

He was flattered by the attention and uneasy with it, too. He'd never craved the limelight nor did he relish repeating his survival story, but he did it anyway, kind of moving into a rote pattern as people asked the same questions over and over. Was he injured in the crash? Had he known search planes were looking for him? What did he eat? How did he survive the snow and freezing conditions? How did he finally manage to escape and make his way to civilization?

And the hardest one of all: What was it like to be home?

The part with Jessica? As well as could be expected leaning cautiously toward great. The part where he'd learned someone may have wanted him dead and might even try again? Not so good.

As the evening wore on and people with younger kids returned to their own homes, Alex found himself in a group of his fellow officers, many of them in uniform as they had shifts to start soon or had just come off of one. Dylan suggested he and the other officers in attendance go outside and Alex wondered if his partner had noticed his discomfort indoors. He hoped not. He didn't want Jessica to see it.

"Before we go outside, I want you guys to look at a photo," he said and they all followed him into his den where he produced the photograph of the man Struthers said might be involved in whatever mayhem was brewing. "I imagine the FBI will share all this with the department if they haven't already, but just in case, I wanted to give you guys a head's up."

"Smug-looking cuss," Dylan said. "Who is he?"

"I'll explain in a minute. Let's go outside, okay?" Alex said, and tucked the photo back into his desk drawer.

The weather had deteriorated in the past few hours and the stars Alex so longed to see had been swallowed up by swirling ground fog that brought a sense of chilled dampness. Still, they settled gamely on the wicker furniture Jessica had somehow taken out of storage while he was gone that day. Obviously, she had not stayed inside with the alarm set or spent her time poring over her students' math papers.

Kit Anderson was the officer who was going to lose his chance at promotion now that Alex was back and he was the first one to speak. "So, I heard you went into work today to make sure you still had a job," he said.

Alex stared at the dark form of his fellow officer. The man's deep voice was tinged with anger.... Maybe Dylan had underestimated how much a promotion meant to Kit.

"What did you expect him to do?" Carla Herrera said.

"I don't know," Kit grumbled.

"Just be patient," she added. "Your turn will come."

Alex studied his folded hands and took a deep breath. A cool breeze blew under the eaves, whisking away the smoke from Chief Smyth's cigarette. The chief had arrived an hour ago with his very own newspaper reporter in tow. He'd posed for a couple of pictures with his arm around Alex's shoulders, made a small speech about miracles and was now lingering long after the reporter had gone off to meet his deadline. The man was obviously lobbying for the job of chief to become his on a permanent basis. The glow from the end of a burning cigarette marked his location off to the side. The other officer present was a guy Alex just met. Hank Jones was a new hire and seemed to be on the quiet side.

Alex felt some of the tension in his neck and shoulders ease as he settled against the wicker. They talked shop for a while and then Alex told them about the visit from the FBI. It was too dark to see expressions, but he could feel a watchful current ebb and flow as he spoke.

"The bottom line is that we're supposed to be cautious while they try to track this person. There's concern he or she is close by. I'm not worried about myself so much, but I would greatly appreciate everyone keeping their eyes open. I don't want Jessica scared or hurt and I can't watch her 24/7."

"Of course we'll help," Carla Herrera said amid a chorus of assenting voices.

"Thanks."

"So they really think your plane was rigged to crash?" Carla asked.

"It looks like it."

"What do you think?"

"I don't know. I mean, I've thought about what happened and I can't make it anybody's fault. I just wasn't myself that day. In fact, I'd thought for a while that I might have been getting whatever stomach bug Jessica said she had." He laughed softly to himself. "Unless I'm the only pregnant man in the world, that obviously wasn't the case."

"So do you remember every moment like it happened in slow motion?" Smyth asked.

"Not really," Alex admitted. "I hadn't slept well the night before." He'd been up arguing with Jess, but he didn't add that part. "And then I got a late start. Well, you remember, Kit, you called me at the last minute for something. I honestly can't remember what."

"Just an address," Kit Anderson said. "I was taking over the Hannigan case while you were gone and I didn't know where the guy's girlfriend was staying."

"That's right, now I remember," Alex said. "Anyway, maybe Nate is right. Maybe I was so disorganized I missed something."

Again, that undercurrent of alarm stirred the air around them. Well, it was an alarming situation.

"But why did anyone want the three of you dead in the first place?" Kit asked.

Dylan spoke up. "Because Mike Donovan had called them to go back to Shatterhorn and help him figure out if there was a conspiracy, which we all now know there was." His voice sounded impatient as though this was old news which it was, at least for almost everyone but Alex. "Mike was killed for his trouble, Nate Matthews was wounded and the speculation is that Alex's plane was tampered with. All by a bunch of patriotic zealots."

"Yeah, I remember now," Kit grumbled, and they all fell into a pronounced and prolonged silence.

Finally, Alex heard the creak of the gate across the wooded yard and wondered who was arriving just as things were breaking up. Sitting forward, he strained to see through the fog. A person approached, footsteps crunching on the gravel. Whether it was the effect of the fog or a matter of stature, the figure appeared short and a trifle squat, wearing bulky clothes, walking with hesitant steps. There was something about that walk and the emerging shape that struck Alex as both familiar and a little spooky.

"Can I help you?" Alex called as the person stopped shy of the steps. Who was it?

"Mr. Foster, is that you?"

Recognition came in a rush. Billy Summers, Jessica's ex-student. And the way he'd walked through the fog just now had triggered another recollection for Alex, but this one drifted outside his grasp. No matter, it would come eventually.

"Yes, it's me," Alex said. "You're a little late for the party."

"Then it's true, you really are alive," Billy said, his whisper tinged with awe.

"Yeah, it's true. How can I help you?"

"I have to tell you something," he said in a rush.

"Sure. Come on up onto the porch." Alex turned in the direction of the burning cigarette and added, "Chief, switch on that other light there by the door so Billy can see his way up here. Come on, Billy, have a seat and speak your mind."

The light went on and everyone blinked against the sudden illumination, even though the fog diffused the brightness. Alex looked down the three shallow steps. Billy was staring up in alarm, his gaze traveling from one officer to the next, eyes wide, mouth agape. It came to Alex suddenly that the kid hadn't realized there were other people on the porch.

Billy had to be about twenty now, a guy with a round face and perpetually pink cheeks. His shaggy brown hair flopped over his forehead and down his neck and was mostly covered by an old cap whose logo had all but disappeared under layers of oil and grease. He was dressed in a black T-shirt and jeans with a dark green windbreaker over all.

"Go ahead and get comfortable, Billy," Alex said. "I want to thank you for all the work you did on this yard while I was gone. It meant a lot to my wife and to me, too. And it will mean a lot to the families of the veterans come Memorial Day. Now, what can I do for you?"

"Mama told me you got back," he said with a sideways glance at Alex and away. He wasn't the brightest guy in town, but he was always friendly and pretty reliable. There was no doubt he had his share of burdens to deal with. Besides his own learning impairments, his mother was a difficult woman who had once been a great beauty. She'd married an out-of-work mill worker right out of high school but the guy died a few weeks after

Billy was born. After his death, rumors circulated she slept around, but slowly those gossipy whispers were replaced by ones concerning her descent into some kind of undefined mental issues that now kept her more or less trapped in the double-wide she shared with her only son. Billy took care of her as well as doing odd jobs at the airport. Money had to be tight.

"She must have read it in the newspaper," Alex said.

"She likes to collect newspapers," Billy said, his gaze lifting to meet the intense interest of the other officers, then sliding away. When Smyth cleared his throat, Billy jumped a few inches.

Smyth was fiftysomething, with a shaved head and a hooked, prominent nose with a tight, strong body thanks to weekend trail biking. His unblinking gaze sometimes reminded Alex of a hawk. Given the cornered look on Billy's face, he agreed with that assessment.

Billy swallowed and tried talking a couple of times, but the sentences ended in stuttering and were difficult to understand. Alex tried to get him to sit down, but he wouldn't or couldn't, nor did he recover his ability to speak coherently. He paced a little, stared at Dylan, paced some more, stared at Herrera, paced some more, darted a quick glance at Chief Smyth.

During this uncomfortable interlude, Alex had a sudden memory of the day his plane lifted off the Blunt Falls runway, something he had completely put out of his mind until that moment of watching Billy aimlessly move around the porch while darting looks this way and that. Add the vision he'd created earlier when he walked through the fog and it suddenly gelled. "You were at the airfield," he said to Billy.

Billy stopped pacing so abruptly he almost tripped on his own feet. "What?" he said.

"Yeah, you were there," Alex said. "In fact, when I came out of the office after taking Kit's call, you were on the field. You'd been deicing someone's windshield, remember? You were carrying the equipment and you were walking toward me during a light snow flurry. In fact, you're the last person I saw that day."

The kid's Adam's apple slid up and down his throat as he swallowed.

"You don't remember seeing Alex?" Dylan asked, hands planted on his knees.

"I forget," the boy said, swallowing yet again. Little beads of perspiration sprang out across his forehead and the redness in his cheeks paled.

"Sounds to me like you're hiding something," the chief said.

"No, no, nothing," Billy sputtered.

"Then why did you come here tonight?"

"I've been helping…helping…you know…Mrs. Foster… with yard work."

"At eleven o'clock at night?"

"No. No. Mama told me Mr. Foster came home. I wanted to see if he was okay, that's all."

"You said you wanted to tell him something," Herrera said.

"I don't remember," Billy said quickly, his voice high and anxious.

The porch door opened and Jessica appeared carrying a tray laden with tall cups of what smelled like coffee, probably in deference to those who still had hours of work ahead of them. Her warm smile faded a bit as her gaze settled on the obvious distress of Billy's expression. Cups slid as the tray dipped. Alex grabbed it from her just in time.

"What's going on?" she asked as he settled the tray on a table.

"Billy came to talk to me," he said.

She looked at the formidable group facing the young man and stepped forward. "Did you ride your bike into town this late at night and in the fog?" she asked Billy, casting him a kindly look.

"Yes, ma'am," he squeaked.

"Would you like something hot to drink?"

"No," he said. "I've got to go."

"Okay," she said softly. "But be careful on that road, okay?"

He nodded, his gaze downcast.

"Come back tomorrow when you remember what you wanted," Alex added.

"Yeah, okay," he said, but he wasted no time hustling down the stairs to beat a hasty retreat toward the gate. The fog swallowed him up after just a few steps.

Jessica looked after him with confusion on her face. "That was odd. He's not usually forgetful."

"The boy couldn't get his thoughts straight if he wanted to," the chief said. "But looking at what I can see of your garden amazes me. Who would have thought the kid had this kind of beauty in him?" He dropped his cigarette butt and ground it out beneath his heel. "The wife just got back from spending a week with our daughter at her college. I guess I'd better get home. And by the way, Alex, I saw your medical clearance on my desk when I stopped by the precinct on my way over here. We'll see you bright and early Monday morning, okay?"

Alex grinned. "You bet."

"I'll walk you out," Jessica said, and led the chief back

into the house. He'd arrived late and he'd used the front entrance. No backyard gates for him.

Dylan got to his feet and heaved a deep breath. "I think the party's over."

"THANK YOU FOR TONIGHT," Alex said as he got ready for bed.

Sitting at her dresser and brushing her hair, Jessica glanced in the mirror where she saw Alex's reflection. "Did you really like it?"

"What was not to like?" he said which she took as a nonanswer.

"Oh, I don't know. After being alone for so long, all these people might have been difficult for you to handle all at once. Maybe I shouldn't have tried to surprise you."

"You did what you thought best," he said. "It was fine."

It was on the tip of her tongue to tell him to stop making nice all the time. She knew he was worried the peace they seemed to have found was too fragile to withstand brutal honesty, but he'd have to get over it if they stood a chance at a real marriage. "How about Chief Smyth bringing a reporter?" she asked, shaking her head. "What is that guy's problem?"

"My guess is that he was trying to score points with the mayor by getting his picture front and center in Sunday's newspaper. The reporter had the look of a guy making a few extra bucks."

She turned to face him, watching as he unbuttoned his shirt. "That was odd about Billy, wasn't it?"

"Yeah. But he's always been a little awkward with people."

"I think seeing all you cops must have unnerved him."

"That's what I thought. All of us have been out to his

mother's place a few times over the years. She's had her share of trouble."

He pulled his shirt off, stood up and unbuttoned his jeans. He was leaner than she'd ever seen him, but stronger, too, the muscles in his chest and shoulders honed by the work he'd been doing to stay alive. She couldn't really imagine what he'd gone through, how he'd survived the first few days of storms and snow with a badly injured leg and cuts on his face. She'd asked him to tell her in greater detail, but he'd glossed over all the facts, dismissing the experience as yesterday's news.

He paused as he sat back down on the edge of the mattress, just in his boxers now. There were scars running up and down his left leg that made her wince when she thought of the agony he must have endured all by himself. And yet he looked younger than he had in years, and incredibly handsome. Every molecule in her body reminded her that making love to him was about the best thing in the whole entire world.

"He was fine until the lights came on," Alex mused. "When he saw everyone he just clammed up. Do you have any idea what he wanted?"

"No," she said. "He's been coming around like I told you, but he doesn't talk a whole lot."

"That's the feeling I got," Alex said. "Oh, and I recalled seeing him at the airport the morning I flew out of here, though he claimed he didn't remember."

"He'll come back tomorrow, then we'll know," she said, getting up from the small chair and walking to the bed where she sat beside him. "Thanks for the anchovies and pickles," she whispered.

He looked into her eyes. "I know how you love anchovies," he said.

She smiled as she bumped his shoulder with hers.

"I'm sorry about not telling you that Nate and I made those plans," he added.

"We got used to keeping things to ourselves," she said. "We have to unlearn all those bad habits."

"Are you going to get mad at me every time I try to protect you?"

"Probably," she said. "I know how you feel," she admitted. "I feel the same way. We've had our problems, Alex, but I've never stopped loving you."

He smiled. "I'm glad to hear that." He raised his hand and ran his fingers through her hair, his gaze devouring her. She closed the distance between them and touched his lips with hers. His were tender, his mouth hot and sexy.

"I've missed you so much," he murmured.

"I've missed you, too," she whispered, and realized as the words left her lips that they were true. She missed the man she'd once known, the man who had loved her, the man she'd trusted with her life and happiness. And now it seemed he was willing to try to find that man again. She knew she'd grown distant, too. They both needed to work.

"I want to make love to you," he said against her ear.

His warm breath traveled through her body like a renegade spark, awakening torrid memories of endless nights of bliss as it burned under her skin. The temptation to give in to her desire for him sent her heart racing and it took a few seconds to trust herself to speak. "I'm not ready," she whispered at last. "I need to think with my head, not my heart and certainly not my body. You know what you do to me."

He smiled slowly. "It's mutual."

"We'll get there," she said softly, and then took a chance that the changes she sensed in him were real. "Being pregnant has reminded me how much I want children," she said, meeting his gaze. "Alex, if I lose this baby, then I want to adopt. You wouldn't even talk about it before, but that's the decision I've reached and I hope you'll at least discuss it with me."

"If you lose this baby," he said, his voice thick, "then I'm open to adoption."

"Just like that?"

"Let's just say that spending one hundred and three nights alone with nothing to do but try to stay warm gives you plenty of time to think. And what I realized was that life is a gift, that living with someone you cherish is a gift. I don't get to call every shot, I have to roll with the punches, we all do. If adoption is the best way to grow our family, then I'm on board. Let's get the pitter-patter of little feet running around here."

She blinked away warm tears. "Thank you," she whispered.

He shifted his weight and settled back on his side of the bed. "Come here," he said, and she scooted up beside him. He pulled her against his chest and flicked off the light.

His skin was warm and musky smelling. He kept running his hand up and down her bare arm, kissing her hair and she closed her eyes, trying to relax. Eventually, she could tell by his breathing that he'd fallen asleep and she was glad.

She'd known the minute he walked in the door tonight that a party was the absolute last thing in the world he wanted. Whereas she'd found the noise and laughter of friends and family comforting after the dire news Agent Struthers delivered, she suspected Alex had found it intrusive.

Thank goodness they'd have tomorrow before the rat race of his job and the last few weeks of teaching hit full force. It seemed forever since she'd had a nice, normal, boring day.

Several hours later, the ringing phone woke her with a start. Alex fumbled with the light and grabbed the receiver as Jessica sat up in bed. No good news ever seemed to come when it was still dark outside. The clock read 5:00 a.m.

Alex spoke in a surprisingly crisp voice, which suggested he was already awake. He hung up abruptly and looked at her. "That was weird," he said.

"Who was it?"

"Frank Smyth. He asked me to go out to Billy's place. Since I'm not technically back at work, he's hoping I can keep the visit under the radar. Don't ask me why."

"Is something wrong?"

"I'm not sure. I guess the chief got a call from Billy's mom but he wasn't explicit about what she said. You know how the chief worries about his public image.... I guess that's why he wants to handle it this way." He leaned over and kissed her lips. "I'll be back before you know it."

"I'm going with you," she said.

"Absolutely not," he said, pulling on his jeans.

She was already out of bed and looking through her drawer for jeans of her own.

"Jess, I'm serious," he insisted. "I don't want you to come."

"You don't want me in any danger," she said, stepping into leggings. Her jeans had been getting a little tight in the waist lately.

"Of course I don't want you in danger," he said.

"From Billy's mother? Really? Anyway, you'll protect me," she said on her way to brush her teeth.

"This is police business," he announced as though that sealed his argument.

"No, it's not," she called from the bathroom, then turned to look back into the bedroom. "Smyth asked you to take care of it because you're not on the roster yet." She watched Alex open the gun safe as she started brushing. He took out his service pistol and put it in a shoulder holster, which he strapped over his T-shirt. They passed in the bathroom door as he went in and she came out.

She shrugged on a light sweater and slipped her feet into moccasins. "Why would she call the chief directly?" Jessica asked as she gathered her hair into a quick ponytail.

"I have no idea," Alex said as he set aside a hand towel. "He just said he couldn't take the call. I don't know why, but I got the feeling he wasn't even at his house."

"His wife just came home, where else would he be? Anyway, the reason I'm going with you is that Billy trusts me. He'll be more likely to talk if I'm there."

"I don't even know if Billy is there."

"Where else would he be?" she repeated as she walked out of the bedroom. After a few steps, she called over her shoulder, "Are you coming?"

She heard him swear under his breath as he caught up with her. It sounded like he said, "Damn stubborn woman." She laughed out loud. At least they'd finally had a genuine honest moment.

Chapter Four

Back when Alex had been on patrol, he'd been called out a number of times to the Summers house for various disturbances. Nothing serious, just one of those situations where occasional loud arguments, late-night noises and unbelievable clutter brought complaints from neighbors.

The last time he'd seen Lynda Summers had been a good three or four years before. That time, neighbors had called because of the five old broken-down cars in her front yard and a putrid rotting smell emanating from the shed out back. It turned out the shed housed dozens of sacks of garbage and at least one dead opossum.

The road that led out to her place was called Blue Point but he often thought it should have a more ominous name as it was narrow and twisty, a challenge to manipulate on a foggy morning before the sun had a chance to burn it away. By the time he and Jessica pulled into the front drive of their destination, they were both tense from the trip.

The lights in the house shone through the fog as the door opened and Lynda Summers stepped outside. "Where's Frank?" she demanded.

"He couldn't make it," Alex told her.

Lynda was edging toward fifty. Time and hard living had eroded her prom-queen looks, though she still

exuded an earthy quality. Her hair was now all but color-
less, wispy and fine, overprocessed. At five-thirty in the
morning, she wore an ivory housedress and fuzzy slippers that might have once been white. The overall result
was unbelievable paleness.

However, much more distracting than her appearance
was the way she had of regarding people with her head
tilted and one eye kind of half-shut, as though she was
trying to discern everything they were hiding. It was
unsettling, to say the least. Even the most virtuous person in the world doesn't appreciate being looked at as if
he's a sleazeball.

"I know who you are," she said at last. "You're that
cop who disappeared. You used to come out here and
give me trouble, didn't you? You cops, I swear, you're
all alike. Your picture was in the paper yesterday. You
look pretty good for a dead man."

"That's because I'm not dead," he said, attempting
humor.

"Everyone thought you were." She cast a long look at
Jessica before looking back at him. "Why do I get the
feeling you were really hiding? Not that I'd blame you.
I think about doing that sometimes."

"What?" he said incredulously. "I wasn't hiding. The
paper explained about the crash."

"You can't believe the things you read," she said. "But
I didn't call you. I called Frank. A long time ago, too."

"And Frank called me," Alex said.

"That jerk." She turned suddenly and, moving way
faster than it appeared she could, retreated into her house.
Since she didn't close the door, Alex and Jessica hesi-
tantly followed.

"What's the problem?" Alex asked, stopping right inside the door because that was about as far as he could

get. Piles and heaps of clothes, stuffed animals, books, magazines, newspapers, dishes and every other possible thing took up all the floor space, except for a couple of narrow paths carved out of the junk that ran down the middle of the room and a path to a love seat and chair situated in front of a television. Some of the walls were covered with sagging shelves crammed with dolls. All those glassy eyes staring endlessly were creepy. Even doorways sported mounds of objects that seemed to burst through the openings like lava from an inferno's fissures. Alex's gut clenched. Being inside was hard for him anyway, and being inside this closed junk pile felt suffocating.

Lynda gave him her one eyed stare as she watched his gaze travel her home. She didn't respond to the question and he wondered if she'd heard him.

Right behind him, Jessica cleared her throat. "Mrs. Summers, is Billy here?"

Lynda's attention turned to Jessica. "I don't think so," she said, stopping to pick up a paper sack full of what looked like dolls still in their boxes and mindlessly setting it back down. "You're that teacher, aren't you. Well, last I saw of him he was headed out to your house."

"He got there about eleven last night," Alex said, "but he claimed he forgot why he came. Do you know why he wanted to see us?"

She shrugged. "He spent the day moping around, muttering to himself like he does. You can't get a decent conversation out of him when he's like that."

"He left our house hours ago," Jessica added. "Are you saying he never arrived home?"

"Maybe he's in his bedroom." Lynda gestured at the doorway Alex had seen earlier, the one piled with junk. Moving carefully through the mess, he approached the door along a little side track, picking his way over discarded clothes. He could see where someone consistently climbed over the pile in the doorway. He found a switch and flicked it on, illuminating a sea of junk. How could anyone sleep in this?

A quick look around revealed a mattress in one far corner with a little lamp on the floor beside it. A couple of blankets and a comic book lay abandoned on the "bed."

"Is he in there?" Lynda called.

Alex retraced his steps. "No."

"Aren't you worried about him?" Jessica asked. "It's very foggy outside and he was on a bike."

"You don't have any kids do you?" Lynda snapped.

"Not yet," Jessica said, as her hand seemed to automatically cradle her abdomen.

"Do yourself a favor and skip it. You got yourself a good-looking guy here. Kind of scrawny for my taste, but a hunk anyway. Why mess up a good thing with a bunch of little brats running around? And try getting rid of them when they finally grow up. Look at Billy. He's a full-grown man no matter what people think and I'm still supposed to provide a roof over his head."

Alex saw anger flash in Jessica's eyes, but she held her tongue.

"Anyway, maybe he got tired and stopped at a friend's house."

"What friend?" Alex asked. "Can you give us a name?"

"That mechanic at the airfield. Tony something."

"Tony Machi?"

"I guess. Billy thinks he can learn by osmosis. That'll be the day. Or maybe those look-alike kids."

"What are their names?" Alex asked.

"I don't know. Who cares?"

"Did you call around or go look for him?" Jessica asked.

"How would I do that?" Lynda said. "I don't have a

single car that runs. You'd think that worthless son of mine could get one of them to start, but no, he just tinkers and tinkers and nothing ever gets fixed. He better get home soon. There's nothing in this dump to eat."

"Maybe you aren't worried, but I am," Jessica said calmly. "Do either of you know where this Tony lives?"

"I can find out," Alex said.

Lynda shrugged again. "I don't go into town anymore." When she abruptly threw up her hands, one grazed a box to her side. The others jiggled and swayed in a rippling effect that seemed to spread across the top layer from one side of the room to the other like a small tsunami. "Billy will be fine. Stop your bellyaching," she said as she ignored the threatening box over her head.

And that wavering tower was just one of dozens, crowding around the room like soldiers on the warpath, determined to take over the house. It was a miracle she could survive in this environment. Maybe he needed to talk to social services Monday morning because if ever a house was a fire and health risk, this place was it. For now, he hitched his hands on his waist. "If you aren't worried about Billy, why did you call Chief Smyth?"

Her answer came in a begrudging voice. "Because I heard a noise out back. It woke me up."

"What kind of noise?" What he really wanted to know was why she felt free to call Chief Smyth in the middle of the night about something that should have gone through the dispatch desk.

"Someone was out there, probably trying to steal something. I turned on a light and the noise stopped. As long as you're here, you might as well go take a look. But don't touch anything."

"Okay," he said, determined not to roll his eyes, which was what he wanted to do. The house smelled—how did

Jessica keep from heaving? She must not have morning sickness. Still, he touched her arm. "Maybe you should come outside while I look around," he said figuring she was safer out there with a potential burglar than in here.

"I'll be fine," she said, sidling away from the teetering stack of boxes.

"You can't get outside through the kitchen door," Lynda said. "It's blocked. You'll have to go out the front way and walk around."

With a last glance at Jessica, he stepped outside where a deep breath of fresh, damp air reinvigorated him. He dug a small but intense flashlight out of his pocket to help thread his way through the yard, which was almost as cluttered as the inside of the house. Evidence of Billy's automotive endeavors littered the path as three cars that looked as if they hadn't moved in a decade stood parked with their hoods open and various engine parts scattered about. There was no sign that Billy had practiced his green thumb on his mother's land.

The sun was just coming up behind the hills, a yellow glow doing its best to break from under the haze like smothered candlelight. For a minute Alex stopped walking and listened. Birds had begun chirping, tree branches hung low and damp from the mist. There didn't seem to be any unexplained noises. He shined his light on the shed and found a lock securing the door through the hasp to which it was affixed. There were scratch marks and gouges on the wooden door as though someone had tried to pry the lock off. There was no way of telling how old they were.

A lean-to had been erected next to the shed and he shone his light there next. It was stuffed to the top with garbage bags and cardboard boxes, used motor parts and heaven knew what else. The light dispersed several rats who scurried off under the debris.

He backed away and shone the light around the yard one more time. As water dripped down his neck, he found himself shaking his head. What in the world would anyone steal in a place like this? Lynda Summers was absolutely delusional.

He walked back to find Jessica standing on the porch, Lynda still in the house by the door. "Well?" she demanded.

"It's possible someone tried to enter your shed. It doesn't appear they were successful."

"That was probably Billy's doing," Lynda said. "He keeps his engine parts out there and he's always losing the blasted key. You look like a drowned rat. Go home and tell Frank thanks a lot when you see him."

"Let us know if you have further problems," Alex said as he reached up to take Jessica's hand and help her down the rickety stairs.

"I TRIED TO talk to her about her son and his living conditions while you were outside," Jessica said as they pulled up in front of a diner they'd last frequented years before. It looked to her that it had changed hands. Bright lights and plaid curtains on the windows gave it a homey, welcoming appearance.

"Have any luck?" Alex asked.

"None. I met her years ago when Billy was in my class. She was odd then, she's odder now."

"What an understatement," he said, holding the door open for her. They were greeted by the delicious smells of coffee and bacon. She thought it must be amazing to Alex to be in a restaurant after months of cooking his own food over a campfire.

Alex called around while they waited for their order to be delivered. He jotted down the airport mechanic's phone number on his paper napkin, then called the man. When he hung up, he shook his head.

"Billy has never been to Tony's house," he said. "In fact, Tony sounded surprised I'd even suggest such a thing."

"Maybe Billy has a life his mother knows nothing about," Jessica said. "One that includes friends. After what we saw this morning, I have to say I sincerely hope that's true."

"Yeah."

Jessica took a deep breath. She was going to be a mother soon. She couldn't imagine ever talking about her child as Lynda Summers had talked of Billy.

"What are you going to tell Frank Smyth?"

"Exactly what happened. I'm hoping he volunteers the reason he was in the middle of such a routine call and why he sent a detective out for something that should have been handled by a patrolman. I can't quite make sense of it."

Their food was delivered right as Alex unfolded the newspaper someone had left on the bench seat. As Jessica buttered her waffle, he groaned. "Look at this," he said, holding the paper so she could see the photo below the fold. There was Chief Smyth with his arm around Alex's shoulder and a big grin on his face. "Chief Frank Smyth welcomes home Detective Alex Foster," the blurb beneath it announced.

"Good heavens," Jessica said.

"There's a whole recap of the same story they ran Saturday," Alex said. "People are going to be sick of me if this keeps up."

She put down her fork as he sliced a bite of melon.

"Alex, how did you catch the fish you ate? How did you cook them?"

"I found fishing gear in the emergency kit I salvaged," he said after swallowing. "Of course, it was touch and go for a few days when I was too sick to fish, but eventually I cooked on spits or flat rocks. The stuff I walked out with, I dried and smoked."

"I wish I had been with you," she mused aloud. "Not because it was a picnic, mind you, just because I could have helped."

"I thanked God every single day that you weren't on that plane," he said seriously.

"How did you keep from getting lost?"

"There was a compass in the emergency bag. The trail between the lake and the camp was marked with a forked tree at the lake side, so it wasn't too hard. What with my leg and everything, I didn't exactly wander far afield."

She chewed silently for a moment before adding, "We haven't really talked about what Agent Struthers told us yesterday. About the call from Shatterhorn to someone here in Blunt Falls."

"I don't know what we can do about any of it until they figure out who the call was made to. We just have to be extra careful." He paused before adding, "Would you consider flying to Kansas City to stay with your sister for a few weeks until this is over?"

"No," she said.

"But—"

"But nothing. I just got you back, I'm not leaving." She didn't add that if she left, she might have nothing to come back to. The threat from some nameless, faceless person coupled with the threat of losing her marriage made leaving impossible for her. "We're in this together, as a family," she said.

He nodded and she was shocked he didn't pursue it. Pleased, but shocked. "Okay," she continued. "Let's move from looming disaster to more mundane things. How about helping me change the batteries in all the smoke alarms today? You weren't here on the first day of spring when we usually do it and I didn't want to ask Billy."

"Sure. But now that you've brought up Billy, I was just thinking that he never came around our house before I crashed the Cessna."

"I know. I hadn't seen him since high school, but like I told you, two or three days after the crash, he showed up and asked if I needed help shoveling snow. Once I gave in and agreed, I tried to pay him, but he wouldn't take any money. How he rode from his place to our house in the snow on that old red bike is a mystery, but he did."

They left the café holding hands. The wind had come up and cut through the fog, made the parking lot a cold, damp, nasty place. Once they got to the car, he turned her to face him. "Do you need to go anywhere else before we head home?"

"Nope." She noticed that he scanned the parking lot every few moments, looking for bad guys, she supposed. She looked around, too. What people were visible through the mist seemed in a hurry to get out of the weather. No one seemed to have a good tan like the man in the photograph.

"Let's just go home and do chores like normal people," he said at last as he turned his gaze to her. His hazel eyes seemed to glow and she realized that each day he was back seemed to erase a week of the time he'd been gone. He was growing familiar again, closer, like before the Labor Day mall shooting and even way before that.

He kissed her forehead and she smiled. "Watch what you say," she warned him, touching his forehead where a pink welt was all that remained of the cut she knew he'd received when the plane landed and he was hit by broken glass. "I happen to have accumulated a long list."

"Great," he said. "Just make sure there's time in there for us to take a nap in the hammock if it ever warms up, okay?"

"And to talk to Billy when he comes by," she added.

"If he comes by."

FOR THE SECOND morning in a row, Alex awoke to the sound of a ringing phone. He answered it quickly, noting as he did that the fog was gone, replaced by heavy, thunderous-looking clouds. May in Blunt Falls was always a mix of weather.

"Yes," he said.

"The chief just called," Dylan said. "We have a dead body out on Evergreen. I'll be by to pick you up in fifteen minutes."

"I can come get you," Alex said. "It would be faster."

"No, I've moved out beyond your house. Just be ready."

Alex got out of bed as quietly as he could, took a quick shower and pulled on his clothes. It would have been nice to start back to work with something a little less gruesome, but you took what you got.

He leaned over the bed and kissed Jessica awake, knowing the alarm clock would ring within minutes anyway. He'd talked to her last night about making sure the house alarm was set and driving a different route to the school, encouraging her to park near others and not wander around by herself. She'd tolerated his instructions better than he'd thought she would and then reminded him that no one had tried to kill her, so maybe he should take his own advice.

"I have to leave," he told her. "We have a dead body."

"Do you know who it is? Is it Billy?"

"I seriously doubt it. Evergreen is a long way from Blue Point. I'll call you later and let you know my plans."

"Okay."

"And don't forget—"

"To set the alarm when I leave. Yes, dear."

He smiled at her and kissed her forehead.

Dylan pulled up right as Alex walked down the driveway. He got into Dylan's dark gray car and they took off as Alex opened a Vita-Drink and took a swig.

"You still drinking that stuff?"

"It's good for you," Alex said. "I'd think you'd appreciate that. Where'd you move to?"

"Eagle Nest."

Alex whistled. "That's the high-rent district."

"I got a deal. They like having a cop around and I like the on-site gym."

Alex looked at the scratched dashboard and added, "I thought someone said you got a new ride."

"I did," he said.

"This doesn't look real new."

Dylan nodded. "It's not. I drove my car to Billings yesterday for a date."

"That's a long ways to go for a date," Alex said.

"You haven't seen the girl. Man, she's barely out of high school."

"Did you check her age?" Alex said.

"Of course I did. She's legal. Unfortunately, she's also a terrible driver. Got rear-ended, so I had to borrow her car while mine gets fixed. Eight hundred and six miles on the odometer and she puts it in the shop."

"Yeah," Alex said, always amazed at Dylan's desire

to bed any female he met. For Alex there was one girl, one woman, and that was Jess. "Time to get to work," he said. "What do we know about our victim?"

Dylan cast him a swift look. "A guy with a metal detector was working the lot at the old drive-in theater when he came across a dead man."

"It's kind of early in the morning for a metal detector isn't it? Was it even light when he was out there?"

"Just barely. It takes all kinds, though. I've run kids out of there plenty of times."

"Maybe they hit someone they didn't know was there," Alex said.

"Maybe. But these kids also do drugs so maybe one of them OD'd and the rest ran off. I'm thinking about the Cummings twins."

The Cummings twins. Was that what Lynda Summers had meant when she said "look-alike" kids? They drove in silence for a moment and then Dylan started talking again. "What did you and Jess do over the weekend?" he asked as he turned onto Evergreen.

"Things around the house."

"I can't believe you're back from near death for two days and Jessica has you doing chores."

"I didn't mind. I just like being with her." He paused a second, thinking back to the day before. "Chief Smyth had me handle an off-the-record complaint from Lynda Summers. She said she heard a noise in her yard."

"Did you find anything?"

"No. Someone might have been trying to break into the shed—I doubt it, though."

"He's had me run out there a handful of times in the past few weeks, too," Dylan said. "What a pigsty."

Alex cast him a long look. "Same kind of thing?"

"Yeah. Almost always it's nothing I can do much about. Last time it was because she was mad at a neighbor who told her they were going to turn her in if she didn't fix up her yard. She wanted me to go read them the riot act. I walked over and calmed down the neighbor. Face it, the Summers house belongs on one of those reality TV shows."

"How did the chief ever get on the receiving end of her calls?

"Believe it or not, his mother is responsible. He told me this one night after a couple of beers. His mother was Lynda's godmother. The old lady—on her deathbed, mind you—made Frank promise to take over as Lynda's unofficial guardian angel. By then Lynda was getting a little goofy. He did as good as he could when he was a detective like you and me, but it was impossible to protect her from everything. Now he's acting chief and he seems hell-bent on making sure her antics fly under the radar."

"I'm not sure he's doing Lynda a favor by helping her avoid reality," Alex mused. "It's a wonder something hasn't fallen on her head and crushed her to death."

"Yeah," Dylan said, "but since Smyth is obviously aware of her predicament, I've decided to mind my own business."

They finally glimpsed vehicles and lights up ahead all pulled into the giant parking lot of the old drive-in theater. Dylan drove slowly through the open gates.

Kit Anderson was one of the uniforms who had responded to the panicked metal detector's call. He had on rain gear which he might very well need within the hour. "We've got guys combing the area for any evidence," he said by way of greeting.

"Get them into a grid," Alex said. "Try to cover the whole lot before the weather breaks."

"Where's the guy with the metal detector?" Dylan asked.

"In the back of my car. He was pretty shook up. His name is Henry Fields and he admits he comes here once or twice a year to see if he can find anything interesting. He says he always wiggles through some loose boards in the back so he didn't notice the chain on the front entrance had been cut."

"Why in the world did he come out here so early?" Alex asked.

"I asked him that. He says there's never anyone around out here when it rains, so as soon as he got up and heard the weather report, he took off. His truck is parked out behind the lot where he left it."

"We'll go talk to him," Alex said.

Kit shook his head. "There's no need," he said. "He already told me everything he knows." Kit was a tall, wiry man who had been a track-and-field star back in high school. He gestured with a long arm. "If I were you, I'd go talk to the M.E.," he suggested, his voice on the raw edge of condescending. "He's been here for quite a while."

"But you aren't me," Alex said softly. "Please join the search and set up a grid, okay?"

"Sure," Kit said, and walked off with a scowl.

"You got yourself an enemy," Dylan said as they moved toward the squad car.

"I guess. I don't want him pissed at me all the time, but there's not a lot I can do because I didn't wind up moldering away in the mountains."

"Are you thinking Kit had something to do with that crash?"

"Hell, no. I didn't say that."

"Because I can't imagine he'd go to such lengths."

"Nor can I." Alex stopped abruptly. "You know, though, in this case he may be right. We both don't need to question our metal detector. I'll go get started on the crime scene before the weather deteriorates."

"Sounds good," Dylan said, and ambled toward the squad car.

Alex approached the crowd of people gathered under an open tent. He'd come to this theater a few times when he was a kid but it had closed decades ago. There was no longer a standing screen or a concession/projector building, just gently rolling ground. In the old days, cars would pull their front ends up on the berms, giving them a clear line of sight to the big outdoor screen over the tops of the cars in front of them. Remnants of metal posts that used to hold the speakers stuck up out of the weeds.

Patrolmen had erected a tent over the body in deference to the deteriorating weather. The victim was facedown in one of the lower spots between the humps. Thanks to the team working the scene, he couldn't see the dead man, just a pile of what appeared to be mangled dark clothing amid a sea of flashbulbs.

"Someone ran over him," the M.E. said as he approached Alex. "More than once, I might add." He turned to the ambulance crew and called, "I'm finished for now. You can get the Vic ready for transport."

"Do we have an ID?" Alex asked.

"Not yet. We've taken his prints, but right now all I can tell you is we have a Caucasian male in his early twenties. There's no sign he struggled, which leads me to believe he was unconscious when he was run over."

"Any signs of drugs?"

"No, but I'll run a toxicology."

"How about a time of death?"

He shook his graying head which was covered with a jaunty plaid beret. "At least twenty-four hours. He's been here awhile."

So he'd died sometime early Sunday morning. Alex thought for a moment before speculating. "I wonder if he walked out here, overdosed on something and fell into a deep sleep or hit his head." Like Dylan said, teens sometimes cut through the chain and came in here at night to race over the rolling lot, seeing just how fast they could go and most of the time, they did it late enough there were few people to see their headlights. If there'd been a sleeping or drugged person in a dark spot, it was conceivable someone ran over him accidentally. However, you'd think they would have noticed a bump and quit after the first hit.

"I'll know more after the autopsy," the M.E. said.

Alex nodded as he looked around. The ground was covered with a layer of weeds that would make getting tire impressions tricky even if it hadn't been raining most of the night.

Alex pulled up his collar as more rain started now. He began the trek down to the body but before he got far, Kit Anderson yelled from the back of the lot near where the screen used to be. Alex changed direction and jogged through the rain. He stopped short as he got close enough to see what had been found near a pile of discarded lumber: a mangled red bicycle.

"I don't think it's been here long," Kit said as Officer Herrera planted an evidence flag near the bike and the photographer began snapping pictures. "There's no rust to speak of."

"Get something over it as quick as you can," Alex said, then turned and retraced his steps. They were loading the body into the ambulance as he gently pulled the blanket away from the victim's face.

Somewhere in his gut he'd known.

"Oh, Billy," he whispered. "What in the hell did you get yourself into?"

Chapter Five

"Take me by the school," Alex told Dylan.

"Jessica's school? Why?"

"Because I don't want her to hear about Billy from someone else."

"Then call her," Dylan said with his typical lack of understanding about sensitive issues. No wonder he went through women like water through a sieve.

"Billy Summers was important to Jessica, especially in the last few months. The kid brought some color into her life and I owe it to both of them to make sure she hears what happened to him from me."

"Use the damn phone," Dylan said impatiently.

"Stop at the school. It'll take ten minutes."

Dylan did as asked, immediately taking out his cell and making phone calls as Alex jogged inside. Probably because of the rain, but maybe because of the run across the drive-in lot, his leg hurt today but he ignored the pain.

He found Jessica alone in her classroom as it was late lunch period by now. She was eating a sandwich at her desk while reading a book.

She looked happy to see him, which warmed his heart to no end, and rose to greet him. He hugged her and held her for a moment, breathing in the fragrance of her hair and the feel of her body next to his, simple pleasures he would never take for granted again.

"Why are you here?" she finally asked, and he requested she sit down.

Five minutes later, tears in her eyes, she blew her nose on a tissue Alex fetched for her. "How did Lynda Summers take it?" she asked. Her voice was raw with grief.

"Chief Smyth said she took it hard," he said.

"Do you have any idea who would do this to him?"

"The drive-in gets weekend action from teens driving too fast and doing drugs. Maybe Billy was in the wrong place at the wrong time. Anyway, I just wanted you to know I'll be late tonight and I didn't want you hearing this from someone else."

"Has he been missing since he left our house?" she asked.

"I'm not sure, but it looks like it. Far as I can tell he was wearing the same clothes. I'll talk to his mother later and find out for sure. Are you okay? I've got a ton to do and Dylan is outside chomping at the bit."

"Go do your job," she said. "And be careful."

"That's what I was going to tell you," he said, and kissed her on the lips. Hers were salty, but sweet, and he hugged her once more.

He didn't tell her about the drug angle Dylan had brought up because he knew she wouldn't believe it, and until verified, it was just a rumor. Dylan had told him he heard that the Cummings twins used Billy like an enforcer of sorts and speculated someone got back at him by giving him some of the drugs and then killing him. Alex just wanted to make sure of the cause of death before they started making up stories.

Within twenty minutes, they were bypassing the air terminal to drive around to the back of the airport. Alex's gaze was drawn to the three rows of privately owned planes and specifically to the spot on the tarmac he'd rented for his Cessna. There was another plane there now.

They parked by the maintenance building and went inside where they found Tony Machi working on the engine of a small aqua-colored single-engine plane Alex knew was owned by a local lawyer. Tony looked up from his work as he apparently heard their footsteps. He immediately broke into a grin and started wiping his hands on a grease rag hanging from an overall pocket.

"Good to see you back," he said to Alex, stepping forward, arm outstretched. "I've been dying to know what happened to the Cessna," he added, his brow creasing. He was a middle-aged guy with a big family, as competent as he was kind and a hell of a mechanic. "I'd just worked on it a couple of days before you took off, remember? And don't think the FAA and every other agency in the country wasn't all over here, looking at my records and books."

Alex introduced Dylan before he explained. "I wasn't feeling very good that day and my memory is shady," Alex admitted. "I recall a sudden drop in the oil pressure, a fire, the engine seizing and the crash. A lot of people are talking sabotage but I don't see how that could be, do you?"

"Did you hear an explosion or something?"

Alex searched his mind. As fuzzy as some things were, he was positive he hadn't. "No."

"Well, I talked to your friend Nate Matthews on the phone. The FBI mentioned him, too, and then there was a lot of talk about that militia group and the way they were staging these horrible shootings on national holidays. You and your buddies were a threat to them, I guess."

"I guess," Alex said.

Tony shook his head. "Memorial Day is coming up—I'm keeping all the kids home. They're throwing a fit because they want to go to the parade with their friends, but I just can't let them do it. We'll go tend my parents' graves like we do every year, but then it's home for movies on the television."

Alex knew Jessica would also go to the cemetery and put flowers on graves of former soldiers and that of her own grandfather, a World War II veteran. It was a tradition in her family, one they had shared over the years. But he hated to hear Tony talk about being afraid for his kids to attend a parade.

"Probably a good idea to stay close to home," Dylan said.

"Yeah," Tony said with a shake of his head. "But kind of sad, too. It's getting so regular folks like me feel they need to carry a gun around."

"Which is exactly the fear these people strive to create," Alex said.

"Yeah. I know, I read that, too." Tony sighed and squared his shoulders. "Okay, give it to me straight. Where is your beautiful Cessna now?"

"Under at least twenty feet of cold lake water. Nate and I are going to dive on it."

"Won't the FAA bring it out of the lake?"

"Yeah, they will. But it's in a remote spot and it's going to take a helicopter and a lot of staging. I want to see it myself before they move it."

"Yeah, I would, too. I'll make a list of things you should look for or check, okay?" Tony offered.

"That's great."

"But that's not why we're really here," Dylan pointed

out. He gestured at a few stools pulled up to a workbench. "Let's sit down. We have bad news."

Tony froze in place. "Is it Noreen or one of my children—"

"Nothing like that," Alex rushed to assure him. "It's about Billy."

Tony shook his head. "I know you were looking for him yesterday. He still hasn't shown up? Well, he's late getting here, too. He has a whole bunch of small jobs to perform and it's getting late. When he does get here, I have half a mind to tell him to get lost."

"That won't be necessary," Alex said gently. "We found his body a little while ago. He's been dead since sometime Sunday morning."

Tony sat abruptly. "Dead? How?"

"I'm not entirely sure. On the surface, he was run over at least twice. But it's unclear why he would just lie there and let someone do that to him."

"An accident?" Tony said. "I mean he rode that bike of his everywhere. Did someone run him down beside a road?"

Thinking they wouldn't really know if Billy actually died at the drive-in until all the evidence was analyzed, Alex kept it vague while Dylan didn't respond at all. "It's unclear."

Dylan added, "Do you know if he used drugs?"

Tony looked aghast. "Drugs? I don't think so. They test employees but Billy wasn't really on a formal payroll. I never saw any indications, though."

"How about friends?" Dylan persisted. "Did people come here to see him?"

"Once in a while, but he had trouble with people, you know. He was impressionable and eager to please most of the time, but then he'd get all sullen and quiet."

"You ever see a couple of blond boys about eighteen years old visit him? They're twins so they stand out," Dylan said.

"Blond, good-looking boys?"

"Yeah, I guess you could call them good-looking."

Tony nodded. "I've seen them. They talk to Billy sometimes. Seemed like odd kids for a guy like Billy to know, but they acted friendly enough."

"Billy came by our house Saturday night," Alex said. "I don't think he was aware there was a party."

"Why did he go to your house?" Tony asked, obviously surprised.

"He befriended my wife while I was away. She got to be quite fond of him. But Saturday night he said he came to talk to me. Then he got scared off by all the cops hanging around and claimed he couldn't remember what he wanted. While he was there, I recalled seeing him here on the tarmac the morning I took off. He was deicing a windshield for somebody else, at least that's the impression I got because of the tools he carried. He didn't remember seeing me, though."

"Ordinarily, I wouldn't have remembered one morning out of a hundred, but that morning stands out on account of what happened to you," Tony said. "No one else took off in a private plane that morning and I don't remember Billy being here, either, at least not until later in the day. Now, two days before, that was a different matter. The kid got here early and stayed late, hanging over my shoulder all the time, even refusing to break for lunch."

"Was that unusual behavior for him?" Alex asked.

"Well, sure. It gets a little cold in this hangar in February, you know, so we're all anxious for a few minutes in what we refer to as the lounge. It's that room back there with a table and chairs. Oh, and a heater. It's where we eat our lunch and Billy was as fond of food as the rest of us. But that day, he stayed here, looking at his little cards as though he was trying to remember something."

"Little cards?" Dylan asked, but Alex was pretty sure he knew what Tony was talking about.

"Yeah, you know, those little white cards my wife puts recipes on, or at least she used to before she got her computer. As long as the directions were real easy, he liked to have them written down."

Alex cleared his throat. "Directions to what?"

"Oh, you know, things like, go get the broom, sweep up garbage, put garbage in can. I don't know what he was looking at that day because it wasn't one of my cards."

"And how do you know that?" Dylan asked.

"Because mine are all pink. They're leftovers from the wife. The one he kept fingering was white."

"What were you working on that day, do you remember?"

Tony shrugged. "Just regular stuff. Engine tune-ups, maintenance checks, you know. It might have been the day I looked at your plane, Alex. Yeah, in fact, I'm sure it was." He frowned for a second. "Sure as heck can't figure out why he'd go to your house at night like that."

"His mother didn't know what he wanted, either. Are you sure he didn't say anything to you about my being back?"

"I haven't seen him since you got back. He didn't come into work Saturday which was unusual for him. The only times he tended not to show up were when he had a problem of some sort he was working through."

"What kind of problem?"

"I don't know, he didn't exactly tell me. I just knew when he was preoccupied. He'd get quieter than ever and go off by himself." Tony sighed as he got to his feet. "The boy had big dreams. I think he was kind of desperate to get away from that house. I gave him rides home when the weather was real bad. His mother was always haranguing him. I don't know how he stood living in that rat's nest."

"I don't, either," Alex said. For the first time, he started wondering about the noise Lynda Summers claimed to have heard in the wee hours of Sunday morning. He'd written it off, but not any longer. Maybe it warranted another look around.

"If you think of anything, let me know," Alex said, and handed Tony a card.

"I will. Damn shame. All and all, I'm going to miss the kid."

"I THINK WE need to talk to the Cummings twins and to Billy's mother sooner rather than later," Alex said.

"Which one first?"

"You go see the twins, I'll go see Lynda Smyth."

"No," Dylan said. "We should stick together."

"I don't think so," Alex said. "Let's drop by the office and talk to the M.E., and then you swing by my house and let me out. I'll get my truck."

"I don't know," Dylan protested. "You heard what the FBI guy said and now Tony is talking about Billy hanging around your plane while it was getting fixed. We stick together."

Alex shook his head. "I'm not budging on this. It's our job to investigate Billy Summers's death and I'm not going to jeopardize what needs to be done so you can hold my hand. Let's stop arguing about it."

"Three months in the mountains didn't cure your stubborn streak, did it?" Dylan said.

"Nope."

By the time Dylan reached Alex's house, they knew

that Billy had drugs in his system at the time of death and that he'd been alive when he was run over. There was still no explanation of how he ended up at the old drive-in except that it seemed unlikely he rode there on his bike as there were no discernible bicycle tracks. And if he hadn't ridden the bike, then someone had taken him. Why? Hopefully Billy's mother or the Cummings boys could shed some light on the matter.

"Jessica isn't home yet," Alex said to himself as they pulled in the driveway.

"Did you expect her to be?"

"Kind of."

"Don't worry. She'll be cautious."

"Yeah," Alex said, not at all sure his partner was right. As Dylan roared off, Alex unlocked the garage and got in his truck. It was the first time he'd turned the key in the ignition since coming home, but Jessica had told him she'd run the engine every few days. The truck started right up and he pulled out of the garage.

As he drove away, he attempted to reason with himself. Jessica was fine, she knew he was going to be late, she probably just stopped by a friend's house.

The pep talk grated every raw nerve in his body.

THE LAST TIME Jessica felt like she did today, she'd been eighteen years old and a freshman in college. It had been the first time she'd been away from home and she remembered feeling so excited she could hardly sleep. All the new people and ideas and parties and conversations made her anxious for each new day.

And then things began to change. It started with an uneasy feeling of being watched, causing her to turn while walking across a field or down a hall to see if someone was behind her, looking over her shoulder with uneasy glances. There never seemed to be anyone interested in her and after a few days of it, she began to think she was developing some major psychological problem.

After a week or so of this, she began getting phone calls from a blocked line with no one speaking on the other end. This was followed by someone turning her doorknob in the middle of the night. She considered contacting the campus police but decided against it, unwilling to go public lest her parents be notified. No way did she want them to panic and demand she come home. A few times she managed to yank the door open, but there was never anyone there. When a bouquet of dead flowers greeted her one morning, she decided it was time to enlist the aid of the dorm resident assistant who helped her set a trap.

The perpetrator turned out to be a boy she had in one of her classes. She vaguely remembered that sometime in the first month of school he had hemmed and hawed in an awkward attempt to ask her out. As she wasn't interested in dating him or anyone else at that point, she'd attempted to defuse the request by joking around and making an excuse to rush off. After that, she'd seldom seen him again. And all along, he had been furious with what he thought was her total disregard for his feelings and had decided to retaliate by anonymously stalking her. After she'd apologized up one side and down the other and he had done the same, they'd avoided each other for the rest of term. She wasn't sure what happened to him after that.

And that's how she felt today as she left the Green Mountain Mall. Like someone was watching. It hadn't started until she finished shopping and was making her way back to her car.

In a replay of those long-ago college years, she found

herself whipping around to check out the people and cars around her. And as before, she saw no one lurking, nothing threatening.

Alex had asked her to not be alone. She'd thought a mall would be the perfect place to search for a condolence card for Billy's mother. At this hour of the day, the place was crawling with people. But now she realized that there were several ways to be alone and one of the most disturbing ways was to be in a crowd of people you didn't know.

Think about Billy's mother, stop thinking about yourself.

Maybe it was because she was in the process of creating a child that the thought of losing one made Jessica so sick inside. But there was also the fact that Billy had been a generous companion with no agenda of his own except to help her. He'd made her world more beautiful, certainly physically with his gardening, but also figuratively by offering undemanding friendship at a time in her life when that was about all she could handle. And now he was gone.

There was that feeling again. Once more she scanned the immediate vicinity, her eyes peeled for tall, tanned bald men in particular. "There's nothing to be afraid of," she whispered to herself as none materialized, but that wasn't entirely true. The FBI don't warn people for nothing.

Where was all her bravado now? Was someone in this sea of cars staring at her through binoculars?

The inside of the car felt like a real sanctuary and she locked her doors, glad no one could see her acting like a scaredy-cat. All this talk she'd given Alex about not being afraid and here she was frightened of absolutely nothing. She picked up her phone to call him and then remembered what he was doing with his day and put the phone down.

Okay. She would not drive directly home. She would drive the opposite direction to make sure she wasn't being followed. With a plan in mind, she took off, checking her rearview mirror frequently. At first there was the usual crush of traffic on the road leading to and from the mall, but the cars quickly thinned out. At the second red light, a station wagon roared up behind her. She could see inside the car. The two teenage girls in the front seat nodded their heads in time with the radio whose music was loud enough to permeate Jessica's closed windows.

No threat there.

The station wagon turned after a few minutes. Jessica veered off into a fancy neighborhood with narrow streets and little traffic. She meandered around until she realized that not only did she feel totally alone and decidedly unwatched, but that she was behaving like an idiot. She headed home.

A half hour later, she let herself inside the house, dumping her briefcase and purse on the chair. With a sigh, she slipped off her shoes and walked across the room to set the alarm. She stopped suddenly as something caught her peripheral vision. Turning, she gasped, covering her mouth with her hands, unable to move.

ALEX DECIDED THE best chance of engaging Lynda Summers in a candid conversation was to arrive unannounced. After all, the day before, she'd told him she never left the house.

She didn't answer her door and a quick turn of the knob revealed it was locked.

He walked around the yard again just to make sure she wasn't outside somewhere and ended up in back.

The big trees stopped most of the rain from falling on his shoulders but it did nothing to stem the stench from the garbage in the lean-to. Once again, the lock on the shed door drew his attention.

Was it possible Lynda Summers had something worth stealing back here?

He walked around the shed, looking for a window and found himself facing a wall of ivy. When he got closer, he could see a window behind the plants and spread the branches a little, getting close enough to peer through the glass while keeping his feet out of the mud in case there were other footprints to be found later.

He could barely make out part of a small room. Shading his eyes from what little glare there was on the glass, the most obvious distinction about the space was how clutter-free it was.

Closest to the window a large model of a red-and-white biplane hung suspended from the ceiling. More or less under that sat a small round table on top of which rested a lamp with a striped black-and-yellow base that brought to mind a bumblebee. A stack of index cards sat next to the lamp. The only other furniture consisted of an old, upholstered chair close to a workbench fronted by a couple of square stools. There were some kind of supplies on the workbench that he couldn't make out.

As Lynda Summers seemed totally incapable of keeping a space this uncluttered, this had to be Billy's hideyhole. But hadn't she claimed he used the shed as a place to store engine parts?

Alex let the ivy close up behind him and walked back toward the house, determined to get a search warrant. Billy had liked written directions—maybe something on those cards would point to his killer.

Once again he stood on the porch and knocked on the

door. Looking through the front window proved fruitless as her junk blocked any view. He took out his cell and phoned her number. Listening closely, he heard a phone ring inside. The woman apparently wasn't home.

He hung up and stood there a second. The phone rang in his hand and he saw Dylan's number flash on the screen.

"I got them," Dylan said, his voice excited.

"Got who?"

"The Cummings twins. I found a piece of torn clothing on their car. It looks like it could have come from Billy's jacket. The whole bumper is a mess like they ran into something. They have no alibi. There are some pills in their glove box, too. I'm taking them in. The lab people and the techs are here. The car will be hauled in pretty soon."

"Wow," Alex said, kind of shocked. "Good work. Did they say how or why they killed him?"

"They say they're innocent. They gave each other alibis that are worth about as much as a three-dollar bill. Listen, I've got to go, partner." He hung up abruptly and Alex did the same.

He needed to go downtown, but first he was going to stop by his house and make sure Jessica had set the alarms. He'd do it sneakylike, so she didn't know he was checking up on her.

Maybe they really had found out who had killed Billy. But Alex couldn't shake the feeling that even if they had, there was more going on than met the eye....

Chapter Six

Alex did his best to check his temper when he found the front-door alarm had not been set. For that matter, the door wasn't even locked. He knew Jessica was home, because her car was in the driveway. He didn't want to bark at her because she forgot the alarm, but such carelessness coming on top of a day like this one made his nerves twice as jumpy.

"Jessica?" he called. Her things had been dumped on the chair and her shoes sat off to one side. He looked around the room, then called upstairs. "Jess?"

Maybe she was in the kitchen. He started to walk to the dining room when the open patio door caught his eye and he veered that direction.

He found her standing still as death in the yard, rain falling on her head, bare feet buried in the grass. By the looks of her hair, she'd been standing there a while. But it was what was all around her that shook his soul.

Someone had ravaged the garden, butchering every plant and flower with what looked like unbridled rage. A million petals lay on the ground, on the paths, on the grass. Crushed, severed stems bent toward the earth, blossoms trampled into the mud. Limbs had been whacked off bushes, leaving raw, jagged edges. From what he could see, even small branches on trees had been bludgeoned. It looked like a giant whirring blade or an ogre with a vendetta had hacked every living thing. The overwhelming scent of devastated flora permeated the air in a sweet, decaying way that reminded him of a funeral.

Jessica finally registered his presence and turned around to look at him. Her eyes were red, her cheeks tearstained, her lips trembled.

He stood before her and she melted into his arms. Great, silent, heaving sobs shook her body as she cried against his neck and he tried to comfort her. If the maniac who did this appeared right that moment, Alex would have gladly beaten him to a pulp.

"Who would do this to Billy's flowers?" she finally managed to mumble through her tears.

But they weren't really Billy's flowers and that's what alarmed him. This was *their* yard, these were *their* plants. Someone had come through their gate and slaughtered their peace of mind less than twelve hours after the man who had created this beauty was found dead.

"I don't know," he said as he tried to comfort her. "But I'll find out."

JESSICA RAN STEAMING hot water into the tub, lying back to cover her shoulders, closing her eyes, her hands resting on her bare, wet belly.

A mere inch or two away, her baby existed in a liquid world of his or her own. Maybe Alex was right. Maybe she should go to Kansas City and visit her sister.

No, she wouldn't do that. There was a feeling in her bones that something was coming to a head. She was not going to abandon the husband who had just miraculously returned to her no matter how many flowers were torn from their stems.

There was a knock on the door and she called, "Come in."

Alex appeared carrying a mug. "I made you some chamomile tea," he said.

She sat up and accepted the mug. "Thank you. I can't seem to get warm."

"Darn rain," he said, perching on the edge of the tub. "It gets in your bones." She smiled as she took a sip of the tea. They both knew the rain had nothing to do with the chills in her body. "I called a gardening service," he added. "They're coming here tomorrow to clean things up."

"Thank you," she whispered, setting the mug aside. "How was all that destruction accomplished, do you know?"

"Our toolshed was open. The only thing I can find missing is the old machete I stored there for when we went camping, you know, the one with the green cord wound around the handle. Unless you got rid of it while I was...away."

"No," she said, "I didn't move it."

"Might Billy have taken it?" he asked gently.

"I can't see why. I was usually here when he worked and I never saw him touch it."

He nodded and they both fell silent. After a few seconds, she took a deep breath. "I owe you an apology," she said.

"For what?" he asked, his expression puzzled.

"For turning into a zombie when I saw the yard. I left the alarm off, I just froze. But it wasn't only because of the flowers or the thought someone had come into our yard."

"It was because it happened right after Billy's death," he said. "I know."

"Was he murdered, Alex?"

"We think so," he said.

"Tell me about it."

"We know he was alive when he was run over. We know he had drugs in his system, enough to cause his apparent unconsciousness. The M.E. identified Rohypnol but a complete toxicology will take longer."

"Rohypnol? Isn't that a date rape drug?"

"Yep."

"Good heavens."

"I know. Dylan found torn clothing on the front grill of a car belonging to Ted and Tad Cummings and there is some damage there including a bunch of dents. There were pills in the glove box, he said, and what do you want to bet that they'll turn out to be Rohypnol? The boys aren't talking much, but the techs have the car and the lab is working on the evidence. There was also paint on the bike and the rear bumper reflector is broken. Part of it's missing. They're running tests on that, too."

"Why would the twins fill Billy with a date rape drug and run over him?" she asked, shivering despite the hot water, despite the tea.

"The drug administered in that quantity would have rendered him unconscious and thus compliant. Do you know the twins?"

"They were never in any of my classes, but they were the kind of boys who stood out. Pranks and shenanigans, never anything serious that I knew of. Certainly nothing violent."

He smoothed a lock of damp hair from her forehead. "You're going to hear this from someone, so I'm going to tell you. There are rumors circulating that the Cummings kids were into small-time drugs and they used Billy Summers to collect money and make deliveries."

"I don't believe it," she said.

"I don't know if I do, either."

"And what does any of this have to do with your plane crash, or are we talking about two different things?"

"I think Billy's death and my crash are connected somehow, but I don't know exactly in what way."

"What did Billy's mother say?"

"She wasn't home," he told her.

"Shouldn't you be downtown asking these boys questions?"

"And leave you? Hell, no."

"You have to do your job, Alex."

"Dylan will keep me informed."

"Did you tell him about our yard?"

"Yeah. On the off chance the Cummings twins had anything to do with it I had to."

"It doesn't make sense," she said, shaking her head.

He touched her again as though he couldn't keep his hands from her. The smoldering look in his eyes burned away a layer of cold.

A sigh escaped his lips. "If I stay here much longer, I'm going to jump in and ravage you. I better go make some phone calls."

"Thanks for being honest and up-front with me about Billy," she said. "I have a very hard time believing anyone would want to harm him." She paused and then added, "I know you're the cop but I have more questions."

"Go ahead and ask them," he said, his gaze lingering on her breasts. "But no promises about the ravaging issue, okay? I may dive in."

She smiled, understanding his banter was tinged with

his desire to reassure her that life was normal despite the current situation. She hadn't expected him to refuse to answer any more questions, but she had steeled herself for the old back-off-my-territory tone that used to stop her dead in her tracks. Thankfully, it was absent and that was heartening. "We don't know for certain that your plane was sabotaged, do we?" she began.

"Not for certain, no."

"And we don't know who the contact in Blunt Falls is, you know, the one Agent Struthers told us about."

Alex nodded in agreement, and she continued.

"Or if this contact is really interested in you, even if they were before. I mean, I understand trying to stop you last February when you were on your way to help Nate and Mike figure out a conspiracy. But the man behind that portion of this terrorism movement is dead now, so what threat are you?"

"It would have to be because I know the contact here in Blunt Falls, the person who set me up," Alex said, alarm igniting his eyes. "Is that what you're thinking?"

She nodded. "You're going to keep at this until you figure out what happened to your plane and your friends."

"Is that what you think?" he asked.

The water was growing lukewarm and she shivered. "What do you mean?" she said.

He fixed her with his hazel stare, the one she always thought she'd hate to be on the receiving end of if she had just committed some heinous crime. "My goal is to figure out what happened to protect you and our baby, Jess. And now it's even more important because my gut is telling me Billy was murdered, too, in the here and now, and that it ties back to my plane crash. That means his death is mine to solve, as well."

"How does his death tie to your plane crash?" she

asked, wishing she could get out of the water, but she
didn't want to interrupt this conversation, so she stayed
still.

"I haven't told you about what the airport mechanic
said about Billy and the plane," he said. "What with the
garden and everything, I completely forgot about it for
a while."

"What did he say?"

"He said Billy missed work Saturday, which was atyp-
ical. So, the first day it's in the paper that I'm home, the
kid doesn't go to work. Tony Machi said Billy hovered
around my plane the day it was serviced. He saw the kid
studying index cards, too, and was in fact alone with the
plane during a lunch break."

"Was Billy capable of doing something to your plane?"

"Not without help, no. But remember, he was looking
at those cards like the ones he asked you to make him
so he could tend the garden the way you wanted. And I
saw a pile of the same kind of index cards in a shed behind his house."

"I can't believe he would do anything to hurt you."

"You're thinking of the Billy who came to our house
and offered you help, who tried to make you happy. But
why did he come to help you, and what did he want to
tell me the night he showed up here during our party?"

"We need to be certain about the plane," she whispered.

He nodded. "Exactly. If we can prove it was tampered
with and that Billy had something to do with it, then
that might lead to figuring out who he was in cahoots
with. I'll call Nate. As soon as he can get here, I'll borrow a floatplane from John Miter and fly us both up to
the lake. I'd better arrange to get hold of some diving
equipment, too."

"Who's John Miter?" Jessica asked.

"A guy Dylan and I met out at the airfield last summer," he said.

Last summer—when they hardly spoke to each other. It didn't surprise Jessica that she hadn't heard of this guy.

"Dylan didn't seem to take to John. I, on the other hand, really liked him. He's not the chatty type, but he's definitely got a certain aura about him."

"What do you mean?"

"He lives out on the lake near Crawfish Point in a house he built himself. I know almost nothing about him because he doesn't volunteer information. He's retired now, but he could have been a Superior Court judge, a priest, a mercenary or a crook. When I ask, he just ruffles my hair like I'm ten years old and tells me not to worry about it."

"Sounds interesting but not your normal choice in friends," she said. She shivered from a combination of cold and nerves and asked what she really wanted to know but had been reluctant to broach. "Alex, do you ever worry about piloting again?"

He seemed to think for a moment. "Right after the crash, I swore I was finished with flying. That feeling seems to have faded. I guess I'll know for sure very soon when I take up a floatplane."

"Take me with you," she said softly.

He shook his head adamantly. "No, sweetie. I don't want you anywhere near that lake. We're going to have to find someplace safe for you to stay while I'm gone."

"You're going to find me a babysitter?" she said, irritated. In so many ways he was letting her in, but when he decided to keep her at arm's length it was very hard to get past him. He was doing better, though. He was trying.

He's going to have to try harder and it's obvious that I need to help him.

"Something like that," he said.

"You frustrate me, Alex Foster," she said, casting him an annoyed look. She started to stand and he caught her elbow to steady her.

"I'm sorry," he said.

"I know you're sorry. I'm sorry, too." She stepped out of the tub. "I know you need to go downtown and find out what's really going on. Take me over to Silvia's house. I'll be safe there. The woman has been a principal for eighteen years. Nobody or nothing gets past her."

"Are you sure?"

"Positive."

He handed her a towel and then gently began patting her shoulders dry with another. It brought back memories of their honeymoon, which they'd spent in Hawaii in a very posh place where their room came with a private lanai complete with its own small swimming pool. They'd spent hours in the sun-warmed water, so into each other that the world had almost ceased to exist. What she wouldn't give to zap them both back to that moment in time....

She turned to look at him.

"You're shaking," he said.

"I'm cold."

"I won't let anything happen to you or to me or to our baby. I promise," he said, sliding his hand against her damp skin to rest it on top of her abdomen. His touch made her dizzy and she leaned her forehead against his chest. "Jess? Are you okay?"

She looked up at him with tears in her eyes. "I can't go through losing you again, Alex. Once was enough."

He pulled her closer and claimed her lips.

THE POLICE BUILDING was bustling with activity when Alex arrived after dropping Jessica off at her principal's house. The two women had hugged and Silvia had promised to lock all her doors. They were going to make a quiche for dinner, she said, and Alex was invited to come back and have a piece. He told her he'd do what he could but not to wait for him.

He found Dylan at his desk, finishing up his paperwork. Dylan loved to catch the bad guys, as he put it. He had little patience for lawbreakers of any kind, let alone murderers.

Chief Smyth poked his head out the door and called for Alex and Dylan to join him.

"What have we got?" Smyth asked, seated at his desk. There was a framed photograph of a pretty young woman that caught Alex's attention. The girl had a great smile and a passing resemblance to Jessica.

"My daughter, Stella," Smyth explained. "She's currently away at college."

"She looks like she's a nice kid," Alex said.

"Yes, she is."

"Where does she go to school?"

"Texas," Smyth said, reaching for the crumbled package of cigarettes on his desk. He knew as well as anyone the laws prohibiting smoking indoors in places of employment and Alex knew he wouldn't actually light one up, but the instinct to do so was apparently very strong. "Why do you ask?"

The real reason was that with Jess's pregnancy came the longed-for anticipation of having a child. It had just dawned on him that girl or boy, this baby who was yet to be born, would someday fly away. He shrugged and said, "You must miss her. I bet you can remember every moment of her infancy."

Smyth scowled. "I suppose," he said, and then repeated his earlier question. "What have you guys got for me?"

They detailed their day, checking notes to bring the chief up-to-date on where they went, who they spoke to, what they saw. Smyth knew about Billy's death, of course, and Alex watched him carefully when he mentioned Lynda Summers hadn't been at home when he went to speak to her.

"She was at the funeral home making plans for the time when her son's body can be released for burial," he said somberly. "I know because I'm the one who gave her a ride." He paused for a second and ran a hand over his bald head. Alex thought he might be getting ready to explain his connection to Lynda, a story Dylan had already related. He could think of no way to cut Smyth short that wouldn't reveal they'd been talking about him, something Alex was loath to do, but he needn't have worried. The chief simply cleared his throat.

"I need to get a court order," Alex said. "I need to check out the shed at the back of the house. I managed to look through a window today and saw the cards I told you about, the ones Billy liked to help him keep directions clear in his head."

"You won't need a court order," the chief insisted. "Lynda will allow me to search anywhere that's necessary. I'll meet you there tomorrow, say 8 a.m.?"

"Why not now?" Alex asked. "There are questions about Billy's activities that she needs to answer."

"Because right now, she is under sedation, doctor's orders."

"Did you happen to ask her if she knew anything about Billy being mixed up with drugs in any capacity?" Alex asked.

"By the time I saw her, I knew about the rumors. They spread really fast on this one. Anyway, I did ask her about the Cummings boys and she said they had come around occasionally, she wasn't sure why."

"What about drugs?" Dylan said.

"She said he might have experimented around a little like a lot of guys his age do but that someone would have had to help him procure them because she didn't think he could do it on his own."

"Do you think that's true?" Alex asked.

"Hell, I guess. She seems to underestimate him, though." He sat back in his chair.

"Jessica is going to want to know if Lynda needs help with her son's burial," Alex said.

"She mentioned they have adjoining sites at the cemetery that have been in her family for years. Now tell me what the Cummings boys are saying," Smyth added. The creaking of the leather made Alex wish he could sit down, but he was too anxious to relax.

Dylan perched on a chair, twisting in a way that suggested he'd hurt his back. The guy needed to lay off the gym equipment for a while. "Alex was detained so Kit Anderson joined me in the interrogation room," he began. "Basically, the boys say they were together almost all of Saturday and Sunday. However, their parents were out of town. Tad says they went to a party Saturday night but didn't stay long. They said they walked and that they talked to two girls outside the drugstore. We're trying to find the girls now. And they both maintain that the car they use to go fool around at the drive-in theater was parked in the far back of the acre their parents own and must have been used by somebody else."

"Did they give the key to somebody else?" Alex asked.

"No. But they claim they leave the key in the ignition at all times and all their friends know about it."

"Is that where you found it?" Alex persisted. "In the ignition like they said?"

"Yeah, I did."

"The M.E. couldn't find any traces of blood," Smyth said, pausing as he now fingered a cigarette lighter with a carved silver metal case. "He was able to match the fibers in the grill to Billy's jacket, though, and the pills in the glove box were Rohypnol, the same as found in Billy's bloodstream. Oh, and there were weeds in the tires consistent with those growing at the drive-in lot."

"Did they test the soil underneath the car?" Alex asked. "It sat out in the rain most of the morning. If there was blood on it, it might have washed off into the soil."

"They didn't find anything."

"What about prints?"

"There are a hundred of them. Every kid in this county must have been in that car at one point or another."

Alex shook his head. "Why would those boys drug and kill Billy? How did they get him out to the drive-in? Are the techs checking the car for evidence Billy was ever in it or that his bike was?"

"They admitted they'd given Billy a ride or two in the past," Dylan said. "Unless we find blood or something, they've got that angle covered. His DNA could have been left behind at any time."

"Is the car big enough to carry the bike?" Smyth asked.

"It would fit in the trunk, but they said they stuffed it in there once when Billy got a flat," Dylan said. "And as for the weeds in their tires, that's tricky, too, because they admit they drive out there sometimes. Hell, I kicked them out myself. What I think is that they arranged to meet Billy at the drive-in to exchange money Billy picked up for them. Maybe they argued, maybe Billy wanted out or threatened to talk if he didn't get a bigger cut. Maybe that's why he really wanted to see Alex, to ask for help with them. Anyway, I think they all did some drugs, and then the twins spiked a soft drink or something with the Rohypnol, then Billy fell into a dead sleep and they either accidentally ran him over or did it on purpose."

"You don't accidentally run over a man Billy's size more than once," Chief Smyth said.

"We have to break their alibi or get them to own up."

"Before their lawyer got there they talked a little. Thank goodness they're over eighteen. They admitted they knew Billy, in fact, they tried to make it sound like they kind of looked out after him and that they even did him favors. They admitted they'd been out to the airport but that was because they liked planes." Dylan straightened his back and sighed. "They didn't give much in the interrogation room even when Kit got a little hot under the collar. Billy Summers is the first body Kit has actually come across and he's taking it kind of hard."

All three men thought about that for a moment.

"Dylan told me your yard was vandalized," the chief finally said, turning his attention to Alex after casting the cigarette pack another longing look. "I suppose we should launch an investigation into that. I'd rather not include the media, however."

"I agree about the media," Alex said. "This has been very traumatic for Jessica. I don't want her subjected to that kind of attention. I also think we can forgo a formal investigation, as well."

"But you guys could be in terrible danger," Dylan said softly.

"I know. I talked to my neighbors before I came in tonight. But you know how the back gate sits out of sight from the street. No one saw anything. And the yard itself was trampled and muddy because of the rain. I checked for a good footprint and couldn't find a single one."

"What kind of tool did the creep use?" Dylan asked.

He told them about the missing machete. "Which would suggest the crime was one of opportunity and not premeditated."

"Are you sure the machete is missing?" Smyth asked.

"Positive. There have got to be easier tools to wield than an old machete but it's about the only thing that would cut plants fast and quietly that was available in the toolshed."

"The question is whether this has to do with the perceived threat the FBI mentioned or is it related to Billy's death," the chief said.

Or both, Alex thought and almost said.

But he didn't.

The conversation he and Jessica had engaged in earlier played through his mind. It was possible someone he knew was behind all or part of this. He looked at Chief Smyth and Dylan, thought about Kit Anderson and Tony Machi....

It just didn't seem possible.

Chapter Seven

Jessica wound up at the school early in the morning because Alex was determined to follow her to work and watch over her until she was safely inside the building and he had an early appointment. He kissed her goodbye, and she watched him drive away through her window.

She knew he was headed out to Lynda Summers's house and that Dylan and Chief Smyth were going to join him. She was glad he wouldn't be alone and she was glad when her class began to fill with students so that she wasn't alone.

She'd taken one last look out at the yard that morning. The devastation seemed worse even though the rain had let up. She wasn't sure what a yard crew could do and she didn't know if she was up to replanting. Alex said he was going to install a lock on the gate, which seemed like a wise precaution.

As the shock of finding the vandalism on the heels of hearing about Billy's death began to wear off, other considerations pushed their way into her consciousness. They'd had a trespasser who had systematically destroyed the sanctuary of their home. Why?

ALEX, CHIEF SMYTH and Dylan arrived in three different cars from three different locations. What was incredible to Alex was that they all arrived at just about the same time.

"Thank goodness the rain let up," the chief said as he got out of his car.

Dylan and Alex joined him on the porch and Smyth knocked. When after several seconds no one answered, Dylan tried looking in the window. Since Alex had taken that route the day before, he knew his partner wouldn't be able to see inside. That's why he was shocked when Dylan said, "It doesn't look like anyone is home."

Alex shifted position and looked in the window. The boxes that had blocked the view the day before were gone.

"Did she know we were coming?" Dylan asked.

Smyth spoke up. "I called her last night and said we needed to ask her some questions and take a look in her shed. She was groggy but I thought she understood me. She mentioned she'd leave the door open in case she nodded off this morning and didn't hear us." He tried the knob and it turned in his hand.

He pushed the door open and called her name. "Lynda?"

Upon entering, Alex turned toward the window that looked out on the porch. The boxes that had towered over the chairs and blocked the window the day before were now in a heap, covering most of the loveseat and big chair. The floor lamp had disappeared completely under the rubble and the television had flown from its table top perch. It lay screen-side down, covered with cable and electrical wires that had ripped from the wall like severed arteries.

But what caught Alex's attention was the sight of a dirty white slipper sticking out from beneath the most ponderous pile of junk. He moved closer until he was sure, and then he began climbing over things, sliding on the trash in his haste. "Over here," he said. "Hurry, she's under all this stuff."

Dylan moved fast, joining Alex, both of them breathing heavily in their attempt to lift the cumbersome boxes off the chairs and free the woman who must be beneath. Smyth shouted cautionary warnings about causing another avalanche. The boxes were unwieldy, weighty with clothing and books, and so old many tore as Dylan tried to pick them up. Their contents spilled everywhere creating more obstacles and mess. All the commotion dislodged the one sure sign Lynda Summers lay under it all, the slipper, which fell to the cluttered floor, revealing a pale foot with bright pink nail polish.

Desperate now but cautious lest they inflict more damage, they moved aside enough rubbish to finally glimpse Lynda. She was dressed in black pants and a pink blouse. Her eyes were closed, her mouth slack and all three men knew she was dead before Alex laid his fingers against her throat to feel for a pulse. He looked over his shoulder and met Chief Smyth's stricken gaze as he shook his head.

It looked as though Lynda Summers's possessions had finally won the battle for her house.

JESSICA WAS IN the process of digging a piece of fruit for a midmorning snack from her lunch bag when the principal, Silvia Greenspan, appeared in her classroom doorway. "You got a call," she began, and for one second, Jessica's heart rate tripled. A statement like that one would have sent her into a tailspin a few days earlier. She set a banana aside and stood up because the expression on Silvia's face finally got through.

"What's wrong?" she asked. "Who called?"

"The emergency room over at the hospital," Silvia said. "They want you to come quickly. Alex has been hurt."

Jessica stood there for a second, trying to take this in, and then she grabbed her sweater off the back of the chair and dug her purse from the drawer. "Did they say how he was hurt or how bad it was?"

"A car accident out on that twisty road north of town."

"Blue Point?"

"Yes, that's it. Connie took the call, but I wanted to tell you myself after last night and everything." By now they were rushing down the hall. "Let me drive you over," Silvia said. "Give me five minutes to cancel an appointment—"

"I'm sorry, I can't wait," Jessica said. Blue Point was the road that led out to Lynda Summers's house.

"Then I'll follow you in a few minutes."

"Fine," Jessica called as she hurried outside. Thanks to Alex's protective streak, and the early time she'd arrived at the school, she had a great parking spot in the front instead of out in the back as usual.

The drive to the hospital was harrowing as her mind raced over the details of Blue Point Road. Had he been hit by another car or had he tumbled over the side into the gorge below? Was he still alive or was she driving to face another nightmare? If someone had hurt him, how would she find that person, because she knew in her heart that she would have to, not only to avenge Alex but to protect herself and thus her child. Had she really told Alex she wasn't frightened for herself? What a load of bunk that was. She was terrified for all three of them.

She parked as close to the emergency-room door as possible and walked inside, mindful to pace herself. All this stress couldn't be good for her baby, she reasoned, plus she was never far from remembering the miracle of being pregnant.

The doctor had told her to be reasonable but to live normally. What was normal anymore? Friends being murdered, vandals, trespassers, terrorists? Okay, so her body had so far cooperated in a way she'd never dreamed it could. Did that mean she should heap more punishment upon it? There was so much at stake.

This pregnancy just had to work out.

The emergency room was crowded with people in various states of trauma, all rushing about. What appeared to be several couples stood clutching each other, their faces stricken with fear as though awaiting to hear the fate of a loved one. Others held small children in their arms while older kids clustered around them, some with cuts and scrapes. Why were there so many children here on a school day?

Jessica stood in a short line until it was her turn to talk to a harried-looking man seated on the other side of the glass window. "I'm looking for Alex Foster," she said, scanning the room, keeping her eyes open for a sign of Dylan or Chief Smyth, both of whom she knew Alex had been meeting with that morning.

"Was he on the bus?" the receptionist asked.

"The bus? What bus?"

"The school bus," he said, and answered a phone, motioning with his finger for her to wait. Then he began digging through papers, apparently to look up something for whoever was on the other end of the phone.

Jessica leaned forward. "What bus are you talking about? Alex Foster is my husband. I got word from you that he was injured in a vehicle accident. He's a police detective—"

The man was completely ignoring her, and she turned

away. There had to be someone else who could help. Had Alex collided with a school bus, was that what was going on? She saw a nurse talking to one of the worried-looking couples and approached, waiting as patiently as she could while the nurse directed them toward metal doors.

"Excuse me," she said as the couple hurried off. The nurse turned to face her and Jessica could see in her eyes that she only had a few seconds to explain things. "I'm looking for my husband," she began, and gave an abbreviated version of what she wanted.

The nurse scanned the clipboard she held in one hand. "I don't see his name. When did he come in?"

"I don't know. I received the call about thirty minutes ago."

"Was he on the Mountain View school bus?"

"I don't think so. Was there an accident?"

"A bus full of kids on their way to a holiday program overturned while rounding a sharp curve on a highway ramp," the woman said.

"Out on Blue Point?"

"No, over by Campton."

Jessica's mind could not wrap itself around what she was hearing. Campton was fifteen miles north of Blunt Falls. What was Alex doing way over there?

"What kind of holiday program?" Jessica asked, suddenly remembering Memorial Day was only five days away.

"I'm not sure. Anyway, they sent us the overflow because the Campton hospital is so small. Maybe he's over there."

"Who would I ask to find out?"

"Wait right here. I'll look around in the back to see if he's in a treatment room and then call Campton. His name is Alex Foster, right?"

"Yes."

"Why don't you sit down," the nurse said kindly. "I won't be long."

There was suddenly someone at Jessica's elbow and she turned, hoping to find Alex. Silvia had arrived and now stood beside her. She took Jessica's arm. "She's right, you should sit down."

Jessica swore under her breath as she retrieved her cell phone. "I'll try calling him," she said. "If he's stuck in a treatment room somewhere, maybe he'll answer."

She punched in his number and he picked up before the ring stopped. "This is Alex," he said.

"Alex!" Jessica closed her eyes for a second. At least he was able to hold a phone and talk. How badly could he be hurt?

"Are you okay?" she asked.

"I'm a little busy," he said. "Is anything wrong?"

"I got a call you were in the emergency room, that you'd been in an accident. Are you telling me you haven't?"

"Who called you?" he demanded.

Jessica tried to explain, and then Silvia got on the phone and told Alex about the call. Jessica sank down on a chair, weak now that the adrenaline rush had spent itself. When the nurse reappeared shaking her head, she told her there'd been a mix-up.

But had there really been a mix-up or had this been a deliberate ruse to—to what? What had been accomplished except scaring the daylights out of her? Did it have anything to do with the busful of children?

Silvia handed her back the phone. "Are you going back to the school?" Alex asked.

"I guess."

"Good. It's disturbing that whoever sent you on that

wild-goose chase knew I'd be out on Blue Point. Go home with Silvia, okay? I have to finish something up here and then I'll come for you at her house."

"Okay. And you'd better call the Campton police and tell them to make sure that school-bus accident was really an accident."

Chapter Eight

As soon as Alex got off the phone with the Campton police, Dylan joined him in the one small clear spot they could find in the cluttered room.

"Everything okay with Jess?" he asked.

For some reason, Alex was reluctant to talk about what had happened until he could investigate it a little on his own. "Fine," he said.

Dylan nodded curtly. He held up a prescription-pill bottle by lifting the plastic bag in which it had been deposited. A few capsules rattled around inside it. "Kit found this near her body," he said.

"Are you familiar with them?" Alex asked.

"Yeah. They're a damn strong tranquilizer. Her doctor prescribed them yesterday," Dylan said. "Five of the ten are gone, which is pretty potent. I wonder if Chief Smyth took her to pick them up."

Alex shook his head.

"Anyway," Dylan continued, "if she'd taken a couple of these and gone to sleep, the whole house could have landed on her head and it wouldn't have roused her."

"Why did the boxes fall if she was asleep and not moving?" Alex mused aloud.

"Maybe her recliner hit them."

"Did Kit find a glass of water in there with her?"

"Not yet. But he's not finished."

"Her son was murdered two days ago," Alex said. "That's why I want her checked for anything suspicious. Make sure you bag her hands," he called to Kit Anderson, who cast him a look that clearly said, *Don't tell me how to do my job.* Buck up, Kit, Alex thought. He wanted to make sure she had died exactly the way it appeared she'd died, and that meant there wasn't any DNA under her fingernails where she'd scratched an attacker or defensive wounds on her hands or arms where she'd fended someone off.

"Where is the chief?" Alex asked.

"He wandered off a while ago," Dylan said, twisting around and stretching his well-built frame.

Alex recalled seeing him do the same thing the night before in Smyth's office, though he sure hadn't spared any effort uncovering Lynda Summers's body. "What's the matter," he joked. "Did you pull something when you were picking up cars or whatever it is you do to buff that physique?"

"I lift weights, dummy," Dylan said with a smile. "You ought to try it sometime. The girls think it's sexy as hell."

"Hmm—I'm going to go find Smyth."

One of the paramedics overheard him and hollered he'd seen Smyth go outside. Alex walked out the front door, anxious to drive to the school and see Jessica with his own eyes.

Why had someone pulled such a stupid prank on her? He could see no purpose in it. He planned to question the woman who had taken the call and see if the incoming number had registered on the phone. He was willing to bet that would be a dead end. Was this prank related to Billy's death and the vandalized flowers? It all seemed like a disjointed mishmash.

He found the chief inside the shed, standing near the

striped lamp. Smyth apparently heard him approach for he turned around, his expression startled. "The door was unlocked," he said.

"The lock was in place when I was here yesterday," Alex said, glancing at the hasp.

Smyth rubbed his chin. "Lynda must have come out here and opened it before she fell asleep last night," he commented. His voice held notes of regret, though the tears that had moistened them briefly were long since gone.

"Did you hurt yourself?" Alex asked when he noticed angry red scratches on the back of the chief's right hand.

The chief immediately stuck his hand in his pocket. "My daughter's cat. Of course she couldn't take him to Texas with her and he hates me. It's nothing. Long as we're here, we might as well take a look."

"Sounds good to me," Alex said, glad to finally get a chance to look around. An extension cord had been strung to connect the lamp to electricity. He switched on the light and immediately looked for the three-by-five index cards he'd glimpsed the day before. They were right where he'd seen them. Using the eraser end of a pencil, he turned the top one so he could read it.

"What's it say?" the chief asked.

"It's directions for planting rosebushes," Alex told him. "This is Jessica's handwriting."

The chief grunted. "Did you see the paper this morning?"

"No, as a matter of fact, I didn't. We were running late."

"There's a blurb in there about your garden being vandalized. I thought we agreed to keep it out of the news."

"We did," Alex said. "I mean, I didn't alert the newspaper."

"Maybe your wife—"

"Absolutely not. No way."

Smyth shook his head. "What's on the next card?"

Alex glanced at the cards in order. All of them held gardening notes except for the pink one on the bottom which gave simple directions for blocking the wheels on a plane. The handwriting on this one must belong to Tony Machi.

"There's nothing important in these cards," Alex said, disappointed. But hadn't the stack been higher yesterday? He searched his memory, trying to recall what had made him think there were well over a dozen cards instead of six or seven.

"I didn't know the kid had the place set up like this," the chief said as he stared around the room.

"It's nice," Alex said. He glanced at the workbench that held paints, glues and pieces of wood along with model airplane boxes. The resulting airplanes Billy had apparently built from the kits were clumsy and heavy-handed, but there were several lined up on a shelf as though he truly enjoyed his hobby.

"First your beautiful garden and now this," Smyth said quietly.

Alex could see no sign of destruction in the shed and wondered to what the chief was alluding until it finally dawned on him that he wasn't referring to the negative energy of vandalism but to the creative aspects of Billy's interests. "He was a man of surprises," Alex said. Had they misjudged him? Was he really a lot brighter than everyone gave him credit for?

But the models weren't without faults and were obviously the work of someone challenged to paint and glue without making mistakes.

"Look at this one," the chief said, gazing up at the big biplane hanging in front of the window.

This plane was different from the others. Not only larger, but the design came complete with details the others lacked and superior overall workmanship. Red paint glistened on the fuselage, while the propeller looked as though it would spin easily if it had been low enough to the floor for Alex to reach it.

"There you guys are," Dylan called from the doorway. He whistled long and low as he looked around. "Wow. This place is a little oasis of calm in a sea of chaos, isn't it?"

"Yeah, it is," Smyth said, looking around. He sighed deeply as he appeared to absorb the details of the small room. "Who would have guessed the boy had it in him?"

AFTER SMYTH SENT Dylan to Campton to check out the bus accident, Alex drove to the Cummingses' house. He'd learned the twins hadn't been arrested, although the D.A. was considering an investigation. He had no plans to talk to them; he just wanted to get a feeling for the lay of the land.

He slowed down his truck and looked at the property. It was easy to see where they must have parked their joy-riding car because of the tracks made by the tow vehicle that had taken it into the police-compound yard the day before. And from what Alex could tell, no one would see that car from the house due to the placement of a large barn between them. It was possible somebody else had taken it unobserved.

He got out of the truck and stared at the house for a minute. It had obviously once been a farm of some kind with a two-story house and a covered porch. It needed a new coat of paint, but things were relatively well kept. He was walking back to his truck when someone called out to him. He turned to see two blond young men coming toward him.

"You lost or something, mister?" one of them asked as they both leaned against the fence.

Alex introduced himself and told them who he was.

"We aren't talking to you," the other one said. "Mom and Dad are at work and they told us not to talk to anyone. Besides, you guys don't listen. We don't know how Billy's clothes got caught in our grill. And it's all banged up because it's a drag car. It's been banged up forever. I don't know when every single dent got made and I don't know how those pills got in our glove box."

Alex looked at them closely. "You guys were friends with Billy?"

"Sure," they said in tandem.

"Billy was okay," the shorter one added.

Alex couldn't think of a single question to ask them that wouldn't be better asked downtown with a recorder playing, so he said nothing. His silence apparently goaded them on.

"He wasn't like other guys," the taller one said. He stuck out a hand and added, "I'm Tad, that's Ted. You're a lot cooler than the psycho bodybuilder who came out here. We used to look out for Billy in school. He was a couple of years older than us, but not older in his head, you know?"

Alex nodded.

"And he didn't do drugs," Ted added. "Okay, sometimes Tad and me dabble a little—nothing hard-core, just weed—but we'd never involve Billy. We were teaching him how to build model airplanes and he was getting pretty good."

"You made the red-and-white biplane in Billy's shed, didn't you?"

Tad smiled. "You've seen it? Yeah, we did that. Well, mostly Ted, but I helped. We let Billy do some of it, too, but he got all upset when we started detailing it in a way that wasn't in the directions."

"Billy liked to follow the rules," Ted said. "Coloring outside the lines made him nervous."

"Well, the model turned out great," Alex said.

"Thanks. I want to ask his mom if we can have it, you know, to remember him and stuff. Do you think she'd mind?"

"I'm sorry to have to tell you that Lynda Summers is dead," Alex said. It would be all over town soon enough.

"How?"

"Some of her belongings apparently toppled over and crushed her," Alex said.

"Oh, man, that's tough," Tad said. "Both her and Billy, huh? That's terrible."

"Funny thing about Billy," Ted chimed in. "He didn't want his mom to know about the shop we kind of created out behind the house. He was afraid she'd take it over."

"Probably a valid concern," Alex said. He knew the D.A.'s office would blow a gasket if he kept talking to these guys, but he was glad he'd had the chance to meet them. They seemed like pretty decent people to him and too straightforward to be killers. Still, you never knew.

"I have to be getting along," he said. "My wife is expecting me." He watched them both to see if they exchanged knowing looks, but Tad just smiled. "That's why your name is familiar. Your wife is the lady Billy was helping in the garden, right? And you're the guy those jerks at B-Strong tried to kill. You were in the paper."

"My claim to fame," Alex said.

A minute later, he drove away. In the rearview mirror

he watched Tad and Ted turn back toward their house. He honestly didn't know if he'd just been conned or not.

ALEX AND JESSICA drove to the airport to pick up Nate that evening. Alex had met her at Silvia's a while ago and they hadn't been apart since then.

Three days ago, both of the Summerses had been alive and well, and now both were dead. It was unbelievable. "Do you think Lynda's death was an accident?" she asked Alex.

He shrugged. "I'm not sure. I'm treating it like a homicide until I am."

She pressed his leg and smiled when he looked over at her. "I want you to know that I've arranged to spend the evening with Silvia tomorrow. When you and Nate get home from the lake, call me and I'll meet you at the house."

"I have a better idea," he said, throwing her a longer glance, this one accompanied by a grin. "Come with us."

"I thought you didn't want me near your lake."

Another shrug. "I just want to have you close by. You don't have to come—"

"I'd love to come," she said. "Will Nate mind?"

"Of course not. It might be kind of boring, though."

She laughed. "If you can spend three months up there alone, I think I can handle three hours. Did you get a chance to ask Tony what to look for?"

"Yeah. He gave me some ideas. Nate got permission from the FAA to dive as long as we buoy the location for them to take a look at later. It's understood we won't remove anything from the plane."

"And the float plane is ready to go?"

"And loaded with dive gear." He frowned as he said, "I'm not telling anyone where or even that we're going anywhere and I'd appreciate it if you did the same." He paused and added, "Did you mention it to Silvia?"

"No," she said, "and that's weird because why wouldn't I? I just didn't. You're not telling anyone at work?"

"No."

"Do you think one of them had something to do with the crash?"

"Of course not, but people talk. Just look at Dylan and his continual effort to impress young women."

"Like his new car?"

"I haven't seen it yet. Some eighteen-year-old in Billings got it rear-ended, so it's in a shop."

"I bet that's the end of that romance," Jessica said.

"Yeah." Alex laughed. "He's incorrigible. Anyway, I'd just as soon not everyone in town knows what we're doing. I just want to check this out without arousing too much curiosity, so I'm borrowing everything we'll need from the guy I told you about."

"John Miter."

"Yeah. We'll leave from his place, not the Blunt Falls airport. I'll just call in sick." He shook his head. "I have to ask you. Did you talk to anyone from the press about our garden disaster? It was apparently in the paper."

"Of course not," she said. "Really, it was in there? That's news? Probably because you're just back home."

"I know," he agreed. "Dylan pointed out the chief himself talks to his pet reporter all the time. He probably let something slip. He does like publicity and he does talk."

"Yeah, he does," she said. "I think we should stop getting that newspaper."

NATE WAS WALKING through the door as they pulled up in front of the terminal. Montana always sported its share of rugged men in boots and Stetsons, but Nate still stood out. There was just something magnetic about his laid-back personality that shone through. Tonight, he carried a satchel in one hand but his other was wrapped around that of a tall woman with black hair and clear blue eyes.

"Who is that?" Alex said.

"I think that's Mike Donovan's daughter, Sarah. Didn't Nate tell you he and she got together while trying to figure out who killed her dad?"

"He hinted around but nothing definite. Guess he wanted to show, not tell," Alex said as he pulled to a stop. "She's sure a heck of a lot prettier than Mike."

Jessica knew that after her father's murder, Sarah and Nate had spent a few very intense days together outwitting a determined killer. And in that time, according to Nate, they'd fallen in love. Since then, Sarah had moved to Arizona to be near Nate and started veterinarian school to fulfill a lifelong dream.

The two of them slid into the backseat, so obviously in love that it made Jessica smile. She'd never seen Nate like this, never seen his eyes dance and his lips twist into a smile every time someone spoke. "I brought my girl," Nate said as they all shook hands across the seat backs.

"I tried to get him to warn you," Sarah said, directing her comment to both Jessica and Alex. "He wanted me to be a surprise. I hope I'm not a terrible inconvenience."

"Of course you aren't," Jessica said warmly. "I'm delighted I'll have some company while these two dive on the plane. Unless you're also a diver, of course, and plan to go down with them."

"I'm not a diver but when Nate asked if I wanted to come, I jumped at the chance," she explained. "I've heard an awful lot about that lake. I want to see it with my own eyes."

"You and me both," Nate said. He gazed at Jessica for

a moment and added, "You look absolutely beautiful. Pending motherhood agrees with you."

She smiled her thanks.

For Jessica, the ride back to the house along with sitting around the table and discussing plans for the next day while eating take-out Chinese food were some of the nicest times she'd had in recent memory. When their marriage began to come apart at the seams, they'd stopped socializing as a couple. She'd forgotten how charming Alex could be when he was relaxed and comfortable, and not having other Blunt Falls police officers around to talk shop with was kind of refreshing.

Not that Nate didn't talk law enforcement. He was a deputy, after all, and he'd been doing that as long as Alex had been in the police department. What they spoke about tonight, however, was pertinent to all of them because they'd all been touched by the delusional madness of the Shatterhorn man with the warped agenda.

And they'd all been left with the knowledge that it wasn't over, that their bad guy wasn't the only crackpot around.

Alex told them about the former employee of the Shatterhorn Killer who had reportedly called a suspect in Seattle about another case and mentioned Blunt Falls in the conversation. "Agent Struthers thinks the reference ties back to someone here in town who was involved with my plane crash," he concluded.

"Any idea who?"

"None."

"Who was this guy?"

"We were given the alias he used in Nevada. William Tucker, sixtyish, tanned, bald. Cold eyes. Do you want to see a photo?"

"Sure," Nate said.

Alex stood and started off to the den. "I'm not sure why this guy would bother coming after me, though. I'm no longer a threat."

"Someone thinks you are," Nate called after Alex, who soon returned with the photo in hand. "Here. Ever seen him?"

Nate nodded. "Once, but not in person and not tanned like this. I saw him on a closed-circuit screen over an intercom. I wondered what happened to him after his boss was hit and killed by that car. I even wondered if this guy was behind the wheel."

Sarah had gotten to her feet and come to take a look. "I don't recognize him," she said.

"You didn't get out of the car, you never saw him," Nate said. He turned his attention back to Alex. "I take it neither of you has seen this guy around here?"

"Not a glimpse," Alex said.

Eventually the conversation led to the events of the past few days. Nate was as baffled as Alex and Jessica by the purpose of the bogus call from the emergency room. This was the first time Jessica thought to ask Alex if he'd heard back from the Campton police—was the school-bus accident really an accident?

"Dylan drove over there and talked to them face-to-face," Alex said. "He came away with the impression there isn't a doubt in the world it was an accident. Children have been targeted before by these kinds of domestic militia terrorist groups, but not like this. Plus the bus was overdue for maintenance and one anonymous source told him the front tire was almost bald. They checked out the driver, too. She's the mother of six and she's been driving for the school district for years."

"But what about the holiday program the nurse mentioned?"

"It was an end-of-the-school-year picnic event at a park."

"You have to ask yourself," Nate said, sitting back in his chair and stretching his long legs, "if the only thing accomplished was frightening Jessica—was that the purpose?"

"But why me?" Jessica murmured. "I'm no threat."

"Maybe you're not a threat, but you *are* the most important person in the world to a man who is," Nate said, looking right at Alex and then back at Jessica. "Your flowers, your husband—your peace of mind. It's certainly affecting how you feel and hence, how Alex feels."

Alex took Jessica's hand in his and squeezed it.

"One more thing that's been bothering me," Nate said, sitting forward and resting his weight on his forearms. "Whenever you describe the plane crash, you get real fuzzy on details."

"I've noticed that, too," Jessica said. "I thought it might be because he hit his head in the crash."

"He had the wherewithal to exit the plane and save his life," Nate said. "And just because he suffered a few cuts doesn't mean he hit his head."

"I don't think I did," Alex said, unconsciously, it seemed, touching the scars on his face.

"It's the time before the crash that you seem vague about," Nate added. "Why is that?"

Alex paused to think for a moment. "I have no idea. I remember being in a funk. It must be that."

"A funk?"

"Yeah, you know."

Jessica looked Nate in the eye. "He means we'd had a big old, hairy argument before he left. We were both in a funk."

They all kind of looked at each other uneasily, and then Nate chuckled. "That occasionally happens to everyone," he said. "Come on, Alex, why don't you and I clean up."

While the guys performed domestic chores, Jessica led Sarah out into the yard. She turned on the floodlights so they could look around.

"It doesn't look too bad," Sarah said diplomatically.

And in a way, she was right. The yard crew had removed the shattered stems and ruined blossoms, pruning things back, remulching the paths and toting away debris until now the yard looked wooded and serene in its way. But it wasn't the riot of color it had been and Jessica could barely stand to look at it.

"I'm sorry about your friend," Sarah added.

"Thank you. He was a nice kid." Jessica waited a second and added, "It appears Nate recovered from the bullet wound okay. Is he 100 percent now?"

"Yes. The doctors were amazed how quickly he healed." She hugged herself and shivered. "Jess, I don't mind telling you. I thought he was going to die."

"It must have been terrible," Jessica said.

Sarah nodded. "That's really why I came. I couldn't bear to have him involved in this situation without me. My coming means we have to leave late tomorrow afternoon because I have a big exam the next day, but it was worth it."

"I totally understand," Jessica said. She liked Sarah, and that was an unexpected treat, too. Nate's last girlfriend had been something of a prima donna with a grating laugh and though Jessica had tried to be friendly, they just hadn't clicked. "Are you planning on having children eventually?" she asked, then shook her head. "Never mind. That's none of my business. I guess I have babies on the brain."

"I don't mind," Sarah said, smiling deeply. "I can't think of anything we want more than a family. My own youth was dominated by an addictive mother and a father

I could never seem to get close to. Children will be my chance to experience childhood again, this time through a better lens. I want to finish school first, though, and even though it seems incredible to me, Nate and I have only been together three months. We're still finding things out about each other." A frown furrowed her smooth brow for a moment, and then she added, "The only thing that blackens the horizon is this lingering threat. And to think that Alex might still be in danger—it's horrible."

"Yes, it is," Jessica whispered.

"Do you think the man who worked on your garden was killed by these people? Was he one of them?"

"No," Jessica said profoundly. "Of course he wasn't. We told you about him. He was a simple guy who seemed to always try to do his best. When he found out I wanted the flowers to put on my grandfather's grave he worked even harder."

Sarah nodded thoughtfully. Then she said, "You must be right about him. There's certainly nothing simple about this situation, is there?"

"There sure isn't," Jessica agreed.

"Maybe tomorrow we'll find some answers," Sarah added.

Jessica nodded but she thought it far more likely they would simply find more questions.

Chapter Nine

They were up before dawn the next day because John Miter's place was twenty miles out of town. It was a quiet, somber drive fueled by nerves, coffee and the inevitable Vita-Drink.

As Alex yawned into his hand, it brought back memories of the day he'd flown off into the blue and not come home for a while. He'd been yawning that day, too. But today the yawns were just yawns. There was no accompanying thirst and lethargy, no mental sluggishness.

If there had been, he would have grounded himself. One crash into that lake was enough for a lifetime.

They took off into a beautiful sunrise and it felt great to soar above the clouds. This was something he hadn't been sure he'd ever do again, but now that he was flying, he knew he wouldn't let fear stop him. He twisted the lid off one of his enhanced waters and encouraged everyone else to join him. "Here's to life," he said, and they clapped the plastic bottles together.

Nate acted as navigator as they flew through the clear blue skies, keeping track of their route on the charts Alex had brought along. Thanks to the FAA, he knew exactly where "his" lake was and sure enough, ninety minutes later, he caught the first glimpse of the river he'd followed to the Bookers' house. From up here, it looked like an easy walk, the gullies and crevices mitigated by height. The truth had been that a two-day walk turned into several times more than that. He'd had to avoid all sorts of hazards including melting snow and the small avalanches that could still be deadly.

And then he caught sight of the lake, a blue gem set in dark green trees, a diamond brooch on an emerald gown. Patches of snow glistened on the peaks of neighboring mountains.

"Is that your lake?" Jessica asked, leaning forward.

He nodded. Then he glanced back at her over his shoulder. "It looked a lot bigger last February."

"Yeah, I bet."

They circled until Nate pointed. "I see the Cessna, over there, not far from the shore."

He was right. The vague but unmistakable shape of the plane was visible beneath the pristine lake water. It had sunk within fifty yards of the shoreline. To Alex, dragging himself across it with a busted leg and during a snowstorm, it had seemed more like fifty miles. And beyond it on the shore, barely visible, he glimpsed the arrow made of rocks that pointed inland toward his camp.

As he'd lugged those rocks into place a few weeks before, he'd imagined it would appear like a beacon to anyone flying over, but in truth, you had to know to look for it—his rocks tended to blend in with all the others. He wished now he'd scattered them before he left. Fact was he'd completely forgotten about them.

He landed into the wind, then steered the plane toward the downed Cessna. Peering into the water and seeing the ghostly white wingspan of his plane down below felt eerily disquieting. This lake, except for some good luck, could easily have been his grave, the Cessna, his tombstone.

And now he was back to a place he'd once planned never to see again.

Nate inflated the dinghy with a CO_2 canister as Alex anchored the plane between the wreck and the shore. When the boat was inflated, Alex ferried Sarah and Jessica to the beach. "I'll go get Nate and our equipment next," he told Jessica, fighting off the urge to ask her not to wander far, to stay where he could see her. Had coming back here spooked him more than he thought it would? Yeah, he decided. Literally, he'd been gone for only five days. But in his head, this place had happened a lifetime ago.

Take that big pine tree right over there. Last winter there had been five feet of snow around it. That was the place he dug out a trench for himself and spent a few miserable nights just fighting to stay alive. A wave of nausea passed through him now, remembering the pain and even more, the hopelessness.

"Where was your camp?" Jessica asked, and he tore his gaze away from the tree.

He waved in a vague direction. "Over there."

"I'd like to see where you lived."

"Where I *live* is in a nice little house with a drop-dead gorgeous woman who is going to have my baby. That's where I live now and that's all that matters."

"Don't be obstinate," she said.

He smiled but he really didn't want to be having this conversation. However, if he didn't compromise, she'd come unglued, so he touched her arm. "If there's time after our dive, I'll give you a personal tour, okay? Or maybe we could just fly over it."

She nodded, her gaze hard to read.

"I'll go get Nate so we can put on our gear."

He faced the floatplane as he rowed the dinghy because he didn't want to see the disappointment on her face. He understood that she wanted to know exactly where and how he'd lived, so why couldn't she understand that it was painful for him? Walking along that trail back to his camp would feel like hiking back to despair. He didn't need to revisit it; he was happy to let it go.

Within an hour, Nate and Alex had changed into wet suits and donned scuba tanks. Pulling the dinghy behind them to tote their gear, they said enthusiastic goodbyes and paddled back out to the wreck. The bright orange buoy they'd attached made finding it from water level a cinch.

"What exactly are we looking for?" Nate said before he bit down on the mouthpiece that would feed air from his tank. With his mask pulled back on the top of his head, his expression was intense. Alex couldn't think of anyone he wanted by his side more than this man.

"Anything to do with the engine and oil pressure. Tony told me to check to make sure the oil-tank plug is in place because of the way the pressure dropped so quickly. He doesn't see how, but maybe it blew. He explained where it is. Hopefully the plane didn't settle with that area in the mud, but the struts broke when I landed so we'll just have to see."

Nate grinned. "You mean when you crashed."

Alex chuckled. "Yeah, well, anyway, thanks to the FAA wanting to make their own assessment, we won't move anything, but we can photograph the hell out of it. Ready?"

In another minute they disappeared below the water, a trail of bubbles marking their spot.

"I'LL BE BACK in a few minutes," Jessica said as soon as she saw Alex and Nate dive beneath the water.

Sarah got to her feet. "Where are you going?" she asked, her head tilted to one side.

Jessica paused, uncertain how to explain. There was no way to sugarcoat it, however, so she just told the truth. "I imagine you've gathered from things you've heard that Alex and I have…struggled. We're just getting back to a place where we can work together, but he still resists. The fact is, just as you had to be here for Nate, I have to be here for Alex even if he doesn't admit it and part of being here is understanding what he's been through. He's so reluctant to talk about it, so anxious to move on. I can't go quite that fast."

"You're going to go look for his camp, aren't you?" Sarah asked.

"Yes. If it were Nate, wouldn't you?"

"In a heartbeat. Do you want company?"

Jessica shook her head. "No, if you don't mind, I'd rather go alone."

"I don't mind," Sarah said. "I'll stay here and make sure their bubbles keep rising to the surface. Do you know exactly where the camp is?"

"He told me the trail is marked by a forked tree on the lake end. I've been looking around and it seems to me that little fir tree right over there has two crowns. But even if it didn't, there's an arrow of rocks on the beach. Alex must have made that this spring when the snow melted, hoping a plane would see it." She stopped talking abruptly as a lump swelled in her throat. He must have felt so alone.

"Just be careful, okay? If you get eaten by a bear, Alex will kill me," Sarah said as Jessica took off toward the trailhead.

As soon as Jessica passed behind the forked tree, the world seemed to disappear. The plants on the path had worn away and the dirt was rutted. It had probably been an animal trail long before Alex started using it.

As the trees and bushes on either side of it closed in, she imagined Alex stumbling, limping down this path. What would she have done? Looked for a clearing of some kind, but not too far from the lake. The lake meant food and possible rescue.

The clearing was suddenly upon her as she stepped around a bush covered with thorns into a space about ten feet by twelve. A campfire ring sat under an outcropping of rocks, and across from it, branches had been woven together to create a shelter against the edge of a cliff. The trails between the two spaces paused at a trio of large boulders, the camp version, she supposed, of a dining room.

And that was about it.

Oh, there were a few scraps around like fish bones and charred wood stakes he must have used to smoke the fish he carried out with him, even a stack of unburned branches waiting to cook another meal. Half of a small rectangular blue-and-white metal box sat on one rock but it was currently empty. Judging from the rust, she wondered if he'd used it to transport water.

What was lacking were all the things she'd spent her camping experiences taking for granted. The sleeping bags, the tents, the pots and pans, and water jugs. There were no paper products like newspapers or magazines, no dishes of any sort except for a few pieces of bark stacked on one of the rocks that looked as though they may have been used as plates.

She stood there in the utter silence of the day, stunned by the paucity of supplies and stimuli. She sat down on one of the rocks, on a spot that seemed to have a natural place for a human haunch, and felt certain Alex had

perched here a hundred times while he cooked his fish
and dreamed of coming home.

Had she secretly wondered if he'd really been up in the
mountains for three months? Had his reluctance to talk
about the details seemed so over-the-top that she'd imagined he might have made some of this up? And wasn't it
odd that glimpsing his plane under the lake and that sad
little arrow on the beach wasn't half a gut-wrenching
reality check as this camp and its almost exclusive lack
of civilization?

After a few minutes, she decided to investigate the
other structure that lay kitty-corner to the fire. What she
found was a small, cozy sleeping area. The floor was
covered with branches topped with a layer of boughs,
she supposed for softness. A pair of worn handcrafted
crutches constructed from tree limbs and tied with plant
fiber leaned against the back wall. Alex had told her he
walked out with his backpack, clothes, some food and
little else, so there wasn't much there besides what nature could provide. She saw the other half of what she
now recognized was the blue-and-white metal medical
box the emergency supplies had come in. This half held a
handful of what appeared to be cold charcoal pieces from
the fire. Hanging from an exposed root above, she found
a small array of sticks hanging from a piece of salvaged
metal. Additional sticks and cones were tied with plant
fiber and dangled from the main structure. She blew on
it and the pieces bumped together and made a pleasant
sound. He'd made himself a wind chime of sorts.

Unable to resist the temptation to try to understand
better, she crawled inside and lay down atop the boughs.
It would never take the place of a good mattress, but it
wasn't bad. He must have used his coat and additional
foliage for more warmth or maybe he'd slept closer to the

fire at first when the weather was colder. She laid her head back and saw that he'd left a small opening near the top she could easily picture being filled with stars once night came and she remembered that first night he was home and the way he'd paced endlessly until finally ending up outside, under the stars.

Taking a deep breath she laid her head down and looked up at the ceiling. For the first time, she saw that he'd made marks along one wall with the charcoal, little lines in groups of five no doubt counting off the nights he'd spent in this camp. But it's what she saw next that literally took her breath.

Up above the lines, easily visible from a reclining position, was a drawing. It would never hang in the Louvre, but it brought tears to her eyes as she recognized her own face smiling down at her.

ALEX HAD SPENT weeks watching the snow melt and he knew that a hundred little streams ran into and fed this lake before escaping out the other side into a river that eventually wound its way to the sea. He'd followed that river to safety, back to Jessica and his life.

But now the task at hand was to check out his poor, wounded plane and he was relieved that although the water was icy cold, it was also clear. Visibility was excellent.

The plane had turned a little as it sank, coming to land on the rocky bottom with the fuselage propped on one of several big boulders. This was a stroke of luck as it meant the engine compartment would be accessible. Beside him, Nate pointed at the area behind and beneath the broken propeller and they kicked their way down.

Looking at his wonderful plane as he descended brought back a decade of bittersweet memories. He'd inherited the plane from his uncle and would probably never be able to buy another. It was insured, but for nothing like replacement cost. That did remind him to snap a few pictures as they drew closer, including the identification or N-numbers near the tail.

They soon discovered the engine-compartment door had been damaged when the struts tore free and the plane skidded on its belly. Nate joined Alex in pulling on the handle, but in the end, they used a multitool to pry the door open and pull it up and back on its hinges. It kind of reminded him of opening a can of sardines.

Things were darker inside the compartment. Nate shone his light where Alex pointed. Tony Machi had told him exactly where the oil-tank plug was located and he levered himself down and around to be able to see if it was still there.

At first he thought it was missing. He snapped a few photos, sure something didn't look right, unsure what it was. He signaled to Nate to move the light to a different angle, and with different illumination, he finally figured out what he was looking at.

The plug was still screwed in place but there was a hole in it. It didn't make any sense. The engine oil would have easily leaked away within minutes through a hole that size and yet he'd been in the air long enough to get all the way to this lake before the situation became catastrophic.

He ran a finger across the opening, then moved aside so Nate could take a look. They took a few more pictures before kicking their way to the top of the plane. Alex studied the cracked and broken windshield for a moment, then peered through the open door he'd used to escape what could so easily have been his tomb.

He noticed his red leather-bound logbook on the Cessna's floor and signaled to Nate that he was going inside. The space was cramped and difficult to maneuver in with an aqua lung strapped to his back and a million of his own bubbles blocking his view. He was extremely careful not to get tangled up in the wreckage as he reached down and snagged the book.

Nate tapped him on the shoulder and Alex twisted around to find Nate pointing at the cabin floor. Alex looked. He didn't see anything noteworthy and attempted a shrug in an effort to ask Nate what he wanted.

Nate held his hand up to his mouth and made drinking gestures, then pointed at the floor again. All Alex could see down there were three or four unopened bottles of his favorite water. He twisted around to pick one of them up and held it toward Nate who took it from him and moved away from the opening so Alex could exit.

They swam away toward the surface without looking back. The FAA would pull the Cessna from the lake for their investigation, but Alex knew he might never see it again.

"Jess?"

Jessica opened her eyes, stunned that she'd actually fallen asleep. Alex was on his knees inside the shelter, right beside her. A wave of guilt washed through her as she looked into his eyes.

She started to sit up. "I'm so sorry—" she began, but stopped as she caught the look on his face as he scanned his humble sleeping space. "I should have waited for you," she finished.

He sat down next to her. He was dressed again, but his hair was still damp and he smelled like cold, fresh water.

"Where are Nate and Sarah?"

"Back on the shore. Sarah built a fire. I told them I wanted to come find you by myself."

She nodded as she blinked sleep away. When he spoke again, his voice sounded contemplative. "It all seems like a bizarre nightmare," he said as he looked around the small space.

"Did you find anything on the plane?"

He told her about the hole in the oil-tank plug. "I also found my logbook and took that. The FAA might quibble with me about it, but as far as I'm concerned it's part diary, as well, and I don't want a bunch of strangers reading it."

"I don't blame you," she said.

"Nate had me grab a bottle of my water, too," he added.

"Why?"

"He's convinced they were tampered with. I don't see how. I bought a six-pack of them the night before and stowed them on the plane myself. There was nothing about them to suggest they were anything but what they appeared to be. Still, we'll get it tested. I've learned to pay attention to Nate when he has a hunch."

They fell silent for a minute until Jessica leaned her head against his shoulder. "I like the way you decorated the place," she said, glancing up again at her own image, drawn in charcoal on a rock face.

They both lay down and looked up. She rested her head on his arm. "I can't tell you how many hundreds of dreams I had about you while I was sleeping right here on this bed," he said. He kissed her brow and squeezed her. "Some of them were pretty damn erotic."

"I bet they were."

"Yeah. And some were terrifying."

"How were they terrifying?"

"I'd dream you were in danger and I couldn't get to you. Once I dreamed you'd fallen through the ice into the freezing water below and I was grabbing for your hand, but you kept drifting further and further away and you never said a word or even struggled."

She pressed herself closer to him.

"But the worst one was when I walked into our house after miraculously getting home and it was empty. No furniture, no nothing, especially, no you."

"Oh, Alex," she said softly.

"Because you see, I thought for sure I'd blown it and that even if I was rescued or managed to get out of these mountains, you would have moved on with your life... you would have let me go."

"But I didn't," she said. She closed her eyes for a second before adding, "I want to tell you something."

"What? Are you all right? Is the baby okay?"

"Yes, I'm fine, it's nothing like that. It's about something I did while you were away."

He looked up at the drawing he'd made of her, then over into her eyes. "I know about the Facebook page."

She took a deep breath. "Oh."

"Dylan mentioned it."

"When?"

"Days ago."

"But you didn't say anything to me."

"There didn't seem any point."

"I could have tried to explain," she said.

He pulled her closer. "You don't have to explain," he said.

"Yes, I do," she mumbled. She took another deep breath. "You can't imagine what it was like to find out I was pregnant right on the eve of your disappearance. I'd dreamed about telling you that news a million times, but then you were gone, and I couldn't bear it. Not just because I loved you, but because this was something you wanted as much as I did and you might never know."

"I understand," he said.

"Do you? I'm not sure I do. It was crazy to think you'd run away from me, but it was also comforting because it meant you weren't dead. If you'd just gotten sick of me, then maybe you were living somewhere and maybe if you were alive, you would think of me sometimes and then perhaps you'd check out my Facebook page. So I wrote that if you could, you should call me. No questions asked, no problems, there was just something you needed to know. In a way it made a ringing phone easier to handle because it might actually be…you."

"I'm so sorry, Jess," he said, kissing her face.

She ran a hand over his cheek, smoothing his hair away from his brow. His eyes glowed as he looked down at her.

"In my head I believed you were dead," she whispered. "In my heart I wanted you alive, somewhere, anywhere. I told myself you didn't have to come back to me if you didn't love me, but you should know about your baby."

"Why didn't you tell me all this when I got home?"

"I was ashamed of myself."

He held her tighter. In a way she wished they could stay in that camp together, just the two of them. "Why were you so reluctant for me to see this place?" she asked after a little while.

"I'm not sure. I guess I just wanted to forget how miserable and unhappy I was most of the time. Having you see it made me feel like it would all seem too real."

"But it is real, Alex, and now that I've seen it and shared it with you, it's more real than ever. And it's remarkable you managed to survive with so little, that you got out alive, that we have a second chance to be together."

He wiped the tears off her cheek. "Until now," he whispered, "I wasn't sure we were together, I mean in a way that would last. But we are, aren't we?"

She nodded as he kissed her, as he ran his hands over her body. "So, where do we go from here?" he asked, his voice as soft as silk against her neck, warm like honey.

She put her hands on either side of his face and looked right into his eyes. "We go home. We find out who killed Billy and Lynda Summers—"

"If they were both murdered—"

"Of course they were both murdered. We find out who did it and we stop them from killing anyone else." She paused for a second as she ran a finger across his lips. "Especially you."

"Especially us," he amended, wrapping both arms around her and touching her lips with his.

His breath was warm and fresh, his kisses intoxicating. She reached up and tugged on his shirt. "How'd you like to make some new memories on this bed of yours?"

"What kind of memories?" he whispered.

"This kind," she said, and slowly started unbuttoning her blouse.

He took over the unbuttoning process. "Are you sure?" he asked. He followed this question with a dozen kisses along her throat.

"I'm sure," she said softly. Those were the last words uttered for quite some time.

Her clothes came off in a hurry, and then she helped him with his. There was something so natural about lying in this bed made of boughs with sunlight glinting through the woven branches, the quiet afternoon ethereal and complete. Only their breathing and the rustle of the dried leaves and twigs broke the silence as they touched each other in all the ways they'd learned over the years brought pleasure, pausing once to just stare at each other in a sense of amazement.

When they were both stripped, he fondled her breasts and kissed them, his mouth hot and intoxicating. She closed her eyes, only to open them when she felt both his hands on her abdomen. He leaned down and kissed her right beneath the belly button, then moved lower. Flames leaped inside her at the touch of his tongue and she frantically reached for him, delighting in the silky smoothness of his body, groaning in pleasure as his fingers ran over her contours.

He entered her when they both reached the point of absolute no return, when to delay another second would be unimaginable. His thrusts were gentle in a way she'd never experienced from him before, as though he was afraid he would hurt her or their baby, and she quickly dispelled him of such thoughts by pushing down on his rear and raising her hips to meet him. She could tell the moment he was lost to reason and she willfully and gladly followed him, swept up in his responses and her own body's greedy need for him.

They lay still afterward, and then dressed each other slowly, with kisses and smiles, both realizing they stood at the cusp of a new beginning in their lives together.

It seemed to Jessica that all they had to do was survive the present and the future was theirs for the taking.

Chapter Ten

By the time they flew back to Blunt Falls and landed on John Miter's lake, the day was drifting away. John met them at the dock where Alex taxied.

John was a good-looking guy of sixty or so with a full head of silver hair and a permanent tan. With a knowing glint in his gray eyes, he helped Sarah and Jessica disembark. "You guys find what you were looking for?" he asked.

"And how do you know we were looking for something?" Jessica asked with a smile.

"I just have a feeling," he said. "Well?"

"I'm not sure. Alex, what in the world is this?"

As she spoke, she lifted the recovered bottle of Vita-Drink whose label had long ago disintegrated. It was still damp although it had been laying in a towel. When she hefted it, her fingers must have slid on the accumulated goo that had attached itself to the outside. The compression of her grasping it produced a tiny spurt of the purplish fluid to hit her on the arm.

"It's one of your drinks," she said, using the towel to wipe away months of slime.

"Is it open?" Alex asked.

She started to twist the cap. The pressure from her fingers released another tiny spout of fluid. "The cap is on tight," she said, "but it's got a leak." By now they were all standing close to each other staring at the Vita-Drink. "You think this was drugged?" she added. "But the cap is still sealed."

Nate took his key ring out of his pocket and separated a tiny flashlight from the keys. He shined it on the bottle. "Squeeze it again, Jess."

She did so and yet another squirt shot through the air and hit Alex in the middle of the chest. "There it is, see? A tiny hole, up high on the shoulder of the plastic bottle."

"Maybe it deteriorated under the water," Jessica said, though her voice hinted that even she didn't believe that.

"That's the kind of hole a hypodermic needle makes," Sarah said as she peered intently.

"You were drugged," Nate said, gripping Alex's arm.

Again Alex stared at the fluid. It looked so innocent.

"Who knew you drank these when you flew?" Sarah asked.

It was Jessica and Nate who laughed. "Everyone who knows him knows he's addicted to these things."

"I wouldn't exactly call it an addiction," Alex said, but he knew his fondness for them was common knowledge at work, at home, at the airport—everywhere.

Alex gently took the bottle and looked at the liquid through the clear plastic. "But I didn't notice a different smell or taste." He lifted his shirt and sniffed the spot the liquid had hit. He could detect no strange odor.

"We need to have it tested," Jessica said. "The police lab—"

"No," Alex and Nate said in tandem.

"I don't want to advertise I took anything off the plane," Alex explained.

"What about your logbook?" Jessica asked. The book was sealed inside a plastic bag.

"That's personal," he said. "I left all the flight information for the feds to find. I don't know if any of the log is readable anymore but like I told you, I don't want some government lab worker going through my daily entries. Nor am I going to admit I took the drink. We'll have to find an independent lab."

He'd been so quiet they'd all but forgotten that John Miter still stood nearby. He spoke up now. "I'll get it analyzed if you want."

Alex looked him in the eye. He might not know a lot about Miter's past—or frankly, anything at all—but he did have a good gut feeling about the guy. "You know of one?"

Miter smiled. "Yes."

"How?"

Miter laughed softly. "Leave it to me," he said.

Nate caught Alex's gaze and Alex could see he was unsure. After all, Nate didn't know John. "I want a sample of it to take back to Arizona," Nate said. "It's better if we split it up."

"I agree," Alex said.

Jessica found a couple of small bottles of seltzer in the ice chest in which they'd packed their lunch, and poured out the contents. Alex transferred a third of the old vitamin drink to one empty bottle, a third to another, and handed them to John and Nate respectively.

"You don't quite trust me," John said, his eyes glinting.

"I don't quite trust anyone," Alex said, "though I deeply appreciate all the help you've been."

Miter's gaze was direct and intense and, truthfully, intimidating, and then he smiled and took the sample. "Smart man," he said, and laughing, checked the twist top.

AFTER THEY DROVE Nate and Sarah to the airport, Alex and Jessica continued on to the Machi house. It had been a long, emotionally draining day for both of them, full of highs and lows and discoveries. And yet Alex felt connected to his life in a way he hadn't in longer than he cared to remember.

He wasn't as certain as Jessica that Lynda Summers's death hadn't been an accident. It didn't seem to him the woman knew much about her son's life even though he lived in her house. What threat could Lynda have posed for anyone unless she was into something herself that Alex knew nothing about? Why would someone murder her?

Had she seen or heard someone that night Billy went missing?

The coroner had said Billy was unconscious when he met his death. There was no proof Billy had ridden his bike to the drive-in. Tomorrow, Alex planned to drive the road between Billy's house and his own, looking for someone who might have seen Billy late that night. Maybe he'd met his attacker along that road. Or maybe he'd made it all the way home and gone out back to the shed without checking in with his mother who it appeared slept in front of the television every night. Maybe Lynda had heard her son's abductor.

"I've been wanting to ask you what the chief said when you called him this morning and told him you weren't coming in today," Jessica said as they pulled up outside a modest house in a forty-year-old subdivision. A few toys lay scattered across the front lawn while a couple of cars and a truck were parked in the driveway.

"I told him I wasn't feeling well. I admit I didn't like lying to him. Frank Smyth isn't as bad as I thought he was. I just had to do this today."

She smiled at him. "You don't sound much like the job-first-at-any-cost cop I married, you know."

"Maybe I've finally grown up. There is nothing more important to me than you and our baby."

"I know," she said softly.

"But it's even more than that," he admitted. "Seeing my plane, listening to Nate, well, you know, the big hits the country has taken from foreign terrorists are terrible and frightening. But somehow, we rally afterward, we declare a common enemy, we convince ourselves, over time, that we can prepare ourselves, protect ourselves." He stared straight ahead, then glanced at her.

"This is different. These people aim lower and closer to the belly, if you know what I mean. Their goal isn't massive loss of life, it's loss of well-being, of the safety of doing mundane things or observing traditional events. It's Americans going after other Americans. It's power hungry people manipulating innocents into thinking with their adrenaline instead of their heads, listening to their fears instead of their consciences. They have to be stopped."

"I know," she said softly. They were silent for a moment before she added, "Your friend John Miter is a little spooky."

"I know."

"I'm glad you didn't give him all that Vita-Drink. If I had to choose someone who might be in on a plot of some kind, I guess he would come to mind."

"He does look the part, I grant you that. But remember, I met him way before Labor Day last year and the fact that Nate and Mike and I got involved in that mall shooting and subsequently everything else was pure chance. Nate and I went to a mall because of a delayed flight with nothing on our minds other than finding something to eat in the food court. Mike told us he was there because he needed new jeans and they were having a sale at one of the stores. It was just chance."

"I'm still glad Nate took some of the water with him."

"And we have the bottle. Okay, let's go talk to Tony."

Tony's wife, Noreen, insisted they sit at the table and have a piece of strawberry pie, an offer neither Alex nor Jessica felt inclined to refuse. She was as friendly and generous as her husband, balancing kids and home like a seasoned pro.

Alex took out his camera, and while they ate pie, downloaded his pictures onto Tony's computer. While Jessica helped Noreen clear away the dishes, Alex and Tony studied the photographs.

"These are pretty clear," Tony said, scanning the images.

Alex used the tip of a pencil to point at the screen. "This is the cap," he said.

"Holy hell!" Tony murmured, leaning closer to study the image. "The safety twist wire is completely gone. And what's that hole? Do you have a better picture?"

Alex scrolled until they found one taken from a different perspective.

"Yeah," Tony said, touching the screen. "That's the hole right there. Straight through the plug. Damn, I wish you could have brought it to me."

"I do, too."

Tony sat back in his chair. "Someone drilled the center out of the plug and replaced it with something else," he said.

"I know. What I don't understand is why it lasted so long before it blew. If it was secure enough to get the plane in the air why did it suddenly give way?"

"Maybe it was some kind of wax," Tony said.

"Wouldn't it just melt when the engine got hot?"

"Yeah, but it might take a while. Once it melted away, though, that would be it. The oil would leak out, the engine would seize—"

"Which is exactly what happened."

"And they might have mixed in some other product that would delay the melting of the wax. There may be residue on the plug. If there is, the FAA will find it."

"But, Tony, how did the plug get there? You did the maintenance yourself and it's not exactly an easy spot for someone to tamper with out on the field."

Tony ran a hand through his thinning hair and shook his head. "The FAA looked through all my stuff, checked inventory lists, the whole nine yards. There wasn't anything missing that should have been there and that includes those plugs. I'd just received a shipment of five in that size, you know the Airtop brand in the red-and-yellow box. I'd used two of them, one on your plane and one on Vic Miller's. The other three were all where they were supposed to be, just like everything else. I'll have to review my records to see where they were all installed and make sure they weren't tampered with, too."

Alex stood behind Tony, who sat in front of the computer, and stared at the images on the screen. He was still staring at them a moment later when Jessica slipped her hand into his.

"Could Billy have switched plugs while you were eating lunch?" Alex finally asked. He felt Jessica's grip tighten around his fingers.

Tony swiveled in his chair and looked up at him. "What do you mean?"

"Think about it for a moment. Could Billy have taken out the plug you put in after the oil change and replaced it with this one?"

Tony turned back around to the screen, studied the photographs, then turned back. "If you mean could he have physically switched out the plugs, I guess, sure, maybe. Let me think. I did that part of the checkup, took a break, came back and finished the maintenance."

"Does that include refilling the oil tank?"

"It would have to. If anyone had tried to switch the plug after the oil was already installed, there would have been a big puddle on the floor."

"I can't imagine Billy could do all that," Jessica said softly.

Tony looked back at her. "It's not really that hard. He would have had to snip the safety twist wire is all, then take out the good plug and put in the drilled out one."

"So someone would have had to give him the doctored plug and pretty clear instructions?" Jessica said.

"Yes."

"And instructed him exactly how to exchange it?"

"Yes. All they'd have to do is Google it." He swore under his breath. "He was acting odd that day. I should have known something was wrong."

"And just so we're clear," Alex continued, "if this is the way it happened, it's possible you wouldn't have noticed the switch when you came back after lunch, is that right?"

Tony was quiet for a second, and then he shook his head. "No, I wouldn't have noticed. I imagine the plugs looked exactly alike unless you were really looking for a difference and I was already finished with that part of the job."

"But how would someone have known exactly what plug your engine took?" Jessica asked.

Tony answered the question. "Most of the Cessna 180s like Alex's came with Continental engines. That would mean drains and equipment would differ from one year to the next. But if someone knew what year Alex's plane was built, the rest wouldn't be hard to figure and with the N-number on the tail, checking it out would be pretty easy."

So it could have been almost anyone, Alex thought as Jessica leaned her head against his shoulder.

Tony once again ran his hand through his hair. "I can't believe Billy would do this. He knew whose plane we were working on." He looked back up at Alex. "What in the world did the boy have against you?"

"I don't know," Alex said, then added, "Probably nothing."

Tony shook his head again.

BLUE POINT ROAD didn't have a whole lot of residences within view of the highway. Places out here tended to sit back from the road a bit, some with heavily wooded areas between the houses and traffic. And one side of the pavement was nothing but a steep fall into a gorge.

Working their way toward the Summers house, Alex and Dylan drove down five driveways. No one was home at two of them, one man had absolutely nothing to offer and the elderly couple at the fifth went to bed every night by nine o'clock, rain or shine.

The last house looked as though it would present another no-one-is-home moment. The road was densely covered with arching trees and Dylan swore under his breath as some of the limbs hit his car. "I just got it back from the shop," he complained. "Cripes, doesn't anyone around here prune stuff?"

This was the first time Alex had seen Dylan's new car and it was a beauty. Built low to the ground, power seemed to ooze from under the hood. In many ways, the car was a perfect fit for the well-toned man who drove it.

"How did you get the car back from Billings?" Alex asked.

"I figured you can get a pizza delivered, you can get a car delivered," he said.

They finally reached the house and knocked at the front door. No response until a woman's voice called from the back. The two of them walked around the well-kept cabin to emerge in a beautifully tended garden that boasted lush vegetable beds as well as walls of climbing flowers. As the growing season started late and ended early in parts of Montana, there wasn't actually a lot of produce on the plants yet but even to Alex's untrained eye, the vegetation looked lavish and healthy.

The owner of the voice rose from where she'd been sitting on the side of a raised flower bed. It had turned into a warm day and she wore a skimpy T-shirt with a flowing cotton skirt and sandals. She'd piled her blondish hair atop her head where it tumbled over her eyes. Her voice was whiskey soaked and her expression was saucy. She was probably in her late forties and holding her own.

"Can I help you?" she asked, the spade in front of her.

"Excuse us," Alex said with a swift glance at Dylan who was giving the woman his customary once-over that seemed to take a week. After introducing themselves, he explained, "We're investigating the death of a man who lived up the street, Billy Summers. We're hoping you might have seen or heard something late Saturday night, early Sunday morning."

"Heard something?" she asked, settling her hip against a potting bench. "Like what?"

"Like a car passing or screech of metal or maybe you saw Billy on his bike?"

"Oh," she said. "No, I didn't. I wish I could help. I know who Billy was. Sometimes he stopped by to see my garden. Not this year, not yet, anyway, and now I hear he's dead, that someone ran over him. That's too bad, he was a sweet guy."

"Thanks for your time," Dylan said as he handed her a card. "If you think of anything, please give us a call."

Her assurances followed them back to the front yard.

"She was holding up pretty good for an old broad," Dylan commented.

"Damn, man, keep your voice down." Alex lightened his tone and added, "What in the world would a real woman see in a clown like you, anyway?"

"Sticks and stones," Dylan crooned.

Once they hit the road, Alex pointed toward the Summers house. "Go that way," he said. "Lynda Summers had closer neighbors we can interview."

"We already talked to them," Dylan said.

"They were questioned about *her* death. I want to ask them if they heard anything the night Billy disappeared. But, frankly, I want another look around the Summers place, too."

"You're becoming obsessed," Dylan said, but then he shook his head. "Sorry. After what you told me you found on the Cessna, of course you're obsessed." He poked Alex in the ribs. "I knew you weren't sitting home sick because I drove by your place and no one was there."

"Why did you do that?"

Dylan shrugged. "I just doubted you were sick and thought you might need help of some kind. Why didn't you tell me you were going to dive on the plane? You told that Miter guy."

"I just borrowed a plane from John," Alex said. "If

he knows anything else it's because he always seems to know exactly what's going on."

"I know. That's what creeps me out about him."

"Anyway, it all came up kind of fast."

"I can read between the lines," Dylan said. "You didn't want the chief to blab it to his reporter pal."

"Something like that," Alex said.

"I still can't believe Billy had anything to do with your crash," Dylan said. "Frankly, the kid didn't seem clever enough."

"If he did, he must have had help," Alex said.

"Yeah. Maybe Tad and Ted Cummings put him up to it."

Alex was about to protest but stopped himself. How did he know what Tad and Ted were capable of?

"Maybe Billy's death didn't have much to do with drugs," Dylan mused aloud. "If the Cummings boys were in on the conspiracy to keep you from going to Shatter-horn, maybe they decided to cut their weakest link—Billy—out of the picture."

Alex glanced over. "What?"

Dylan shifted position which seemed to cause the car to sway. Sitting next to the guy in the low-slung car was like sitting next to a bulging muscle. "Think about it," he said. "Didn't that B-Strong organization in Shatter-horn use young males about Ted and Tad's age to do their dirty work?"

"They trained them as gunmen who then terrorized malls and picnics and parades," Alex said. "We'd better check them out for any kind of club involvement."

"Is there a B-Strong around here?"

"From what Nate said, there's no longer any B-Strong clubs anywhere. They were disbanded after what they were doing came to light."

Dylan parked in the yard. The old double-wide already had a sagging look of abandonment about it, like the weight of its interior was pulling the roof down and in. There was a sign on the door telling people the property was condemned and to keep out.

"Things move fast," Alex said.

"They sure do," Dylan said as he rubbed a tiny scratch on his hood with a finger and swore under his breath. "Okay. I'll take the two houses down there, you get the three up the street."

They went their separate ways. The first house Alex came to was owned by a small, ancient-looking woman. She tried to think back to Saturday night or early Sunday morning, but Alex could see it was a lost cause.

"I don't go outside after dark," she finished. "There's that woman next door and her odd son. Have you seen what a mess she keeps that place? It's disgraceful. I have half a mind to call the mayor."

There was no one home at the house next to hers, and at the house farthest away, he found several people sitting around the yard drinking beer. Figuring out which person actually owned the place took a while and produced no results. Alex walked back to the Summers place. Unless Dylan had better luck, this line of inquiry was going nowhere fast.

He waited in the yard for Dylan to return for five long minutes and in that time, he had the strangest feeling that someone was watching him. He walked completely around the house and saw nothing, didn't even hear anything but some birds chattering up in the treetops.

Eventually, he decided to take another look at the shed while he waited. It was once again locked, and Alex played around with breaking it open to look at the model airplanes and the room one more time. Instead he walked around to the back where he saw evidence the lab crew had tried to lift footprints from under the window. Stepping carefully to avoid the last of the yellow crime-scene tape, he moved the ivy and peered into the room.

His gaze was immediately drawn to the stack of index cards beside the lamp. He was almost positive there had been more there the first time he saw it, though he couldn't say why that thought persisted. He closed his eyes and tried to picture it the way it had looked the first time he'd seen the room. The striped lamp, the cards by the base, all the way up to the bottom of the first yellow line.

He opened his eyes. That was it. The cards topped out down low on a black stripe. The stack was shorter than it had been before Billy died.

"What are you doing?" Dylan asked.

Caught by surprise, Alex jumped a few inches. Then he told Dylan about the index cards.

"Are you sure?" Dylan asked.

"Well, I guess I wouldn't bet my life on it, but I'm pretty sure."

"Maybe Lynda took some of them when she came to unlock the shed," Dylan offered.

"And that doesn't make sense, either. If she was so grief-stricken she was on sedatives, why would she have walked out here by herself to unlock the shed and then come inside to investigate? Why would she do that?"

"From everything you and Frank Smyth have said, I get the impression she wasn't aware of what Billy had done to the inside of the place. Maybe it caught her off guard. Where did we come up with the scenario that she came outside to unlock it?"

Alex thought for a second. "Chief Smyth surmised it. We don't know for sure." What caused him to pause was the fact that he'd found Smyth inside the shed when he came looking for him the day Lynda died. Was it possible he'd slipped some of the index cards into a pocket? He'd actually been standing next to the lamp and table.

But why do it with everyone there when he'd apparently enjoyed free access to this place? And wouldn't taking those cards amount to a cover-up, either for himself or someone else? Was Alex really thinking that the chief of their small police department was involved in all this?

He tried to recall the man's politics as he moved aside for Dylan who had been straining to see into the room over Alex's shoulder. But he didn't know Frank that well. He'd never been to his house or said more than a greeting to his wife or met his daughter. Still, could a man be part of something so sinister and not reveal it in his everyday life?

If he was clever enough.

This was impossible.

Again Alex thought back to the day before yesterday. He'd commented on the scratches on the back of Frank's hand. He could visualize the chief subsequently shoving that hand in a pocket. He'd been wearing the kind of jacket someone wears when they ride a bike, close fitting, not bulky at all. Wouldn't Alex have seen the general shape of a half a dozen or more cards if they'd been in one of those pockets?

Dylan walked away from the window and Alex took his place for one last glimpse. This time he noticed a small vertical seam on the rounded side of the table. He'd taken it for a defect, but now he wondered if it indicated an inset drawer. Why hadn't he paid more attention to it when he had the chance?

"All we have are questions and more questions," he

muttered to himself. He glanced at Dylan. "You were gone quite a while. Did you find out anything?"

"Nobody was home anywhere," Dylan said. "I swear, this neck of the woods empties out during the day. I'll catch them tomorrow night." He popped a knuckle or two.

"Why not tonight?"

"I have plans."

"Are you driving all the way back to Billings to see your new girlfriend?"

"How'd you guess?"

"And you have the nerve to call me obsessed."

"Get in and relax," Dylan said with a laugh.

Alex slid into the luxurious car, but the relaxing part wasn't as easy to accomplish. On the way back into town, he found himself checking his side mirror, trying to see if they were being followed.

He never saw a thing but he was almost certain someone was there.

Chapter Eleven

Jessica was as restless that night as Alex was. Neither of them could stand staying inside the house. Since their own yard still held too many upsetting memories they tried a walk. Even that didn't settle their nerves.

They finally decided to drive to the store and order the flowers for Memorial Day. That process ate up a whole forty-five minutes. They were waiting in a long line to buy a sandwich for dinner when Alex's cell phone rang.

"It's John Miter," Alex said as he scanned the screen.

What followed was a short conversation where Alex hardly said anything but listened intently until he muttered, "No rush, we're not at home. Thanks."

"Was that about the Vita-Drink?" Jessica asked as he pocketed his phone. She'd unconsciously lowered her voice as though the people in line behind them had the slightest idea what they were talking about. It was just sometimes hard to remember that not everyone was caught up in the same confusing drama they were.

"John's friends at the lab just got back to him. Nate is right, the drink was drugged." His voice was toned way down, too. "He'll email the results to our home computer sometime tonight."

"What drugs?"

"A whole laundry list of pharmaceuticals. Something

to relax muscles, something else to make you sleepy—
it was probably the combination of them that made me
queasy as well as tired that morning. It's a wonder I
didn't pass out."

"Who could have done this?" she asked.

"I picked up the water at the store the night before
the flight. It was locked in my truck in our garage until
I got to the airport the next morning. Someone either
doctored the bottles there or switched them with previ-
ously altered bottles that morning, and the only time I
can think either of those things could have been done
was when Kit called me at the airport and I went inside
to take his call."

"Why didn't he call on your cell?"

"He said he was at home and he didn't have that number. Let's see, I remember him complaining that he hadn't
been able to reach Dylan. Anyway, it was a miserable
morning weatherwise, cold and nasty and the only other
person I saw on the field was Billy Summers."

"But you said he was cleaning a windshield or something like that."

"Deicing, I think, but I didn't see him working, I just
saw him carrying a bunch of stuff."

"Coming or going?"

"He was coming toward me while I was walking to
the Cessna."

"So you think he could have been carrying your original water bottles?" she whispered.

"They could have been in the toolbox," he agreed as
he dug out his keys. "Let's get out of here."

"Where are we going?"

"Blue Point Road. You game?"

"Absolutely," she said.

ALEX STOPPED AT the first of the three houses Dylan had struck out with that afternoon and was relieved when someone was home. Jessica sat in the car as he conducted the brief interview, which didn't turn out to help a whole lot because the guy admitted he fell asleep to a blaring television every night.

The second place appeared to be abandoned but the man who answered Alex's knock at the last house was a different story. He claimed he'd heard screeching brakes late Saturday night.

"What time?" Alex asked.

The guy was in his late forties, tall, wearing a bib apron printed with the slogan Will Cook for Sex. He explained he had to flip a steak on his indoor grill in exactly four minutes. The aroma of sizzling beef wafting from the kitchen started Alex's stomach rumbling.

"After midnight. The clock in the bedroom is broken but I'd gone to bed at twelve and I heard the brakes before I actually fell asleep."

"Did you see anything?"

"I looked out the window. I think I saw a couple of lights like headlamps a little bit south of here, but it was really foggy and I'm not sure. That road is treacherous on a bad night." He glanced at his wristwatch. "It's time to turn the T-bone. You need anything else?"

Alex handed him a card. He got back in the truck, and together he and Jessica drove south, stopping often to look at the road. About four hundred feet along, Alex found what he was looking for and got out to check the pavement.

When he got back inside after taking a half dozen pictures with his cell phone, Jessica raised her eyebrows. "Well?"

"There are tire tracks like a vehicle makes with a sudden stop, but there's no way for me to know when they were made or by who. I'll call downtown and get someone out here tomorrow to process them just to be on the safe side." He was thinking the adjacent terrain deserved a once-over, as well.

It was still light outside, though the shadows were deepening when they pulled up in front of Billy's old house. Alex was surprised to find a tractor and a large Dumpster out front.

"What's with the equipment?" Jessica asked as Alex parked his truck.

"I don't know," he said. "I wonder who will end up with this place."

"What would anyone do with it?"

"I can't imagine. Probably knock it down once it clears probate. The land must be worth something. Come on, let's make sure no one else is around, and then take another look at that shed, okay?"

They both got out of the truck and Alex took Jessica's hand. He wasn't sure exactly how they'd managed to go from lovers and friends to frustrated near enemies, and he also wasn't sure how they had managed to get back on the right track with each other. Perhaps they owed this second chance to the plane crash which was kind of ironic when you thought about it.

But wonderful, too. It was hard to believe that they would soon be parents at long last.

"Which room are we going to turn into a nursery?" he asked suddenly.

She looked up at him and smiled and he leaned over to kiss the top of her head as his arm slipped around her shoulders. "I thought the one right across the hall from ours," she said after a moment.

"Do we know if it's a girl or boy yet?"

"Not yet. The ultrasound that checks bone length and organ development also reveals the baby's sex. It's in about a week."

"Which do you want?" he asked, stopping to pat her stomach area and look into her eyes.

"I couldn't care less," she said. "How about you?"

"One of each," he said lightly as he stepped onto the front porch and knocked, then tried the knob. "It's locked," he announced. He looked through the window, too. The place looked different than it had when he'd last been there which was right after Lynda Summers's death, as if more of the boxes had been shifted here and there. No doubt the paramedics had had to rearrange things to get Lynda's body out of her house.

"Let's go around back," he said.

He called out as they walked around the house, not wanting to surprise anyone, but there wasn't anybody there.

The shed door was secured just as it had been earlier that afternoon, with a lock threaded through a hasp. "Wait here a second," he said, and sprinted back to his truck where he took a toolbox out of the covered bed and carried it back to the shed. Setting it on the ground, he dug around in it until he found a screwdriver.

"Alex Foster, what are you doing?" Jessica asked, her eyes wide.

"I'm taking the hasp off the door because I don't want to break the lock."

"Is that legal?"

"Not technically."

"In what way, then?"

He removed the last screw from the old wood and the hasp came free. "I think Billy tried to kill me."

"I know you do."

"And I think he must have had help and I don't know who that person might be. That makes trusting anyone except you a little tricky. Plus there's a tractor and a rig out front. On the off chance I missed something in this shed, I plan on taking a look before it's too late. Stay here."

"Who's going to watch your back?" she said. "If we're caught, maybe we can share a cell."

Alex laughed as he stepped inside the shed, Jessica right behind him. The laughter died immediately. Billy's bastion of uncluttered order looked as though it had been hit by a tornado. Glass sparkled on the floor in front of the shattered window and the little striped lamp had been smashed to pieces. The round table lay on its side next to the overstuffed chair that spilled its foam rubber guts.

"Someone has been in here," Alex said unnecessarily. As he righted the table, he noticed something was missing and looked around the room.

"This was Billy's space?" Jessica said.

"I know it's hard to believe, but it used to look like a little oasis next to everything else around here," Alex said.

"Why would anyone destroy it this way?"

"It looks to me like someone was looking for something."

"I wonder if they found it."

"If it was part of the red-and-white biplane that used to hang over the table, it appears so. The plane is gone and I don't see its pieces on the floor."

"There are other models."

"This one was different. Much larger, better constructed."

She stared at the ones that had survived the attack. "He was capable of being very creative," she said.

"Yeah."

"When I think of how meticulous he was with the garden—you know, Alex, I'm going to replant it. I can't let whoever did that to Billy's work get away with it, especially when they also wrecked this sanctuary. I mean it has to be the work of the same person, don't you think?"

"It sure appears to have the same wanton destruction-for-destruction's-sake quality about it," he agreed.

"Yeah. Well, I'm going to make our yard beautiful again, you know, in his memory."

"That's a good idea," Alex said. He looked down at the table and used his fingers to feel for the groove in the table apron that he'd noticed from the window. "I was right, it's a drawer," he said, kneeling in order to check it out and watching he didn't cut himself on broken glass. He turned the table a little and slid out the drawer that seemed to have a spring mechanism instead of a knob or handle. "This seems shallow," he said.

"Is there anything in it?"

"Not much. I don't want to leave prints on the contents, though. I should have brought gloves."

"Wait a second," she said. "I just saw an open box of latex gloves over in the mess on Billy's workbench."

"Don't touch anything," he cautioned. "I'll get them. I was here two days ago so my prints are easy to explain away but yours might be a different matter."

"That's why my hands are in my pockets," she said. "I'm married to a cop, you know. I figure stuff like this out."

He grabbed a couple of gloves so he wouldn't destroy any evidence that might be in the drawer, and stopped to kiss her forehead before he once again knelt in front of the drawer.

"Okay. There are a few blank index cards, a couple

of pencils…not much else. Frankly there doesn't seem to be room for much else."

She knelt beside him, touching her belly as she did so. "For the first time, it feels like there's a baby between my chest and my knees when I bend over," she said, and they exchanged excited smiles. She studied the drawer before adding, "Is that a false bottom?"

"Yeah, I think it is," he said as he withdrew his knife. Wishing the light were better, he inserted the blade at the front edge of the drawer bottom and immediately felt the thin wood wobble. He removed the few things that had been scattered atop the false bottom, then carefully slipped the wood out of place.

They found themselves staring at a hypodermic needle and three small empty medical vials whose labels Alex recognized as the drugs John Miters's lab had confirmed were injected into the Vita-Drink bottles.

Beside him, Jessica's sigh sounded like a very soft, sad refrain. "I didn't want to believe it," she said.

"Look," he said as he lifted the needle out of the drawer to reveal an index card covered with simple illustrations and directions. "Here's how you load a needle with the drugs and then inject the contents into the high shoulder of a plastic bottle. Sound familiar?"

"Of course it does."

He slid the entire drawer from the table and gestured at the index cards. "Is that Billy's writing?"

"I don't think so. What are we going to do with all this?"

After shifting the drawer into position under his arm, he helped Jessica stand. "I'm going to call downtown and get a crew out here," he said, grabbing his phone from his pocket. "I'll stay with everything until someone arrives.

The place has already been broken into once tonight, we can't walk away and leave it unguarded."

"Actually," she said with a fleeting smile, "it was broken into twice."

"You and your technicalities," he said.

"What do you want me to do?"

"I want you to drive to Silvia's house. I want you as far away from all this as you can get." He pulled out his phone but before he could place a call, her fingers lit on his arm. He looked down at her.

"I'm not leaving you here alone," she said. "You should know that about me by now."

He did know it. He just wanted her to be safe and that meant away from this shed.

"Just make the call," she told him.

He nodded, but before he could tap even one number the window beside them shattered. From the corner of his eye, he saw a missile fly into the room. It hit the chair and immediately burst into flames. "Get out of here!" Alex yelled, pulling on Jessica's hand. The fire quickly spread to the wooden floor and then to the worktable where it ignited the solvents and paints stored on the shelf.

They reached the safety of the outside right before a small explosion inside the building signaled the beginning of the end. They ran to get as far away as they could.

Alex handed Jessica the drawer and pulled out his gun. She stood with her back against the house, her face pale in the weakening light. She clutched the drawer in one hand while she took her cell phone from her sweater pocket with the other.

"Are you all right?" he asked her.

"I'll live. I'll call the fire department."

"Stay here," he added, and took off to the front where he could hear what sounded like a far-off motor. Their attacker was getting away. By the time Alex rounded the corner, the yard was clear and nothing looked one bit different than it had since they entered the shed. The tractor still stood off to the side, the Dumpster beside it, Alex's truck pulled in close to one of the wrecks that occupied the side yard.

His head pounded with the images of what could have happened inside that shed, not to himself, but to Jessica and their baby. He'd thought earlier about irony, and how saving his marriage might have actually hinged on being stranded in the mountains for three months.

But now it occurred to him that coming home might have put a whole host of people in jeopardy. Billy and Lynda were dead, the Cummings twins were under investigation, his wife had been scared out of her wits half a dozen times.

He returned to Jessica, unsure what to do to protect her except to disappear again…and that was not an option. She'd set the drawer aside and found a garden hose and had turned it on. He took it from her and aimed the water higher into the flames.

"Did you see anything?" she asked.

"No," he said. The water pressure wasn't great and seemed to be having no positive effect, so he switched his efforts to making sure the blaze didn't spread to the house, the trees or any of the abandoned cars that stood nearby. It was a relief to hear screeching sirens. Within minutes, firemen had taken over, the bomb squad was waiting nearby and police cars started arriving.

Alex explained that what he'd seen was a Molotov cocktail, a gas bomb made out of a beer bottle, gasoline with a burning rag as a wick. He didn't add what everyone there knew—such things were easy to construct out of universally available materials. Anyone could have done it.

Kit Anderson acted fidgety and ill at ease as he ran around doing his best to take charge. As soon as he could, Alex steered Jessica toward his truck. The smell of a fire and the resulting ash was never a pleasant one, but with all the burning garbage in the lean-to, this one was particularly noxious and he didn't want her exposed to it.

Kit caught up with him. "Where are you going with that?" he asked, gesturing at the drawer and its contents tucked under one of Alex's arms.

"Downtown," Alex said succinctly.

Kit held out his hands. "I'll take it."

"No, thanks," Alex said, and continued walking. Kit trotted behind him.

"The chief said I should handle this kind of thing," he insisted.

Alex turned and looked over his shoulder. "The chief doesn't even know this stuff exists."

"Well, not what you're holding in particular," he said, "just evidence in general."

"Let me get this straight," Alex said. "The chief told you not to allow me to transport evidence?"

Kit looked uncomfortable as he shuffled a bit. "Yeah."

"Too bad," Alex said and kept walking, relieved when Kit fell behind.

He paid close attention to the road and was relieved when he saw the landmark he'd chosen, the broken branch on an old oak tree, and subsequently the tire marks on the roadbed. They would be easy to find again in the daylight. He searched his mind for the feeling that someone was watching him, but it didn't come like it had earlier in the day. At least there was that.

A few minutes later, Jessica touched his arm. "You're pretty quiet," she said. "What are you thinking about?"

He glanced over at her beautiful face illuminated by the dashboard lights. "Why would the chief tell Kit to make sure I wasn't handling evidence?"

"Maybe Kit was lying. Maybe he just wants to control everything."

Alex thought for a moment longer. "No, I don't think Kit was lying. The guy doesn't exactly have a poker face." He thought for a few seconds longer and added, "You know, the first part of the equation is relatively simple."

"What equation?"

"The beginning, back when someone wanted me and Nate and Mike dead. We represented an immediate threat to the Shatterhorn Killer. I think he overreacted. He got someone to try to run Nate off the road when he was on his way to Nevada to meet with me and Mike. They got someone else to sabotage my airplane. And then they drove up to Mike's house and shot him dead.

"If things had gone according to their plans, Nate would have died in the desert north of Vegas in a car accident. I would have slammed into a handy mountain somewhere or imploded in the middle of a desert and there wouldn't have been a lot left of my plane. Forensics being what they are now, the government may have uncovered a conspiracy but it would have been a lot harder and if everything else hadn't happened the way it had, they might not have even looked for one."

"But Nate didn't die," Jessica said, her hand warm on his thigh, her voice very soft.

"No. And no one else has tried to hurt him since then. It appears he isn't a threat anymore."

"Someone is sure trying to get you," she said.

"Yeah, but by the oddest backdoor methods. Ruining

our garden, killing the guileless kid they set up to sabotage my plane, perhaps killing his mother because, well, I don't know why. Add that fake call to the emergency room and frightening you—it's crazy."

"And it's escalating," Jessica said. "There was nothing tentative about lobbing a bomb into an occupied building."

"But if they just wanted me dead, why not kill me? Shoot me, stab me, you know. Why all these antics? Get it over with already."

"Be careful what you say," she told him. "The universe may be listening."

THEY AWOKE YET again to a ringing phone, only this time it was Agent Struthers. "I'm in kind of a hurry but I wanted you and your wife to know we just got word that the man known as William Tucker is actually named Charles Bond. He was thought to be dead, one of several victims in a very messy terrorist attack in New Orleans several years ago. He obviously survived the terrorist attack and used the opportunity to disappear. There's nothing to tie him to that attack and in fact, the people behind it were caught, tried and convicted. But Bond apparently took on a false identity and moved in with his ex-brother-in-law, aka the Shatterhorn Killer. It now appears Bond is the one who's been pulling the strings."

Alex rubbed the sleep from his eyes and muttered, "Do you know where he is now?"

"Unfortunately, no. His last call was yesterday and he mentioned leaving Seattle. He didn't give a clue to his destination."

"Okay," Alex said with a sigh. "Is Seattle still on alert?"

"Absolutely. He's proven he doesn't have to be around

to cause mayhem. He's pretty good at coaxing other people to do it for him. There's another lead suggesting the target for a Memorial Day attack in Seattle is a big food-and-wine festival. Security is being tightened."

"I hope they get the bastards," Alex said.

"So do we all. But it makes sense that after Nate foiled the parade attack a year ago, Bond might be hot to try the same thing on a different one. Use caution, Detective Foster. Stay alert."

"I will," Alex assured him. After turning off the phone, he met Jessica's nervous gaze and put his arms around her, nuzzling her neck. "You're the best thing that ever happened to me," he said softly.

"Oh, Alex. Was that about William Tucker or whatever his name is?"

He put his hands on her shoulders and held her a short distance away so he could look into her eyes. "His name is Charles Bond." He told her what Struthers had said.

"Then he could be on his way here?"

"Here, there or anywhere. Who knows?"

Tears spilled onto her cheeks and she buried her face against his chest.

He kissed her hair and raised her chin so he could look in her eyes. "I'm here for you, sweetheart."

She nodded. "I just want it to be over. And I thought if he was behind our yard and the emergency-room stunt and then the bomb last night, well, at least we'd know who our enemy was. But if he's been in Seattle…"

Her voice trailed off and he finished the sentence in his head, *then it could be anyone.*

She put her lips against his. "I love you so much, Alex."

He kissed her again, losing himself in her tender warmth. And then the nature of the kisses changed as they often did, grew deeper, longer, merging into one long cacophony of sensation that awakened every part of his body. "It's still pretty early," he whispered with a rasping voice while cupping one of her succulent breasts in his hand, dipping his head to lick her nipple through the silk of her gown.

"Let's make the most of it," she said, and pulled him down on top of her.

SOON AFTER, ALEX joined the team investigating the tire marks he'd found on Blue Point Road south of the Summers house the night before. Dylan showed up a few minutes later and walked beside Alex.

Alex's attention was divided between searching the ground for some other sign of mishap and the sight of Frank Smyth's car pulling off to the side of the road beside the police van. A spray of gravel suggested the chief was either in a hurry or distracted. He jumped out of his car and began talking to the techs.

"I heard about what happened to you and Jess last night," Dylan said at last. "I was too far away to respond."

"I know you were," Alex said, watching the chief. "Smyth didn't show up, either. We left so Kit could play detective all by himself."

"Well, I want you to know something," Dylan added.

"What?"

"I've been thinking about everything that's happened to you and Jessica. I took it all too lightly. Hell, man, you guys could have been killed last night. From now on, I have your back. I'm going to get to the bottom of whatever is going on or die trying."

Alex looked closely at his partner. He wasn't used to the serious tone he heard in Dylan's voice and it touched him. "Thanks," he said.

"Sure thing. And I mean it. However, you do realize the tire tracks on the roadbed could have been made days ago, like even when you were still up in the mountains."

"I know. I can't believe I've been home a week."

"Neither can I. And I want you to know that I would have gone back to those houses tonight like I said I would. You didn't have to do it for me."

"I know. I was just restless and needed something to do. You know, one of those places is totally empty."

"Guess that explains why no one answered the door."

The chief came to a stop near them, pausing for a second to shield a cigarette with his hand while he lit it with his trusty lighter. "I heard you were out here," he said, addressing Alex. "I also heard what happened last night. Is your wife okay?"

"She's fine, thank heavens," Alex said.

Smyth's thin lips all but disappeared off his face when he scowled and he was scowling now. "What were you thinking, taking her with you?" he growled.

Alex almost blurted out something like, "You think I'd leave her alone?" Only trouble was, the chief was right. He'd endangered her, not protected her. He should have hustled her out of that shed the moment he saw the broken window. Instead he said, "It seemed like a good idea at the time."

"Well, it wasn't. Furthermore, Kit Anderson reports the hasp on the door of the shed had been removed. I take it you're responsible for that, too?"

"I was just looking around," Alex said. Once again the image of Smyth standing close to that dwindling stack of index cards played in his mind.

"By breaking and entering?"

Alex didn't respond. He was angry and he wasn't sure he had a right to be.

Smyth jabbed the air between them. "I'm told you made a deposit in the evidence room last night."

"I found a drawer in that little table in the shed," Alex explained. "There were directions for how to fill a hypodermic needle with drugs and inject it into a plastic bottle so no one would know the contents had been tampered with. Maybe the lab can lift fingerprints or analyze the writing. It could help the government with their investigation."

"If you haven't jeopardized the provenance of that evidence," Smyth said sternly. "You should have handed it over to Kit."

"Since when do I hand evidence to Kit?" Alex asked.

"Since now."

There was a moment of silence, broken when Dylan cleared his throat. He looked at Smyth. "Where were you last night, Chief?"

"Not that it's any of your business, but I had a meeting," Smyth said as he rubbed his bald head.

Alex took a deep breath. "The shed is destroyed, right?"

"Totally," Smyth said.

"It's true I broke into it, but someone else did it first only they came in through the window. The place had been ransacked. The only thing I could see that was missing was the big model of the red-and-white biplane that used to hang over the table. The Cummings twins helped with the model and they were anxious to get it back, so someone should talk to them."

"We may be able to use that in further questioning," Smyth allowed. "I had them in yesterday for another round of interviews. I can't say they divulged anything new. Neither one of you mention this to anyone else, okay?"

"Okay," Alex said. "I should also mention the FBI

reports the man known as William Tucker is actually Charles Bond. They have currently lost track of him."

"You spoke to the FBI?" Smyth snapped.

"Yeah."

"Did you mention what you found?"

"No, not yet. The agent was in a hurry and I thought you should be part of any exchange of that kind of information. I'm sure they'll be contacting you."

"Yes," Smyth interrupted. "I should think so." He nodded decisively. "I have another meeting this afternoon," he said, zeroing in on Alex. "We're busier than a mosquito at a nudist colony getting ready for God knows what disaster. I can't change any of that but by golly, I can change this. I want you to step back."

"What?" Alex said, stunned.

"Let Dylan and Kit handle this case. You're off it."

"But—"

"I think all that time in the mountains made you forget you're part of a team. And I'm in charge of this team, not you. Stop going off like some lone wolf looking for glory. And if I hear you're tampering with anything at all, there will be hell to pay. When I think what a reporter could lead with when it comes to this…well, it doesn't bear considering."

Alex blinked a couple of times. His mind raced to make sense of what he was hearing. What in the world was going on?

"I don't want to have to give you a reprimand or time off, but I will if I have to, no matter what happens to me."

Alex met the chief's gaze and did his best not to appear defiant or challenging since he figured that would just make things worse.

"I'll see you later," Smyth said to Dylan, then stalked back to his car and took off.

"What was that all about?" Dylan demanded.

Alex shook his head, bewildered. "I really don't know. Maybe he's got trouble at home or something."

"He's too pious to have trouble at home. Mr. Goody-two shoes is all about smoothing things over."

Alex had never heard Frank Smyth described that way. "You sound like you know him pretty well. Do you know his wife, too?"

"Not really. They're both involved in a lot of civic and church activities. Word gets around."

And Dylan always seemed to have his ear close to the ground. "Well something is bothering the guy," Alex mused. "Maybe he feels bad Lynda died the way she did after he'd promised his mother he'd watch out for her. Is he handling her estate?"

"What estate?"

"You know, her house—"

"The chief owns everything," Dylan interrupted. "The land, the trailer, the whole nine yards. Lynda lived in it for twenty-some-odd years and there's no record of her paying a dime in rent."

"How do you know all this stuff?" Alex asked.

"It's a matter of record, buddy." Not to be deterred, Dylan continued. "Did you notice the equipment out there?"

"The tractor and Dumpster? Yeah. When did you see it?"

"I drove by this morning before I got here. Our trusty chief is getting ready to level that dump. He's had it declared a health hazard and rumor has it, he's hurrying things along to get it demolished. Makes you wonder what's he's hiding, doesn't it? And who is he meeting with that he won't name? Why so secretive?"

Alex wasn't a big fan of idle speculation, although he

couldn't help but be interested. Was the chief involved in something dangerous? There was absolutely nothing to go on to suggest such a thing. So Smyth was acting surly—that didn't make him a criminal.

But why had he all of a sudden called Alex off this case?

"All I'm saying," Dylan said, "is that I'm keeping my eyes open. Be honest, what are you out here looking for?"

Glad to get off the topic of the chief, Alex resumed his systematic search of the terrain. "I'm wondering if Billy was hit on his way home from my house last Saturday night. It was crummy weather and we know his bike didn't get to the theater by itself. It's a long way to go in the fog."

"I'm sorry, but this seems like a fool's errand to me. If someone hit him out here, why move him to the theater and not the hospital?"

"The only reason I can surmise is they wanted an out-of-the-way place to finish him off. I'm pretty sure someone really didn't want him to talk to me."

"If you're right about Billy being involved with your crash, why in the world would he want to talk to you the minute you got back to town?"

"I'm not sure about that." Alex caught the glint of sunlight off of a piece of metal down in the gulch off the steep roadbed. He scrambled down the slope, Dylan on his heels. He slid a couple of feet on some shale and knelt to examine his find, a small piece of red plastic encased in chrome.

"This looks like part of a taillight housing off a bike," Alex said, and then his shoulders stiffened. The dirt around them had been disturbed with parallel tracks as though something, or someone, had been dragged up the gully. It wasn't visible from above. Rain had washed most of it away, but from down here, it was pretty obvious. A small, darker patch of earth off to the left under the cover of a bush made his stomach roll. A combination of intuition and experience kicked into gear.

He'd be willing to bet that dark patch of dirt had been saturated with blood. Billy's blood. Had the boy been hit, tumbled down the slope, laid here bleeding until someone dragged him back up the slope and drove him and his mangled bike away?

Beside him, Dylan groaned as though Alex had spoken all of this aloud. "I'd better get the techs to go back over the Cummings twins' car," he said, his voice subdued. He glanced at Alex and added, "You better let me handle this now. You heard what the chief said."

"I don't care what the chief said," Alex stated boldly. "I'm in the middle of this, which means my family is in the middle. I'm not backing off for anyone."

"But—"

Alex looked his partner in the eye. "Maybe it's because I'm going to be a father, I don't know. But this is about more than me. This is about our country and our freedom to make decisions. It's about our future. I know that sounds kind of over-the-top, but it's the way I feel. On a broad level, this is your fight as much as mine, I get that. But in my heart, this fight belongs to me."

Dylan nodded once, his gaze impenetrable. "Okay," he finally said. "If that's the way it is, that's the way it is."

"That's the way it is."

Chapter Twelve

As it was the Friday before a holiday, school let out an hour earlier than usual. Jessica had seen an ad about a sale on garden plants over near Campton, and with the sun shining and an extra hour of free time, she asked Silvia Greenspan to accompany her on the ride to the nursery.

"It's supposed to be sunny tomorrow and I want to be prepared," she explained.

"I just can't right now," the older woman said, holding up a stack of papers. "It's almost the end of the year and I have a ton of work."

"Don't worry about it," Jessica said. "It's only a half-hour drive and I'm restless again. It seems I can't sit still lately."

"I was like that when I was pregnant with my youngest," Silvia said.

Jessica headed out of town with a light heart until she drove by Billy's house and caught sight of the burned-out hulk in the backyard. The place looked depressing in the rain, the equipment waiting nearby like vultures hovering over a rotting corpse.

She looked away at once. Being pregnant demanded optimism and hope, it demanded faith in the future and a positive attitude and she was tired of being afraid.

Once at the garden center, she chose plants already

established with set-on buds to hurry the bloom time. She mimicked the choices she'd chosen for her yard several weeks before when she gave Billy instructions. She started toward the checkout line, pushing a cart laden with pots of impending glory. It looked as though she and Alex would spend their Memorial Day vacation digging in the dirt.

If he got a vacation. With one confirmed murder and another death hanging over their heads as a possible homicide, to say nothing of a potential Memorial Day bloodbath, nothing was for sure.

As for why she still felt sentimental over the death of a young man who it appeared had gone out of his way to try to kill the man she loved—that was harder to pin down than the flowers. There was just some part of her brain that couldn't combine the image of Billy, the kid out in the garden, and Billy, the guy sneaking around Alex's airplane, doing his best to make sure Alex didn't have a chance of survival.

Maybe it *was* Tad and Ted who had organized all this. Maybe they used Billy. Maybe they were into drugs. Maybe, maybe, maybe.

Her phone rang and she smiled when she saw the call was from Alex. It was four o'clock and she couldn't wait to see him again. She answered it and the call immediately disconnected. She knew she had the mountains to thank for that, and she was glad she'd texted him her plans before taking off. At least he wouldn't worry about her.

Still, a gnawing pit opened up in her stomach and she debated returning the plants to their shelves and driving back into cell range. At that exact moment she felt the first fluttering kick of her baby and she touched her abdomen in awe.

This was the moment she'd been waiting for, and a rush of pleasure bathed her in what felt like sunlight. She smiled and her resolve strengthened. Life had to go on. There were these issues now, there'd be others later. In a way, the destruction of her garden had been like a metaphor for life—just keep going. Fix what's wrong, replace what's lost.

The clerk was an attractive blonde in her late forties. "You're going to be busy," she said as Jessica approached with a rolling cart covered with plants. "I hope you have a van or something."

"My car has a big trunk," Jessica said.

"You chose a nice variety," the clerk added, and she began scanning the bar codes.

"Someone destroyed our garden and we're starting over," Jessica explained. "Pity these won't be blooming in time for Memorial Day."

"Why?"

"Because I take flowers to the graves of veterans on Memorial Day, to honor my grandfather, you know?"

"Oh, my gosh," the woman said. "So do I. Red, white and blue?"

"If possible."

"But I live over in Blunt Falls," the clerk added.

"I do, too," Jessica laughed. "Hey, maybe I'll see you there."

"That'd be great," the clerk said.

"I go midmorning," Jessica added.

"I do, too," the clerk said, accepting Jessica's credit card. "Do you have a big yard?" Jessica explained what had happened to her flower garden. As she spoke, the clerk's eyes got wider and wider.

"That's terrible," she said. "It's so much work to create

something beautiful and then to have it wantonly destroyed, makes you wonder what the world is coming to."

"Most people are good and decent," Jessica said with conviction. "Some aren't, but they're in the minority." *At least I hope they are,* she thought, embarrassed that she'd gotten so serious.

"Yeah, you're right, but I do have to say there are more than a few creeps lurking in the corners. Either that or I'm just a creep magnet. Well, is there anything else?"

"Nope. That should keep us busy."

ALEX WENT INTO the office the next morning to finish up paperwork he'd started earlier, before the chief got so adamant about him staying out of things. It was Saturday and with some shock he realized he'd been in this same office one week ago today making sure he still had a job. In a way, he was back in the same position.

But what he really wanted to be doing was helping Jessica plant her new garden. He'd unloaded the car for her the night before and while his plan had been to discuss the chief's confusing behavior with her, he'd backed away from the subject. She'd been in a great mood, happy and full of plans and chatter about a nice woman she met. She'd felt their baby kick for the first time and they spent an hour that night lying in bed with his hand on her abdomen waiting for him to experience it, as well. So far, no luck, but that would change.

"I didn't expect to find you sitting here smiling to yourself," Dylan said as he perched on the edge of Alex's desk.

"Just thinking," he said.

"About Jessica, no doubt."

"No doubt," Alex agreed. "Let me see your report."

"I don't think so," Dylan said.

"Why not?"

"Because you got warned off the case or have you forgotten?"

"I haven't forgotten."

Dylan stared at him a second, then shook his head. "Buddy, I'm going to be blunt. Before your crash you admitted to me you and Jessica were thinking of breaking up. Then you come back and discover she's pregnant. You can't walk away even if you want to."

"I don't want to," Alex said.

"Well, man, see, that's the thing. What about her? I mean, she was so sure you might have run out on her that she placed that remark on Facebook. You show up, what's she supposed to do but give it another shot? I know she wants to stop working for at least a year or two, you told me that. She needs your paycheck to make that happen. If you keep pushing, you could lose your job. Have you thought about what that might mean?"

"Are you implying she'd leave me?" Alex asked.

"I don't know," Dylan said as he glanced up. His expression changed. Alex looked to see what had caught his attention and found Smyth approaching.

"The bottom line is that it doesn't matter," Alex said softly. "I have to keep digging. There is no option. I told you that."

Smyth paused at Alex's desk. "Digging for what?" he said, eyebrows furrowed, eyes glinting.

"Nothing," Alex said. "We're planting a new garden and that takes digging."

"The newspapers will eat that up."

"The newspapers could care less."

"I heard about what you found out on the road," Smyth continued. "What part of 'back off' didn't you get? You better go home before you jeopardize this whole investigation."

"Listen," Alex said, "I know I stretched the letter of the law the other night when I entered that shed…"

The chief shook his head. "You broke into private property and took evidence."

"That would have been destroyed if I hadn't taken it." He met Dylan's gaze because it was on the tip of his tongue to add that if the chief owned the place then what was the big deal? But Dylan seemed to know what Alex was thinking and his expression clearly said to tread softly.

"So help me, if those Cummings boys walk because you messed things up, Montana won't be big enough for the two of us," Smyth barked. "And by the way, just so you don't take me for a gullible fool, I know you weren't sick a few days ago, I know you dove on your plane, I even know you took a bottle of water out of the cockpit. That's probably another case you messed up, this one for the government. You're on quite a roll. I'm not going to reveal my sources so don't bother asking."

"Okay, I won't," Alex said.

"For both of you," the chief added, "the next two days are going to be busy with patrols at the parade and over at the fairgrounds where they've got some citywide rummage sale going. Lord almighty, why can't people just stay home? We're all pitching in for this. But for now, for today, Alex, you get out of here. I know how you like to dig in the dirt."

Dylan shook his head as the door closed behind Smyth. "I'm going to follow him."

"I don't think that's a good idea. He's acting strange. Did you tell him about the plane?"

"Not me," Dylan said. "Could it have been your friend?"

"You mean Nate?"

"No, the other guy. John Miter."

"I don't see how. I don't think he and the chief even know each other."

"I've seen them talking," Dylan said.

"When?"

"I can't remember. While you were missing. Just on the sidewalk or something." He pushed himself away from Alex's desk, which seemed to groan in relief and added, "I'll call you when I discover what the chief is up to."

Alex left soon after. He sat in his truck for a minute, unsure what to do. He kept thinking back to Billy.

The kid must have been drugged after he was hit, perhaps to keep him quiet while the perpetrator found a way to transport him to the drive-in. What had Lynda Summers really heard that night, and, if she was murdered, why?

His gut told him the Cummings boys didn't have anything to do with Billy's death. All sorts of people knew where their car was kept and that the key was left in the ignition.

Had the piece of Billy's jacket found on the car gotten there when his bike was hit out on the road, or later, at the drive-in?

His phone rang and he saw by the number on the screen it was the lab. He was surprised the lab techs were working over the weekend, especially since it was a holiday weekend.

"What are you guys doing in?" he asked.

"I just came in because I knew you were anxious about this. We'll finish testing on Tuesday. Meanwhile, the reflector you found came off Billy Summers's bike. We're going back over the Cummingses' car. So far, no blood.

In fact, dents and weeds notwithstanding, oh, and those pills, there's nothing other than the fabric caught in the grill to tie it to Billy Summers."

"Judging from the roadside, he must have bled a lot," Alex said.

"It would seem so."

"How about the paint on Billy's bike?"

"Not a match. Same color, but different paint. There are a lot of red cars in the world, you know."

"Keep me posted," Alex said, wondering how long it would be before Smyth spread the word for them to do otherwise.

He drove around for a while, nervous about going home and letting Jessica see how uptight he was. He had to figure out a way to get a handle on things. It had started raining and the windshield wipers beat a monotonous thump-thump as they cleared the windshield. In some strange way, he was reminded of being in the Cessna, alone, high above the earth.

What had he overlooked? There must be something.

What did it mean that Frank Smyth owned Lynda Summers's land and home, and did it mean anything special that he was apparently ready to plow it under as soon as possible? The place was a dump; who could blame him for wanting to get rid of such a health hazard? Tuesday morning, Alex needed to check the property deed for himself.

Was the chief warning him off the case because he was afraid Alex would find something that tied him to one or more deaths, maybe even to domestic terrorism?

And…how important was Alex's job? How much could he push without jeopardizing it? If he lost employment or went on unpaid leave, it would be impossi-

ble to find another job of the same caliber in Blunt Falls.
They'd have to relocate.

He thought of what Dylan had said. Was Jess giving
their marriage a chance solely because of his paycheck?
There was no forgetting the way she'd acted when he
first got home, as though she was undecided how she felt
about him. He could remember the way she'd nervously
folded clothes rather than sit next to him.

His phone rang again. This time he saw that it was
Dylan calling and he realized he'd been driving aimlessly
for over an hour. "Where are you?" he asked.

"Just saw the chief leave the bank with a briefcase that
had to be full of money, what else?"

"Maybe he emptied his safe-deposit box," Alex said.

"Or maybe he made a big withdrawal. But why? Just
wanted to let you know your trusty aide is on the job."

"Thanks," Alex said, and hung up. He'd pulled over
for the call and now as he edged back into traffic, that old
feeling of someone tracking him hit yet again. Searching his mirrors, he looked for anything out of place, but
traffic looked pretty much like it always did midday Saturday and he could see nothing amiss.

What was he doing out here alone when Charles Bond
could be driving into town, up to their front door? He
made an abrupt turn and went home.

JESSICA SAT BACK on her heels and admired her handiwork.
She doubted the garden would ever again look as it had
under Billy's tender care, especially since there would
soon be a child digging in the dirt and playing in a sand-
box, but the promise of flowers in the months to come
pleased her down to her soul.

It was a lonely weekend despite Alex's attempts to help
her. When he was home, he was distracted and when he

was at work, he just kind of disappeared. Since this was the weekend before the targeted Memorial Day, everyone at the station was pulling extra duty. Billy's murder had slipped to a back burner, on hold until after Monday, Alex explained, but there was something about the way he said it that made her wonder if he was being completely frank with her.

On Sunday, she picked up the flowers from the store and spent much of the day making small bouquets, tying them with red, white and blue ribbons and storing them in the refrigerator for delivery the next morning. Alex had said because he had parade duty later in the day, they would have to go very early so he could be with her. That was fine, she didn't care when they went, although the thought crossed her mind that she would miss seeing the nice clerk from the nursery.

Monday dawned overcast and nasty with promises of thunder and rain to come. "I guess it's a good thing we're going out to the cemetery first thing this morning," she told Alex.

"No kidding. I have to be at work by eleven, so we should leave right after breakfast."

They ate a quick meal and opened the closet for rain gear. She was zipping her slicker when Alex got a call and the look on his face as he took it made her cringe inside.

"Change of plans," he said after a few terse words. He grabbed his service pistol from the top shelf of the closet and slid it in the holster. "I have to go."

"Where? Who was that?"

"Dylan. He needs me right now."

"I'll go with you," she said.

"No. I'm sorry, but this is too dangerous. I'm not going to put you in jeopardy like I did with that bomb."

She pulled the coat closer around her body and held it.

"You're scaring me," she said. "What does Dylan want?" As he stared at her, she all but stamped her foot. "Be honest, Alex. I know something is wrong."

"He's been following Chief Smyth."

"What? Why?"

Alex seemed to have to struggle to get the words out. "Because the chief's been acting odd. Toward me. Nasty, almost. Dylan swore to get to the bottom of it and now he says Smyth is out at the Summers place and he's not alone."

"Who's he with?" she insisted.

"Dylan says it's either Charles Bond or his double. I seriously doubt this is the case, but I do have to go. You wait here. I'll be back as soon as I can."

She nodded once, unwilling to send him off worried about her, but just as determined to go about her life. What was her option? Sit here alone and wait for news Alex had been shot? *No, thank you.* "Be careful," she said.

He kissed her. "I'm sorry I kept this to myself. I should have shared it with you."

She kissed him back and sent him on his way, but there was an old familiar ache in her heart.

ALEX DROVE AS fast as he dared. He couldn't wrap his head around Smyth and Bond meeting at Lynda's house of all places. The skies just kept growing more and more ominous and the weight of the clouds seemed to mirror the weight in his own heart.

He'd think about Jessica later. For now he made himself blot out the look of disappointment he'd seen in her eyes.

Twenty minutes later, he pulled up on the other side of the hedge outside the house. Dylan had pulled his car behind a dense copse of trees and was mostly out of sight. Alex was surprised his partner had chosen such a spot because of the inevitable scratches to the paint.

Alex moved quickly and silently toward the property, stepping over the yellow police tape that had been broken and now dangled down into the mud. Smyth's sedan was parked close to the double-wide. There were no other vehicles in sight, though the acrid smell of the fire still filled the air. The yard was muddy now where fire trucks had disturbed the soil a few nights before. Had whoever Smyth been meeting with already left?

"Psst…" Dylan said from a couple of feet away.

Alex hotfooted it to the bushes behind which Dylan stood. His partner was wrapped in a dark slicker, his face and hair wet, though the rain had just started to gently fall. "They're in the kitchen," he said.

"Maybe we could sneak around back—"

"No, I tried that. You can't hear anything. The front door is ajar. We'll have to chance going in."

"But there's only the one car," Alex said. "Did the meeting break up?"

"No. Smyth stopped at that motor lodge outside of town, this guy got in and they drove out here together."

Alex delayed. If Smyth caught him spying on him, he'd have a major fit. Worse, he'd probably fire him outright and he'd probably have just cause. Entering a building unlawfully, trespassing now.

"You're right to hold back," Dylan said suddenly. "Listen, you stay here. I'll go…"

"No," Alex said, his mind snapping back into focus. He pulled out his cell and put it on Vibrate, shoved it back in his pocket. This was about way more than Billy's murder or Lynda Summers's death. If Frank Smyth was involved with the militant terrorists responsible for killing Mike and all the others, responsible for putting a bullet hole in Nate and terrorizing Jessica, then this was Alex's fight. Job or no job, future or no future.

"Cover me," he said as he pulled his pistol. He crept up the steps and across the threshold, Dylan right behind him.

The house greeted him as it always did, with boxes still wobbling on top of one another, bags of junk still overflowing. If anything it appeared more squalid than ever and it certainly smelled worse as years of garbage continued to rot in the corners. He breathed through his mouth so he wouldn't gag, then turned and met Dylan's gaze. He signaled for Dylan to stay put and tiptoed toward the kitchen, sliding on a pile of overturned magazines, catching himself by grabbing the wall. He stood without breathing for a moment, sure he must have been heard, but there was still no sound coming from the kitchen. He continued forward, deeper into the house, where the light had trouble penetrating and the smell got worse and worse.

The kitchen was new territory to him, but here, too, movement was restricted by rubbish. It appeared there might have once been stacks, but now things were overturned, upended as though they'd fallen or been pushed aside during a fight. Two open bottles of beer, both half-drunk, occupied the only clear drain-board space and from the beads of moisture on the glass, it was obvious they were fresh.

Where were the two men? Had they battled their way out to the backyard? He could see a corner of the door and it appeared closed.

The place smelled like hell. If that wasn't the stench of fresh blood, he didn't know what was and it raised the hairs on the back of his neck. He rounded the counter to a relatively clear spot and stopped dead in his tracks.

Frank Smyth lay in a pool of his own congealing blood, which had also sprayed and splattered everything around him. The poor guy looked like he'd been through a meat grinder. There was no way he could have survived, and even as Alex knelt to feel for a pulse he knew there could be none. An unopened briefcase lay close by.

So, Smyth had met with Bond. They must have been in it together. Bond must have decided to cut his losses and get rid of Frank. Maybe they'd been using this house as a meeting spot. Maybe Lynda had gotten in the way.

All these thoughts bombarded his head in the time it took to get back to his feet and turn around. Dylan stood behind him, his weapon drawn, as well. He lowered his arm as his gaze darted past Alex. "Oh, my God," he said, pointing to a corner. "What's that?"

Alex looked around the room again and there by the door he saw something that sent a chill down his spine.

A machete lay on the floor. A machete with a dark green cord knotted around the handle. His machete. The blade was covered with fresh blood. He walked over to the discarded weapon and leaned down again to make sure. It was his, all right. His initials were written in indelible ink on the shaft.

He felt a cold round pressure against the back of his head. "Put down your gun and stand up. And so help me, if you try anything I will make sure Jessica faces a worse fate than the chief."

Dylan's voice. Dylan.

"What the hell are you doing?" Alex said, but he knew. No wonder Dylan was wet and covered with a raincoat. He must have been covered in the chief's blood and washed it off before calling.

"Put the gun down," Dylan repeated, and emphasized his remark with a jab to Alex's head.

Alex set the gun down on the floor and stood. Dylan kicked it aside where it spun out of Alex's reach.

"Did you do this to Frank?" Alex demanded. "Why?"

"Oh, Alex, don't be so dense. Who do you think is Charles Bond's Blunt Falls accomplice? Come on, dude."

"Are you behind everything?" Alex said, trying to merge his partner, Dylan Hobart, with this lunatic.

Dylan nodded. "All the little mishaps and innuendos, Jess's race to the emergency room, the garden, a couple of deaths…this and that, yeah, that's all me."

"Are you trying to tell me you got Frank Smyth to drink a beer with you, then lay down on the floor so you could hack him to death?"

"Frank was coming here with a briefcase filled with money because someone threatened to tell everyone he was Billy Summers's father." Dylan grinned. "You didn't know that about our chief, did you? It's true. He and Lynda had a thing for a while. I guess it was before he found religion. Hell, maybe it's *why* he found religion. He got Lynda pregnant about a month after he knocked up his wife. God forbid his precious daughter ever find out."

"How can you possibly know this?" Alex said.

Dylan smiled. "Lynda may have let herself and her house go, but she was still good for a hot time on that couch of hers. Frank did me a favor when he kept sending me over here to calm her down. Sometimes she indulged in a little postcoital chatter. Amazing what a sex-drunk woman will tell you."

"I don't believe it," Alex said.

"I like them older. Young hotties are for show-and-tell. Anyway, I pretended I'd shown up to meet you here, too, got Frank to unwind a little by drinking a drugged beer and then used your machete to whack him. He didn't put up much of a fight and everyone knows you've been a little high-strung since you got back. Frank even talked to the mayor about suspending you. I guess you got wind of it and decided to take him out."

Alex tried to wrap his head around the craziness. "Why would Frank want to suspend me?"

"Because he is, or rather, *was,* under the impression you vandalized your own yard and then made sure you kept yourself the center of attention. He also thought you were hiding evidence like this machete. He was beginning to think you might even have killed Billy Summers yourself. He's a gullible man, no matter what he said. He'll believe anything you tell him if you tell him in the right way."

"Then it was you who set Billy up to sabotage my plane," Alex stated matter-of-factly.

"It wasn't hard. I made it sound like a prank and I gave him a little money so he could work on his models. And then the little jerk found a conscience and started following Jessica around like a lost puppy. By the time you got home, he couldn't wait to spill his guts and confess."

"Which you couldn't let happen."

"Not so much. I ran him down after your party. He was cut up pretty bad but he wasn't dead. I had a few of those Rohypnol pills we took off that loser last year in the car. Two little forget-everything pills threw Billy for a loop. I'd seen a tarp out at the Summers place, so I drove there to get it. Didn't want my car to get too dirty. I think Lynda saw me. She kind of hinted she did and I knew sooner or later, she'd get chatty with someone else. I knew I'd have to get rid of her soon so I did. Anyway, when I got back, Billy was trying to claw his way up the hill. I knocked him out, dragged him and his bike up the hill, wrapped him up in the tarp and stuck him in the trunk. His bike went in the backseat." He paused for a second and shook his head. "It was a tight fit. And then I thought of the drive-in theater."

"Billy was never in the Cummingses' car," Alex said. "You planted the evidence when you went out to question them and then you started rumors. That's why there's no blood on their car. And your girlfriend wasn't rear-ended in Billings. You needed an out-of-town body shop because the front was damaged when you hit Billy."

"Aren't you the clever one? They brought it back to me the day you flew up to the lake. Great timing."

Alex shook his head. "You're part of these domestic terror groups? You, Dylan? I had no idea you held such deeply seated beliefs." As he spoke, his phone vibrated with a text. It might as well have vibrated on the moon.

Dylan barked a laugh. "I'm not some crazy crackpot like Bond and the others," he said. "What they do is certifiable. If people are stupid enough to cave to their tactics, so be it. I participate solely because of the money, plain and simple. New cars, steroids, pumping iron, sex, excitement, it's all the same. You were supposed to disappear forever, that was the plan. A Boy Scout like you is problematic for an entrepreneur like me. I was delighted when that loony in Shatterhorn paid me to screw with your plane."

Alex's mind was still playing catch up as past events demanded examination under this bright new light of discovery. "You weren't on a date Thursday night," he said. "You were here breaking into the shed. Why'd you take the biplane?"

Dylan shrugged. "I'm toying around with hooking it back to the Cummings boys. 'Keep your options open,' that's my motto."

"Then you watched Jess and me discover the drawer in the table that you missed. You wrote the directions for Billy, your prints might have been on that card. You threw the Molotov cocktail to get rid of the evidence."

"To get rid of the evidence and to get rid of you," Dylan stated, his eyes hard, the bantering tone now absent. He lowered the aim of his gun to Alex's knee. It was the one hurt in the crash and it suddenly throbbed like hell. The gun barrel inched up to aim at his groin next with similar results. "Now, with Frank dead and you about to die by a bullet from his gun, I can spin things any way I want."

A layer of sweat broke out on Alex's brow. How could he have known and worked with this man for three years and never seen the cold-blooded egotism behind his eyes? "Forensics will be all over this," he said. "There are no powder burns on Smyth's hand—"

"Won't matter," Dylan said, pulling a cigarette lighter from his pocket. Alex recognized it as belonging to the chief and he knew the man's initials were engraved in the metal casing. "You know, any other guy would have said, 'Screw this, I'm taking my wife and moving away from here,' but not you. So I put a bug in Frank's ear. He got the impression you were messing with this case so he'd look bad and you could have his job.

"Then he started getting blackmail letters and you got credit for those, too. I gave him the same drug I gave Billy, the rest of which they'll find in your pocket. Well, if there's anything left of you, that is." He held the flame next to a pile of newspapers that immediately began to burn.

"Dylan, think about what you're doing. Not just to me but to the country."

"I'll be the new chief by tomorrow," Dylan said calmly

as he threw the lighter across the room. "I'll get rid of the index cards and explain you and Smyth away." He picked up the briefcase. "So long, buddy. All your high-flying ideals are for nothing. It's too late. You can't stop what's going to happen. You should have stayed in the mountains."

The deadly sound of gunfire cracked the air. Alex gasped before he realized he hadn't been hit. Instead, Dylan crumpled to the floor with an unholy scream and a splatter of blood. Alex immediately slid himself across the room to grab his own weapon, exploding to his feet, ready to fire.

And met the steely-eyed gaze of John Miter, armed to the teeth. He stood over Dylan's prone, writhing body, an impassive expression on his face. Blood covered Dylan's now empty gun hand and his wounded thigh. Invectives and empty threats spewed from his mouth.

"The fire is spreading," John said matter-of-factly.

Alex glanced over his shoulder. In the midst of the adrenaline-charged past few seconds, he'd all but forgotten about the flames; now the crackling, smoky blaze was already too big for them to extinguish without help. They both grabbed one of Dylan's arms and hauled him upright. John snatched the briefcase and the three of them stumbled their way out of the burning double-wide.

"What are you doing here?" Alex asked John as they erupted into the fresh air.

"I've been watching your back ever since we tested your Vita-Drink," he said. "Nate kind of asked me to keep an eye on you."

"You're the one who's been following me."

"When I can. You shouldn't have known I was there, though. I must be losing my edge."

Alex slapped his shoulder. "I never saw you," he

assured him. Dylan had slumped onto the wet grass and now Alex leaned over him, catching his collar in one hand. "What did you mean it's too late?"

Dylan smirked through gritted teeth.

"Is Jessica in danger?" Alex demanded, grabbing Dylan by the collar.

Dylan groaned. "Jessica. She's all you ever think of. No, you moron, Charles Bond is here. What's going to happen is bigger than your precious little wife."

"How do you know Charles Bond?" Alex demanded.

"We go way back," Dylan said, some of the bravado resurfacing. "Back to before New Orleans. We lifted weights at the same gym but he was an old guy, at least to me. I thought he was killed in the explosion just like everyone else did. Could have knocked me over with a feather when he called here a few months ago."

"Was he behind the bombing that supposedly killed him?"

"No way. It was just a lucky break as far as he was concerned. Gave him a nice, clean start. Then he fell in with his brother-in-law in Shatterhorn and climbed aboard the crazy zealot bus. He tried to coax me into helping him by talking about ideals. When he finally started changing the language to money, well, that's when I started listening."

"Is he going after the parade?" Alex said, just about ready to smash Dylan's nose into his face.

Grimacing, Dylan waited a second, then nodded.

"You go, I'll stay with him," Miter said as the fire inside the trailer blew a window. "I'd appreciate you telling your buddies not to shoot me when they get here."

Alex dropped Dylan and ran to his truck. He raced downtown with his heart in his throat while placing call after call. First the fire department, then the mayor's office and Carla Herrera. Kit Anderson was in charge of the officers patrolling the parade that would start in less than two hours, so his call came next. Then Agent Struthers who promised to beef up federal law-enforcement involvement.

The only one Alex couldn't reach was Jess.

Chapter Thirteen

The cemetery was surprisingly well visited in spite of the drippy skies, explained, in part, because of preparations underway for a graveside ceremony at the top of the hill. Workmen had raised an awning over a freshly dug grave. An elderly woman in a long, dark coat stood watching them, head bowed, gloved hands resting atop a cane, framed by a nearby crypt and the dark silhouette of trees.

Jessica easily found her grandfather's grave situated close to an old grove of oaks. "Here you go, Grandpa," she said, setting the first bouquet of the day in his flower holder. She paused, as was her habit, to draw on memories of him, but her thoughts immediately darted to Alex, and she took out her phone to text him. She wasn't surprised when he didn't respond and crossed her fingers that he was safe.

"Hi," a woman said, and Jessica looked up to see a blonde in a black raincoat walking toward her. She carried a basket of small bouquets much like the one Jessica held as well as an umbrella.

Jessica recognized her from the nursery. In a way she was glad to see her; in a way she was too distracted to even think about making small talk with a near stranger.

"Are you okay?" the woman asked.

Jessica nodded.

The woman touched her arm. "My name is Nancy," she said. "Is there anything I can do for you?"

"No, I'm fine," Jessica said as her attention was drawn to the sight of a hearse driving through the cemetery. A long line of cars with dimmed headlights followed behind. "My husband is...working," she explained as she watched the procession, which was hard not to view as ominous. "I...I miss him."

Nancy nodded with understanding, her gaze following Jessica's. "That's one of the reasons I'm here," she said, nodding toward the hearse. "The service on the hill is for an army nurse who died last week. There was a big write-up in the newspaper about her. She's credited with saving the lives of two dozen orphans during the Korean Conflict."

"I didn't see the article," Jessica said, glimpsing the older woman in the black coat slowly walking away from the new grave. She still leaned heavily on her cane as though the weight of the world had settled on her thin shoulders. "I haven't read the paper lately."

"I read about her last night and thought I'd pay my respects," Nancy said. "Want to join me?"

Jessica started to refuse, then changed her mind. Nancy seemed to be easy company and she didn't want to be alone. "Thanks, I'd like that. By the way, I'm Jessica Foster."

Nancy's brow furrowed. "That name sounds familiar."

"Well, I did charge all those plants."

"No, it's not that. Wait, is your husband a cop?"

"Yes. Do you know him?"

"No, not really. I just met him a few days ago. He was with a walking muscle named Dylan."

Jessica nodded. "They're partners."

"Are they close?"

"I suppose."

Nancy nodded, giving Jessica the distinct feeling she was holding something back.

"Let's walk on up the hill," Jessica said, curious now.

As they approached the awning and the growing crowd, the older woman in the long coat had almost reached the crypt. As she slowly turned and surveyed the gathering she'd just left, her gaze met Jessica's. Jessica sucked in her breath and looked away.

"What's wrong?" Nancy said as she opened her umbrella to ward off the increasing rain.

"Nothing," Jessica said, darting a glance over her shoulder.

The old woman stood in front of the crypt, seemingly oblivious to the weather, lost in thought.

BY THE TIME Alex arrived downtown, traffic was already plugged. He parked in a loading zone and ran along the sidewalk to the fountain outside the courthouse where he'd arranged over the phone to meet Kit Anderson. Kit's usual air of superiority had been shaken in the wake of learning what had happened to the chief and that the man no one wanted to ever come to Blunt Falls was allegedly already here.

"I called Campton," Alex said by way of greeting. "They're sending over all their off-duty police to help."

"The sheriff's department responded, too," Kit said. "I think there'll be more police here than spectators, especially if this rain gets any heavier." He shook his head. "I still can't believe Dylan killed the chief."

"Among other things," Alex said as his phone rang. It was John. As he answered it, he remembered the text that had come back when Dylan held the upper hand

and things looked really bad. He'd check his messages after this call.

"Your buddy started to laugh after you left," John Miter said.

"Why?"

"That's what I wondered. He didn't want to explain what was so funny until I accidentally stepped on his shot-up hand. I can be so clumsy."

"Who the hell are you, really?" Alex said. "Tell me the truth."

"I'm John Miter, an old retired guy who likes to fish."

"You know what I mean, John."

There was a slight pause and his voice dropped. "Let's just say I know my way around people like this. Anyway, what I wanted to tell you is that I don't think anything is going to happen at that parade."

"Because?"

"Because Dylan finally choked out that you were going to the wrong place."

"Do you believe him?"

"I don't know for sure, Alex, but there was another nasty laugh like he'd put one over on you and then the ambulance arrived, so he clammed up. Are there any other events planned for the day?"

"There's a citywide rummage sale at the fairgrounds. I'd better get more people out there, too."

"Or here's another thought. What if this Bond guy isn't coming here at all? What if Dylan is still yanking your chain?"

"And what if he's not?"

"Okay, I see your point. Good luck," he said and disconnected before Alex could belatedly thank him for saving his life. He checked his messages immediately and saw that Jess had tried to contact him. The first text told him she was at the cemetery, that she loved him and hoped he was okay. The second one said that she'd run across an important graveside service for a former army nurse and she was going to attend. She'd contact him afterward.

The cemetery.

A former soldier, a hero, laid to rest.

The Shatterhorn Killer had never killed in volume. It was the unexpected terror and the erosion of confidence and hope he was after. Alex began running. Thunder crashed the sky. A bolt of lightning followed soon after. Maybe the parade would be called off. If so, that would send more people to the indoor rummage sale. He called Kit and told him to make sure to think of that should the parade fizzle out. He said he'd be gone for a few minutes but refused to provide an explanation.

His intuition was in high gear now and there was no turning back. It was a long shot, way too remote a possibility to call people away from the more obvious choices, but there was no way in the world he could keep himself from making sure.

His phone rang as he drove the truck out onto the highway. The cemetery wasn't far and all the traffic was going in the other direction so he knew he'd make good time, but he also knew Jess's second text had come fifteen minutes earlier—how had he missed that? And why wasn't she answering now?

He answered without looking at the screen. "Foster here."

"Alex?"

"Jessica," he said with such profound relief that it knocked his breath away for a second.

"Where are you? Are you okay?"

"Didn't you get my text? Never mind. I'm at the cemetery. Listen, I have to tell you something about Dylan. I met this woman—"

"You don't have to tell me about him," Alex said.

"Yes, I do."

"I already know about him. This is important. Are you at the graveside service you mentioned?"

"I'm standing apart so I don't bother anyone with this call."

"I'm at the gate right now. Where is it being held?"

"At the top of the hill. Why are you here? I don't understand. What about Charles Bond? Did you see him?"

"Listen to me carefully. I've got this gut instinct that Bond may target that funeral. Please, just trust me. Have you seen anything or anyone unusual?"

She paused for a second. "Not really. I'm looking around now. There's a crowd of people here under a sea of umbrellas. Mary Rivers's pastor is speaking about her years of service. The thunder stopped but it's raining like crazy and we're all getting soaked so I imagine they'll cut this short. Wait, I don't see the old woman. She must have left."

"What old woman?"

"There's a tall elderly lady here wearing a long black coat. She was near a big crypt a few minutes ago. Oh, wait, okay, I see her. She's walking toward the ceremony. Man, she's moving fast."

Alex frowned. "Why did this lady catch your attention?"

"It was just that her eyes... Well, I mean, when I looked at her earlier, it was like she looked right through me, like I was invisible. And her eyes were so dark and bright, they were kind of possessed. And now she's moving three times as fast and not using her cane—"

"Are you sure it's a woman?" Alex said, pulling the

truck to a stop down the hill. He immediately jumped out. He could see the gathering up the slope but it was raining too hard to make out details. He quickly darted between gravestones, charging his way up the hill.

Jessica's voice wavered. "Of course. And yet, I don't know." A slight pause, and then a gasp. "That's not a cane."

"Listen to me, baby," he said urgently. "Get down low right now, down as close to the ground as you can. I'm on my way." And then he suddenly heard shots in stereo, both over his phone and from up the hill. Jess screamed once and fell silent. He stuffed the phone in his pocket as he pulled his weapon. He heard the sickening thud of more shots as he dashed up the slope as if his feet were on fire.

He erupted on the top by the crypt. Everyone in attendance had either started running or had hit the ground. What appeared to be an old woman stood over them, an assault rifle in her hands, her back to Alex. He silently moved toward her until he was only six feet away. All of a sudden, her gunfire ceased.

"Bond!" Alex yelled.

The old woman turned and came into focus as Charles Bond in disguise. He'd popped out an empty clip and as he stared at Alex, he jammed in another.

"It's over," Alex said. "I know about your brush with terrorism. This isn't making anything better."

Bond didn't respond.

"Put the weapon down."

Bond reached forward to charge the rifle.

Time was up. Alex fired.

Bond immediately fell to his knees and then twisted and landed on his back, faceup. Alex approached cautiously, his pistol pointed at his target.

The killing shot had hit Bond in the forehead, knocking the wig askew, revealing a bald head underneath. Even in death, Bond's eyes burned as the rain washed blood over his face. After taking the rifle, Alex was happy to turn away.

But what met his gaze was sobering. Those who hadn't run or hidden behind tombstones lay on the ground, their dark clothes and the pounding rain making bloodstains hard to see. People who hadn't been hurt were beginning to tend to those who had. Groans and whimpers increased. While he walked among everyone, he looked for Jessica but couldn't find her. He took out his phone and placed an emergency call. He didn't want to stop the police efforts underway at the rummage sale or the parade on the off chance there was another attack but they needed ambulances out here at once.

When he hung up, he did a one-eighty and that's when he finally saw Jess. She was kneeling over a woman, and he veered off in her direction. The victim looked vaguely familiar. Jess held her scarf against the woman's throat. He kneeled down next to his wife and she looked up at him, tears in her eyes.

"I got to her as fast as I could. Is she—" she began, her lips trembling.

He checked the woman's wrist. "No, she's not dead. Her heartbeat is strong. Keep applying pressure with that scarf. You're doing fine." He snatched an open umbrella lying on the ground nearby and held it over both women. The welcome sound of sirens reached them and their gazes met. "Are you okay?" he whispered.

"I think so. That old lady was really Charles Bond, wasn't it?"

"Yes," he said.

They both looked around the cemetery as people came to the aid of those who'd been wounded. Ambulances arrived, and finally a team of medics came to relieve Jessica of her task and transport the woman to the hospital. Alex sent the umbrella with them.

As they wheeled her away Jessica turned to him. She was wet and pale, tears mixing with raindrops, relief and sadness at war in her eyes. His heart melted at the sight of her. He'd thought he'd lost her. He ached to hold her and yet he was oddly frozen, waiting for something he couldn't name.

"I'm sorry I got annoyed you weren't sharing things with me," she mumbled. "I was afraid things were slipping back to how they had been. But that's not going to happen."

"No, it's not. Never again," he said. "I was struggling with Smyth. Dylan had been playing us against each other. It was confusing and I retreated into myself. But it wasn't like the old days. I swear, it wasn't. I just needed time. And as it turns out, time was the one thing we didn't have a lot of."

"No marriage is perfect," she said softly, wiping rain out of her eyes with her fingers. "No relationship comes without struggles and compromises," she continued, gripping his hands. "The bottom line is that we love each other and we want to spend our lives together. Right?"

He pulled her tight against him. Their lips met and for him, at least, the sun burst through the clouds.

"Take me home," she said against his neck.

ALEX HAD TO go back to work, of course, as the mayor had appointed him temporary chief of police and there were a million loose ends to iron out. He'd told her about what happened out at Billy's old house during the drive home, and she was still shocked by all of it.

She'd watched the evening news and knew an attack at a Seattle food-and-wine festival had been averted. Maybe it was finally over—for now, anyway.

It surprised her when Alex walked in the door at seven that night. He looked ragged and worn but his smile warmed her. "I didn't expect you so early," she said, patting the seat next to her on the sofa.

"It will all still be there tomorrow," Alex said, yawning into his hand. "I'm done with it for tonight."

She took his hand and pulled him down to sit beside her. "Was there any more trouble in town?"

"No, thank goodness. The parade was canceled, the rummage sale went without a hitch. It was just the cemetery. Unfortunately, four people were injured. It's incredible the casualty toll wasn't higher. Makes me wonder if this wasn't Bond's swan song."

"What do you mean?"

"I wonder if he was tired of the scheme he was playing out. People were getting wise to his tactics, the fear angle had turned into anger. There was no hope he could influence people the way he wanted. I know these domestic militia terrorists groups are informally linked, if at all, but I think maybe in Bond's case he wanted out and this is how he chose to do it. Most of his bullets seemed to fly high and wide."

Jessica shivered.

"How is your friend?" he asked.

"She's going to be okay. They admitted her to the hospital and I went to see if she needed anything. Her parents had arrived by then." She looked closely at Alex and added, "She lives really close to Billy Summers. Did you know that?"

"I thought I recognized her. She's the gal with the great garden."

"Her name is Nancy Dill. She's also the person who told me about Dylan. That was before you told me everything else about Dylan."

"What did she say?"

"She told me that Thursday afternoon, Dylan came back to her house after you two had left."

"Must have been when I asked him to question neighbors he claimed weren't home. Damn, no wonder he didn't know one of the houses was abandoned."

"She said he was polite and charming. She told him to come back later for a beer. When he came back he was different. Full of himself, bragging about all his exploits, grabbing at her and making it clear what he wanted. She slapped him and told him to leave and he did. But she saw him pull off to the side of her driveway and run into the trees. That kind of made her nervous so she grabbed her keys and drove into Campton to spend the night with friends. She didn't know about the bomb or the fire."

Jessica studied Alex's strong profile. "When I heard her story, I realized he might have run through the woods and broken into Billy's shed. The timing was right. And that suggested he was the one who threw the Molotov cocktail. That's when I called you."

He nuzzled her hair. "I've never been so glad to hear anyone's voice before in my whole life." He pulled her to rest against his chest, his arms around her, his face close to her ear, his breath warm and comforting against her skin. "The last ten days make the time stranded in the mountains seem peaceful and soul affirming by comparison. How about we fly up there when the baby is old enough and camp on the lake?"

"I'd love that," she said. "Would you introduce me to the people who rescued you?"

"You bet."

"Nate called while you were gone," she added. "I told him what had happened. He and Sarah are flying back up here this weekend. He wants to hear all the details."

"That's great news," Alex said, sighing deeply.

"Alex, I can't believe John Miter saved your life. Who is he really?"

"I asked him. He wouldn't tell me."

"I guess we'll never know."

"As a matter of fact, I asked Agent Struthers about him. Once he stopped chortling, he swore me to secrecy except to you. John Miter is ex-CIA. He was a cold-war agent."

She looked up over her shoulder at him. "He was a spy? A real spy?"

Smiling, Alex nodded. "Apparently a damn good one, too."

"Let's have a little dinner party when Nate and Sarah get here. We'll invite John," she said as she positioned Alex's hands on her abdomen. "Maybe Silvia would like to come, too. Don't you think they'd make a good pair?"

He laughed. "A high-school principal and a retired spy. Why not?"

"Junior is having a frisky evening," she added with a murmur. "Maybe you can feel something."

They sat still for quite a while. To Jessica, the baby's antics were pronounced but when Alex failed to comment, she began to suspect he'd fallen asleep. Checking to see if she was right, she found herself looking at his face the moment the baby let loose with a big rolling kick. His lips curved and his eyes crinkled. "I bet you a dollar there's more than one in there," he said before kissing her forehead.

She nuzzled her face against his neck. "You're on."

* * * * *

A sneaky peek at next month...

INTRIGUE...

A SEDUCTIVE COMBINATION OF DANGER AND DESIRE

My wish list for next month's titles...

In stores from 18th July 2014:

- ☐ Evidence of Passion – Cynthia Eden
- ☒ Hunted – Beverly Long
- ☐ Bridegroom Bodyguard – Lisa Childs
- ☒ KCPD Protector – Julie Miller
- ☐ Secret Obsession – Robin Perini
- ☒ Blood Ties in Chef Voleur – Mallory Kane

Romantic Suspense

- ☐ Cavanaugh Strong – Marie Ferrarella

Available at WHSmith, Tesco, Asda, Eason, Amazon and Apple

Just can't wait?

Discover more romance at

www.millsandboon.co.uk

- ❤ WIN great prizes in our exclusive competitions

- ❤ BUY new titles before they hit the shops

- ❤ BROWSE new books and REVIEW your favourites

- ❤ SAVE on new books with the Mills & Boon® Bookclub™

- ❤ DISCOVER new authors

PLUS, to chat about your favourite reads, get the latest news and find special offers:

- 🗗 Find us on facebook.com/millsandboon

- 🐦 Follow us on twitter.com/millsandboonuk

- ❤ Sign up to our newsletter at millsandboon.co.uk

The World of Mills & Boon

There's a Mills & Boon® series that's perfect for you. There are ten different series to choose from and new titles every month, so whether you're looking for glamorous seduction, Regency rakes, homespun heroes or sizzling erotica, we'll give you plenty of inspiration for your next read.

By Request

Relive the romance with the best of the best
12 stories every month

Cherish™

Experience the ultimate rush of falling in love.
12 new stories every month

INTRIGUE...

A seductive combination of danger and desire…
7 new stories every month

Desire™

Passionate and dramatic love stories
6 new stories every month

nocturne™

An exhilarating underworld of dark desires
3 new stories every month

For exclusive member offers go to
millsandboon.co.uk/subscribe

Which series will you try next?

*Awaken the romance
of the past...*
6 new stories every month

*The ultimate in romantic
medical drama*
6 new stories every month

MODERN™

*Power, passion and
irresistible temptation*
8 new stories every month

MODERN tempted™

True love and temptation!
4 new stories every month